The Exiles.

Backlash against genetic engineering had resulted in their banishment to a parallel world. All they had to do now was survive. Between the hungry wildlife and the prejudices that had come with them, it wasn't going to be easy.

The Gods.

The test kids for genetic engineering, they'd gotten every single improvement, every experimental gene . . . and lifted ESP, telekinesis and telepathy out of the background noise and into something all too easily thought of as magic. They'd opened the gates to new worlds, and sabotaged the equipment when they escaped with the last of the exiles. They'd been sarcastically called gods on Earth, where they were virtual slaves. Here they were free—of everything except the possibility of genuine godhood.

Other Titles by the Author

Wine of the Gods Series:

Outcasts and Gods

Exiles and Gods

The Black Goats

Explorers

Spy Wars

Comet Fall

A Taste of Wine

Dark Lady

Growing Up Magic

Young Warriors

God of Assassins (2014)

Short Stories:

Writing YA as Zoey Ivers:

The Barton Street Gym

Chicago

Demi God

Exiles and Gods
Three Novellas

Pam Uphoff

Table of Contents

Exiles and Gods

Pam Uphoff

Chapter One

21 January 2117

Hartford, Connecticut

About half the school bullies were standing around the exit to the bus loading area. Quite the unwelcoming committee. Chris decided that this would be a good day to walk home. After all, it hadn't snowed since Sunday, all the sidewalks would be shoveled and clear.

Why didn't my parents tell me?

The results of his routine physical prior to trying out for the football team last summer had come as a shock. Back in California they'd never tested DNA; he hadn't realized they did it here. Not that knowing would have changed anything. He hadn't realized he had anything to hide.

They just said I was "special" and "talented."

There were kids around the front entrance too, but he didn't recognize them, and they were mostly short. Freshmen and sophomores. Waiting to be picked up by their loving parents.

Chris eeled through the crush and angled down the steps. Ignored the whispers behind him.

"That's him. The monster."

The freak. Part animal. The boy with the genetic engineering.

A car drove by, the window dropped down as it passed. "Hey Frankenstein, catch this!"

Chris dodged what he diagnosed as the dregs of a latte. He'd had a lot worse thrown at him since he'd plummeted from a sought-after junior varsity star to a not-legal-to-compete genetic abomination. Next year he could drive himself. Only Seniors were given parking tags for the school lot. Chris already had his license, all he needed was to earn enough money for a car. And gas. And insurance. Even his parents were showing signs of fighting down prejudice; they weren't immune to relentless propaganda. People shunned them because they'd had their first child engineered. He was strong, healthy, good looking, smart, athletic . . . monstrous. His two younger siblings hadn't gotten any engineering at all, as the parents bent to the public switch in opinion about genetic engineering.

They've started looking at me like I might murder them all in their beds some night. Like I'm the kid gone bad, on drugs, or in a gang.

He crossed the main street, ignored the honking and rude comments from the cars stopped at the red light. The light changed, and they all honked and yelled again as they passed him. One car swerved and splashed slush from the gutter. He dodged and they all laughed. The high tones of girls. He didn't look to see who it was. It hardly mattered.

At home, the TV was on, some girly show his sisters loved. "I'm home." They ignored him. Old enough to catch the flack about the unacceptable older brother, too young to really think it through. Desperate to separate themselves from him, to be accepted by their peers as normal.

I understand wanting to be normal.

He tossed his backpack into his room, and raided the fridge for food. Peanut butter and jelly, glass of milk. Everything else was fresh veggies and tofu. And Mom had complained about having to buy him cow's milk. She wouldn't even buy the new vat grown meat. Maybe he ought to forget the car and just use his money to buy himself real food. Maybe if it snowed more, he'd earn enough money shoveling walks around the neighborhood to do both. He whipped through his homework and then pulled out his last library book.

Have to go to the library again tomorrow. Maybe Mom will drop me off when she takes the girls to ballet.

He managed to lose himself in a space opera until his door crashed open.

"There you are!" Sibyl Dunmeyer was dressed for success in a red suit. Tense and obviously unhappy.

He sat up straighter and closed the book. *What's wrong this time?* "Hi Mom. How was work today?"

"Great until someone told me the news." She hunched her

shoulders.

"What news?" His stomach flopped over.

"The vote. The Congress got the genetic engineering bill out of committee and voted on it today."

Chris sagged back in disbelief. "They didn't pass it!"

"Of course they did. And the Senate will pass it as well. No one wants to be on the record as supporting . . . dangerous . . . people." She blinked suddenly. A tear broke loose and tracked down her cheek.

Crying? Mother crying? It must be anger, or shame. "So they're actually going to exile us?" Then he swallowed, tried to think. He felt like he was floating on a cloud of denial.

Or realization.

"I mean, me."

Then he scrambled to soften the offense. "I mean, anyone with engineering. Good thing I'm plenty old to be on my own. I'll be seventeen, maybe eighteen, before anything actually happens."

Mom shook her head, helpless, not denying. "I can't live in a howling wilderness. And what would your father do? He's a stock broker. And the girls?"

"Brook and Pet would hate roughing it. I, on the other hand, will enjoy every minute of it." Chris fought down his gorge, fought back tears.

"We'll help you, help get you . . . things. Supplies." She wiped an angry hand across her cheek, smearing makeup. "You'll be fine." She clutched the door. "We do love you . . ."

"It's just that you custom ordered your perfect baby boy. And then they changed the definition of perfect." Chris looked beyond her, and spotted his father. "I know you can't take the girls there, frontiers are no place for little girls."

His dad's hand tightened on Mom's shoulder. "They say they'll be opening gates once a month. So after the first month, send us a list of things you need. We'll bring it to you, have a family vacation for a month. It's not like we'll never see you again."

Chris nodded, unable to force more reassurances from his mouth.

"I picked up dinner, let's go eat." Dad led Mom away.

Chris closed his door quietly. And concentrated on not getting sick. Tears didn't count, when there was no one to see. After a few minutes he forced himself to wipe his face and go sit with his family. He didn't have much of an appetite.

It snowed overnight, two inches of wet slush, that threatened to freeze as temperatures kept dropping. He grabbed his shovel and headed out in the pre-dawn to clear the driveways of the three clients who left early, then the rest of the driveways, then he started on the sidewalks that ordinarily he'd have left for after school. Mr. Fergusson sent him away, Mrs. Burns fussed and paid him early, as if she thought the government would whisk him away tomorrow. None of his other regular clients came out, so he worked in peace, ignored the school bus as it passed. It wasn't as if his grades mattered any more.

At home, alone, he started researching the parallel worlds. They were all Earth, of course, with some slight difference in their natural history that had split them off into a present that was just across a dimensional fold. Trans World Travel was the company that had invented the mechanisim that opened gates between worlds. They'd previously been NewGenes, the company that had made so many genetic discoveries, years ago, before genetic engineering was made illegal. Same managers, same board of directors. Same stockholders, mostly some Chinese family.

Now they get to screw me all over again.

The scenes they showed of Gaia, the first colony, were pretty. Scenic. Quaint little villages with small garden patches, the observatory up on a mountain. A few big swaths of grain fields to provide the bulk for the reformulators. They had automated kitchens in the communal cafeterias in each village.

They were colonizing the worlds where humans had never evolved, but that had split away recently enough that the animals were roughly recognizable. No dinosaurs.

Chris sighed. It looked really boring, and he'd bet there was going to be someone in charge of all the children. His only hope was to delay going until he was eighteen. Several private colony companies had lists of what they recommended their members bring with them. Chris blanched at the hugely expensive items. *I am so screwed, the parents won't buy me an RV. Maybe a jeep.* Chris contemplated what he'd heard from his parents, about their current financial situation. The wonderful old boat they'd sold before moving across the country had never been replaced. *Maybe a motorcycle. Off road variety.*

The phone interrupted further studies. The Vice Principal for Junior Boys informed him he'd better be sick, else he would be truant. The man managed to get a tint of sympathy into his voice, but was unmoved by Chris's claim of immunity from school attendance requirements, as a non-human. "Get here for fourth period."

Chris wolfed down lunch—more peanut butter and jelly—and started walking.

He was greeted by the school football star. "Hey, Dunmeyer, haven't they thrown you off the planet yet?"

Chris managed a smile. "Eat your heart out. No more school, all the land I want. Fishing, hunting. No parents. *Major score.*"

Hector actually looked taken aback. "Your parents aren't going?"

"Course not. Geeze, the little sisters are all natural. They wouldn't fit in at all." Chris walked past the jerk and kept going.

The looks he got from people after that changed. A bit. Some sympathy, some envy, some pity. But mostly just the usual unthinking prejudice and bullying.

A week later, the Senate passed the bill without changes.

The President signed it. And made a big to-do of it; he spoke about keeping the human race safe, about sensible limits on science. Chris listened in disbelief. No apology to the kids he was kicking off the planet, no remorse for families torn apart.

Two weeks later, the letter came. Apparently the government knew where all the genetically engineered people were. It sounded like a lawsuit. Or perhaps an arrest warrant. "Subject is reported to have been engineered to contain Happy Kids, Inc. genetic suites BTSS and F23." His Dad filled it out, admitted that his "minor partial child" would be unaccompanied. That the child was not a member of a commercial colony group.

It only took the government four months to organize the exile.

Apparently they wanted it done and over with well before the elections. Some people tried to run, some people tried to hide their kids. The government gathered them all up, mostly with a fair amount of "stuff" for colonizing a raw frontier. Chris's parents had spent some serious money outfitting him, but stopped short of buying him a vehicle. Which rather limited the amount of stuff he could take.

The federal agents were anonymous behind mirrored sunglasses. They slung his two big plastic trunks into the back of the SUV without looking in them and gestured him in. Good. He'd been afraid they'd confiscate his arsenal. He'd hugged his Mom (stoic) and sisters (crying), shaken his father's (trembling) hand already. He picked up his backpack, filled with the government recommended traveling kit, and got in the back seat. He didn't look back. A pane of something clear, and probably bullet proof, separated him from the front seat. He eyed the doors. No handles on the inside. *I'm just a kid. How dangerous do they think we are?*

They drove off without talking, took the interstate, but exited on the other side of town. They wound around to a huge house in an obviously rich neighborhood.

"Wait right here, kid." As if he had a choice. But at least one of the agents had finally spoken to him.

Chris nodded, silenced and intimidated, even though he tried hard to channel a heroic character from one of his favorite books. He couldn't see any people at the house. Well, a curtain twitched a bit. The agents returned, toting more plastic trunks. A second trip. Two kids being exiled? Then the screaming and crying started. Two *little* kids. One broke away and ran for the house. The agent scooped him, no, her, up and carried her at arms length to avoid the flailing and kicking. The second kid tried a sit down strike, and was scooped up, as well. She didn't scream, just pushed, leaned as far away from the agent as she could. They were shoved in the back and the door hastily shut. The tantrum continued, unabated even when she rolled off the seat and onto the floor. The feds jumped in the front and the car pulled away.

Chris blinked at the girls' hair. "Wow. Blue. How old are you two? You're kind of small to be tossed out of the nest." He had to raise his voice over the temper tantrum. He met the scowling gaze of the other girl. "My parents sent me away too, but at least I'm big enough to manage on my own."

Scowl.

The temper tantrum thrower took another deep breath but just blew it out with a catch of a sob at the end. "Mommy doesn't love us any more. Steven said we were just stupid *pets* and they ought to just put us down like unwanted *puppies*."

"Steven's our step-father. " Scowler added. "Not our real one. We don't have a real one. Mommy just wanted cute little babies with peacock hair. That was before she met Steven. Now she doesn't want us anymore. They want a *real* baby."

Chris eyed their hair. Yeah, when a light hit, it was iridescent and almost purple.

"And Steven said we shouldn't be allowed to go to school. Which is stupid because we can already read." Temper Tantrum climbed up onto the seat between her sister and Chris. Scrunched up against her sister, who was pressed against the door.

"Yeah, everyone calls us morons, but we're actually smarter than most of them. I'm Chris Dunmeyer. What are your names?"

"I'm Sky and she's Sea." Tantrum thrower matched her sister's scowl. "Way. That's Mom's old last name. Steven doesn't want us to use his name. We're five."

"We're twins. We were made this way on purpose." Sea's scowl wobbled toward truculent.

"I'm sixteen. Almost seventeen. I think my parents would have come, if I'd been their only kid. But I've got two little sisters, and they're just normal kids. Mom and Dad . . . stayed to raise them." He had to look away.

Tantrum, Sky rather, reached over and patted his arm. The silent sympathy had him blinking back tears himself.

The agents got back on the interstate and sped up, heading to the far left lane. Apparently three was their quota of kids.

Chris looked out at the dimming light of evening and wondered how far they'd be going. A warm weight leaned up against him. The two girls were both asleep. He remembered when his sisters were young enough to just crash like that. And refused to cry. He diverted himself by looking at the agents. "Are you taking us all the way to Wisconsin?"

The driver took off his sunglasses, and met his eyes in the mirror. "No, we're meeting a bus in Springfield. They've got all the kids from Boston already aboard. I heard the bus is fixed up for you kids to live in, and it's supposed to have a whole bunch of cutting edge tech, an auto-kitchen and a mini fabricator."

Chris bit his lip. "That's good. I guess we'll need that, until we get gardens going and so forth. Hunting and fishing."

"Some of the adults will have hunting rifles and so forth." The other agent chimed in.

Chris nodded. "I have my fishing gear." *And two rifles, two shotguns, and lots of ammo, but I'm not going to bring that to your attention.* "We'll be fine. Although I think they ought to have let the little kids stay until they were a bit older." Chris sat back and stared at the dark landscape and the bright lights of the other traffic.

In Springfield, they waited for half an hour at a rest stop before the bus from Boston arrived. Chris helped with the trunks while a woman led the cranky twins away. The trunks were all shoved into the luggage hold of a very odd looking bus. It was a cylinder, give or take the wheels and the rather minimal ground clearance between them.

"Shaped so it will fit through the gate." The agent stuck out his hand. "Good luck, kid."

"Thanks." He shook hands, and then climbed into the bus. Inside there were nice big seats, a single row down each side.

His assigned seat was up front, behind the driver. The driver looked at him over his glasses. "You must be Chris."

"Yes, sir." *I don't have to be polite, anymore.*

"There are only five of you with driver's licenses. Watch what I do, you'll be taking over soon enough." The driver turned away, pulled a lever and the door sighed closed.

Chris gulped. Drive this huge thing? "You're not going through the gate?"

"Hell, no. You kids are on your own."

No nanny. No teachers. No foster parents. "Holy Toledo."

The girl in the front seat on the other side nodded. "They're just throwing us through the gate, they figure we've got enough stuff to make a go of it. I'm Milly. Amelia Prentice." She looked older, like a senior, or maybe even a college student. *She must be seventeen, else she wouldn't be on the bus.* Thick wavy brown hair, bright blue eyes in a tanned face. She waved at the three girls in the seats behind them; they all eyed him with disfavor. "Lillian Marshall, Ariel Wyss, Jamie Uchida. The five of us are theoretically in charge of the bus and the kids. Are those your sisters?"

"Nope, never met them before." They were all pretty, like the popular girls that never wanted to have anything to do with him. Actually, the fat ugly girls hadn't either. Oh, well.

Lillian snorted. Bright green eyes, red hair. Her slightly tan skin was about as pale as the genetically engineered came, some combination of Political Correctness and the suntan craze of twenty years ago. Both extreme whiteness and extreme blackness had been left out of the genetic engineers' palate of skin colors. "We hoped Chris was short for Christine, and we females could run things sensibly. I suppose you think boys should be in charge?"

Only when the girls have stupid attitudes like yours. "Nope. I'm going to go off and live in the wild. You four can be as in charge as the rest of the kids let you be."

A giggle from further back. "Yeah! We are *not* swapping our parents for perpetual babysitters."

Jamie leaned out and glared. "Shut up Mallory. We're just worried about the little kids. *You* can get into all the trouble you want."

A bunch of them looked as old or older than he was. "Only five of us have driver's licenses?"

Mallory scowled. She was tiny and blonde, with no figure to speak of. Female gymnast type, made to order. "My parents didn't trust their little monster with a big dangerous car. There was a kid that was in a wreck, killed two other people . . . it sort of poisoned the whole state about us driving. They didn't take the older monsters' licenses away, but us young ones? Forget it."

"Well, if we do very much driving, over there, you'll all get to learn." Milly turned her attention back to the front as the driver put the bus in gear and pulled out.

In the empty stretches between towns, the driver pulled over and let them all take turns behind the wheel. They didn't get much turning practice, but they got a feel for the weight and responsiveness of the bus, as they sped up, slowed down, and changed lanes. Huge powerful engine, massive weight. Chris loved it. It felt so powerful. But not nimble.

They picked up a few more kids in Albany. Roslyn and Lance could drive, the rest were younger, or hadn't learned.

By the time they got to the Trans World Travel headquarters, they were all relaxed and comfortable with the handling. They slept on the bus, lined up with a wild miscellany of vehicles. Just ahead of them, a mooing mass of cows was crammed into a trailer made of steel bars, two horses stood stolidly in a separate section at the front. The man driving it cursed not being able to drive through immediately and fetched water and hay for the animals. The bus driver and the woman who'd been minding the little kids wouldn't let the kids out either.

Not that they needed out. They had two bathrooms, a fab

machine and a kitchen in the back of the bus. The seats reclined till they were nearly flat, and swiveled to face either the window or the seat across the aisle. Facing the aisle, the trays could be pushed up and shoved a bit to the side, so they all met in the middle. Chris temporarily swapped seats with Jamie so the four girls could play card games. Chris walked back and checked on Sea and Sky. They perked up to see an almost familiar face, and showed him the kitchen. It was pretty easy to learn the controls, and he produced cookies to share around with the other kids.

Lillian snorted as he distributed them. "Did you notice they're not programmed for alcohol? They gave us a 'child safe' kitchen! They're still controlling us."

"Never fear, someone is sure to start a still." Chris grinned. "I read how it worked once, I'll give it a try if we develop a desperate need to get drunk and rowdy."

Besides Sky and Sea, there were four boys under ten, five boys and four girls between ten and fifteen, and the other twenty-seven of them were older than that. Chris wondered if the older bias reflected the growing unpopularity of genetic engineering. *Or the younger the kids, the more likely the parents emigrated too. Or both.*

Mid-morning the government people walked the line, got everyone woken up and their vehicles started up. The driver and the nanny got off.

Milly sat behind the wheel, and inched forward with the line. According to their instructions, she tried to stay close to the trailer full of cattle in front of her, as the line lumbered forward and built up a bit of speed.

Lillian scooted up to Milly's seat. "Remember, hands off the wheel the moment we get to the wheel guides for the gate, get ready to start steering as soon as we pop through, and do not stop."

Milly nodded. "The cows will go left, I go straight ahead, the car behind veers a bit right, and everyone is happy . . . Oh. My. God!"

Chris gawped at the spinning hoop of light and leaping lightning arcs. "Keep driving. Straight ahead. There are the guides, take your hands off the wheel . . . " The bus dived into the electrical whirlwind. A subliminal impression of a roaring torrent of light . . . and out into sunshine. The bus dropped at least a foot, the under chassis hit the ground and scrapped. Then they bounced over lumpy bumpy grass. The cattle trailer ahead was wobbling badly. The driver wasn't about to try veering. "Edge to the left, I don't think that guy dares to turn at all." The bus jounced left, then she swerved hard as the trailer brakes lit. The bus swayed, and Milly turned the wheel back to steady it. Chris winced at a scrape and glanced back. Behind them, cars were appearing out of a glowing circle, but the circle was moving away from them, spreading the cars out further.

"Okay. You can stop now." Chris took a deep breath, and stepped up to open the doors.

And down onto a whole new world.

"God damn it, you hit me!" The driver of the cattle trailer climbed down from his big Dodge dualie and stomped back to look at his cattle. Nothing showed on the pipe construction. "Stupid kids can't drive, no wonder your parents dumped you."

Chris traced the long scrape down the side of the bus. "I thought the gate would be holding still, not moving like that. I guess that made it impossible for you to turn left, like you'd been instructed. You're lucky we didn't rear end you. In as much as we'd been instructed to drive straight and not stop until we were way far away from the gate."

"Listen you little shit . . ."

Chris felt like every horrible moment for the last year was about to shatter his skull. From some detached observation point he heard himself. "Going to call the cops? You're the one who'd get a ticket. Call a lawyer? Sue us? You'll have to start a government, form up some courts, elect a judge, and pass some laws. And there's forty-two of us and only one of you. You're out voted." Chris turned back to the bus. "Asshole."

"Why you little . . . " The man started toward him.

The screaming body fell out of nowhere. Hit the ground between them. A man, naked but for some greenish slime all over and a blocky cage-like helmet over his head.

Lillian shrieked, and Chris was startled into motion. The man twisted on the ground, gasping for breath. He was big, muscular, looked like some weird Martian Warrior from a sci-fi story. All he needed was a big shiny sword and a loincloth.

Lillian screamed again, Chris turned in time see her knocked flat by another slimed and helmeted body. This one female. Screaming along with Lillian. Confused shouts drew

Chris away from the first man. Two more men. They writhed on the ground, clutching the weird helmets and screaming.

Movement behind him.

A redheaded young woman trotted between vehicles, and crouched down beside the first man. His screams dropped off into panting gasps.

"What the heck? These are total immersion sensory helmets. With *implants*. I've never heard of such a thing on a *person!* Why on Earth would anyone . . . oh. Are these the gods? The animals that were used for test runs of all the genetic engineering? I'd heard people call them kids, but I didn't realize they looked so . . . human."

Chris gulped. "They are humans. And they aren't kids anymore." In fact, this one was huge. He touched the helmet. "Is this how they controlled the gates? They said a few absolutely crucial monsters would be staying behind. I guess they decided these four weren't needed."

"Four?" The doctor or nurse or whatever she was, raised her head and spotted the naked woman on the ground. She'd curled up and gone quiet. The redhead checked her quickly, raising an eyelid with her thumb. "They've both had some sort of brain trauma. Not quite like a stroke, it's symmetrical. Minor. I hope."

Chris tried to concentrate on the woman's bald head, not the green slimed nakedness.

The doctor climbed to her feet and trotted over to the next man. He looked older, dark skinned, African features, bald under the cage that held his head. Chris looked back at the first man. Also bald. Or his head shaved. A deep tan, his face wasn't covered with goo. His eyes, as they blinked, were dark, nearly black, just a warm rim of brown around the outside, and enough flecks to tell where the pupil was.

He got his elbows under himself and sat up.

Jamie hustled over, and talked to him. He looked around a bit, and spoke. "It looks like a nice place. And it smells free." He sank back down and his eyes closed.

There were thin wires, hundreds of them, it looked like, running from helmet to scalp. Chris's stomach twisted. "Do they have things stuck all the way into their brains?"

The redhead was back. "Yes, or at least, laid out on top of the brain, in contact with it. They do that to monkeys, to rats. Not *people!* Can you kids keep an eye on them? I'll get my hospital set up as quickly as possible."

Chris let out a relieved breath at that. *A hospital. A doctor.*

"Sure. Can we move them into the shade?" Mallory glanced at the man, then looked away, blushing.

"Certainly. Try to not wiggle the helmet, and don't let them pull on any of the wires." The doctor hustled away.

The cattleman snorted, climbed back into his dualie and started it. Chris grabbed the naked man's shoulders and hauled him a bit further away from the trailer. It wasn't easy, with the goo. And he was heavy. Muscular as well as tall.

Ariel came out with blankets, but hesitated. "Will that slime wash out? We don't have many extra blankets."

19

Chris shrugged. "Use mine. I packed a sleeping bag."

They shifted the other unconscious people over closer.

Chris and three other boys heaved the last man onto the blanket, and they carried him into the shade of the bus.

One Black, three White. One woman, three men. Political correctness falling from the sky. He shivered, the spurt of humor fading. *All treated like experimental animals. Where are they from? What's going on?*

Other people started shifting their vehicles, and Chris heard people talking about staking claim to land. Most of them were heading off to the right or straight ahead along the rough line of vehicles. West? North? Chris walked around to the back of the bus and climbed up the ladder. The top wasn't flattened, he had no idea why it had a ladder. But it gave him a wider view. They were in the middle of a rolling grassland, with a few trees here and there. On the horizon to the right of the bus he caught the gleam of light on water, the blue of deep water. A line of darker vegetation probably marked the shoreline, or a forest along the shore.

It looks like a nice place. And it smells free. Chris wasn't sure what free smelled like, but like the man below, he was free now. *All I have to do is decide what to do with all this freedom.*

"Is that the ocean? Or a really big lake?" Jamie had climbed up behind him. "If it's fresh water we should claim land on the shore, don't you think?" She was another blue eyed blonde, but tall and, umm, with a well developed figure.

"Maybe. We'll look at the ground and see if we can tell if it floods." Chris turned and took a slow survey. "There's a stream that way, see the line of trees? The other way looks pretty dry. And rocky, maybe sandy. "

"Yeah, all the people who landed over there are driving this way, and over toward the lake." Jamie looked down. "Here comes the doctor. I wonder if she needs an apprentice?" The girl scrambled down the ladder. Chris followed, and was promptly drafted to help set up an Army surplus mobile hospital in a big canvas tent. And transport the four people with their weird helmets. He fled before the doctor started doing anything.

From the top of the bus he looked around again. He looked down, to judge how the shadow of the bus was changing. *Should have kept a compass in my pocket.* He decided the lake was north, the dryer lands east and the stream, west. To the south, the rolling grassy hills added trees as they rolled out of sight. *Lots of room, no need to rush to claim land until we find out what the climate, and especially the drinkable water situation is.* No more people were coming from the east, and just a few dozen vehicles were in sight, spread out. People wandered about.

Like lost puppies, wondering what to do.

What do we do?

After a couple of hours, Jamie came out, looking excited. "The doctor said I was very steady, and that she'd help me study to at least be her assistant, and maybe a doctor myself, depending on how we eventually accredited things like that. She said they'd probably have a college, and a medical school eventually."

Chris nodded. "Umm, those people?"

"The doctor said they'd probably be all right. She said the implants were organic, and would dissolve, so she just clipped them off below the skin. She said there's no ongoing trauma that she can see, without CAT scans and so forth. They're starting to wake up." She flapped a hand in farewell, and trotted back into the hospital.

Chapter Two

9 June 2117

Anyone's Guess

He was in a tent.

Harry frowned, wondering how that had happened.

"Awake finally, are you?"

"Gisele!" Harry frowned. Beyond that instant recognition, very little stirred.

"Do you know your name?" She stooped over him, petit and shapely.

"Harry, and you are Gisele, aren't you?"

"Am I? I haven't been too certain." A big bandana covered her head, all her hair concealed. He couldn't remember what color it was. Her facial bones were excellent, the bright blue eyes, superb.

Another woman bustled up, a young one with green eyes and red hair in a pony tail. "Now, here's another one of you awake. Thank goodness. Really, we hadn't thought you gods were going to be coming with us. Did they exile you, too?"

"I, I suppose so." *Gods?* Harry looked around. "Where are we?"

"We're calling it Exile, because, well that's why we're here. They called it Extension, from some geologic thing they spotted with a satellite. I heard the lake to the north is fresh water, so maybe it's one of the Great Lakes, except we don't know if the geography is the same or not."

"Oh?" Harry lay back shakily. *What is a great lake, other than big? And who are "they?"*

"Only three more of you still unconscious." The redhead burbled on. Was it nerves or did she just talk constantly? "Two here and one way to the west. Goodness, we were hoping we wouldn't need to set up the hospital so quickly." She looked around. "Army surplus M.A.S.H. unit, you see?"

It didn't *look* mashed. Harry turned his head and saw more cots beyond his.

"I don't know why they didn't remove the implants and helmets before they sent you, but someone said they thought you had to have them to control the gate even as you went through." She flashed a light in his eyes and nodded, apparently satisfied with whatever she saw there. "That sounds an awful lot like they were shutting down the gate, but maybe they can do it with regular people now, or computers, so they got rid of every last one of us."

Harry couldn't keep up with the rush of words. He blinked, lost.

"Do you know these men? Do you know their names? This one keeps fading in and out of consciousness. The other fellow hasn't so much as twitched yet. I don't know what those implants did to you."

She helped Harry up, and steadied him as he staggered

over to the next cot.

"I, I. He's always in trouble. I don't . . . I don't know his name. He looks drowned. Puffy and nasty. Was he bald? I don't remember bald." He looked over at the other man. "Romeo, but that was a joke. He looks funny bald. All his girlfriends are going to complain. Rom Eww? Oww?"

"That's it!" Gisele said from behind him. "Romeau. It has been on the tip of my tongue all day."

"All day? How long have I been here?"

"We all arrived yesterday about noon, and it's nearly sunset today. The days are a few minutes longer, our watches are practically useless."

He remembered watches. Yes. He looked at his wrist. "Good grief!"

"Yes, they depilated all of you for the immersion tanks. If you'd been in longer, your skin would have adjusted." The redhead looked at the unconscious men in pity. "At least they aren't screaming any more. I think something interfered badly with the contact circuits in your brains. Maybe passing through the gate. At least they were organic conductors, they'll dissolve gradually over the next year or so. I cut the connectors off at the outer skull surface."

Harry looked at the man on the bed. Tiny dots of scabs were scattered across forehead and scalp. Harry refrained from feeling his own head. What he could see of himself looked like he'd been immersed in water for days. His dark skin was splotchy and peeling in damp thin sheets. He didn't look quite as chapped and drowned as the other two. He touched a loose flap and pulled carefully.

"Don't do that. It'll make sores."

"Yes, Ma'am." He snuck a sideways peek at Gisele. Yes, under makeup she had the same skin . . . mess. The bandana was explained, then. He felt his own smooth scalp, and hoped to hell it wasn't permanent. Yep, little bumps from . . . contact circuits on his brain? His stomach roiled and he shivered. *Brain damage. That's why I'm not remembering right.* He looked out at the bright sunshine at the end of the row of beds and thought about running away, as far as he could travel, and wondered what he would find.

"The old shortwave radios work. We've gotten reports in from up and down the line. From here to the end of the line, there are three other clumps of you guys. These two and a fellow at the very end are the last ones left unconscious."

"Who?" Harry wondered what she meant by the end of the line. What line? "Err, Miss?"

The woman blushed. "Ginny Wacolm. Doctor Wacolm. I had just started my residency when all this . . . Let me get my list. I wrote them all down, figured you guys all knew each other . . . They don't all know their complete names. Dr. Mercy Green and Ms. Abram and Martie Branson are all at the furthest east location. Then someone called Chance and a teenaged boy named Richie are a bit closer. Michael, Edward Virtue and Barry Virtue are about a thousand miles to the east of us. We think, calculating from the time their sun rose this morning.

Those last two are pretty sure they are brothers. The other unconscious man is young, maybe a teenager, blond with very strikingly colored eyes, gold in color. He's in the far east."

Harry shook his head. The names didn't seem to mean anything to him. The nice Dr. Wacolm led him back to bed, and he slept and had dreams about moving, going, traveling far away and always finding new things, new people.

In the morning they fed him and put him to work. He followed orders, and dug holes where required. Tamped in fence posts and stretched rolls and rolls of barbed wire.

He gradually picked up information. They had just arrived here from somewhere else, and were scattered in a long line across the prairie. Instead of all getting together, they were instead coalescing around favorable spots every few miles. The nuclei of a hundred towns. And the people who didn't want to coalesce were going north or south, away from the roughly east-west line of arrival.

"A new world" they called it. No mention of rockets or spaceships. Apparently everyone had driven here with their families and possessions stuffed into their cars and trailers.

Harry whimpered and gave up trying to understand.

Romeau staggered out to join him at dusk. "That last fellow is sort of awake, too. Gisele asked if you could come take a look at him, after we scrounge something to eat. Why didn't we bring any food? Everyone else did."

"I, wasn't there a bubble?" The thought fled as quickly as it had come.

"Oh, yes, my Temple of Love." He looked around baffled. "I had a dream about putting it up on top of a hill somewhere. Fully automated kitchen."

When Harry thought about looking for a bubble, his head hurt. He accepted a bowlful of beans from the rancher he'd been helping all day, and split them with Romeau. He wasn't very hungry.

Back at the mashed hospital, the last man was sitting up in bed. "Wolf something." He looked up and frowned. "I should know you. I'm something Wolf, maybe."

"Old." Harry said suddenly.

The young man lit up. "That's it. Old." He lay back with a sigh of relief. "I hated not knowing my own name." He drifted off to sleep.

"Hmph. Old Wolf? He doesn't *look* like a Native American." A woman he hadn't met, frowned down at the man in the bed. "I suppose he's a bit tan, like an Italian or something. But then all you highly engineered people are tannish."

"What's a native american?" Harry glanced at his arm. *That's a heck of a tan. I think I'm . . . black? That's not right either. I'm obviously brown.*

"Why it's someone from one of the Indian tribes. You know, Cowboys and Indians?" She looked hopeful, but Harry had to shake his head. A chunk of knowledge, gone. Maybe it would come back, like a lost cat.

It was warm outside, and he and Romeau withdrew from

the other people, with their families and neighborhood groups, with their cars and all their possessions. Their thoughts and emotions. They lay in the long grass and stared at beautiful bright stars, millions of them. A falling star streaked across the sky.

Whatever had happened, had happened. They were alive, and the stars were bright.

Sometime later Gisele and Old Wolf joined them.

"It's too noisy," the man said. "They all get mad and yell in my head. I dare not relax."

Gisele nodded. "I have trouble shielding too. Every time I relax and almost fall asleep I hear weeping."

"We need to . . . go away." Harry said. "Far enough that we can't hear anything."

Romeau sighed. "Can we start now? I can't sleep."

Old Wolf stood up, stretched, then staggered. Harry felt the faint jolt and froze.

"Earthquake." He cleared his throat and straightened. "Just a little one. I grew up in California."

Old Wolf straightened from his crouch. "Yeah, it was too brief to be a big one far away. The bigger, the longer it shakes. California . . . I think I've been there." He leaned and peered into the darkness.

Harry followed his gaze. Something large and dark moved toward them. Wolf made a squeezing gesture and tossed a small fireball that direction.

The lion was huge.

Flat to the ground as it stalked, it froze in the light for a moment, then accelerated up the hill toward them. As the fireball fizzled out, Harry spotted other moving patches.

He threw a fireball of his own, but missed. A bloody line erupted across the lion's face and it collapsed.

"Slice them." Wolf made a hacking motion. "Like cutting metal."

"Metal?" Harry didn't remember cutting anything, and tried another fireball.

A lioness the size of a small horse flinched away as the fireball fizzled and died. Harry backpedaled, gathering power in his hand, trying for more time to get enough power compressed. In the confused darkness, the power, the fire, gleamed off a mouthful of teeth. He threw the glowing handful as the beast reared in front of him. He ducked, the weight knocked him flat, and claws raked.

Pain like an electric shock shot through his body. He frantically fought his way out from under four hundred pounds of lioness. The animal twitched, stilled. It was quiet and dark. Another fireball burned briefly, as Gisele tossed it upward.

Six dead lions. Four shocked and bloodied gods.

Harry collapsed, trying to slow his descent. The pain was focused on his right leg. The dim light mercifully dulled the colors. That dark fluid didn't look nearly as frightening as blood . . .

Gisele hunched like an old lady and crept over to him. "Let me see your chest Harry. And your leg. Damned reflexes, she got you good. Lay back down."

"Chest?" He looked down. More dark fluid.

Wolf produced a medical kit of impressive size and a flashlight from thin air.

All the fluids turned suddenly red.

Harry closed his eyes, shivering. "Damn. Have we even forgotten about predators? Are we insane, just walking around out here?"

He heard the snip of scissors. Jumped as a burning liquid added an all new layer of pain to his leg. Then tight wrappings. Then the painful liquid hit his chest.

He gasped, and opened his eyes, tried to concentrate on Wolf.

"I guess we should have been more alert. Has everyone else forgotten too? Or . . . did they just arrive?" Wolf scanned out into the darkness, with his eyes closed. "There are other predators out there. We'd better warn people."

Harry looked at the lioness, close enough to touch. He eyed the faint drift of smoke from her mouth and empty eye sockets. He propped himself on one elbow, to see more. Romeau examined another lioness with a burn through the chest. The other four lions were laying about in parts.

Slice? Like an invisible sword? Harry sank back down, woozy. *I'll have to learn how to do that.*

Wolf produced a stretcher from nowhere, or possibly a bubble, and he and Romeau carried Harry back to the Mashed Hospital. And abandoned him there as a horse's scream and many running hooves broke the night's silence.

It was a long night. Harry could only listen. Any attempt to help would just get in healthy people's way.

By dawn the animals that hadn't bolted straight through fences were tightly corralled and guarded. Everyone had slept in their cars.

In the morning, after a quick consultation, everyone agreed to move to the western side of the pastures already fenced and barricade a small valley with a sizable stream.

Chapter Three
10 June 2117
Camp on the Exile World

Fortunately the bang of the rifle frightened the predators, because Chris wasn't sure he'd managed to hit a single one of the long low shapes circling the hospital just beyond the limits of the lights of the cars, trucks and bus surrounding the building. Two of the girls had little handguns. He had the only rifle on the bus, and shooting at moving shadows in the night was different than the target practice he'd managed to get in over the last two months. Lance climbed up and relieved him, but no matter how wistful the looks, Chris wasn't about to hand the rifle to someone who'd never fired a gun.

"Just yell. I'll be right out." He climbed down and found Milly reorganizing the bus.

"Girls back here by the kitchen, boys up front. Little kids in the middle, boys forward, girls back." She wrinkled her nose. "There are eight empty seats, I put them all at the very back, by the bathroom."

"I see. Umm, yeah, that tent of mine looks a little impractical, all of a sudden. I guess we'll be sleeping in here for some time." Chris yawned. "I've got to sleep. If anyone sees anything at all that even might be a lion or hyena or leopard or .

. . " he broke off as she made a rude gesture. "Well, you'll probably have to kick me to wake me up. But first I'd better clean the rifle." He yawned, and forced himself to get out the cleaning kit. *Suddenly this gun is very important. And I really need to be sure it stays in working order.*

His sleep was disturbed by the occasional sound of hooves. Half the horses, cattle, and sheep people had brought with them had escaped. It looked like they were getting most of them back, though.

When he finally gave up and got up, it was midday. The hospital was being dismantled and packed.

Jamie glanced over at him. "We're moving a bit west, to where there's a stream, and more trees. We're going to circle up and start building a wall to keep the predators out."

Chris eyed the foursome of cows being trailed by an exhausted horse. He did a quick double take at the rider. He dropped his voice. "Isn't that one of the, you know . . ."

Lillian snorted, behind him. "Naked guys. Gods. Whatever. Yeah. They sort of remember stuff, but they're way screwed up inside their heads. They aren't even sure about their *names*." She tossed her head. "And don't even think about inviting them into the bus. They're grownups, they'll take over. And, well, I suppose being a boy the dangers of strange, mentally unstable men wouldn't occur to you. But don't think you're immune." She tossed her head again and marched off.

Chris sniffed disdainfully. But he fetched his rifle and walked out ahead of both the bus and the RV that was packed full of hospital. The bus wasn't built for rough country; the bottom of the luggage compartment scraped several times, but they never quite high centered. They even got across the little stream and into a position on the crest of the opposite ridge, as part of the village's temporary wall.

A big fat guy was yelling at everyone, and getting them almost organized.

"Those lions can jump right over most of the cars." Chris had to admire the way they were all, umm, en echelon, so their lights would shine out and cover a considerable area.

"You will sleep in your cars, all the livestock will be inside and loose. They will be running around, and damn near as dangerous as the lions. Stay in your cars unless you have a weapon and can use it." The fat guy put his bullhorn down and accepted a drink from a woman who waved and pointed as she talked.

Inside the bus, a couple of the girls were working the kitchen, and food started circulating. Chris checked that Sea and Sky were eating (of course; the girls had probably fed the little kids first) and then climbed up on top of the bus.

Lance and Mathew were already up there.

"I wish they'd made the roof flat." Chris balanced over to them. The cylinder of the bus was big enough that it wasn't that much of a problem.

Lance grinned. "I wish I had a rifle."

Mathew nodded.

Chris cleared his throat. "I have another, and two

shotguns. I just learned how to use them a couple of months ago . . . We could ask someone for lessons, but what if they just take the guns?"

"I hate being a kid." Mathew made a face. "How about you giving us lessons with one rifle and one shotgun, then we'll look semi-competent when we ask for further lessons. So they can't claim they're taking them for our own good. And if they do take them, they don't get everything."

"Good idea." His attention switched back to the fat man and the argument going on around him.

"I caught them, I ought to at least get something for my work." A man in a Padre's ball cap was glaring from the fat man back to the truck driver asshole.

The truck driver was shaking his head. "They're my cattle. They're branded with my brand. They're mine. My animals are all I brought with me, and both the horses are dead, and probably the other half of the cows. Thank you very much for catching them, but no, you can't have them."

"Mike, that's the way it's got to be. Property is property. Now, I saw some local critters that looked like big damn longhorns. As soon as we're safe, we can have a round up. Catch a bunch of heifer calves. Cross them with domestic cattle, and we'll all be set."

The ball cap man tossed his hands in the air and walked away. ". . . risked my life to help that asshole . . . "

Lance snickered. "Boy is he ever bad at making friends."

Chris turned away. "That's not very smart of him, we all . .

. need . . ."

The first of the "gods" was outside the circle of cars. The big muscular man. All he was wearing was a pair of pants, ugly green scrubs that ended about mid calf. The helmet was gone, his bald head and naked back looked scabby and nasty. He had a military style rifle in his right hand, not ready to fire, even though he was clearly stalking something.

A patch of dappled shade moved, turned into a leopard that clearly didn't like being treated like prey. It turned to leave, but the bald man made an abrupt gesture with his left hand. The leopard leaped up in the air and came down in two pieces. The head rolled away, and the body twitched and spurted blood.

Chris sat down abruptly, scrambled to not slide off the bus.

"What did he just do?" Lance gawped out at the dead leopard.

"How did he do that?" Mathew's voice turned gleeful. "Magic. Just like the rumors."

"Telekinesis and teleportation and telepathy and stuff. ESP. It's science, not magic." Lance retorted.

Chris choked faintly. "No. He must have thrown something. There's no such thing as magic, and dressing it up with made-up latin words from a science fiction book doesn't change that. It's not possible." He rolled over and scrambled down the ladder. *All the novels I've read, all the times I wished it was real . . . Don't go wonky, Chris. This is a dangerous place, and you haven't had a good night's sleep for . . . three days? Something like that.*

He sat down abruptly in the long grass. "I have passed through a dimensional gate to a parallel world full of savage beasts. Why am I caviling about magic? I'm in one of my books."

Jamie dropped down beside him. "And you are talking to yourself. What a night! I . . . helped do stitches in Harry's chest. The real doctor did the ones in his leg, man, that lion came close to killing him! They did kill a couple of people. And there were a bunch of other injuries, too. The hospital is nearly full. We're just lucky the predators mostly went after the livestock."

"Yeah. I didn't think about, well, landing someplace really dangerous."

She nodded. "I remember the vids of the dinosaur planets."

"Yeah. It could have been a lot worse. Stupid company. Did they actually explore here?"

"The company, or the government? Did you know the government threw some of the company executives through the gate and then took over the whole place?"

"The government?"

"That's why there were so many soldiers around, on the other side. And maybe the people who were handling the gate didn't know much about the gods. There were some people here, I heard them talking about driving to something they called a beacon, to report that some of the gods came here. I think the gods weren't supposed to come. I think they escaped. What if they really do need them to operate the gate, and we can't go back?"

Chris blinked at her. "We never could go back. Ever."

"But we could mail order stuff. Our parents could change their minds and come. They could at least visit us." She was starting to cry, and he wrapped an arm around her and let her bawl into his shoulder for awhile.

It wasn't a bit romantic, like in a book. Her eyes were red and her nose was running, and he didn't have a hanky to offer her. When they started chivvying the cattle and horses into the barricade of cars, he nudged her. "C'mon, we've got to get back to the bus. It's going to be wild in here, tonight."

Chris didn't remember the leopard until midnight.

It wasn't magic. There's no such thing.

Chapter Four

10 June 2117

Unnamed camp, Exile World

"We need to catch all the lost livestock." Harry scowled at his leg. He could barely walk. *All I can do is talk!* "Before they all get eaten by god knows what."

Romeau perked up. "I know cattle and horses. Damn, I wish Sungold was old enough to ride." A vertical line creased his brow. "Except I seem to have misplaced him."

A young man walking by heard him.

"Come on. If we can catch the horses, I'll loan you one. Leo Harding."

"Romeau . . . something. Old Wolf and you know Harry. And Dr. Gisele . . . something. God, I hope our memories return. These holes are disconcerting."

Harry relaxed while Wolf prowled, rifle in hand.

The man looked quite bad; hairless and scabby. Tall, muscular and dangerous. When he found a leopard, he killed it with that "slice."

That night the predators stayed away. Perhaps they'd cleaned out the local prides and packs. Harry sighed. That probably meant all the surrounding packs and prides would move in.

At dawn Romeau saddled up and rode out again. They needed to find all the loose livestock that had survived two nights out there.

Harry scowled at his leg and turned to watch Old Wolf, out beyond the circled vehicles.

Waving his hands. Backing away as an entire building slid out of nowhere.

Harry grabbed his crutches and limped up the hill. Stared at the low modern building. "That's redwood, isn't it? From California."

"Yes?" Old Wolf frowned. "I . . . might have gotten it there." He walked up the steps and across the porch. The interior smelled fruity, the first room was large, with barrels racked along one side, tables, wine racks, glasses.

"This is a winery, isn't it?" A young man had followed them in. Boy. Sixteen years old, maybe. Wide-eyed, he looked younger.

"This looks like a tasting room. I've toured wineries." A young woman stepped in carefully, as if she expected the floor to disappear.

More people peeked in the door.

They explored, and found rooms with glass and metal vats, presses, bottling equipment. An office and bedroom on one side. A fully automated fabber kitchen on the other. Laundry room, bathroom. Several other rooms, unused. An unfinished attic.

Harry squinted. "What is in those bubble things?"

Wolf frowned, looked where he was pointing. "I'm not sure." He reached and pinched one.

The black animal startled back, then stopped and looked around.

"Why do I have a horse in my winery?" Wolf looked baffled, but reached out and scratched the animal's neck. "And how am I going to get it out of the attic?"

"He looks like a baby. A big one, mind you." The young woman proffered a tentative hand. "I'm Milly Prentice."

"Old Wolf. That's Harry."

"Chris," the boy put in.

Other introductions circled. The horse was escorted out. It had no problem with the stairs.

They got some odd looks as the building drew everyone's attention.

Harry eased himself down in one of the chairs on the front porch. He could hear the comments circulating.

"They're gods. Of course they can do magic."

"There's no such thing as magic. It's . . . an odd effect of the genetic engineering."

"They look disgusting."

Harry pried open an eye. "Don't you kids have parents you could go help?"

A general shuffle. Chris got juggled to the front to be the spokeskid. "No. Our parents didn't come with us. The government people split us sudden 'orphans' up into bus loads, with enough of us old enough to drive and sent us through."

"Damn. How many of you are there, and what supplies do you have?"

"Forty-two. We have clothes, hand tools, seeds and a few weeks worth of food. A small fabber and auto-kitchen."

Old Wolf shook his head. "Good thing they stopped making babies five years ago, otherwise there'd be little ones too."

"They stopped making babies?" Harry's alarm collapsed as the kids started laughing.

"*Genetically engineered* babies." Chris wiped tears of mirth from his eyes. "That's why they exiled us. They think we're all freaks, especially you gods."

Harry bit his lip. "There was a . . . gate?"

"To a parallel world." Milly waved at the prairie.

Yes. They were exiled, but how did we four get here? They drove through a gate and we . . . hitch hiked? Looking over the kids, Harry estimated their ages to run from Milly's and Chris's upper teens to a blue haired pair that looked about five. "We'll all band together and survive. Walls first. Then cabins."

"A store." Miriam Wilson was a tiny woman, slim and athletic, in the way of girl gymnasts. "I'm starting a list of everything everyone is going to order, when the gate opens again. I'll order a bunch of stuff to add to the stock we brought to put on the store shelves."

Harry blinked. "Oh. Right. Once a month all colonies get a connection to Earth, right?"

"Right. That should be in a month, twenty-six days, actually."

Jack Otts was big man in every sense. Darker than Harry, nearly as tall and much wider. "That's too soon. I need to get all the livestock owners to register brands before we get any more arguments about who owns which damned cow. Then we need to co-ordinate with all the nearby villages, get an agreement to honor brands. We should get an order out for branding irons as soon as possible." He shrugged. "There's always the month after that. I just don't like the idea of starting with fights over ownership of all these strayed cows."

"Surely we've got a blacksmith around here somewhere." Romeau protested. "We should do as much as possible ourselves."

Miriam nodded. "We need to make things locally; transportation is going to be a problem. The magnetic anchor is at the western-most end of the line. I've been talking on the shortwave, getting orders and payment information straight with the lady who has taken charge there. We figured it's at least a thousand miles, but if there aren't any major rivers blocking the path, we can probably get in enough of a road and temporary bridges to send trucks for our stuff, the next month. But what about the groups that landed further away? It's going to be a problem, getting stuff to the far east."

"We need a boat." Harry looked north, to the lake. "I wonder if all the lakes are connected."

"I think I have a boat." Old Wolf glanced at his bubble-filled winery.

"The far east and the near east are both on salt water bodies." Jack shrugged. "When I saw the lions, I thought, Africa, but those fresh water lakes aren't the Mediterranean. From what people have told me on the radio, there's no outlet to the West, just a river on the east end."

Chris bit his lip and blurted out. "I don't think you gods were supposed to have come. You may need to hide, if a search party comes through, looking for you."

Romeau and Gisele swapped startled looks, and then they both nodded.

"I don't think you'd better plan on that gate." Old Wolf frowned, obviously trying to remember. "I think we may have been a necessary part of the gate mechanism. So when we escaped we may have broken something."

"Broken . . . " Miriam looked at him, wide-eyed. "You mean we won't ever be able to go home? George and I were just going to pioneer for twelve years, until the boys were grown up and established. Then we were going to retire in Vermont. Visit for a month around Christmas every year." She looked around at the raw beginnings of a primitive village in horror. "Do you have any idea what old age will be like in a place like this?"

People had been listening, and gathered closer.

"Retirement? What about childbirth?"

"What about electricity?"

"What if we can't find oil nearby?"

"Are you saying we're stranded here? Forever?"

"What have you done?"

In the back of the small crowd a man snorted. "They're building another trans-dimensional gate in Pennsylvania. Remember? It won't be finished for another two years. But no one is stuck here forever. The next generation of computers will render your live assistance unnecessary."

Harry looked over the intervening heads. The man looked familiar. Oriental. "Chou. You're one of the Chou's aren't you. In accounting or something."

The man glared. "Yeah. Want to make something of it? With luck, once they get the gate up, I can get permission to move to the world that most of the family was exiled to."

"Most . . . Other world?"

"Fried your brain properly, didn't you, Frankenstein? Yeah, they sent all the engineered to five worlds. The family planned on finding a nice one just for themselves, and wound up arrested and shoved through randomly. I was on vacation. By the time I got home, everyone else was gone." He gave a disgusted snort. "Two years."

Harry nodded, vague memories, knowledge without context started surfacing. "There were protocols . . . if you were stranded. Marooned. Fire up the beacon on the solstice, summer or winter, because that could be found easily enough. They said that the week after was when they'd search for people. Weren't there classes?"

Old Wolf nodded. "Right, how to track the sun and identify the solstice. The beacon needed to be boosted if possible. Batteries or a generator. They'd start searching on the solstice, and for a week after."

The stolid man stepped up beside Miriam, nodded. George, her husband. "Well, we'll all just have to get by with what we brought for a couple of years. Not the best situation, but hardly a disaster. And anyway, you could be wrong. Maybe the gate is just fine."

Old Wolf opened his mouth, then shut it.

Harry kept his mouth closed, and didn't say anything about, oh, sabotaging the beacon so they wouldn't wind up wired back into the machines. Leaving the matter alone was the best idea. When the gate opened, it would be time to worry about the personal dangers. Today they had other challenges. "So, getting back to building, which we need to do, with or without a gate, how are we going to build this barricade?"

A man of about thirty nodded. "There are plenty of trees. We need to start cutting them and ditching to plant the poles."

Wolf walked off to the side of the patio and stared at the ground. Chopped twice with his hand then gestured, as if inviting a guest in. A strip of ground obliged, flew into his face and exploded all over the patio.

The kids laughed and they all crowded around to see.

Harry estimated the hole three feet deep and twice as long. A foot wide.

The man cleared his throat. "Yes. Just about like that. Perhaps I'd better round up some people with saws. I'm Dave, by the way."

Old Wolf concentrated on the ditching, while the chain saws roared in the forest, and their single harness-trained team of horses hauled the long trunks to the ditch. A young woman named Muriel had a tractor and started ditching on the other side of the little valley.

Harry organized the orphans. Then more children gravitated his direction. He put them all to work. They packed the dirt in around the poles, fetched and carried supplies for the other groups, took water to the workers, and in a few hours, sandwiches some women were making. The littlest kids spent most of their time running and playing, making instant friends. The teenagers spent half their time eyeing each other, too socially inept to simply walk up and introduce themselves. Well, not immediately. The groups slowly merged, then new groupings started showing up. The little kids wore out, and Harry parked them in Wolf's tasting room with a movie on the vid screen there. Star Wars, the third remake, his own favorite. *Of all the things to remember clearly.*

All day long, riders returned, herding exhausted cows. Harry spotted Chris trailing after a thin girl to check on some big tame red and white cows. The boy ran off to the bus, and returned with a first aid kit. Ah yes. Kindness to animals. One of the easiest ways to a girl's heart. Although kittens were usually easier than cows. One of them kicked. Chris landed on his butt, while the girl giggled.

The wall lengthened, log by log.

Romeau rode in with a dozen cows. He gave the winery an

odd look. He was back in a few minutes. He walked to the end of the completed wall and pulled out a ... building.

"Temple of Love" was engraved over the wide columned front porch. The Grecian style white marble edifice had a full catering kitchen, two large open rooms and an ornate apartment in the back.

Harry limped through it all and smothered laughter. "Romeau, this is not a house, this is a wedding chapel. It even has a honeymoon suite. Probably rents out with a generic semi-religious person with a license to perform marriages."

"Me?" Romeau looked doubtful. "To be honest, I don't recall ever sleeping in a round bed." He shrugged and invited everyone to sleep indoors.

Harry looked down at his bandages in disgust. *I want to go, to explore this new world. I want to see everything. Instead, I'm stuck here, not even able to help. We could get run over by predators, or for that matter, elephants. We're guessing about how tall to make the walls, what if we're wrong? We'd be stuck inside* with *the lions.* He shook his head. "Stop emoting, Harry." *Talking to myself now? Well, hardly the strangest thing about me. What I need to do is build a good, large house for these kids, and get them well set up and independent before I take off exploring. Which will have the added advantage of giving me a home to come back to.*

Home.

It seemed like a foreign concept. Like something he'd never had before.

Chapter Five

1 July 2117

Town under construction, Exile

"They may have had their brains scrambled by the gate stuff, but they aren't dangerous to us. I don't see any sign of a desire to own us or control us." Chris surveyed the pack of kids. The four littlest were collapsed in a puppy-heap with a couple of the girls hovering over them. Scary to see otherwise attractive females going gooey in the brain. The tall native grass was tromped down in a circle beside the bus. Most likely they'd sleep inside again, even if the walls were finished today.

"I think we can depend on them to fend off other controlling people—like those teachers—while we steer them in the right direction. And they do need help. Hell, they need keepers."

Ariel, who was not interested in the littles, nodded. "I think it was the wires in their brains. I think they messed something up when they ripped loose."

Chris shuddered at the thought. "Nobody ought to be allowed to do that."

Mallory nodded. "It's slavery. Worse. They were treated like animals."

"They're part animal. So are we, but not as much." Lillian

sniffed.

"One or two genes." Milly frowned at the other girl.

"They're people. They aren't animals." Jamie crossed her arms. "Gisele is *brilliant*. We talked about medical school."

"Oh, enough." Chris waved the gods' defenders down. "If they come to arrest them, we'll hide them. Or just watch for goons and warn them. They have a whole world to get lost in. And they can certainly take care of themselves."

"I'm not so sure about Harry, he needs help the most. But those building techniques are awesome." Matt was another of the almost eighteen year olds. "I think we should get Harry to open a . . . well, if we're headed for a Medieval existence, call it a Tavern and Inn. As we grow up, we'll move away, and then Harry can rent rooms. Be the Barkeeper. It'll be a good job for him if his leg doesn't heal right."

That got nods.

Milly added, "He looks so old. The others look, well, I suppose in their twenties. But we need to keep an eye on Harry. He's a nice old guy."

Right. We'll just adopt the most powerful and scary people I've ever met. Chris waffled.

Lillian shrugged. "We'll keep an eye on Gisele as well, she goes all odd sometimes."

"We'll make sure Harry and Gisele have got homes. Anyhow, we'll all want places for our own, as we get older. For now an inn sort-of-thing would let us have some privacy and freedom, and still take care of the little guys." Chris looked at his scribbled notes. *I hope someone knows how to make paper.* "Next thing: they're talking about school and college. I wasn't learning a thing in high school. I think we can just quit at about fourteen or fifteen. Work for awhile, figure out what we want to be, then either start college level classes if we can find an expert, or just apprentice, get the lectures while also learning hands on. Like Jamie working in the hospital."

Since that got twenty-seven of the thirty-eight kids who were awake, out of school, it was generally approved of.

The other eleven kids scowled. One of them, Dane Kyber, nodded reluctantly. "That sounds about right, but right now we need to earn a place here in the village as equals to any adults. We need to work, build and own our own homes, with or without this tavern of yours. And we especially need to stick to these gods, and learn how to do magic." *Kid was pretty smart, for fourteen.*

"But . . . " Benita frowned. "I just had my diabetes gene fixed. I'm not magic."

"What suites do you have? Do you know what company did them?" Milly drummed her fingers. "I researched most of the companies. My laptop will have the suites they were all offering, if it still works after being tossed around by that landing." She got up abruptly and climbed into the bus.

"How long will your batteries last, though?" Dane followed her.

"I've got a solar charger, but still, a couple of years and computers will be useless. Something is bound to break." She

53

pulled a backpack out of the crammed vehicle and lugged it back outside.

"So? That means we need to produce something we can sell on Earth, so we can buy stuff."

Chris craned his neck and watched the screen over her shoulder. "Yeah. So, this list of suites, I've got the Happy Kids BTSS and something . . . F23?"

"Ooo! Bigger, taller, stronger, smarter! That's got improved antibodies and multiple enhanced cancer response, too. And the male power gene. Plus F23. That's a cosmetic thing, hair color, eye color, natural skin tones, nose shape. Happy Kids made most of theirs additive instead of replacement. So you've got your Dad's nose, slightly modified and so forth."

Chris sighed. "Mom's nose, actually. So, Mom and Dad never told me I was genetically engineered. Guess they were afraid I'd tell someone. Or afraid of what I might do, if I tried, you know, stuff. Like kill from ten feet away with a wave of your hand." He started to wave his hand, and tucked it hastily in a pocket.

Milly shrugged. "The power genes, because of the god controversy, were removed from their standard suites at some point. Fifteen years ago? And nobody *ever* did the double power genes for kids who belonged to someone. No gods 'out in the wild,' so to speak, except the early university experiments. Some of us may have two copies of the Witch gene, but that's a dominant, so two doesn't give us any more oomph than one, doesn't make me a Goddess. Lots of parents left out the power genes on purpose anyway. Anyone with BTSS2 doesn't have one unless they specifically asked to have it put back in. For NewGene . . . And let me see if I can find out when Number One Kids did it . . ."

"They didn't really call them Witches and Magicians. That was the media's fault. They went all sensationalist and ruined it for everyone." Lillian scowled, and read over Milly's shoulder.

Eventually they organized and sorted themselves out.

"Thirteen Witches, twelve Magicians, and two people with that substitute California Kids tried to call Wizard. It didn't work very well." Milly looked around at them. "We need to ask for magic lessons."

Chris shuffled his feet, his stomach flopped over. "That's why we were exiled."

Milly nodded. "I know, but think! Now we're on a World where most of the kids have engineered genes."

Chris nodded slowly. *Iris was exiled, that means she's engineered. Or her brother. Or both.* "And about half of us with power genes. If no one is prejudiced, then we could use it for anything. Openly. I wonder what we can do? I wonder if the gods know? As soon as we've got the wall up, I'm going to ask them."

Milly nodded. "*We're* going to ask them."

The bus had a shortwave radio. Lance fiddled with it, not broadcasting, but listening in as other people talked about what they were doing. Most of them had lost livestock, and were building walls as fast as possible. One place had a large river, and crocodiles. They also had three gods, and the person on the radio sounded a bit dubious. A group right on the lake reported that the water was very cold, and that they'd seen an iceberg. Three villages said they were on salt water bodies, and that the fishing was excellent. A man from here, what had Harry called him? Chow? Or someone who sounded a lot like him, talked about the possibility of the gate having been damaged, and how it could be two years, or more if there were construction delays, before the new gate was finished. That brought a storm of comments from everywhere. Chow commented that everyone ought to be especially cautious around the mentally unstable 'gods' and that when the gate was open they ought to arrest the gods and send them back. That increased the storm. Few people spoke in defense of the gods. Chris finally elbowed his way to the radio.

"Do you approve of slavery? You think the way you were treated was harsh? Exiled because of a few engineered genes to keep you healthy? These sarcastically named gods were legally not human. They had no civil rights. They were property. They were used for experiments. Raped. Murdered. Drugged. They had brain implants as if they were animals in an experiment. They escaped.

"And maybe they *were* necessary for the operation of the Gates, but nothing, *nothing*, excuses the way they were treated. You don't like it here? Remember what the alternate was?

Sterilization. No right to vote. Some places you weren't allowed to drive a car. Tell me, does a person who was treated the way you were treated have a right to bitch because *these* people escaped much worse conditions?

"Of course you have that right. You just won't get any respect, *slaver*. You are indeed less than human. You are a disgrace to the entire mammalian phylum. You sicken me."

He slapped the microphone back into Lance's hand and stalked out.

A couple dozen of the bus kids gawped at him.

"Wow."

He didn't look to see who he'd impressed. Or horrified.

***

The next morning, Harry shoved himself to his feet and headed for the nearest grove of trees. Limping, but without crutches. "Wolf, come show me that slice of yours." Before he was halfway to the trees, he wished he'd brought the crutches.

A hardwood sapling was his first victim. With a staff to lean on he started felling the straightest of the trees, the spell cut away limbs with ease. He passed out about noon and woke in the Mashed Hospital, again.

"That was a brilliant idea, Harry." Ginny Wacolm beamed at him. "But you need to pace yourself. Use outside power sources as much as you can, and stop when the inner power is low. Your Indian friend showed all the other magically able how to do it."

"I thought we four were the only gods here?"

"You are, but we've got some people with a single power gene. They can do this as well as you lot can."

"Oh. Of course. I didn't think. Good." When he tried to get up she pressed him back down.

"Dinner in half an hour or so, and a good night's sleep, for you. Tomorrow you can get back to over-doing."

A couple of the boys trotted in to check on him. "Everyone was worried." Brandon frowned at Harry's head. "Lady Gisele said you weren't really bald."

"And she said she wasn't bald either. Then she went and cried on Romeo's shoulder. She's worse than my big sister." Pete scowled fiercely. "And I don't miss them."

Nine years old. How could his parents send him away?

"And the Old Wolf said we should bring you home for dinner. All the boys are camping out in the attic. Some of the girls are going with Lady Gisele to the Temple until she builds a house." Brandon was about the same age. Showing a bit more hurt, but perhaps feeling a bit less.

Harry levered himself carefully out of bed and took his time climbing the low hill to the winery. The Old Wolf had pulled two beds out of nowhere and stuck them in his back rooms.

"That one's all yours. Romeau's taking the other. I've got twenty boys sleeping on the floor upstairs. Gisele's got fifteen girls across in the Temple. The older girls are still in that bus. I think they think we'll enslave them, or steal their bus, or something."

"We're going to need a hotel for them all." Harry wrinkled his nose. "Maybe a boarding school."

"Tavern and Inn." Brandon looked around and shook his head. "Harry, you should think about living there, too. You know you'll outgrow this room almost instantly."

"And then you can mentor all the older kids, and be a male role model for the younger ones." Dane stuck his head in the door.

Harry snorted. "Kid, you are proof that it is possible to read too much. What are you? Twelve?"

"Fourteen. You know, a bunch of us kids have power genes. With a bit of training, we could be serious assets to the village."

Wolf eyed the boy. "Can you gather power?" He compacted a ball of light between his hands.

Dane squirmed. "Are you doing something?"

"Yep. You're still a bit young. I couldn't do it until I was sixteen, almost seventeen. But I should start teaching some preliminaries. Meditation. Yoga and Tai chi."

"Karate! And how about sword fighting, if we're headed for medieval times?" Dane's enthusiasm flooded back. "Do you know how to sword fight?"

"Is that why you have the black colt? To be a war horse when he grows up?" Pete brightened as well. "He's going to need a stable this winter, you know."

"We could build stables onto the Inn." Chris's voice came from beyond them.

Wolf and Harry swapped grins.

"I think we're being managed, Harry. So, where do you want your inn, tavern and stables?"

Harry snorted. "I suspect it'll go wherever the kids want it. And children cannot have a tavern. They can have a restaurant."

They didn't let him share the night watch, either. Bonfires and rifles at ready. But the lions, leopards, wild dogs and hyenas stayed away.

***

Chris gave a brief lesson in shotgun handling to all the bus kids. And worried about whether his buckshot would stop a lion. The loaded shotgun was left by the driver's seat, in case of emergencies. "Nobody touches it, otherwise. Until all of you get more lessons, and some target time." He mentally increased the order he was going to place for ammunition, when the gate opened in a month. If.

By late the next morning, the wall was complete to the north, west and south. The two buildings crowning the west ridge were built into the walls. The east wall was going up fast. Gates, roughly centered in each wall were a bit of a problem. The farm gate hinges seemed to be holding, they'd just have to brace them shut until they got a blacksmith shop up and working for the brackets they needed for a crossbar to secure it at night. Inside the wall, they had a confused mass of cars and livestock.

Jack Otts kept trying to organize the chaos.

"Cattle and sheep pens to the north. Then a nice broad street running north and south, and another running east and west. Anyone who wants to have a shop, you get a lot on one of those streets. Everyone else gets a parcel back behind them." He frowned a bit at the two buildings on the ridge. "Guess we'll just ignore them for now."

Chris, once again the designated spokes person waved a hand for Jack's attention. "We're a group of forty-two kids whose parents didn't emigrate. We want to build something with long term use potential." Milly had written a speech and made him memorize it. "A big inn, maybe a stable on the back, a hall for meetings. Us kid's will live there for now, and move out as we grow up—more than half of us are sixteen or older. Then the town will have a place for travelers to stay. Maybe a restaurant, or . . . something." No doubt she'd read him the riot act over his ad libs.

"Right. We'll put you on one corner of the two main streets. The other corners we'll leave empty, for an eventual Town Hall, maybe a church, library or school on the other corners."

Chris blinked. No arguments? No charge?

As other people called out suggestions or demands, Otts pulled out a bunch of stakes and survey gear. He put everyone to work, and soon enough, had them all moving their cars to their plots. Chris watched, a bit awed. *Sometimes someone who knows what needs to be done just steps up and yells enough to get it done.*

***

"So? When do you think you'll start planting your grape vines?" Harry frowned out at the sunset. Over the last week they'd hauled rocks and laid them out for a patio behind the winery. It made a nice meeting spot for the gods, and however many people came by. Up on the hill, they had a long field of view to the west.

The predators had quickly learned to stay away.

Or perhaps they had killed them all.

The older kids, Jack Otts, Muriel Westfarlin and Phaedra Shandy were regulars. Both the women's husbands had declined to follow their wives and children into exile. Tonight Miriam Wilson had come with them; she and her husband George still planned to build a store—once there was something to sell.

"We don't even know what time of year it is here." Old Wolf paced like a big cat. "The vineyard will have to be outside of the walls. There's no room inside. Keeping the antelope away is going to be hard. And for all we know, there will be elephants."

"It was June when we left Earth." Dane looked up from a book on architecture. "I doubt we could do a dimensional gate if the planet wasn't in the same place in the same orbit. Although with the days four minutes longer, we may not have the same rotational speed as Earth, and that may be why the gate was wobbling all over like it did."

Gisele and Wolf eyed each other uncertainly.

"It was wobbling?"

"Yep." Chris sighed. "It spread us out, which is nice."

"It got kind of scary when it started raining naked bodies, though." Dane's eyes flicked toward Gisele, and he visibly suppressed a smile. "Good thing there were only four of you and you only fell about five feet.

Muriel cleared her throat. "I've got an auger, I can drill holes for your vines, if you don't want to use the voodoo thing for it. Bill and Jerry both have fruit saplings they need to get in the ground soon." She had her youngest daughter in a basket, asleep at her feet. The other two were inside watching some horrible cartoon. Harry occasionally wondered how Old Wolf had acquired such an odd collection of shows. The man himself didn't remember.

Jack nodded. "We'd best start allocating land out here. Originally, it was just going to be, fence it and register it and it's yours. But between the predators, and the pests, everyone wants to be close in."

Wolf stared out at the twilight plains. "The vines don't need to be so close to the wall." He flicked a quick grin at Muriel. "I forgot about the voodoo thing. I can probably protect them. Jack, why don't we get together a town meeting, elect you mayor officially, and decide on a land registry and plan. Maybe close in, ten acres, a mile away forty, two miles, a hundred and sixty acres. Three miles away, and you could start allotting square miles."

"Yes, something like that." Jack frowned at the gods. "And eventually we'll whittle down the predators and the deer and the antelope or whatever will be so afraid of us that they won't come near. But what about bugs? Fungus? We're going to have to import fuel, fertilizer and bug spray. If we can. It's beginning to look like we aren't going to find much oil or natural gas here."

"Which is going to complicate farming enormously. And at the rate villages are combining, there's going to be some large concentrations of people to be fed."

Jack snorted. "Even the people who think you lot are dangerously insane part-animals admit we got the barricade up in a quarter of the time other people took. Those magic techniques of yours, you need to teach them to everyone with the right genes." He looked wistful. "My grandkids have some, I think." A widower, he'd accompanied his daughter, son-in-law and three grandchildren. "Magic. I'm damned glad you're here, and frankly, the way they treated my grandkids? I'd just as soon they never contact us again."

Old Wolf nodded.

Harry didn't care for himself, but it hurt a bit to wonder if the parents of the so-called orphans had had regrets and made plans to come over, a chance now forever lost. If they showed up in two years, would even the youngest kids care any more? *I can't substitute for a parent, but I'll help this collection of lost boys and girls as much as possible.*

***

Milly and Lillian were talking to two girls Chris didn't know, and summoned him with a wave.

One of the new girls giggled. "Hi, I'm Cleo, and this is Cecilia. We just got here."

Chris nodded. "People keep coming this way, I dunno why."

Cecilia rolled her eyes. "You have walls. It's safe here." She looked about eighteen, blonde with big brown eyes.

"That's it? It's going to get really crowded if people keep coming, umm, why didn't you just build your own walls?"

She wrinkled her nose. "We tried. We ran out of gas for the chain saws, and people didn't want to syphon their cars, and anyway, by the time we got to Wisconsin, we were running a bit low."

Cleo was blonde too, her eyes a clear pale blue. "You guys seem to know what you're doing. That's . . . irresistible. I mean, you're starting to plow, the lions didn't get your cows, you've got buildings." Cleo looked around. "Two months ago I would have laughed at a crappy little third world shithole like this. I was old enough to be on my own. I can't believe mother talked me into coming with them."

65

Chris bristled. "It's not a shithole. I take it you aren't engineered?"

"Eww, no! Just my stupid little brother." Cleo eyed him and edged away. "You are, aren't you?"

Cecilia stopped smiling at him.

Typical. He'd really hoped he'd left that behind. "Better get over the attitude. More than half the people around here are engineered. Or better yet, go back to Earth if they get a gate open again."

They flicked a glance behind him. He turned to find Iris and two other girls walking up. They'd all come with their parents, but he'd met them a couple of times. And encountered Iris as often as he could make it happen.

Iris looked over Cleo, then Cecilia. Stuck her nose up in the air. "I'm engineered. I'll live longer than you, and be healthier than you. My teeth are straight, I don't have zits. And I don't have brunette roots showing."

"You don't have the really bad genes, do you?" Cleo was red faced, embarrassed and getting mad, judging by her changing expressions.

Cecilia looked Iris up and down, then the rest of them. "You look normal." She sounded dubious. "For a bunch of freaks."

Chris stood as tall as he could, which wasn't tall enough to look down his nose at her, but he gave it his best try. "I have tons of engineering. I have the power genes." He held his hands out in the warm sunshine, and imagined squeezing the heat into a glowing ball of energy. "I am a magician." The palms of his hands glowed. A fainter glow formed a sphere above his hands.

Milly was gawking at him, her embarrassed flush paling. Iris and her friends stared.

Cleo and Cecilia started laughing.

"What a loser!" They turned together, and walked away.

Chris stared at the glowing ball in his hands. Hot but not painfully so. More like a welcome relaxing heat. He tried to shake it off. It stuck to his left hand, but his right still glowed a bit, too. He pictured it darkening and going out. It glowed.

He swallowed panic. "I think I'll go talk to the gods, excuse me."

Milly hovered over him all the way to the winery. Empty. Out the west gate to take a look around. He spotted Wolf up on the next ridge and strode out to where he and Romeau were pointing at things and talking.

They glanced around, and stiffened at the sight of his still glowing ball of warmth.

"I can't make it go away." Chris shook his hand.

"Touch the ground. Imagine it soaking into the ground like water." Old Wolf knelt beside him.

Chris crouched and grounded both hands. The light seeped reluctantly away. He swallowed. "So, do you guys teach magic?"

"We'll start this afternoon." Old Wolf glanced at the sun, then at Milly. "Can you do that?"

Milly held out her hands and tried to gather sunlight. Her hands just shaded each other. Her shoulders slumped.

Romeau shrugged. "Gisele says that she and the other goddesses mostly used their spare Y chromosome and the Mage gene. She said Muriel and Phaedra get their power in some other way. I think we'll need to split everyone up, with all you girls learning as much from Muriel and Phaedra as from Gisele. Talk to the three of them, about lessons."

Milly brightened. "I'm going to go talk to them, right now." She headed down hill.

"Chris, why don't you round up any boys who know they have the power gene and are fifteen or older. Not just your group, but the other kids as well. We'll hold a meeting in the winery . . . say in two hours."

Chris looked at his hands. No redness, not even a sunburn's worth. "Right. Two hours." He walked back to town, thinking. He knew who had the power genes on the bus. The other kids? Ugg. Probably a bunch of them would be like Cleo and Cecilia. He looked around and spotted a bunch of teenagers hanging around the far side of the stock pens and walked that way. A couple of the gang stepped out to intercept him.

He raised his voice just a bit. "If any of the guys here have the power genes, there's going to be some classes on how to use it, up in the winery, in a couple of hours."

"Listen you little abomination . . . "

Chris turned and walked away.

"Yeah, you better stay out of our territory." One hulk

yelled after him, but didn't pursue.

Probably just because it's broad daylight.

He made a circuit around the town. People were building little cabins; the few larger, more ambitious ones were lagging behind badly. Chris made note of that. Start small, plan to expand.

There were gardens everywhere, looking pretty healthy. Little kids playing tag, running and laughing.

Not bad for a third world shithole. Maybe they should build a suburb for all these new people. Better yet, show them how and let them build it themselves.

Lance and Mathew could also already do the "gathering power" thing once Wolf had coached them. And some of the adults, as well, but most of them had already learned things like that tree cutting slice. The Gods split all of the magic students up into groups, according to whether they could "collect power" or not.

Which put Chris in a group away from Iris. He'd just have to find another way to spend time with her.

***

Their peeling, nasty, skin healed, but their hair didn't grow until Wolf remembered something about making his hair grow faster, and Gisele took his technique and made it into an odd jumble of words and phrases that she said twisted her

69

thoughts the right direction to do what she wanted done.

Romeau heard it and shook his head. "Oh no. That just won't do. Let me see . . ."

"Growing, growing, growing

Keep that hair on going

Sooooo loooong"

The little kids burst into laughter.

"That's silly." Rob looked offended. At fourteen he was apparently of the opinion that he was too old for silliness. "That's a cowboy song. I heard it on the radio. Did you always have to say silly things to do what you wanted or is this new, since you came here?"

The gods looked around at each other.

Gisele frowned. "It helps shape the telekinesis or telepathy or whatever you want to call what we're doing. We always started with silly rhymes. I suppose that eventually we got so used to it that we could just twist the thoughts that way, without the words." She shook a finger at Romeau. "No. Scratching. I think that silly song will work better than my mishmash. Hmm, even the 'flowing hair' hand movements help. How odd. I suppose when it comes down to it, we're trying to communicate with our subconscious. Whatever works is good. We'll just have to be silly until we've got the feel of it down pat."

Rob rolled his eyes.

Shortwave radios had been on every list of every colony company, so they were commonplace. Old Wolf had four. That he'd found so far.

People started music shows, told stories, read books. Told jokes (often dirty).

Harry limped out to the newly planted fields every day, pushing himself.

And every day they felled trees or plowed fields and experimented with the fortunately large selection of seeds a number of people had brought with them. In the evenings they listened in on the shortwave radios to the other groups. Dinner tended to be communal, as they frequently killed multiple critters that came to eat their crops. Wolf kept the kids out from underfoot in the evenings with lessons in karate and tai chi. Gisele tried various herbal mixtures for mosquito repellant and salve for various rashes. And added a few bits of rhyme.

And every night they traded off keeping the watch fires burning, and watching for predators and pests.

Places were starting to have names. A few villages were named after people, or the cities they'd called home. But most of the exiles seemed to have concluded that they were in northern Africa, and the lakes were a much altered Mediterranean. Approximate place names started springing up, all along the south shore. The lakes became Lake Morocco, Lake Tyro, Lake Ionia, Lake Malta, Lake Egypt. In the west, the villages became Gibraltar, Tangier, Oran, Algiers, Tunis and their own town became Tripoli. In between them, and further south, there were dozens of smaller villages, collections of small farms, and people were still moving around. Some moving further away, some joined the dozen larger towns. Tripoli was growing.

To their east, a thousand miles or so of scrub and arid semi-desert was uninhabited. Michael, Barry and Edmund had named their town Cairo, and claimed the river it was on was the Nile. Then Red River, and another long gap to Kuwait, Karachi and New Bombay. And there the line of the settlers ended, and another accumulation of "gods" had landed.

"There probably weren't more than fifty thousand people in the last roundup of genetic frankensteins, all of us who came to this world." Leo stared out over the rolling grasslands. "My parents had a genetic propensity to diabetes and high blood pressure fixed in me. When my fiancé found out I was engineered, she dumped me. Hard to believe she'd have preferred me sick. Anyhow, with you four, that makes it one thousand eight hundred and twenty people crammed in here. Hard to believe that makes us one of the big towns. Everyone else is getting together in groups of one or two hundred; there must be over a hundred villages strung out along the path of the gate."

"We'll probably consolidate further, as we get a grip on survival, and start having time for things like school." Wolf nodded back at the village. "The kids are having a wonderful vacation, but we don't want to forget everything. They may talk about going medieval, but I'd rather stay in at least the middle industrial age. Some of the teenagers are old enough to be getting college level classes."

Romeau nodded. "But first we work on that survival thing.

Now that the palisade is up, I'm going to start hunting. Food, but also I think we should aggressively trim back the predators."

Harry nodded. "Bring me some hides, I've read up on tanning. Now to see if it actually works."

"At a distance, unless you're planning on something magic to deal with the smell." Wolf was sharpening a wooden point on a very primitive spear. "Do you think we could magically get iron ore hot enough to refine it? I've seen a lot of red rocks, but I haven't a clue what iron ore actually looks like."

Leo snorted. "We've got a couple of geologists. They're carrying on about not being able to find any coal, and they keep driving off, wanting to find tar sands or seeps so they have some indication of where to drill for oil. We're running short of fuel, fast."

"We'd better save it for the tractors. Now that the grain has sprouted we'd better figure out how to keep the deer and antelope and rabbits and everything else out of it." Harry narrowed his eyes. "What about compulsions? Can we give the local wildlife a compulsive fear of our fields?"

Leo grinned. "Can you scare the bugs off it? I like the idea, but can you really do it?"

"Interesting thought. And charms to keep our livestock close?" Wolf started doodling on the ground with his spear. "How about weather? We should really work on that."

Harry nodded. "Any time you spot something different or interesting, especially rocks, bring some back, and I'll work on it. Everyone will work on it." He scowled at his leg, where the lion slashes were slowly healing. "I'll be able to get out and hunt in another week as well."

Gisele made a rude noise behind him. "You behave, or it'll take even longer to heal. I've found some nice sand for making glass, and I'm working with the women of power on levitating it as soon as we melt it. So we'll have window glass for the winter, assuming we need it. Peter and Harriet McCullough have a pottery wheel, and they dug a pit for firing, so we're good on housewares, so to speak. We need to work on fabrics and paper. If we don't find oil, then we'll need beeswax or tallow for candles. I'm running a list, tell me anytime you think of something we need."

Leo shook his head. "The kids are bringing in all the branches of the trees we cut for the wall, we'll have plenty of firewood, even though we weren't actually planning on doing so much of the cooking that way. We need to figure out how to make charcoal. With that and limestone we should be able to make iron. With a bit of experimentation."

"Good. In the mean time, we're finally running low on meat, so if some of you gentlemen enjoy hunting, please do. Now."

"Yes ma'am!" Romeau paused to kiss her, then followed Old Wolf across the pasture, angling southeast. Their young horses galloped up to them, and followed.

Leo shook his head. "Whoever gelded that chestnut ought to be treated similarly. But we'll be glad of the draft stallion, if we don't find oil."

"Can we run the tractors on vegetable oil? Or alcohol?" Gisele pointed to a log cabin being built outside the walls. "I told Marshal his still was going to be outside the village, so he didn't burn everything down. And we should have corn oil in, what? Three months?"

Leo nodded. "If you lot can keep the pests out of it. And a bit of rain twice a week or so would be nice as well."

"Pioneering is a bit of a challenge." Gisele looked around at what was fast looking like a secure little frontier town. "And we gods weren't well prepared."

"Well enough. We're glad to have you, and your magical abilities and training. Don't glare. Magic is close enough. And I think you're underestimating Old Wolf, he keeps pulling the damnedest things out of his attic."

"Very well, one of us seems to be fairly well prepared, and so long as we can keep hunting, we won't starve." Harry flexed his leg and grabbed his walking stick. "I think I'll go think about how to scare off bugs."

"I'll help. Those bug repellants . . . " Gisele followed him out to look at the fields of young wheat.

By the end of the day they'd come up with a simple vocal to stimulate the mental manipulation for repelling all animals, as well as one that seemed to be able to break up nitrogen and water for a scant bit of ammonia to fertilize the crops. The power requirements were so low Gisele persuaded a couple of the unpowered young women to try them. They promptly made songs out of the rhymes and went dancing and laughing through the fields, fortunately watching where they put their feet. The young men were drawn to them like flies. Harry made sure they were armed, and spent some of their time looking for predators.

"We're going to grow into a very strange society." He watched Gisele carefully soaking the bandages off his leg.

"Yes. I need to figure out how to boost people's immune systems, and repair systems. I don't like the looks of this. It's taking too long to heal."

"Think about what you'd like to see. What should the cells be doing? How could you twist them to do it?"

"Humph. More T cells, to the injury site, for starters, and the repair . . . the cells at the edges ought to be becoming less specifically a specific tissue and edge back toward a stem cell. Then they should multiply enormously, then get all specific again."

"Think about how it would feel, how a cell would feel, fading back into the past."

"Feel? I know how it's done, chemically. It's just a little twitch, to restart the body stem cell process, that's fairly well understood." Gisele sat down, looking dreamy eyed and absent for a long moment. "And triggering cell reproduction. Humph. Yes." She waved a hand at his leg. "That should help, unless you dissolve into a gooey grey mass of stem cells."

Harry chuckled a bit nervously. "We aren't exactly following proper test protocols for any of the things we do.

Perhaps we should think carefully and proceed slowly."

Gisele looked down at his leg. "What the hell am I doing? Telekinesis on a microscopic scale? Assembling the enzymes or ribosomes that are needed? That's what I was *picturing*. Was I forcing a pattern on the cells' internal mechanisms to make them manufacture what I think you need?"

Harry shrugged. "I'm not sure that rationalizing it will make a bit of difference. Although I suppose if you believe it could put a bit more oomph into it."

"I should work out a verbal trigger, so anyone with . . . Harry, are we making *magic spells*? Have we always done things by magic? I swear sometimes if I stop paying attention, the past just slips away. The other women don't have this problem. And they're magic too. Muriel and Phaedra and I can get together like some story book coven and do things well beyond our individual abilities."

"That's right. Trios, no, Triads, wasn't it? For women, and three Triads is a pyramid. Men work best in fours and eights."

"A compass rose of magicians. I remember someone saying that." Gisele frowned. "A very logical young woman. She analyzed what was going on, and made the fellows line up according to the compass points. And sometimes she'd shift them around, and it always made the magic stronger. I wonder who that was?"

"Mark and Derry have power genes. Maybe, with Wolf, Romeau and me we can try a few major tasks."

"Eight, Harry. Add in a few of those older boys as well."

"Yes. I was thinking about what to teach the kids, setting them up for independence. I shall have to add group magic drills to the plan."

"We already know how to do a great many things. It may be that we already know all of this. The bug repellant, the medical usage. Maybe we just don't consciously remember." Gisele's brows drew together as she hunched her shoulders. "I don't like this not-remembering. What did they do to us, that we can't remember?"

"And who are *they?*"

***

Harry found himself hovering over the shortwave. The village of Gibraltar kept the beacon turned on. The one month anniversary of their exile came and went. Another week passed, and the gate did not open.

And some internal tension Harry hadn't noticed eased inside his chest. Perhaps in two years they'd be hunted down like animals, but for now they could concentrate on . . . now.

Chapter Six

1 August 2117

The Lake, Exile

Old Wolf's boat was a totally impractical huge speed boat with a huge fuel-guzzling engine. It was longer than the Owens they'd sold when they'd moved from California to Connecticut. Chris remembered days and weekends out on the bay, up the river, trips up the coast when the sea was calm. His Dad teaching him navigation . . . He blinked back tears, and concentrated on the boat and trailer. Fortunately, Old Wolf had thought to take this bubble outside before he popped it. Chris suppressed a smile, thinking about it in the attic.

They borrowed Leo's truck and backed its trailer into the stream where the bank sloped into deep water. It bobbed in the current, fairly begging to be taken for a spin.

Chris swung aboard and checked it out. "Fuel tank is full, wow, an auxiliary tank. Should have a cruising radius of several thousand miles, if we don't blow it all trying to see how fast it can go. How about it, Harry? Want to visit your fellow gods to the east?"

Harry limped up and shook his head at it. "What an insane thing to bring here!"

"You could check out what they're doing, with spells and

so forth, without straining your leg." Chris pointed out. "By the time we get back, you'll be even further along magically, and practically all healed." *It's as healed as it will ever be; Harry needs to learn about boats.* "And as it happens, I know about boats, and will be pleased to take you anywhere you want to go." *And hope I remember the navigating by the stars stuff.*

Wolf chuckled. "Go, Harry. I'm tired of watching you constantly trying to do too much. Keep the speed down and you'll have plenty of fuel to get to Cairo and back."

The corners of the older god's mouth twitched up. "All right. But when I get back, I'm damn well building a sail boat."

They packed, loaded a minimum of food and fishing gear into the tiny cabin, and left at dawn. They dawdled down the lakeside, then, more confident of the boat, turned north to find the other shore. The wind got chilly, and they started seeing floating icebergs. Small, but Harry stayed well away from them. Near sunset they found the glacier, filling a valley and running back into the tall peaks. A few hardy pines found root space in the rocky coast, but there was nothing else to be seen. They turned southeast and motored until full dark, then drifted. In theory, at about the same pace as any icebergs, so any encounters would be slow, and probably do no damage. Chris tossed a line over and pulled in a huge bass. He filleted it, while Harry looked for a way to cook it.

"Nothing. Big fancy boat without even a hot plate." Harry eyed the fish, then held out his left hand. Hesitated. "Wait. Put the fillets on this oar, and hold it out over the water."

"Fireball?" Chris tried to not twist the oar and dump the fish. "Is this a good idea, Harry?"

"I'm hungry." Harry grinned and tossed a modest sized fireball. There was no pressure when the fireball hit the oar, but the fish sizzled and the oar darkened and charred around the edges. Chris brought it all back, and Harry scooted the fish onto plates. Steam hissed, as Chris plunged the oar into the lake.

"Perhaps we ought to go ashore to cook." He sniffed the fish, hot and flaky. Perfect.

Harry nodded. "If you insist."

"Yes. Then you can teach me how to do that without me accidentally blowing up the boat."

"Good point."

They traded off the watch, flashed the big battery powered spotlight around occasionally. No icebergs. The next night they slept on the south shore and dined on some sort of lake salmon. The third day they anchored offshore. Harry wasn't very agile, with his wounded leg, but Chris decided to swim. He climbed back aboard in haste as a large shadow moved purposefully toward him.

"Crocodile." Harry watched it carefully as it surfaced. "The snow and glacier melt from the north keeps the deep lake cold, but the shallow southern shore . . . It looks a bit sluggish, must be why we haven't had any up our creek."

Chris gulped. "I'm surprised there aren't crocs up every creek, they're pretty warm. A lot warmer than here."

"I'll bet this is just a straggler from the Nile. I wonder if the smaller streams freeze in the winter?"

"Suddenly, I hope so. However, if the Nile is in the same place as on Earth, we ought to be there tomorrow. Of course, with the days slightly longer, I may not be calculating the distances right." Chris glanced glumly at his instruments and charts.

By noon the next day they were trying to follow the largest streams through a delta covered with head high grasses and reeds.

The streams merged gradually into a broad powerful river, and just upstream they found Cairo.

In Cairo they found religion.

Chris eyed the twin ziggurats askance. They weren't huge, but they towered over everything else. Looking out across the broad river, the delta, the cliffs that ended the greenery so abruptly, he rather thought that this town was well named. It was the largest town yet, easily double the size of Tripoli. They were farming the east side of the river, and the town was on the east bank, up on a rocky hill. The ziggurats were at the top, with a plaza in between, centering a regular grid of roads. There were no walls around the town. They had sailed pasts hundreds of miles of desert before reaching the delta. *The desert must be enough of a barrier to allow control of predators in the valley.*

By the time they'd cruised up river to the docks, two men were waiting for them, with a crowd of onlookers staying well back.

"Well, well, if it isn't Massa Harry."

Harry blinked. "Drat. One of them had red hair, the other one was blonde. They'll be nearly impossible to tell apart, bald." He raised his voice to carry across the narrowing strip of water. "Barry and Edmund. Figures you two would stick together."

"The Sigma brothers, forever together, forever at war. Welcome to Cairo, fellow God."

Chris tossed bumpers overboard, and leaped out to tie off the boat without any attempt on the part of either brother to help. Harry stepped onto the wharf and looked the brothers over. Chris thought they both looked like they'd been lifting weights, and as if they ought to have gone easier on the food as well.

"I hope you remember that it was meant sarcastically, when they called us that." Harry sounded a bit disturbed.

"Oh, we remember. But it's such a lovely idea, we've decided to keep it." The one on the left spoke.

The other one grinned. "Isn't that what every country needs? A benevolent God and an Evil God? I'm Barry, the God of Virtue."

The first one snickered. "And I'm Edmund, the God of Vice. Very fitting, don't you think? Come on up, we'll treat you to a welcoming feast suitable to the God of . . . Travel, I think would fit."

"Absolutely not!"

"Oh yes, very nice." Barry turned and faced the crowd. His voice rolled over them as if amplified. "Our brother God, Harry, the God of Travelers honors our City with his presence. Prepare a feast!"

The crowd cheered and started breaking up.

Chris grabbed luggage and followed Harry, hanging well back. The brother gods were getting his hackles up, and he'd just as soon not draw their attention. He'd felt a lot of spells flowing out with the speech. *Are these self-appointed Gods controlling their subjects with magic?* The thought sent a chill down his spine. *They're not really gods, but they could be damn realistic tyrants.*

***

The party started quickly, with tables being carried out into the plaza with practiced ease.

A horseshoe of large ones, with covers and flowers and big chairs went up on a raised platform in the middle of the plaza.

"How often do you have feasts?" Harry watched the people, scampering to obey and felt sick.

"Once a month, minimum." Barry grinned. "Everyone has a great time. See? Everyone brings food, the store keepers set up booths. Musicians. We've figured out how to brew beer—or something close enough. And wine. We're using magic to control the process, and did you know you could change the time ratio on bubbles? We can get it from ten thousand to one all the way to one to twenty, the other direction."

"Speed aged our first wine." Edmund looked smug. "Damned good stuff."

"You have grapes?" Wolf's first small harvest had been just a couple of weeks ago, his first wine still in big glass jars, fermenting away.

"We used every fruit we could get our hands on. Peaches and cherries, wild stuff growing on the delta and up the valley. Everyone just loves it."

Harry eyed the two ziggurats. "I thought Michael was here, too."

Edmund waved the thought away. "The God of Just Deserts was not simpatico. We made him go away."

"Damned dogs. I don't like dogs that smart. I think he stole them." Barry scowled and Edmund laughed.

Barry gestured at the northern ziggeraut. "Come and see the Temple of Virtue. Most of our fun is out-of-doors, so it's actually quite basic. Throne room, spa, bedroom, servants quarters."

Harry climbed the steps and wrinkled his nose at the throne, set up on a raised dais. "Servants? Look, it's all well and good to show off a bit with your skills, but surely you aren't really setting yourselves up as gods?"

"Why ever not?"

Harry eyed the walls. "How did you build this, anyway? I don't see any seams."

"Magic." Barry grinned. And squeezed the arm of the stone throne, molded it like putty.

Harry felt what he did, pure applied power, no silly rhymes here.

"Ah, Sylvia, our guest needs a bath before the feast, and, I think, a touch of your healing magic."

"Healing? Are you a doctor?" Harry eyed the young woman. Mid twenties, perhaps, slender apart from the obvious pregnancy. Green eyes, blonde hair.

"Massage therapist. Now that I've learned how to call up the magic to help, I can fix all sorts of things. Your shoulders look tense, and you're limping. How about a quick shower, then I'll work on all that, then a nice long soak."

All the tightness and pull in the deeply scared leg relaxed under her kneading fingers, and the itchiness in the chest scar faded away. He nearly fell asleep, until her touch became seriously intimate.

"You have scars here, as well. An old surgery, like the other gods had. All fixed now. Why don't you take a long soak until the feast is ready." She moved away before he embarrassed himself by finding out if she was being professional or seductive.

He tried to relax in a tub sized for company, but his brain kept conjuring up thoughts of magic as a force of coercion. He gave up, and climbed out of the steaming water.

Clean clothes turned out to be tunic and toga. *Mixing their Mythos a bit, aren't they? I do hope there aren't any gladiatorial contests planned.*

No, just acrobatics, music, food, way too much wine that went straight to his head and then parts south and Harry found himself deep into what looked like a city-wide orgy as a pretty young woman refilled his cup then climbed all over him. It was dark, torches were guttering, the woman was eager . . .

***

They all ignored Chris. He carried the bags silently. And gazed wistfully at the beauty who was rubbing Harry down with scented oils. And spells. He saw Harry's eyes narrow, as he analyzed what the woman was doing. Chris listened in, mentally, but it just didn't make any sense at all. Harry was nodding like he understood. Chris sighed, and decided this was when he ought to duck out and leave Harry alone with the babe.

There'd been quite a few teenagers out there, helping set up for the party. He ought to clean up himself, and track them down. See if they were learning magic, too. When the woman led Harry off to another room with a steaming hot pool about the size of a Jacuzzi, Chris nipped back into the first room and took a shower. Washed clothes with the scented soap and dressed in his last clean outfit. His 'good clothes' in fact. He shook his head over the state of Harry's clothes and washed them too. Then he laughed at the heap of wet stuff. He rolled it up awkwardly, threw it over his shoulder and humped it back down to the boat.

A dozen teenagers were drooling over it. He gave them a tour, such as it was, and hung clothing everywhere to dry.". . . so I suppose we'll have to mothball it for lack of gasoline when we get back."

Two boys and a girl had their heads down under the raised decking that formed the top of the engine compartment. Others were looking over the instruments, and a gaggle of girls were in the tiny cabin, admiring the woodwork and cabinetry. The sun was just hitting the horizon, but the breeze was so hot and dry Christ flipped all his draped wash over and let the other side dry a bit.

"How do you get along with your God? Are you his personal servant, or do you just keep the boat for him?" The girl had the tell-tale deep tan and red hair of the genetically engineered.

"Umm, Harry isn't like your gods. Our gods help us, and teach us."

That got him some skeptical looks.

"Really? Like, you can do magic?"

Chris gathered power in his hands. The kids stared. He tossed a fire ball out over the river. "Want to learn how to do that?"

Nods all around, and nervous glances toward the city. Chris looked around. "Why don't we go down to the last dock, there, where we won't bother anyone?"

That got everyone moving.

And they caught on really quickly to gathering power. Chris remembered enough of what Muriel and Phaedra told the girls about their way of doing it that they could figure it out. They tossed fireballs at passing crocodiles, and learned push and pull, and the start of shielding. Thinking about the setup here, Chris concentrated on teaching mental shielding.

One of the girls whispered something to a boy. He nodded and ran off.

The girl grinned impishly. "The gods always serve special wines and terrific food for the parties. I figured we ought to bring some down here, and have our own little orgy."

"Orgy? They don't actually, aren't actually going to . . ."

They did.

And they'd figured out some interesting things to do with magic.

Wow.

***

Harry had the hangover from hell the next morning. He was far from the last to crawl out from under a table. He righted the nearest chair and sat down. Surveyed the grounds. He didn't see the cute serving girl from last night. Assuming he actually would recognize her. And it had gotten quite dark and, umm, active under those tables. He couldn't swear who, or even how many women he'd made love to.

A loud laugh rang out and he winced.

"What? A God without a good hangover cure?" Something poked him over the ear and the pain faded.

Harry rubbed his eyes and looked around. "Good morning Edmund. What the hell did you put in that wine?"

"A little something to make sure we don't get too inbred,

you know."

"You mean so you can screw as many women as you want to?"

Edmund laughed again. "That too, which Barry justifies by remembering that we had all our genetic errors fixed."

"And our vas plugged as well." Harry staggered to his feet and looked around. No signs to the nearest public bathroom. Hardly a surprise.

"What, didn't Barry sic his favorite healer on you? Ha! I see that he did. You're all fixed up again. Congratulations."

"I don't think anyone . . ." Harry looked down at his leg. Flexed it. No pull of adhesions, no feeling of weakness.

Edmund grinned. "Let's find Barry. I know he'd hate for me to give you the tour without him. And much though I hate to admit it, his bathrooms are better than mine."

The tour covered a lot of land under cultivation.

"What's your population? You must have several hundred square miles under plow." The grain had been harvested, cattle grazed in the stubble.

"About five thousand. Give it another year and it'll be larger, the women don't seem to remember about contraceptives." Edmund snickered.

Harry tried to keep a neutral expression on his face. "Do you have spells to keep the pests out? I've been giving lessons up and down the lakes. They are very low powered spells. I suspect you two would love seeing the unpowered girls dancing through the fields throwing the spells around."

Barry scowled. "Well, yes, I suppose. But then Edmund would just take advantage of more of them."

Edmund laughed. "Don't be fooled by his appearance of rectitude. The God of Virtue resists temptation, but falls well short of perfection."

"I see. Shall I give your people lessons while I'm here?"

"We have anti-insect and anti-fungus spells ourselves, and the bubbles should store the grain with no loss to rodents at all. We prefer to not empower the little people. Come see the size of the crocodiles in the river. Hard to believe they're related to the ones back on Earth. Or the other Earth, I suppose I should say." They stopped at the top of a five foot drop off to a sandy beach.

"They look more pre-historic to me." Barry pointed at what Harry had assumed was a rock outcrop.

Harry stopped dead and stared. "That thing must be forty feet long! Do you stay completely away from the river?" The creature's broad, armored head was about as long as Harry was tall. Massive and powerful. Lots of teeth.

Edmund laughed and swatted Harry's shoulder. Harry stumbled forward, and slid down the sandy drop. It was just a few feet forward, and a few feet down . . . but the croc raised its massive head and turned toward him.

Enough fun and games with the evil twins.

Harry stepped around at enough of an angle to throw a quick vertical slice that cut the croc's spine with a single gesture. The beast's head dropped back to the sand with an audible thud. The body barely twitched. Blood pooled beneath it, stained the water and drifted down stream.

"They eat the tails in Louisiana, don't they?" *Where the hell is Louisiana?* Harry fought to remain nonchalant, shrugging as he labored back up the steep sandy rise. "You should clean the big ones out though, before you have a bunch of children running around."

The pair exchanged glances, and walked him back to his boat. Chris was there, thank goodness, and started untying lines. "Thanks for the hospitality. And the party. Oh, and do you know this one?" He sang Romeau's hair growing song, and grinned at the expressions on the brothers' faces. He turned and stepped aboard. Chris pushed off. *The people here are going to have to deal with the brothers, themselves. Somehow. Perhaps when I return, I'll manage to sneak in a few lessons.*

He started the engine and turned for home.

***

Harry made Old Wolf put the speedboat back in its bubble.

He showed the others the healing 'spells' Barry's masseuse had used on him, and the rock manipulations. Gisele was impressed by the improvement in his leg—and challenged. Both horrified and amused by the spells he'd copied from the wine. "Some of these spells will be useful, if only because I can work out their opposite effect."

Chapter Seven

30 August 2117

Tripoli, North Africa, Exile

". . . and get everyone registered for school."

Chris looked around in dismay. The woman had teacher written all over her. Elementary teacher, actually. He relaxed a bit, as he walked over to join the conversation. "I suppose the younger kids will be needing to learn the basics. Probably half of us are older, though. We'll either apprentice, study on our own, or wait for someone to organize a college."

Iris's eyes widened as he stood up to authority. The bus girls just looked around and nodded. *I guess we all had bad parents, and lost our dependence early.*

They'd built a "play yard" for the littler kids. Too many cows, horses and cars around to let them run wild. They traded off keeping an eye on them, and the parents had taken to bringing their own kids by to play. The mayor was starting to refer to it as "The Park", which at least meant it wouldn't get taken for city hall or something.

Chris wasn't the only teenage boy to notice that the babies seemed to draw the girls. Iris came by regularly, some times with a neighbor's kid she was minding, but sometimes just alone.

"Apprentice!" The teacher recoiled. What had she said her name was? Mrs. Gilligan. Like she was already asserting her authority, and they were too young to use her first name. "I really don't think we could possibly train doctors and lawyers with an apprenticeship program. And then there's the legal situation, what with well, salaries and housing and discipline. No, no, I don't like that idea at all. We'll be opening a school. Schools. People keep trickling in and joining the town. As of this morning, with that new little group, there are over two hundred children here. We need a school now."

"Who are you counting? Twenty-seven of us are over fifteen, and not interested in pointless repetition. The rest, the teenagers just need math and science, in case they want to 'tag around after' a doctor or a nuclear physicist or a geologist. The younger ones will need a whole curriculum."

The teacher had been getting stiffer with every word he spoke. She summoned her most authoritative tones, in a high volume. "Every child under eighteen will attend . . . "

"No we won't." Chris got up and walked away. And ignored her orders to return. *I am not a child.* He glanced back, Ariel was leaning on the fence, talking to some boy he didn't know, ignoring the teacher. Everyone else had left. He wished he'd seen which direction Iris went. *Drat.* He circled around toward the livestock pens. Maybe she was visiting her cows. Two of her dad's six cows had been her FFA projects, and were just big pets.

Several of the older Bus Kids were in a group by the east

gate.

He veered over to warn them. "The teachers are organizing. I tried to make it clear that no one over fifteen was going to attend. She's pissed. Beware."

Lillian rolled her eyes. "Oh yes. I do so need Advanced English, US History, Pre Calc, and German 4. Do you suppose they'll try to organize PE?"

Lance leaned over and whispered in Milly's ear. "How about some sex education?"

She giggled. "Abstinence based, Buster." But she didn't move away from him.

One of the boys guffawed. "I won't ever go back to school. Between farming and hunting, we'll be living the good life."

Not the brightest fellow around. Not that he doesn't have a point. I need to learn how to hunt. Hmm. . .

Chapter Eight

1 September 2117

Tripoli, North Africa, Exile

Wolf eyed the three boys, suppressing a smile. *They aren't boys any more than I was at that age.*

"We need to learn to hunt, and we noticed you were lacking some crucial equipment."

Christopher Dunmeyer had emerged as the leader of the kid pack. He, Lance Vesely and Mathew Lindon looked stubborn.

Wolf swapped glances with Romeau. "I've got to admit that actual hunting rifles and shotguns do seem like sensible sorts of things to bring on a hunting trip."

Romeau snorted. "Longer range than magic. Less scary than your military weapons. Guess we'd better bring them along."

Wolf enjoyed the hike out into the wilds. He followed a thin game trail, pointing out the most obvious signs, hoof and paw prints, scat, to the boys and assigned them each a direction to concentrate on watching. They paralleled the stream that ran through town, staying above it, and occasionally climbing a tall hill for a longer view. The rifles and the shotgun were examined, demonstrated. They weren't carrying much ammunition, but targeted bushes at fifty feet received a pair of bullets from each boy. Out on the plains they could see several small herds of several types of antelope, and a distant herd that was probably zebra. Heavier trails led down to the stream, and they settled down, downwind of one and waited to see if dinner would come to them. The two young horses stayed close, dropped their heads to graze. *Can't beat that for looking innocent.*

"You three are all eighteen?" Wolf looked the boys over. They all glowed to his inner vision.

"I just turned seventeen." Chris frowned. "That doesn't matter any more."

"Well, it does, but not necessarily for the same reasons. You are all three able to gather power, and use it for a few things. Your strength will grow with age. Let's see if you can do a few things that will be useful for hunting."

He and Romeau took all three boys through relaxation and focusing exercises. Recalling the old chants brought up flashes of personal memory. Of learning the chants . . . no. Inventing the chants. *We were the first, but we won't be the last.*

The boys knew several of the physical effects spells. Chris was impressive, with both physical and mental shields. So Wolf turned to the mental effects spells.

Unnoticeable. Sleep. Fear. Those three were enough for now.

Magic lessons were pushed to the back as the afternoon

sun drove animals down to the stream to drink. Sable antelope, wildebeast, impala. The zebras were only partly striped, and he couldn't remember the right name for them . . . The boys picked targets, took aim, and on whispered command fired. Wolf and Romeau took out one apiece from the fleeing animals. Chris glowed at his clean kill, and Lance paled as the Wolf quickly finished off his wounded impala. Matt's target had gotten away clean, and apparently uninjured.

With four good sized carcasses, even field dressed, the young horses received quick lessons in dragging crude frames. They expressed trepidation with head, neck and ear motions, but hauled the meat back toward town without a single bucking fit.

Romeau eyed them. "I think they understood your explanations."

"Don't all horses?"

The boys all grinned. Romeau shook his head. "Even I remember that much!"

Old Wolf shrugged. "Well, these two did. C'mon. If Harry can tan these hides, we ought to make some proper . . . things to drag."

"Travois. If we don't find oil, we're going to be trying to figure out how to make wagon wheels pretty quick."

After a mile, Old Wolf dropped back and discouraged a pack of hyenas from following them home. They dragged in the south gate as the sun touched the horizon, and turned the meat over to a small army of butchers and cooks. Several families were talking about cooperatively building a proper hygienic butcher's shop. The Bus Girls had built a big outdoor grill from rock, with clay to plug the gaps, topped with metal grids as large as they could coax from the small fabber.

With over a thousand people here, the antelopes wouldn't last long.

"We'd better count on hunting every day, and training the kids."

Wolf met Romeau's eyes and nodded. "Let's split them up, magic and not. So they all get the lessons they need. And co-ordinate with any other hunters, so we don't interfere—or worse—with each other."

Between hunting, tending his new vineyard and karate lessons, Wolf almost didn't notice how much time Muriel spent in his vicinity. And how attractive she was.

***

"It's a genetic mutation, deliberately bred for. Domestic cattle don't need horns."

Ira Penner was a farmer and a rancher. In addition to the six cows that had survived the first predators, he now had seven calves. Polled Herefords, red and white.

Iris Penner was beautiful. And also a witch. Her older brother had had a few problems fixed, but no power gene, no special suites of strong teeth and intelligence. Their parents had gotten a bit more daring with their second child. Then, when the prejudice had set in, they'd moved, kept quiet about the kids' engineering. The government had still found them.

"I thought I'd just show Iris the signs, so as she matures, she'll know when she's ready for lessons." Chris tried to look casual and friendly as he turned away from the cows.

Her parents frowned at Chris. They hadn't invited him into the little log cabin behind them. Once the chatter turned from cows to magic and daughter, the welcome mat for the young man who'd stopped to admire the big cows had instantly disappeared.

Ben, the brother, scowled. "There no such thing as magic, and it doesn't get the chores done. Iris goofs off enough as it is. She don't need a swelled head."

The mother sighed. "All the boys chase after her, no wonder it's turned her head."

Ira snorted. "And anyone with any sense will breed *those* bad genes out. Iris won't be dating any of you so-called magicians."

Iris rolled her eyes. "Daddy! He's just showing me some ways I can do more work."

"And stay away from those 'witch' girls. You're a good Christian, not some devil worshipper. Everything that boy just told you? You couldn't do it. So remember. You can't do it, so stop thinking about it." Ira split a scowl between Chris and his daughter.

"I thought you like that nice Harding boy? He's got horses and cattle, both." Her mother chimed in. On the wrong side, unfortunately.

Iris's eyes lit. "Oh yes. I want a horse."

Chis wished her eyes would light up like that for him. A horse? If she wanted a horse, then he'd just have to catch a wild one and tame it for her.

Chapter Nine

15 September 2117

Tripoli, North Africa, Exile

The gardens were still producing like mad. The "Compass" of the Wolf, Romeau, Derry, and Mark with various teenage boys had figured out how to make it rain, and even better, how to make it stop.

"Chris and Lance are strong enough to lead their own Compass, pretty soon. Matt and Tyrone are good too. Young Dane is the surprise. He's good at figuring things out, he was a science nerd in school, knows all about weather. He's not the strongest mage, but he sure makes a group effective." Wolf paced, stared out at the dark clouds overhead.

"It's all air pressure, heating volumes of air so it starts rising, pulls damp air in off the lake and voila! Then we do the same further off, so it's pulled away from us. It's quite a trick, none of us can do it alone. We'll show you, and maybe you can pass it around to other villages, if you can find at least four men with power genes." Romeau smirked a bit. "Gisele is a bit miffed that her Triad can't do it."

Harry bit his lip. "Anyone can do the pest spell, but the fertilizer one works best for women. Do you suppose . . . no, it's probably just a matter of the small sample size. Probably we'll all have strengths and weaknesses."

Romeau grinned. "Or witches and magicians may be different things altogether. I feel like I'm living in a storybook, except when I forget and think this is all I've ever known. I don't have a problem remembering things since we got here. But everything before is a bit slippery." Romeau was in high demand. He'd performed five marriage ceremonies, three of them in other villages. Two babies had been born while Harry was away. Their village was looking like a success.

Harry frowned down at his feet. "What happens if we lose our memories altogether?"

"We ask people whose brain are in better shape than ours."

"And who do we ask in a hundred years? You know we all have genes that are supposed to lengthen our lives." Harry grimaced at the thought.

"Well, how long is long? The genes were experimental. Double the usual life span? Triple? Unless they got it wrong and we die early. And if everyone else has forgotten where their grandparents came from, we might as well, too."

And if we live very long, forgetting might be the kindest thing. Harry couldn't make himself say it aloud.

***

"Hi Iris. You here for the tai chi? Or the magic?" Chris tried to keep his voice casual. She glowed almost as brightly as

Gisele. She made those girls in Cairo seem ordinary. Unfortunately, she wasn't anywhere near as forward as they had been. Wow.

She ducked her head shyly. "You know my parents don't approve of the magic talk. I think I was a snap decision, since regretted. They're very religious."

Chris chuckled, like he thought she was kidding. There were girls moving into position around her, and he faded back. He was one of the advanced students, anyway, and ought to be over on the other side of the Dojo, otherwise known as the winery's front lawn.

He watched her out of the corner of his eye, and admired her form. And figure, and face, and glowing golden hair.

He noticed half the other guys were as well. Drat. He needed to get out and do things, lift himself out of the common crowd and into visibility. Maybe he'd get a heifer out of the round up. If not the first cattle drive, the second.

***

Harry looked down the hill, where they were starting to muster for the cattle drive.

Wild cattle drive.

Some people were trying to call them aurochs, after the wild ancestors of their own domesticated cattle. Only time and attempts to cross breed them would tell if they were the same species, for some loose definition of species.

Romeau strode down the hill. He'd be going with the mounted party, to start the drive. The rest of them would split up and on foot, attempt to steer the herd into the trap. The cattle were migratory, they were moving south, coming out of the mountains to the north, and swimming the river. The bulls had come first, now the cows were moving.

They were after young heifers, the calves born in the spring, and old enough now to be weaned. They hoped to trap enough to parcel them out, one heifer for everyone who participated in the drive. If they didn't have enough, they'd hold a lottery. Ditto if they had extra.

The ranchers had all lost cattle. Several cattlemen had lost all their stock to the predators in the first days after they'd arrived, and were hoping to start over. This would only be the first drive, not the last. Enthusiasm was high, and close to a quarter of the population marched out, confident of their herding prowess.

Harry kept an eye on the eleven kids from the bus who were helping. *I need to stop calling them kids. They're all seventeen or eighteen. And six of them are armed, although I doubt Milly and Lillian's handguns would stop one of these critters.*

They'd hunted enough of the aurochs to appreciate the size of them. And the size of their horns. Romeau called them longhorns on steroids, but their horns didn't spread to the sides, they curved forward, more like a bull-fighting bull. On steroids.

They'd built a big corral, with wings to funnel the cattle into it. Then they spread out in a thin line. They were carrying spears, and had things to flap, hopefully to turn the cows without having to get dangerously close. In theory, if they kept it slow, didn't initiate any sort of stampede, they could just walk the cattle into the trap.

Harry eyed two small herds that had crossed and gotten ahead of them. About twenty cows and calves total. If they could trap four or five little groups at a time, gradually build up their herd...

The horsemen headed north, and the wait began. Knowing nothing about cattle, Harry and the bus kids were all out toward the end of the line. The people who knew what they were doing were closer to the corral, where the cattle might start realizing they were being trapped.

"Don't look so worried, Harry." Milly grinned at him. "We've all got Romeau's cow calming spell. It's the people with no magic or no training that ought to be nervous."

Harry snorted. "I'd feel better if I believed a word you lot tell me about this 'Texas' Romeau is supposed to be from." He straightened. "Here comes the first batch, and they don't look happy."

Two horsemen were on the little herd's flank, but the beasts seemed more inclined to drop their heads and charge than be herded. As they watched, Vito spun his horse away from a charge and loped in a distant circle around the herd. The eight cows formed up around their calves, horns pointed outward. The horsemen withdrew, stopping and waiting. The circle broke up, the cows heading away from the riders, toward the trap. The riders kept their horses to a walk, and at a distance that just barely threatened the cows. The cows kept trying to turn south, the riders kept trying to force them to move westward as well. The circus moved off to their left, gradually working closer to the thin line of people. A few shirts were waved. Despite the distance, the cattle stopped, milled about nervously. Then turned and trotted off to the west. Harry relaxed. *This is going to work.*

The next herd he spotted was well off to the west, shuffling along quietly with Romeau trailing behind.

Chris snickered. "Guess that spell works."

A cloud of dust heralded the next herd. The dimly seen cows charged straight at them. No amount of flag waving or spells changed their trajectory. The kids started heading for the shelter of thick tree trunks.

Vince stood waving his flag a moment too long before scrambling for cover. Four shots snapped from a grove of trees. The cow closest to Vince buckled, chin hitting the dirt then rolling to a stop. *That* turned the herd. Harry dodged for safety, and checked that everyone was safe. The breeze cleared the dust away. One dead cow, a bunch of impressed children. Hell, he was impressed too.

The boys were experienced, and set to butchering the cow.

The day wore on, with occasional sightings of cattle, some being chivvied into the trap, three more groups stampeding over everything in their path. As the sun set, they all pulled in, to check the total in the trap.

Romeau sauntered over, leading a bay mare. "Eighty cows, sixty-two calves. So roughly thirty heifers, this time. I suspect the lottery will be fierce, just remember we can do this as often as we want to."

Romeau was put in charge of separating out the heifers, by universal acclamation. He put the bus kids to works, extending the area under the calming influence, and the cows and male calves were sent on their way. The heifers all got vaccinated, dewormed and inspected.

Lillian won a heifer in the drawing. Vince looked relieved, the rest disappointed. Harry had to admit that he hadn't actually wanted one, but Romeau looked a bit disappointed. Wolf had just shrugged. He'd also killed a stampeding cow. Two people had been injured, but no one badly.

"Not a bad day's haul." Leo wiped his forehead. "Now all we have to do is get them back home."

Romeau grinned. "There are those things we call bubbles. I think this would be an excellent time to put them to use." He reached and plucked absolutely nothing from thin air.

Harry squinted. It was a bubble, like the ones in Wolf's attic. And now that he was looking for them . . . "Huh. They're all over the place."

Romeau chivvied heifers while Wolf and Harry caught bubbles. Everyone, even the kids with magic boggled, and apparently couldn't see the bubbles at all. It was a spooked crowd that followed them home and watched them retrieve the heifers and turn them loose with the domesticated cattle.

***

Then Harry got back to important things.

His first boat was actually a raft.

Adequate for fishing, but not the sort of thing he wanted for a long trip. As he got better at tanning hides—his first experiments were burned as public nuisances—he started thinking about ways to magically waterproof both rawhide and leather, and he managed to impress Wolf with his first canoe.

He went west first, taking along a load of window glass. It was a long paddle up the lake to the next village. Over a hundred miles, at a guess. The glass was very welcome, and they told him the head of the lake was just twenty miles on.

"There's a short river in the northwest, linking to another lake. I think there are a dozen villages along there." The recently elected mayor pointed north. "And the Alps have grown. Some of the people that arrived at this end moved north, across the river. They thought maybe there'd be fewer lions where it was cold."

Harry stayed long enough to teach everyone the various "magic" techniques they'd developed. The one to get the bugs off the gardens was especially appreciated. They'd given up on the first fields outside their walls.

The river was sluggish enough for him to paddle up it with

little trouble. He traveled from village to village, rarely staying longer than a week, teaching anyone who was interested all the "spells" they had worked out, and learned a few new ones. He kept a journal, and drew maps, kept a rough census. And he noted how many of the settlers were genetically engineered, and how many powered. They'd stopped automatically inserting the power genes over a decade ago, so the number of . . . Lord he hated using the terms Witch and Mage. The number of kids who would be strong telies tapered off at twelve years of age, but then the second generation, and even a few third generation children started filling the gaps. Rather a lot of the powered children had been abandoned by their parents and were living in groups in the big cylindrical buses.

"You look worried." The local doctor eased down to a seat on a rock near his.

"Well, perhaps a bit apprehensive. But maybe I should be hopeful, instead. As a group to strand away from modern society, we're pretty good. Lots of us with strengthened immune systems and so forth. I'm wondering what the next few generations will be like, though."

Another man chuckled, as he joined them. "And no prejudice against the engineered. I'm not, but I got a slew of things fixed in my kids. My wife died of cancer, but my kids and grandkids won't. They're smarter than I am, they'll be taller and better looking. And they still manage to look a bit like Vera, and if you squint really hard, me. Very prettied up."

A man snickered. "And so many of us are doctors! I swear,

every village must have one or two."

"And lawyers." The doctor shook his head. "You can see them sweating, resisting the impulse to sue the hunters on behalf of the wildebeests." There was general laughter, and they sat and talked as the sun dropped to the horizon. Then they all migrated back inside the walls. Food and drink started showing up, and the speculation on the future continued. All in all they were minimally bothered by the thought of being marooned here.

Damn good neighbors.

As were the other villages.

"If those lions mean this is Africa, then the straights of Gibraltar are closed." This village had decided to go for the Medieval feel, and elected a High Sheriff. A big genial man who'd come with his two children and three grandchildren.

His wife rolled her eyes. "It's a different world. We ought to rename the continents."

"It's supposed to be a parallel Earth," the High Sheriff returned, stubbornly. "Those bullies we kicked out, they came to be near the beacon. Talking all the time about parallel worlds, and which one they wanted to move to. Most of them wanted to go back to Earth."

Harry bit his lip. "Earth? Who were they?"

"Parents, adults who'd had a breakup with an engineered spouse, or walked away from kids who were engineered. Older brothers and sisters, who'd been dragged along. People who ought not to have come in the first place."

"So far, there has been sixteen women and twenty-five men." The wife smiled ruefully. "With such a small population, I tend to keep an eye on the gender balance here. So I noticed it with them. They weren't balanced at all."

"Which worries me." The High Sheriff frowned. "I'd hate to see them start raiding for food or women."

"In any case, that first group talked about the beacon, about how they'd go back home, as soon as the gate opened." The wife made a face. "I figure we did Earth a favor, taking them away, but frankly, I'd druther they'd been left behind. They've settled south of here, I think, through the hills and out on the Atlantic coast."

"With luck, the government will get the gate working again, without you gods, and they can all go back." The High Sheriff grimaced. "I doubt it will happen."

Harry stared over at the beacon. "It's been . . . I don't know whether to say it's already been five months, or to be amazed that it has only been five months. A year and a half, give or take, before the new gate is finished."

"What will you do?"

Harry pulled his eyes away from the beacon. "If they can open gates, then they won't need us any more."

"You hope."

"Yeah." *A year and a half. Summer Solstice. Remember, and be prepared to run for it. This is one thing that we can't afford to forget.* He eyed the beacon. It would make his life so simple, if something were to happen to it. He turned away from temptation.

Harry hiked the ridge of "Gibraltar" and viewed the "Atlantic Ocean" from the heights. He didn't go any further south. He didn't want to meet these putative rebels.

But salt. Yes. He hiked down to the shore and experimented with magically separating it from the water, and decided boiling it away was slower but less painful. He returned well laden, shared a bit of it with the village, and suggested that they had a valuable trade commodity just thirty miles away.

The return trip was faster, the current, however sluggish, was with him, and he stayed only a few days at each village along the route.

The ladies of his own village were delighted with the salt, and began salting and preserving meat. There seemed to be a lot more people than he remembered, and a second stockade was under construction two miles northwest.

***

The magic and hunting lessons and construction continued through the fall. Slice turned out to be a handy spell for cutting hay, and as the tractors started running short on fuel, they switched from baling hay to stacking it. By hand. Then scooping it up with a bubble, for later use.

Then the corn was ready to harvest, and needed a lot of hand picking.

The wheat was sliced and scooped up, to be run through a thresher run off of Muriel Westfallen's tractor.

There was a good chance that job would have to be done by hand, next year.

"And keep coming to the meditation and tai chi classes." Old Wolf called after her. "It's a good idea to learn how to concentrate and visualize before you have enough power to be dangerous.

Old Wolf was pretty slick, complimenting Muriel, playing with her kids. Carrying her sleeping kids "home" to her RV, and kissing her goodnight in plain sight of everyone.

Chris gave the compliments some thought and managed to stammer out a brief version of some of them, Iris blushed, and seemed pleased to see him whenever he showed up.

Chapter Ten

15 October 2117

Tripoli, North Africa, Exile

Harry curtailed his trips when the weather turned suddenly cold, and the first storm front of the winter hit. Three days of chilly rain turned everything to mud, and finished off the gardens.

Wolf kept up the hunting and lessons in martial arts to anyone interested. And magic lessons for all the boys who could gather power. Gisele, Muriel, and Phaedra were giving magic lessons to the girls.

Gisele cackled at his surprise. "I may be the oldest Goddess, but there were plenty of women engineered to have a single power gene, or single type of power gene, before they decided to cram everything possible into me."

"I thought the female gene meant the women could have only daughters?" Harry glanced at the kids.

"The four boys are all in vitro engineered. Happy Kids used the women's genes—and their husbands'—and the women bore the children normally, it's only Y bearing sperm that gets attacked. Once conceived, a male embryo is safe." Gisele sniffed. "Of course both their husbands used that as an excuse to abandon their families. Disgraceful. Look at Muriel, a wiggly five year old boy, a two year old and a baby! Out here alone in the wilderness."

Harry chuckled. "Wolf seems to like them all. I don't think she'll be single for very long." He turned back to the original subject. "So they're magic, and so are their kids."

"Yes, and about hundred other adults and teenagers, and thirty kids. Almost ten times as many people are engineered in non-powered ways. So less than half of us are normal."

"If that holds for all the villages, normal for here is going to be very different."

"Especially a few generations from now. The vast majority of the non-engineered are adults, here with their engineered children, and not planning on having any more. Perhaps a third of the youngsters are normal, siblings of the engineered."

"Planning and reality may differ. We don't have access to modern medicine, that is to say, contraceptives."

Gisele cackled again. "We're working on a spell for that one as well."

Romeau snorted as he walked in. "You should have started earlier. These teenagers! I've got five upcoming weddings, if the families will stop the name calling and settle down."

"No magic abortions?"

Gisele sighed. "I can make a death spell. I've tested it on animals. Can I cast it inside a woman without killing her, too? Pretty small target, a tiny clump of cells. I could probably do it if I wait until the baby is big enough to kill just a bit of the heart or brain, keep the field of the spell definitely inside the baby."

Wolf nodded slowly. "How do you avoid affecting the tissue in between?"

"Exactly. I'm practicing with animals, and it makes me sick to think of killing a baby so far along. Karen's six months along, and I can feel the sleeping thoughts of the baby. It would be murder, brutal and cold, to kill that innocent child." Gisele hunched her shoulders.

Harry was suddenly reminded of an elderly woman. *This is what Gisele will look like at eighty.* He turned his thoughts back to the matter of pregnancies. "Couldn't you, oh, knock it loose? Jiggle everything around within tolerances the mother can handle?" Harry worried that one over. "I can sense—locate—people. But I've never tried to detect organs."

"I can see small stuff like that. And do delicate telekinesis." Wolf was frowning. "I sort of remember an aneurism, someone dying of a stroke."

Gisele looked up, eyes bright. "Were you able to save him?"

Wolf hesitated. "Actually, I think I caused it. On purpose."

"Oh. Dear. I think the other doctors, the ones without their medical knowledge scrambled, are secure in their jobs, for now." Gisele shrugged. "We're all teaching by example, and talking about a college, but no one's done anything yet."

"At least we'll have an elementary school going all winter, whether the kids like it or not." Romeau grinned. "And not is the answer. I suspect they'll appreciate it more once the really cold weather hits . . . if it does. We're pretty far south."

***

Harry made several shorter trips up and down the lake, trading with the people of the three nearest villages. On his last trip, Phaedra accompanied him, and hobnobbed with the women in the other villages. Several times he saw them practicing magic, always in threes.

He added working in circles of eight to his own magic lessons. So odd, how men and women worked differently.

Chapter Eleven

25 December 2117

Tripoli, North Africa, Exile

The Inn grew in fits and starts. Smaller than they wanted; a great big dining room and kitchen but only a loft upstairs under the high peaked roof. But it was weather tight, with a marvelous fireplace, before Christmas.

The fabber was worked over time, making presents. Two each for the little kids, one each for the older ones. The Inn was enclosed enough that they could hold a party during the day. Break out some games, play music, eat too much . . . the little kids sobbed openly, and Chris wasn't the only one trying to not remember real Christmases at home with his family.

The next winter storm roared down from the north with little warning. The temperature dropped off the cliff and rain turned to ice, then snow. The livestock crowded into the few sheds that had been finished, and the gods bubbled a lot of them. It seemed like a sensible thing to do . . .

Three days later the weather warmed, the bubbles emptied, and a frenzy of barn building started. A big public one, for all the people who owned just a few animals, smaller ones for the ranchers with small herds and bigger plans for the future.

"If that was a taste of the local winters, we're going to need to close off the sheds, and I'm not sure the hay will last." Vito fussed, but at least he worked and knew what he was doing.

There were a couple of whiners that were neither polite nor able.

Chris shoveled manure in the public barn twice a week, swapping dishwashing chores with Lillian. It had nothing to do with Iris Penner stopping by to coo at the wild heifers. Really. Regular applications of calming spells helped the critters accept people, but they were noticeably nervier and less friendly than the domestic heifers of the same age.

"We can bubble the bulls and the stallions, but that's just five animals out of five hundred. Well, we can bubble as many as we want, but they won't be growing up or gestating while they're in there." Romeau finished Sungold and turned to brush the patiently waiting Jet.

"Ha! You just solved one of my worst worries." Leo grinned. "I have cows that will be dropping their calves in March. It might be a good idea to bubble them for a month or two, make it May for calving. June was warm, when we arrived, the grass mature. The wild heifers, on the other hand, I'd like to see keep growing all winter. Breed them next fall and see what we get the following spring."

That idea spread like wildfire, and half their animals disappeared as the next storm's clouds loomed across the lake.

It was the worst of the winter storms so far and dumped five feet of snow on them.

Old Wolf demonstrated a new use for bubbles. He bubbled the bus, and moved it so the door coincided with the door of the closet under the stairs. Then he attached the bubble edges, and there it was. The whole bus. In the closet.

That sparked a burst of innovations.

As they got out between storms and chopped down more trees, both for firewood and for lumber, they built rooms for themselves.

The upstairs loft turned into two short hallways, lined with tightly packed rows of windows, keeping the glass makers busy. The wooden rooms were built separately, encased in bubbles except for the window hole and the doorway. Installed, the bubbles turned the upstairs into tightly packed rows of doors, each opening into a generously spaced room with a window.

It was disturbing, to say the least. The kids laughed and moved in. Old Wolf finally built two long hallways, with holes for doorways spaced ten feet apart, bubbled the hallways and installed them over the packed doors.

Harry shook his head. "It looks fine, on the inside. So long as you don't remember seeing a lack of building extending out the back, before you walked in."

The kids voted, and named it the Fire Mountain Inn, for no apparent reason, beyond perhaps, the vid they'd watched the night before in the Chapel.

Romeau moved back into his Temple of Love, and Gisele did not move out. She found a nook she claimed would grow herbs, come spring, and studied the medicinal uses of everything anyone had seeds for. And how to increase or duplicate the chemical effect magically. Harry moved into what was supposed to be the wine cellar of the Fire Mountain Inn, swearing he wasn't going to live in a bubble. The kids teased him, and loved their rooms. Harry shrugged and decided they could take their rooms with them, when they grew up and wanted to be independent. "I can build proper hotel rooms and put them in the vacant door and window holes. And in the mean time, I'd better think up a spell that will prevent anyone from noticing the lack of exterior wings."

The dining room of the Tavern turned into the much delayed school, and the gods insisted the older kids read college level texts and discussed them with them regularly.

And they practiced magic. Invented magic. Shields. Push, pull, and slice. They couldn't figure out invisible, but managed to be very unnoticeable. Chris worked hardest on the calming and charming spells. He still needed to catch a horse. Two horses. One for him, one for Iris.

Gisele was remembering more of her training. She might have been a doctor, but she seemed to know a lot about genetics as well. She handled the biological subjects, talking with the older teenagers, and several adults with an interest, and helped in the hospital. Seven births and two deaths. Heart attack in one case, and an accident with a chainsaw.

The other gods worried less about their mental state. Old Wolf drilled them, gods and orphans and anyone else who showed up at the winery, in martial arts twice a week.

There were complaints about petty thievery, and glances sent toward "all those unsupervised teenagers, living in what is practically a bar. It was bound to happen."

Since Harry's first attempt to brew beer had been weak, tasted nasty, and had been finished off by the adults within a month, Chris figured the thief was more likely one or more of the *other* unsupervised teenagers, the ones who met out at the public barn and bought the even nastier stuff Marshal Wallace fermented and distilled.

Chapter Twelve

April 2118

Tripoli, North Africa, Exile

Mark Lawrence, one of the men with a power gene and some friends had been working on bending and shaping wood. A mix of steam, magic and painstaking care. They could meld boards together so tightly only the change in grain testified to their one time separateness.

In the spring, Harry used their techniques on a larger hull.

"It needs a dragon on the front."

Harry grinned at Wolf. "It does look a bit like a Viking long boat, doesn't it? I'm thinking a simple square sail will save me a lot of paddling, without needing a deep keel. Since no one's got an actual harbor or dock, I have to get in close to shore so I have to keep the shallow draft."

"You could add a umm, catamaran? No, that's not right. Pontoon? No. Damn my brain. A cross arm with a float. Whatever the word is." He grinned suddenly. "Oh, the expression on your face! Okay, I won't say that again until you've tipped over."

"Outrigger." Harry growled. "Vikings do not have outriggers."

"Ah. Thank you."

The lake was twice as long east-west as north-south, with broad slow rivers connecting it to other lakes. They had enough contact, village to village by shortwave that Harry found himself carrying cargo and people from place to place. *Viking* was much admired, and he suspected would soon be much copied. He experimented with mentally redirecting the wind. It was almost as exhausting as rowing; he limited his use of it to times when the wind was blowing from almost the right direction, and the power needed to shift it minimal. And when he lacked companions to grab the second pair of long oars and work for their passage. At every village, he stayed long enough to teach Slice, Unnoticeable, Pesticide, Fertilizer, Heat, Light, Fireball and Levitate. To tell the women to work in threes, the men in fours and eights.

To the east, Harry skipped past Cairo without stopping.

He was relieved to find Michael alive and well in the next large settlement. And even more relieved to find the ordinary people in charge.

"They named it the Red River, even though it's not red. But the river has got to be approximately the Suez Canal and the Red Sea." Michael leaned down and pet one of his dogs. He had a handsome pair of black german shepherds, a great dane and a boxer. He hadn't pulled a single asinine trick yet. His pale, almost white hair gleamed in the Arabian sun.

"We're spread out all over, but we swap and trade regionally all along the curve of the Israeli Coast and over the mountains. The next settlement is Kuwait, clear across Arabia, then Karachi and New Bombay. No one's actually been to any of them, but we talk on the radio all the time. Too far across the desert, and yours is the first seaworthy craft I've seen."

"You can't go overland? We were wondering about the Middle Eastern oilfields. I'm afraid I didn't put a shortwave in the boat. Wasn't someone going to go take a look?"

Michael snickered. "That might have something to do with the millions of square miles of natural asphalt and near surface tar sands they talk about in 'Kuwait,' perhaps?"

"Damn. One of the geologists was talking about all the earthquakes and a highly active lithosphere." Harry nodded at the waterwheel to change the subject. "You look like you're doing well."

"The town is. We power a small core of the city. Hospital, school, city hall and a couple of factories. If we can find enough iron and copper, we'll build another one, and really get going. A couple of people had electric cars, and they've formed a taxi service. Oh, and we pump water to the holding tank up there. Everyone has running water in their home."

They'd been strolling as they talked. A man strode around them and gave them an unhappy glare as he marched passed. The dogs all hackled a bit. The man tripped and staggered into a woman carrying a canvas bag of rolls.

When Harry would have stopped, Michael just grabbed his arm and steered him onward. "I get blamed for everything that happens around me. So I try to not be around very much."

They ended up at the top of the ridge the city was built on.

Michael waved his arms at the land on the other side. "We pump water for the fields and orchards. Those mountains over there have copper ore and they've found iron to the south. They figure they can build another alternator in a year, and start a second town to the north where we cut all our lumber."

"You've done . . . "

"They've done. Not me. Them."

Harry looked at him in exasperation. "How are they cutting these trees, Michael? Making glass? Keeping the bugs off the crops?"

"Chainsaws. Charcoal and sand. Pesticides."

"There's a lot that can be done with magic. I'll show you, and anyone else who can gather power."

Michael looked surprised. "I'm the only one. The engineered here can only do very simple low powered things. I'll introduce you to the Committee on Magic. Everything here is committees."

All appointed by the Town Council. Harry stayed in his boat at the wharf, there being no facilities for visitors at all. Michael lived ten miles out of town, by order of the Town Council, on the recommendation of the Committee on Magic.

The committee was clearly unwelcoming. Harry discussed the pest and fertilizer spells first, went on to those useful in hunting, the woodworking and leather making spells. They allowed him to teach a small selected group of adults. Michael showed up most days and watched from a distance. He made people nervous and gathered the blame for all clumsiness. The

Committee thanked Harry for the lessons, then showed him the door.

"That's the first time I've seen you smile, Michael."

The tall man shrugged. "At least now I see that I'm not being singled out for exclusion. No gods welcome here. I guess I'll go somewhere with no other people at all."

"Would you like to sail around the peninsula to Kuwait and then on to New Bombay?"

"I'd just make your boat sink, or a storm blow up and drive it onshore."

Harry finally admitted defeat. "You are just going to have to cheer yourself up, Michael. No one can do it for you."

"I'd wish you smooth sailing, but it might doom you."

"I'll see you on the return trip, Michael."

The tall youngster just shook his head and walked away.

The Red River was swift but deep enough to not be too dangerous during the day. The shores were unremitting desert for close to a thousand miles. Harry fished and cooked over small fires of wood he'd brought along.

Chapter Thirteen

Spring 2118

Tripoli, North Africa, Exile

" . . . and if the women aren't going to shovel manure, why should they get a heifer in the roundup drawing?"

Chris looked at Ben and shook his head. "Some of them do, like your sister, and some of them trade, like Lillian. I mean, I just hate washing dishes, especially when it involves forty-two kids." He racked his shovel. "And with the cattle out to pasture every day now, the manure volume is down to half or less. So it's even less work than it was all winter. And if they help with the roundup, they get into the drawing."

Ben shook his head. "You are so soft on women, let them run everything."

"I let them run themselves. Instead of trying to take over and order them around."

That got him a sneer.

If he wasn't Iris's brother, I'd totally ignore his existence.

Still without a heifer, Chris decided it was time to try his other tactic.

He stalked the wild horses carefully.

Projected the calming spell as hard as he was capable of. Added unnoticeable.

They paid him no more attention than if an antelope had wandered among them. There were two prime targets. He couldn't judge the mares' ages, but they were huge and round, due to foal. Now to find out if this would work . . . He tied off both ropes to the closest trees. Slipped a noose over one mare's head, then the other, quickly, as the first raised her head in alarm. They both shied back and the calm broke with an almost audible snap.

Chris shielded for all he was worth. He got knocked flat, rolled around, stomped by the stallion . . . and emerged shaken but unbruised.

With two frantic mares flailing about, falling and scrambling back to their feet to throw themselves at the end of the rope again.

Chris kept his distance, and waited for them to learn they couldn't escape. He'd put knots in the rope, a large one to keep it from choking them, a small one that would keep the noose from falling open. Their first panic had pulled the end loop over the small knot, and they were in the bag.

It took them a long time to admit that. They were wild, not feral, like a mustang. There'd been no thousands of years concentrating the genes that made domestication possible. Mousy gray, with dark stripes down their backs and double slashes of black over their withers. He studied them carefully, and finally decided one was a bit taller than the other. "Right. You're Mutt and you've Jeff, and I doubt I'll ever be sure which one of you is which."

His voice panicked them all over again. He really wished he could do that bubble thing.

They finally calmed down enough to be susceptible to the Calm spell, and he untied them. He moved them carefully from grove to grove. Tying them often, so he could relax the spell and recuperate.

He camped, and his tiny fire spooked the exhausted animals *again.*

Romeau rode Sungold into camp about midnight. He whistled when he saw the mares. "Excellent. I've thought about doing that but never got around to it."

Chris yawned. "They haven't broken their necks yet, but could you bubble them? I'd like to get home in less than a week."

He did, and helped build two small sturdy runs for them, behind the Inn.

Chris fed them hay by the handful, all day, for days, and layered on spells, and they remained wild animals. Minimally socialized, never really tame. He registered a brand, and used magic, a reverse of the silly hair growing spell to mark both mares. And the colt and filly they produced a week after he'd gotten the mares home. He tried, hard, to imprint on the foals. They were a bit friendlier than their mothers, but . . .

He bred the mares to Jet, and moved them out to the larger pastures, to make room in the pens for the next batch of wild heifers.

Milly shook her head at him. "Still trying to impress that

Iris Penner? You could have a hundred head of cattle, and still fail."

"She likes horses. She spent tons of time trying to make up to the filly." Chris scowled at the fast disappearing horses. Hopefully they wouldn't run right through the barbed wire fence. He had a nasty suspicion he was going to need his calming spell to catch them again.

Chapter Fourteen

18 June 2118

New Bombay, West Coast Indian Subcontinent

Ms. Abrams dismissed the senior calculus class, and closed her folder. Math, science and basic logic were the only subjects she trusted herself to teach. History was hopeless with the holes in her memory, and even English was a bit iffish. She was very careful in her preparation for science, so she didn't overlook something obvious, but she seemed to be adjusting to the new person she was.

New Bombay, from the very start was beautiful. The four gods had split the responsibilities of governance among themselves. Mercy had appropriated the hospital and Pax the police and courts. Marty had taken over all city planning and approval of buildings. And they'd built them, working together. Magic worked quite well on stone.

Abrams had gladly picked up the schools. If anything needed to be run logically . . . Basic education, then tracking to either vocational training or university prep. The University was a bit thin on professors, but by building the hospital as an adjunct to a medical school, she'd managed to recruit two doctors to be the medical school. Marty had designed a building for the school of law, she was going to have to talk to the exiled lawyers about how to organize it. The geology department was run by a rather rude texas oil man, whatever that was. He'd been silenced by the blocky, random "crystals" stack that was the science building. Marty had basked in the man's total bogglement. She had biology, chemistry and physics professors, one of each, and she lectured in philosophy and taught math at the college level as well as in the high school. Art was a major department all its own, of course. Marty also managed the public museum. Richie managed nothing what-so-ever.

It was all very grandiose for a "city" of twelve thousand people.

Most of them hunters and farmers and farm workers.

Abrams remembered enough history to know that at the Medieval level it took ten people working in the fields to support a single urban specialist. She hoped they'd kept enough tech to do better than that, once they had everything organized. Pest control alone should tip the ratio in their favor.

She trotted down the steps (graceful, sweeping white marble) and headed down the street toward the University. She planned to expand the University into the current high school buildings and grounds, and build multiple local high schools as the city grew.

But the way Marty built, it would be a good while before they outgrew their current quarters.

Bright colors resolved into Mercy, trotting down the street toward her. She was getting quite alarmingly large. She'd been impregnated with engineered sperm prior to the Exile.

"You must be nearly due." Ms. Abrams continued her speculation aloud as the other woman got within hearing range. "It's been almost twelve months since we arrived."

"Yes, the doctor said if I didn't start labor within a week she'd induce. I really should have declined the honor, but who knew this was going to happen?"

"Indeed. And we have no idea what the normal gestation is for a Goddess. Brave of you, to be the first." Abrams said no more, as her recollections of the pre-Exile were rather dim. The only strong one involved the lack of someone. She couldn't even remember his name. But he wasn't here.

"At any rate I came to talk to you about Harry."

Abrams looked at her blankly. "I don't believe I have any students named . . . "

"No, no, no! Harry. He's one of *them*."

Abrams frowned at the shorter woman. "One of the people who exiled us?"

"A traitor." The deep voice was directly behind her.

She spun around and frowned at Pax. She hated it when he snuck up on her.

"He's one of us, a God. But he worked with them. He thinks we won't remember. So act nice but be on your guard."

"He's here?"

Pax looked down the Street of Exile to the harbor. "The Viking boat with the square red sail. An undersized Viking longboat. I'm shocked it's actually sea worthy."

"I dare say he hugged the coast." Abrams still couldn't

remember anything about a Harry. "Should we walk down and meet him?"

"Much though I dislike seeming to give him any honor, I'd as soon control who he talks to." Pax hunched a shoulder and set off down the hill.

Mercy scampered after him and Abrams followed at a more deliberate pace.

Marty walked out of the Department of Performing Arts building and fell into step beside her. "Do you remember him?"

"Not a glimmer." Until she saw him. He'd been in a suit, not these raggedy khaki things. She remembered fury, screaming, terrified and sick. The emotions, not the reasons. It was going to be difficult to judge. Emotions were poor things to base a decision on, but apparently that was all she was going to have.

***

After the tiny seaside fishing village of Kuwait, New Bombay was astonishing. White marble buildings, broad paved streets. Landscaping. Dramatic shadows and highlights in the early morning sunshine.

No wonder Karachi and all those smaller villages shut up shop and moved here.

Everyone walking, not a car or horse in sight.

Harry lowered his gaze to the harbor as he approached. The *Viking* wasn't the largest vessel there, but the largest looked more like a barge than anything he'd want to take on the ocean, himself. Pax glowed like the sun, hair and clothes golden. Harry kept his mental shields down, in case the man had anything else to say. He could feel speculation from the brown haired man to Pax's left. The woman on the other side bubbled with chaotic emotions, her poorly organized thoughts underlain with self interest. With a start, he realized there was a second woman. No emotions at all. Faint intellectual curiosity.

At a gesture from Pax, a pair of boys scampered to catch his lines and snug him up to the marble pier. *Wish I had more bolsters. This could be tough on the wood.*

He stepped ashore. "Paxal, nice to see you again. Marty, Mercy and err..." He recognized the woman now, but in his memory she was screaming at him. Spat on him.

"Abrams." She frowned. "Yes. I remember that emotional encounter as well. Odd that I can't remember what triggered such an emotional outburst." She stared at him.

Thoughtful? Watchful? Utterly indifferent? He couldn't tell.

Mercy gasped faintly, a hand going to her abdomen. Harry blinked. He'd been concentrating so hard on the mental impressions her shape hadn't registered. Now it did, with faint alarms. Marty and Pax drew back from her a bit. Abrams was as indifferent to her as to Harry.

Harry stepped forward. "Are you all right Mercy? I hadn't realized, well, that any of the Goddesses could have babies."

"I agreed to an experiment. I was inseminated before the

exile." She gasped and leaned on his proffered arm.

Over twelve months ago? Harry tromped hard on his cynicism. "I think it's time to get to the hospital. Are there any cars still running? Wagons?"

"Bah. We don't allow things of that sort into town, dirty the air or poop in the streets. Walking is the healthiest exercise. And labor, especially first labor, takes hours. I will walk to the hospital." She steered Harry around and started walking.

Behind them, he could hear Pax asking Marty something about a rural police station. Abrams, when he glanced back, was pacing along the Viking, studying it.

The route to the hospital took them past a high school. The University of New Bombay. Across the street, City Hall. All done in white marble, Grecian style, whatever that meant. The term had drifted up out of his battered mind, unaccompanied. Mercy was silent, concentrating inwardly, or perhaps frightened. He couldn't read her at all, now. They turned. The hospital was a block beyond City Hall, perhaps part of the University. He supported her through the front doors.

The girl manning the reception desk gawped, eyes going wide. Then she bolted through a door behind her. She was right back, and orderlies with a stretcher right behind her. Mercy was whisked away with a constantly increasing flood of personnel.

"Impressive reception." Harry glanced over at the girl, once again the sole occupant of the reception area.

"The Goddess of Mercy owns the hospital, and takes a personal interest in every aspect of it."

"Really. Well, where can I wait, and stay out from underfoot?"

She eyed him dubiously.

Not fair! I swam and changed into clean clothes before I entered the harbor! Clean or not, he was pretty ragged. He straightened. "I am Harry, the God of Travelers. I will wait for my friend."

She gulped. "Of course." She ducked back through the doors, and again returned quickly. A teenaged boy followed her, this time.

"Take him to the father's waiting area."

The lad led him up three flights of stairs. *They carry pregnant women up three flights?* A corridor opened out on the right. Lots of seating, facing out, into rooms where women paced or lay. Or screamed, in one case. *The Goddess of Mercy takes no pity on fathers. They get an overdose of women in labor.*

He spotted Mercy being carried into a separate room and looked around. The lad had already left. The three men chewing their fingernails looked like they had problems enough of their own. Harry walked further down the hallway. He caught Mercy's voice, sharp and commanding from one room. On the other side, a windowed room with cradles. Two occupants, at the moment. More rooms further down. An open door and sobbing.

"Just let me go home. Bad enough my baby wasn't perfect. Too much work for little or no return, indeed! That hag. How dare she decide my baby's fate."

"She was merciful, she doesn't believe in prolonging pain and suffering."

"Bethany wasn't hurting, just . . . Oh, go away. Or let me leave."

"The doctor will be seeing you and your husband this afternoon."

"Get out of here. Leave me alone!"

Harry walked on. Came to a dead end, turned and walked back. A nurse was hustling out of the occupied room, red faced and bustling about to expend emotions.

"I guess, without modern medicine, infant mortality will be rising." Harry ventured.

The nurse hunched a shoulder at him. "We can't support people who'll never be productive. Can't have people like that reproducing."

Harry felt ill. "So you kill infants with . . . problems? Or sterilize them? Or is it the mother that you sterilize?"

"Mother and father both. The baby would have died in a few days anyway. The Goddess just made it painless and quick. Merciful." She hustled off.

Harry walked back to the open room. "Excuse me? Why don't you get dressed and walk out. Right now. Change your name just a bit."

"I, I . . ."

"Where's your husband?"

"He'll be by after work, and they'll do him, us, then." Tears welled.

"Are you well enough to walk to where he works?

"Yes. Yes!" Uncertainty changed to determination.

Harry walked out, stood for a moment listening to the women in labor. *I'm surprised there are so many babies, they must have been conceived within a few months of the Exile. People running out of contraceptives, or the Gods wanting a growing population?* He thought about Gisele and the spells she was devising. Energy to support the effort, a web of spells that relaxed some muscles and strengthened others. Took the edge off the pain. He whispered the gentle poems a few times, then walked on. The sounds quieted behind him, and then as he walked back, the squall of a newborn baby. He whispered the poems, stopped outside Mercy's door for a round of them. Paced.

Another baby, then the last in the large delivery room. He paced for another hour before the cries came from the private room. He waited, chewing fingernails himself, until Mercy waved him in through an open door.

She had a glow of pride, accomplishment. She waved at the cradle as he peered. "My daughter Grace."

"She . . . well, she looks like a newborn. I dare say she'll be a beauty soon enough."

Mercy snorted. "Flattery, Harry? I must look a wreck."

"You look triumphant."

She smiled a bit smugly. "Go away Harry. Find the others and tell them I'm fine, and the baby, of course."

"Of course."

Somewhat at a loss, he wandered back past City Hall and spotted Marty and Abrams walking out. They were indifferent to the news about Mercy and Grace, discussing a proposal to electrify the city as they walked.

"Perfectly feasible, it just takes a turbine on the outfall of a dam." Abrams said.

"But do we want a society that depends on electricity, rather than the power of mind and body?" Marty countered, turning up a walkway.

And when it comes to the power of the mind, you will always be on top, won't you Marty? "I see you've gotten away from Classical designs." Harry frowned at the upside down pyramid. The ground floor was a square, about fifty feet on a side. The second floor was cantilevered out over it by ten feet or so. The third floor added another ten feet all around.

"I've put my living quarters in the basement. Want to come and see my private museum? I'm attempting to recreate high society, but it's an uphill battle." Marty fanned himself, a faint sarcastic smile on his face.

"Museum? I'd love to see what you have. Did you bring it from Earth, or is it all new?" Harry tried to sound neutral. He had no doubt but that Marty's idea of high society had himself on the top tier. Mercy and Pax as well, no doubt. His eyes strayed toward Abrams. He didn't like the specific memories he could recall. Would she talk to him? Would she remember the same things from her point of view?

Marty led the way into the museum. Polished wood floors. Expensive rugs. Subtle lighting that drew the eye to the pictures on the walls, the statuary. The pictures gave Harry a feeling of recognition. And doubt. *They can't be the originals, just excellent copies.* His memories of Earth were so shallow, he felt no surprise that copies were available, while having no idea how it was done. The statuary was realistic, natural and breathtakingly detailed. A handsome young man, joy and laughter on a face just breaking into a smile. A horse, magnificent and bold, ears half back in warning. A snake, coiled to strike. All in bronze, no marble. A girl on the cusp of womanhood, balanced between caution and boldness sat on a bench, playing with her hair.

"Well, Marty, your tastes in art are impeccable. I'm a bit surprised by the lack of modern art, though."

Marty shrugged. "This is my personal museum. No doubt public museums will appeal to broader tastes."

Harry nodded. *Where did he get all these? Did he bring them with him, like Wolf and his winery?* He made a face.

"Problem?"

"Just remembering Barry and Edmund. They would call you the God of Art."

"God of Art? Oh. My."

"Oh. Indeed. I'm not at all comfortable with their nonsense. I remember that the term god was sarcastic when applied to us. I remember that we were virtual slaves."

Abrams had been following them silently. She spoke now.

"I remember you as one of Them. I remember screaming, throwing things at you. But I don't remember why."

Harry frowned. "My memory is bad as well. I think I was older, an adult. Most of you were children, with circumscribed rights. I think I was trying to change things from the inside . . . and I have a nasty feeling it didn't work."

Abrams snorted. "Indeed. I believe it was Wolf who got us all away."

"And him the perennial troublemaker." Harry smiled a bit. "I guess he gets designated the God of War. Will you be the Goddess of Logic?"

"I will be content to be a Professor of Logic, thank you." She turned away and frowned at a peaceful arrangement of horses and trees. Willows wept, and mares lounged, half asleep. "How did you get that through your doors, Marty?"

"In a bubble."

"Oh. Of course. I should have realized that. I think it's my favorite. Drowsy, content, safe."

"I shall have to design a fountain around it, perhaps place it outside the Art Department building." Marty looked thoughtful. "Those one way flow pipes of yours would be useful for fountains, don't you think?"

"Yes, they would."

Harry frowned. "One way pipes?"

"Yes, a very useful spell, all water in a pipe is urged in one direction. With a pressure shut off, mind you. My first plumbing exploded impressively." A faint smile crossed

Abram's face.

That led to a discussion of spells, and over the next few days, demonstrations of men in fours and eights and women in threes and nines. In a city of twelve thousand, there were almost six thousand people with engineering, close to a thousand with a single power gene. It was rather intimidating to think of over a hundred 'Compasses' and 'Pyramids.'

Just as well so many of them are kids. There's time for a smaller number of adults to organize training and usage, before the main swell of children can access that power. Hopefully they won't have battles over the weather. Harry thought of bar brawls, gang fights, wars, fought with fireballs and slice. It was not a good thought.

Mercy released herself from the hospital and invited Harry to stay in her home. A mid sized mansion, not over done. Tasteful. With servants who scurried to sew him a new wardrobe, and take over the care of the baby.

Two weeks into his visit, Richie Xi showed up.

He eyed Mercy's daughter with trepidation. Shrugged. "She'll be a lot more interesting in sixteen years."

Mercy's eyes flashed. "Richie likes to go hunting. Of course it takes weeks, and involves parties nearly every night. It's a wonder they bring in any meat at all. How many people came along on your hunting trip, this time, Child?"

Richie grinned, unrepentant. "Couple hundred. Must have friends along, and cooks, and people to set up the tents and take care of the horses. And clothing."

Pax snorted. "Oh, I thought they were there to do the hunting."

Richie laughed out loud and walked out without answering.

"No manners at all." Mercy sniffed. She reached out and snared a bubble, popped the baby into it and attached it to the wall beside her. "So, Harry, where are you going to settle down? Whose side are you on?"

"Side? What sides are there?" Harry frowned at the bubble. "Is that good for her?"

Mercy rolled her eyes. "There's virtually no time in there. If I double layer the bubbles I could leave her in there for centuries and she'd think I'd just closed and immediately opened the bubble. There's no reason for motherhood to inconvenience a goddess."

"Sides, Harry." Pax shifted forward. "Are you on the side of the gods who rule, or the gods trying to pretend they're just regular people?"

"Are you insane? With the number of kids with power genes, we'll be swimming in gods inside of a couple of generations." Harry shivered. "I saw what Barry and Edmund are doing. Are you doing the same?"

Mercy laughed. "Heavens no. We're much more subtle. We want real power, not an orgy every month. Those two are fools. We have a city council and a Mayor to look good and deal with the paper work. But I run the hospital. Pax the courts. Abrams the education system, and Marty the planning council.

The government does what we tell it to do. And we make sure everyone is reasonably content and safe and that's all anyone really cares about."

"What does Richie run?" Harry tried to shake his brain into action.

"He in charge of idiots. He takes all the restless youngsters and would be youngsters out on hunting trips where they can do their worst and harm no one but themselves." Pax snickered. "He likes it because it keeps him away from all the middle aged women who climb all over him, here in town. They say he makes them younger, and they are relentless; we're quite short of unattached men. There must be a dozen or so of them who are pregnant now, but he claims they can't possibly be his. Like most of us, he was sterilized. No doubt I'll be saving his financial ass in court, soon enough."

Harry boggled a bit. Richie as the Fountain of Youth? *And who cares?* His cynical side raised its head. *These two may carry on and act like they're running the show, but are they? Really? Like Barry and Edmund, they may be in for a rude awakening. And Marty, Richie and Abrams aren't here to support this claim of being the power behind the throne. Apart from this conceit, they've got an excellent basic city setup here. I should study it, copy it when I get back home.*

"And in any case, we're the only gods and goddesses there will ever be. Remember? Witches have only girls, Mage power is inherited father to son, on the Y chromosome. There will never be any more double sourced babies." Mercy smirked and glanced at the bubble. "Even my own daughter has only the witch X chromosomes."

Harry nodded in relief. *No matter how obnoxious, tyrannical or kind, we are not immortal. Eventually we will die and the rest of the human race will be free of us.*

He sought out the others, to see how they felt.

Richie laughed. "Me? In charge? Fat chance. Someone else should do the hard work, while I attend the parties and try to get into the pants of something young and interesting. Why is it only the old crones chase me? The young ones ignore me." Harry thought the women hanging around in Richie's vicinity were quite attractive, even though obviously older than Richie. *And he complains!*

Art shrugged. "They're barely the same species we are. Why should I care how they organize themselves, so long as I can do whatever I wish." His eyes tracked across the people walking by. "Ugly. Look at them. They're all so ugly. All I want is to preserve beauty at its peak of perfection."

Abrams treated it like a school assignment and dissected the idea. "In theory, light handed, behind the curtain, leadership by the most qualified would be good. Of course we aren't talking about the most qualified, are we? Mercy, Pax and Marty? Pardon me while I laugh."

Harry did laugh, then. "I'm not sure what is most offensive, the highly magical putting on airs and acting like they are above the law, or the least magical accepting their place at the bottom rung of the ladder."

"The latter, if you've any sense." Abram's abrupt retreats into cold logic were starting to bother him. "Yes. It bothers me as well."

Not to mention the mind reading.

"Sometimes I feel as if society as a whole is squeezing me into a role, whether I want it or not, whether I even understand what they want. Look at us, all of us. People want mercy, but cynically they think it comes with a price, a catch. And you get Mercy, down at the hospital, relieving parents of the burden of raising children with extreme needs. They want Peace, but they think it will have to be imposed from above. Look at the way Pax is behaving."

"You're talking about the collective subconscious. A universal belief in Archetypes. In fact, you sound a bit like Barry and Edmund."

"Yes. Vice and Virtue, but they cynically don't believe in true Virtue, so Barry back slides and then tries again. Apparently Virtue is seen as trying to resist horrible impulses, not in not having them in the first place. Vice, combined with power, is unrestrained. Michael is Vengeance. Karma. Would you like to bet that if we ever have a War, Wolf will somehow wind up in the middle of it?"

Harry shook himself. "However interesting the theory, I somehow doubt it'll affect our actual actions. But I'll think about it."

"You do that, Dan'l Boone."

"I'm not . . . "

"The ever-traveling, self-sufficient frontiersman?"

"That's how I am by nature, it's not imposed from outside."

"No? Enhanced, perhaps? Or piggybacked upon a strong characteristic?"

Harry hunched his shoulders in rejection.

Abrams was the only one who walked him down to his boat.

At least they didn't try to feed me to the sharks.

Chapter Fifteen

13 August 2118

Tripoli, North Africa, Exile

They finished building a town hall. Finally.

And then they started trying to organize an election.

"They're too young to be voting." Ira Penner shot a glance across the square toward the Inn.

"And what about those gods. They're why we all wound up out here. They shouldn't even be here." A big man, red faced with sunburn.

"Nobody magic ought to hold office. You can't trust them. They're magic. We know all about that sort of creature." This one was skinny and dark. "What they did to our wives and daughters."

Chris winced. "You're from Cairo? I think we've all heard about how those two so-called gods behave. You're right, that powerful magicians can abuse their authority. But anyone powerful can do that. What we need is to keep would-be tyrants out of power. With or without magic."

"You're one of them!"

"I'm engineered. I know about prejudice. And we need to avoid it, for any reason. Race, language, genetics, age, wealth. Origin. You live here, now, so you ought to have the vote."

"You're just a kid." Ira Penner spat on the ground, and glared. "You and your 'Magic' friends."

"They've worked their butts off, not that you've ever so much as thanked them. I ain't big on praise, myself, but I can see who's goofing off and who's working." Vito Richardson glanced at Ben Penner. "And who does the least he can get away with when someone is watching, and squat other times."

Chris gawped. Mr. Nasty Rancher was backing him up?

"Tell you what. We'll make up a ballot. Everyone who wants one, gets one. In a booth, alone. Then they turn it in. At the end of the day, we tally them up. And if some of them just have flowers and butterflies some kid drew on them, so what?"

"So, how do we decide what goes on the ballot?"

Jack Otts fanned a sheaf of papers. "Just like this. We're going to tack these petitions up on the wall. Anyone can write one up, and post it. Then people can read them, and sign on the bottom, or the next sheet. Keep each one brief, because I think we need at least ten percent of the, well, sorry Chris, adult population to sign 'em before they get on the ballot. I've got a bunch of basic laws. Stealing and killing, and whatever. Yes, Leo, your brand laws are down on paper. I'll start by putting these up. Five hundred signatures and it's on the ballot. Nobody better even think about tearing one down. So? Comments?"

"What about the Mayor's office?" someone called.

"It's up for grabs. I know I got elected by a simple hand vote, but that was when there were maybe a thousand people here, including the kids. We're close to ten times that now, so we need paper ballots."

"How are we going to print ballots?"

"There's six fabbers in town. We'll get it done."

"Who does the counting?"

"Volunteers. Shall I count you in?"

It went on for hours. The mayor took some of the suggestions, rejected others. In the end a rough agreement that anyone thirteen or older could vote. Penner looked put out, but he grudgingly gave way.

The next day, Chris spotted him nailing up papers on the wall. He waited until the man had left, then walked over and joined the people already reading them. Use of magic illegal in town? Use of mind control punishable by ejection from the town? No alcoholic beverages sold on Sunday? Women to dress modestly?

"Taxes! Is that man insane? How the hell do you tax a barter economy?" Chris threw his hands up and stalked off. *Magic illegal. Son of a . . .*

Milly fell in at his side. "Dress modestly? Yeah, right. But you know, we really do need some sort of money. Swapping I.O.U.s isn't working very well, now that we're a lot bigger. Nobody knows who the original person is, whether he's good for it, or a dead beat."

"And there've been some claims of forgeries, too." Chris scratched his chin. "I can't work metal, like you witches can. Do you think you could make coins?"

"Oh . . . Now there's a good idea. But we'd have to have some sort of central bank that, umm, bought the coins from us?" Her eyes narrowed in thought.

"No. A government that paid you to make the coins, and your word to make only as many as they ordered." Chris grinned. "I wonder if the money could be marked, magically, so it couldn't be counterfeited?"

Lillian and Ariel slipped out of the crowd.

Lilian raised an eyebrow at Milly consorting with a man.

Ariel grinned. "What's up? You two look like your plotting something."

Milly nodded. "Yep. A bank, money. Come along, witches, we need to talk about this. Do any of us do any artwork? And we need to write up a petition about it, too."

Chris fell back. Metal, he regretted to say, was still women's work.

Old Wolf had figured it out, and could do it fairly well. Even the other gods were clumsy at it. The rest of the men were just pathetic. The women acted like it was child's play.

Infuriating.

Of course the women couldn't do weather work. Or wood.

So it all averaged out, in the end.

Lance and Matt started studying the older men's wood working skills. Then Vince and Tyrone suggested they build a boat and start trading up and down the coast. Hugh, Dane and Javier pitched in, and Chris made it a full "compass" and what the eight of them working together could do to wood was nothing short of awesome. They made small fishing boats for practice while Chris dug into computer files for boat designs, and they settled on a fifty foot single-masted cutter for their first trading ship. About the only thing they argued about was whose girlfriend their ship would be named after.

***

One of the petitions was to build a jail, driven by a spate of thefts. Some of valuable items, some of increasingly rare luxury items. Jokes about the women who stole each other's pretty undies made the rounds.

Until Cassie was attacked. Hit over the head, raped and left unconscious behind the public barn.

Then petitions for a justice system, courts, judges, and as a starting point, a sheriff.

Both sheriff and judge were added to the slate of offices they wanted to fill. No one registered for the judicial race. Two men vied for the Sheriff's post. Ira Penner was elected.

***

The late crops could use the water, so no one formed up to chase the clouds away. Huge, billowing high thunderheads. Brilliant white, darkening as they built, spreading, thickening, moving in from the lake. A gust of cool air stirred the trees, thunder rumbled in the distance, and the day grew dark and gloomy. Chris hurried to finish all his barn chores. Easy enough, with almost all the animals out to pasture. Today he helped extend the fencing outside the barn, so they could split up the cattle for more efficient feeding, according to the experts. They hung the last gate as the first big fat drops hit the ground. He was soaked before he made it through the doors of the Inn, and headed straight to his room to change. Back in the dining room, the kids on serving duty had already lit candles.

"Good thing we're cooking on a wood stove." Neil plunked macaroni and cheese down in front of him. "I'll bet the electricity would be off, if we had any. Milly wants opinions about the cheese, it's local, not fabbed. It think it's pretty good."

Another crash of thunder rattled the windows.

Chris nibbled. "Good, nice and sharp." He took a forkful and eyed the steamed broccoli. *Vegetables. I still haven't escaped from having to eat vegetables.* He ignored the green thing and dug into the mac.

Karina and Elnora hustled in, dripping.

"Man, it's wild out there. The cows and horses are running all over the place."

Chris swallowed. "We'll have to go out and check them for barbed wire cuts after this is over. I hope they don't go through the fences." He winced a bit at the thought, but all the cattle ranchers had tall tales about what spooked cattle could do, fences, cliffs, rivers apparently no obstacle once they panicked en mass. *I'd never see those mares again.*

Three hours later he'd changed that to *I'll never see those mares again* as he stretched wire to repair the breaks. Riders were out searching for the hopefully tired but not injured or eaten escapees. Roughly half their cattle were gone.

When they finished the fence, Chris started walking south. He stuck to the better drained ridges. He sighted several groups of animals being herded homeward. Spotted a trio of cows huddled in a grove of trees and waved down Romeau to point him at them.

"I suppose Sungold is much too smart to panic over a bit of thunder?"

Romeau grinned. "Of course. The fact that he and Jet took refuge from the storm in my front room had nothing to do with it."

The horse nodded his agreement. Chris grinned and hiked on. Romeau's front room was large and bare, except when they brought out the folding chairs for a wedding. *Wish my horses had that much sense. Or socialization. No telling how far those critters went. In fact, they may still be going.*

He camped, damp and uncomfortable despite a fire, and circled around, checking for the hoofprints of cattle and horses. He spotted one of the polled hereford cows with her calf, and two wild heifers with big V brands on their butts, and circled to carefully aim them back toward home. He managed to not spook and stampede them again, and turned them over to Leo around noon.

"We've got most of them back, or accounted for. Lions and injuries . . . lost five for sure. Vito'll be glad to see these two. And Ira might even start talking to you again."

"Maybe." Chris shrugged. He doubted it would make much of a difference.

He made a long sweep around further west, but his wild mares were long gone.

And the first time he saw Iris, she was chatting one of the 'normal' boys.

Just as well I've got the boat, and trading as a backup occupation. I don't seem to be getting anywhere as a rancher.

Chapter Sixteen

15 August 2118

At Sea

Greatly daring, and with the wind behind him, Harry sailed west, directly across the Arabian Sea, then followed the coast of Arabia to the Red River. The river was his first serious barrier. The warm winds from the Ocean at his back were barely sufficient to make way against the current. Then the winds shifted and a cool breeze from the north had him anchoring along shore and learning how to heat rocks to cook the fish he caught.

It gave him too much time to think, and review his visit to New Bombay. Mercy with a Hospital, Logic with a University, Peace with a police force and court system, Art with a museum full of statues. Babies in bubbles. Harry slapped his forehead. "Idiot!" He caught a bubble, slid it over his boat and started hiking. It was a long way to the town of Red River.

And a very thin welcome.

Michael was gone. His dogs had killed an eight year old boy.

Harry walked on to the north and then west to the lake, and a welcome return to sailing. He crossed to the north shore and found wild places that had never been seen by man. Places that called to him to be the first. He turned east and following whims and dreams, found Michael and his dogs.

The man paced, restless. Haunted. The dogs slunk. Sad eyes on their master. "I can't stop it. Things happen around me. And every once in awhile I can read someone's thoughts. And the dogs just . . . That boy . . . Was I supposed to tell his mother that he'd killed the baby she'd given birth to six months ago? That he was angry that she was pregnant again and planning on killing that baby too? He wasn't the first person the dogs killed. There was a pedophile . . . they *ate* him. Everyone assumed he ran off. It's going to be like this wherever I go. I can't stop it, there's nothing conscious about it."

Harry winced. "I see. I don't like what's happening to us. I think we're being molded into the Archetypes. War, Peace, Logic, Art, Explorer. I'm going to check on Cairo, see if Barry and Edmund are still playing at Virtue and Vice. Would you like to come?"

Michael laughed. "Certainly. It sounds like *they* deserve me. Bad Karma on the hoof. I should never have left there."

The trip across the lake was mercifully quick, as all five of his passengers got sea sick.

Harry greeted the brothers cheerfully. "Still here, I see. Have you gotten over your god complexes?"

"Complex, no, we're actually very simple gods." Edmund

eyed the dogs, huddled behind Michael. "So, you dogs brought your servant back?"

Michael smiled faintly. "No, that's cats. Dogs are man's best friend. Well, that's arguable, where mine are concerned. A bit too much of the collective subconscious focused on them, I'm afraid."

Barry snickered. "I think your 'karmic field' is funny, Michael. You must show us how it's progressed with time. Edmund and I have been tracking our own growth with considerable interest. God really isn't a misnomer, anymore."

Michael gritted his teeth. "Harry, you'd better not sail without me. I don't fit in here."

Edmund snickered. "Well, since we're all still friends, let's have a party." He turned and walked away.

Harry hesitated, then followed. *Why did I come here? Do I really want to know what they are up to, now?*

The plaza was lined with booths, produce and hand made goods for sale. Not terribly well constructed. The end one collapsed as they walked past. Michael sighed.

Barry shook his head over two men arguing; when the first fist swung, he waved a hand and they both sank peacefully to the ground.

"I've got to learn that one." Michael muttered.

The two brothers climbed to the top of the central platform.

"Today we are graced with the presence of two of our brother gods. We shall have a feast tonight. Prepare!"

Edmund's amplified voice rolled over the plaza, and Harry heard faint echoes from further south.

Can they hear him all the way out in the gardens and grain fields? Harry shivered and walked around the plaza. He traded copper and iron ingots for supplies for the remainder of the journey as well as trade goods. They had some nice cloth here.

"Are those coffee beans? Real coffee beans?"

The pretty girl manning the booth smiled. "Yes, and we have cocoa powder now, too. It's still a bit rough, but I think we've just about worked out how to process it."

"And they have tea in New Bombay. The world is now complete and acceptable." He spent the last of his witch-manufactured metals and loaded the boat.

Michael viewed wares from a cautious distance. Embarrassing utterances and arguments followed in his wake, pratfalls occurred, and items were dropped, generally fragile ones. The dogs eyed the people warily, but the brothers never seemed to have any problems with clumsiness, however much they laughed as it spiraled out from Michael's vicinity. *It doesn't seem to touch them. Or me, now that I think about it.*

As the sun dropped toward the horizon, tables started appearing on the plaza, and then food. Harry winced at the thought of another drunken, magic involved orgy.

If Michael doesn't affect me, I ought to be able to shed the brothers' effects too.

Harry bought a bottle of wine from a merchant, and took

it with him to the head table as the brothers toasted the visitors and started the feast rolling. Harry avoided their wine, and managed to shield the women in his vicinity. He left the dais as soon as he could, and headed south with a following of anxious women. They kept drifting off and returning carrying babies, and many were also trailed by husbands. Upriver far enough to be out of the brothers' area of influence, he relaxed.

"So, how about a class in mental shields? And anything else you're interested in, and might need, once you've figured out how to get rid of that pair?"

One of the women snorted. "They keep the insects off the gardens and the fields. Can you show some of us how to do that? Trading *them* for starvation doesn't seem like the best of ideas."

"I don't have the power gene, but my son will." The second woman's voice dripped disgust; the baby boy she was carrying was a redhead, an odd contrast with her brunette tresses. "But I really don't want to have to wait a generation to get rid of those perverts."

"Oh yes. You don't even need the power genes to do the pesticide and fertilizer spells. I'll teach them to all of you. And those of you with the power genes, do you know about working in teams? Three women together? Four or eight men? Let me show you . . . "

Teaching the basics. Again. Why haven't I ever written them down? A manual of magic practices? I hate to leave them with so little instruction.

"Right. Women and men have different areas of expertise."

The coffee-and-cocoa woman was there. The baby girl she was carrying had a noticeably darker complexion than her deep tan.

"Why don't you put all the babies kind of in the middle, where you can keep an eye on them?" Harry half closed his eyes, and could easily see the women with power. "You, you and you. Try holding hands. And you three . . . " He scooted a baby out of the way and felt an odd zing. Like nothing he'd ever felt before. Like falling in love for the first time. Like the first time he'd touched a woman.

Like holding my child for the first time.

He blinked at the child's dark skin and put the little girl down carefully. Stepped away. That . . . zing of recognition. Real or imaginary? He was utterly certain the baby was his.

Harry worked with them all night, and left them out there, practicing in coordinated "Compasses" and "Triads." The women with no power memorized the garden songs, several of them taking notes, so hopefully they'd remember all of them, and which of them did what.

Harry hoped he could return to the city before the brothers missed him. It turned out he needn't have hurried.

The party had gone sideways, the plaza was empty except for a few slumbering or passed out drunk bodies. The only movement was up on the dais, where . . . several dozen matrons were demanding that the gods give them powerful children.

Barry and Edmund were surrounded by the older women, and clothing was definitely optional. Harry spotted Michael and circled around towards him. He was stinking drunk, sitting in a circle of exclusion and laughing at the brothers. His dogs were laughing, too, but from twenty feet beyond the far side of the dais. Was that the "safe zone" around these drunken idiots?

"You and your fucking damned karma!" Edmund shoved one of the old women away and climbed to his feet. "Effing damned God of Just Deserts! I'm not finding this amusing." He wrestled a pair of pants away from a woman who looked old enough to be his grandmother.

Harry snorted. "Are you admitting that you deserve what's happening?" He concentrated, envisioning a bank of magic blocking fog creeping across the group. The nearest woman staggered a bit, backed away looking horrified, and fled. The others started looking around, their gazes sharpening.

"Very funny." Barry fought his way out from under a woman, and joined his brother, facing Michael and Harry.

Edmund was scowling at Harry. "That suppression effect right there is not something we want anyone around here to remember." With a wave of his hand the women surrounding them collapsed. "Nice, the way a stun spell interferes with short to long term memory conversion, isn't it? The perfect Date Rape drug, should the two of us need any such thing." He frowned. "I think you two should die. You've just made yourselves into a threat to us."

Barry nodded. "How about chopped to bits by a friend?

Sounds good, eh?" He threw back his head and spread his arms, theatrically. "God of War! I summon you!"

Something quivered in the air, some force, some potential that seemed to encompass the whole world, a flood of choking invisible power. An odd breeze swirled up a bit of dust, a funny shape that he might have imagined . . .

***

Chris scowled at the red rock. No matter what he did, it was still just a red rock. Old Wolf was getting pretty good at refining metals. The women, especially the older women were awesome. A pulling gesture of their hands, and the rock crumpled, sand falling away from the rusty redness, then they pulled the oxygen right off and they were left with a powder of pure iron. That they could shape into anything they wanted. They were doing it with copper as well, and everyone was using the new coins, or solid bars of a useful metal. Chris thumped the rock down and picked up the sword.

"It's probably not good for anything. Iron, not steel. I was just experimenting with making shapes." Wolf was brushing his big stallion. Jet was probably less than two years old; he'd be even bigger in a couple of years when he quit growing.

Just a big friendly pet. Chris sighed. He occasionally caught glimpses of wild horses. Possibly his. Hopefully their next foals would be, well, a bit like their sire. And maybe he could even catch them.

The black horse nudged the man, who grinned and vaulted lightly on to his back.

Romeau shook his head sadly. "When that horse is finally old enough for you to do something with him, he's going to be wild and fierce, untamable. You ought to handle him more often."

"You're just hoping he'll buck me off."

"Well, most people at least have a halter and reins. And saddles make things more comfy for both horse and rider."

Chris extended the sword. "You ought to make armor, too."

Wolf threw back his head and laughed. He brandished the sword, and Chris thought he could almost imagine armor.

The black colt reared suddenly.

Then they both disappeared.

***

. . . looked just like a rearing horse, black, saddled and bridled in black and silver. The knight on his back wore shining silver chain mail with dull black breast and back plates. A silvered helmet with a black plume. The cheek pieces and nasal were covered with black etchings. His gleaming sword was held aloft. The big horse touched down.

"God of War! Kill my enemies!" Barry pointed at Harry and Michael.

The God of War turned and looked at Harry. Looked down

at himself, as the giant warhorse snorted and pawed.

"Good grief! I *clank!* Harry? Where the Bloody Hell are we?"

Harry boggled. "Wolf? What are you doing here? How did you get here? And when did you make the armor?"

Barry stalked forward. "I told you to kill my enemies!"

"Edmund? No, you're Barry. I thought you were the good twin?" Wolf tucked the sword under his left arm and pulled his helmet off. Stared at it in disbelief. Ticked it with a fingernail to hear the metallic ring.

"I summoned you, damn it. DO MY BIDDING!" Barry put magical projection into it.

"Bugger off, you idiot." Wolf's comment was indifferent, his attention on his armor.

Edmund prowled around horse and rider. "It worked. I told you I was summoned."

"You said you did as you were bid!"

"It was something I enjoyed, immensely." Edmund circled, his left hand out of Wolf's sight.

Barry stalked forward. He was glowing with power.

Michael's boxer leaped forward silently.

The black horse lashed out with a hind foot and connected solidly with Barry.

The dog's leap knocked the knife from Edmund's hand and staggered him into the horse's side.

Wolf fumbled the helmet, dropped it and snatched the sword as the horse spun away from the men and out into the open.

Edmund waved a hand at the men and women laying around in drunken stupors. They started rolling over, climbing to their feet. Staggering toward Harry and Michael.

"Harry, can you get back to your boat?" Wolf grabbed the reins. "I think we need to get out of here." The horse high stepped over unconscious women and turned to view the people now moving toward them.

"The horse won't fit!" Harry started backing away. Some of the moving bodies were between him and the quay.

"I'll bubble him, get going, the faster the better." Wolf frowned at Michael. "Do I know you?"

"Call me Michael, also known as the God of Just Deserts. Tell your horse to not step on my puppies." Michael turned and staggered toward Harry.

Oh right. He's drunk. Harry remembered something . . . high school football? He lowered head and shoulders and charged at a closing gap between two local men. He knocked them right off their feet and kept going. A woman threw herself down in front of him. His leap caught a fold of her linen dress and he hit the ground hard. He rolled over. A man with a club swung at his head, but the club fell from nerveless hand as his eyes rolled up. Wolf galloped by, his sword trailing blood. He took out two more men, then galloped back to help Michael's dogs remove all threats. Michael helped Harry stand, and they staggered downhill, mutual support. The dogs followed, looking back, teeth showing.

At the wharf, they tumbled aboard. The horse skidded to a halt at the edge and Wolf leaned to slice the lines. The ship started drifting away. The dogs leaped the gap with ease.

The black stallion reared again . . . and was gone.

Harry swallowed to equalize pressure in his ears. The world suddenly looked normal, no huge magical *thing* blanketing everything. Less bright. More real. The bodies uphill were suddenly horrible, not part of some play, some fantasy. Innocents, controlled by the brothers, used as weapons, and killed by Wolf and the dogs.

He blinked at the empty pier for a long moment. Then he ran out the oars and started putting more space between himself and anything the twins might come up with.

"Harry? Do you know how to teleport?" Michael looked more stunned than drunk.

Harry swallowed. "No. I didn't think it was possible."

"I'll definitely come with you to Tripoli after all. I want to know what Wolfgang just did."

"Wolf . . . gang?"

***

Jet touched down, and froze.

Wolf lowered his plain iron sword in a series of jerky movements. They were back in front of the winery. Romeau and Chris ran up and stopped, as if afraid to touch and see if they were real.

He swallowed. "How long were we gone?" No armor, no saddle or bridle. He slid off the colt, who didn't seem to be as large as he'd been just a moment ago.

"Maybe fifteen minutes. What happened?" Romeau froze, staring at the sword.

The horse ducked his head and laid it against Wolf's chest, as if looking for reassurance. Wolf looked at the blood dripping from the sword, and it dropped from nerveless fingers. He wrapped his arms around the horse's head and leaned on him. "Oh. This is not good."

Chapter Seventeen

30 Oct 2118

Tripoli, North Africa, Exile

It happened again, four days later.

It was early morning, the sun was barely up. He was tending his grapes, checking, almost ready for harvest . . .

Then he was on the rearing horse, armor, sword, the works. In a village. At least two houses ablaze. A screaming woman being dragged away by a man with an AK in his other hand. The man's eyes widened as he spotted Wolf. He released the woman, brought the AK around . . .

Shield. Wolf knew how to shield. And did it as the gun coughed. Stinging pain up his arm, then jolts as the rest of the burst was bounced. Jet charged forward and he swung the sword, coordinated with the shields so he could . . . chop the man's head off. He jerked back in shock. *I don't even know what's going on. Was he rescuing a hysterical woman?*

Galloping hooves beyond the smoke. He rode toward the sounds. Cattle were being driven off. Stolen or saved from the fire? Another woman, screaming, being hauled onto a horse.

He took aim with Jet and rammed them. The girl fell free, landed on her feet and bolted for the burning house. The other horse was staggered. The rider cursed, and kicked it into a gallop, out the gates. Silence, relative silence.

Then he thumped down in his vineyard.

He jumped up and scanned around. Jet trotted up, from the end of the row where he'd been grazing. The horse, was sweating and smelled of smoke. A twinge of pain, and he looked at his left forearm. A long straight rip, dripping blood. Not deep. He teased a bit of metal out of it. A deformed steel ring, such as one might find in chain mail.

Romeau questioned him while Gisele muttered and tried some herbs and spells on his arm. "If it was still dark there, it must have been one of the villages way to the west. One of us will need to go there, ask about what happened, and who those raiders are." He stood and paced. "I wish Harry'd hurry up and get back. I want to hear his version. Dammit, we're not gods. How can someone summon us?"

"I think it's the collective subconscious." Gisele tied off the ends of a rather bulky bandage. "Do you remember when we arrived? I felt like the whole world was in my head. I shut them out, first the strangest ones, then even the ones I agreed with. But I think we gave them access to our brains. And our abilities."

"I can't teleport." Wolf wiggled his fingers. "It was a pretty shallow cut, for all this wrapping."

"I'm testing a mixture of herbs and spells on you. Leave it on for a couple of hours—in fact, come back here then and let me see it. It might need stitches." She turned away, then glanced back at him. "And when you figure out how to teleport on purpose, come teach me. It sounds really handy."

Romeau fingered the distorted ring. "I don't understand why this ring didn't disappear with the rest of your imaginary armor. And next time, be quicker with a shield. Can't have the God of War getting killed. Ruin all our reputations."

***

Harry and Michael landed the next day.

The dogs ran around in a paroxysm of joy, to be on solid land again. Until Vito snapped at them to stay away from the livestock. They eyed him hungrily, and Michael hastily called them to heel.

The Bus Kids laughed, and plied the big dogs with snacks from the butcher shack.

"We're still hunting nearly every day, so there's plenty of offal and bones." Matt handed out huge bloody femurs, and the dogs settled down to gnawing.

There was a crash from the kitchen. Michael winced. The dogs got some fresh pancakes. The second round made it to the table intact, and Michael dug in. "I don't think I've kept a meal down all week. From now on, I'm walking."

Harry grinned; the nearest dog growled faintly.

Romeau walked in and slapped down his note pad. "So, tell me all about Cairo."

"What about it?" Harry eyed him. "What are you doing?"

"Analyzing a very odd thing that happened to Wolf. Now

stop asking questions, I don't want to lead you."

Harry and Michael swapped glances.

"Well, Harry, so much for it being a hallucination."

"Talk. Start at the beginning."

"Well. Michael sailed across the lake with me. We landed in Cairo . . . "

They talked for hours.

"God of Just Deserts? Who invented such a cracked Pantheon? I trust they didn't give me a name."

Harry snickered. "This from the god who lives in the Temple of Love? Performs all the marriages around here?"

"Oh no. I'm no cupid."

Snickers all around.

Michael'd been eyeing his dogs, as they got restless. "Look, I'm about to overstay my welcome, so it's been nice seeing you all again, even though I don't remember you worth beans."

Harry got up too. "You know, we're a lot more concentrated than Red River was. I'll bet you could live far enough away to not affect everyone twenty-four hours a day, and still walk into town whenever you wanted to."

"I think I need at least ten miles, maybe twenty, between me and anyone else." Michael whistled his dogs in close.

"Well, I happen to know where there's a spring to the east of us, probably a bit over ten miles away. And you still haven't opened up the bubble on your shoulder. I'll show you the spring, and you can experiment with that distance, eh?"

A pack of teenagers, mostly boys, mostly not magical,

sneered at them. "Look another moron with brain piercings and delusions of godhood."

The dogs stiffened, hackles rising.

Michael sighed. "Harry . . . did it ever occur to you that I might deserve myself? And my dogs. *Heel*."

Out of the gates, the four dogs ran ahead, and Harry winced as they eyed the cows.

"Poor cows deserve nothing but pity. They won't bother the cows unless a really nasty character owns them." Michael lengthened his stride though, and Harry angled them to the southeast.

The land was rockier and dryer, the limestone rising to the surface and getting wind carved into odd shapes. Michael relaxed, and Harry realized his leg wasn't hurting at all. *I really wish someone other than Barry had provided that healing, though.*

"Do you think we have any responsibility, for what Barry and Edmund are doing?"

Michael shook his head. "No. I mean, no more than if they were magic-less tyrants whom we'd never before met. We . . . have a responsibility to, oh, hell. I don't know. Start a war? Not hardly. But . . . okay, while I was drunk it was really funny, all those older women mobbing them. But no one should have the ability to *make* people behave like that."

"I think you were just twisting their siren call to all the young pretty women."

"I shouldn't have had *anything* to do with it."

They walked on in silence. A slight dip in the surface, with a grove of trees surrounding the oasis. Not that they were in a full-blown desert, but . . .

"Oh, nice."

The dogs leapt into the pool. It was about twenty feet across, and an antelope leapt away on the far side. The dogs floundered out and gave chase. Michael laughed and fingered the bubble on his shoulder.

He turned and walked out to the east side. "Every foot of additional insulation is important. And something tells me I need a wide open space for this."

He also had a building. A big one. A mansion, ornate and . . . huge. He'd even grabbed the front patio. Two water fountains, each with a pair of naked nymphs trying to pour water over each other. A ballroom. A small movie theater. A huge dining room and auto-kitchen on the second floor. Thirty-eight bedroom suites on the third floor. In the basement, tiers of marble seating around a platform.

"Theatre in the round." Michael's forehead wrinkled. "I can't remember the name. Some famous Broadway actor. He did a few movies, but mostly live theater. He died, and about eighteen heirs were squabbling over the will. So I took it all."

"It's . . . uh."

"Yeah. Pretty funny, especially for one man and four dogs, out in the desert. I wonder if I can get the fountains working?"

Harry laughed, and showed him Abram's one way pipe flow spell.

Chapter Eighteen

5 November 2118

Trading on the Lakes

Harry didn't linger long in Tripoli. He took another load of glass up the chain of lakes. He found his basic spells had spread, and that new groups of magicians were forming, and starting to work collectively. Some villages had been abandoned; generally he found the people in the next successful town.

One small village was burned to the ground.

He found the survivors in Gibraltar.

"I don't know why I yelled that." The woman had the speckled complexion of someone recovering from multiple small second degree burns. "But there he was, the God of War. He cut that man's head right off! Then he galloped off and saved Jackie."

A girl of perhaps eighteen nodded vigorously, in the background. "I've started carrying a knife, in case they try to raid here."

"We were out hunting, most of us men. We left before dawn, as soon as there was any light to see by. At first we thought they must have a spy inside, but they might have just been lucky. Picked the right morning to hit us. They had clubs, didn't actually kill anyone, but some of the kids had some bad burns." The old man tossed a worried glance at the small huddle of women and children. "I liked the idea of just us four families out there. But it won't work. We'll have to stay here or move to one of the other large towns. Start over. Not quite from scratch, but we lost half our livestock. Bastards."

"All the clothing we weren't actually wearing, linens and bedding, furniture." One of the other women sighed. "Every single one of those stupid chickens. The grain, the hay."

Harry told them about the other large towns that were attracting people along the lake shore, and when they decided they wanted more distance between themselves and the bandits, he spent a week ferrying the families to Algiers while the men drove their surviving cattle overland.

In Algiers, Harry worked with the local magicians. They were getting very strong, figuring out things themselves. Thinking back, Harry realized that most of the towns that were growing had power users. Either a "pyramid" of witches or a "compass" of mages. Often both. And multiples of each. Or gods. Red River and Gibraltar were the only exceptions he could think of, and Gibraltar wasn't growing very fast. *Even Red River had Michael there, for awhile.*

Cause or effect? He studied it, talked to people.

The towns seemed to be coalescing around the more powerful magician groups. The men were calling their groups "circles" or "compasses" and they all found eight people worked best, joining together to apply concentrated power where needed. The women—now calling themselves witches—still found three-woman groups to be most effective. For large projects they used three groups of three, and adopted the terms triad and pyramid. Like the men, they were codifying and analyzing their abilities.

How much tech can we duplicate with magic? And if the answer is "a whole bunch" where does that leave the non-magical?

Chapter Nineteen

December 15, 2118

North Africa

The cart thumped down off a big grass tussock with a loud snap.

Chris snickered as Jet stopped with a disgusted snort and looked around.

The Old Wolf jumped down and glared at the wheel.

"We've got to be doing something basically wrong." Dane said. "I think we need the spokes angled so they brace the rim out of the plane of the wheel."

"I suppose we'll try that next," Wolf growled. "Hey! God of Travelers! Do you do road-side service, like Triple A? We could use a . . . "

The weight, the denseness, as if the air was suddenly thick with potential silenced them all.

A bright reflection off armor . . . Roman, perhaps, or something odder, stranger.

Harry stood there, bright brass chestplate, leather kilt, something white and robe-like under it all, sandals strapped up over his ankles, bare legs. Spear in his right hand . . .

"What the bloody hell is this?" Harry stared down at himself, then up at Wolf.

Dane frowned. "Whoever designed your armor doesn't seem to have realized the pharaohs didn't use much in the way of armor. Or the Ethiopians or Auxumites. Or wherever they think you came from. That's not right for Roman, either."

"I'm from California." Harry growled.

"Ah. Hollywood armor."

Harry shot Dane a glare, but there might have been a quirk of lips in there. He turned and looked at Wolf. "How did I get here?"

Wolf started chuckling. "I prayed—or possibly cursed—in the name of the God of Travelers. Tag! You're it!"

Harry glared. "You are as cracked as your spoke." One last flash of sun off the breast plate, and he was gone.

"Huh." Dane eyed the empty spot where Harry had been standing. "Do you suppose we can summon the God of Love, or the Goddess of Health?"

No wording worked. They gave up when they started laughing at the ridiculousness of it all.

"How can you possibly have a Love Emergency?" Chris subdued his snickering. "Now, a medical emergency, I could see. But if this really is an effect of the collective subconscious, well, they know we don't have one."

They propped up the cart and used Dave's woodworking spell on the broken spokes. They stayed out four more days, storing all the field dressed game in bubbles, and failing to spot Chris's mares.

Back in town they sold the meat to the butcher shop, a cooperative effort now of three families, in exchange for a combination of IOUs and the new coinage.

Chris paused at the doorway of the Inn. The atmosphere was a bit tense. Lillian and Milly were glaring at each other. Several other women stood about, slightly to one side or the other, in something that looked a lot like taking sides.

He edged away from the door and over to a pair of girls. Benita and Larita were watching, wide-eyed, but back far enough to be out of the confrontation.

"What's the problem, and should I barge in or stay out?"

"Out," Benita hissed. "Lillian says the witches should never have anything to do with men, except to get pregnant. Milly says there's no reason to not get married."

Her little sister whispered. "Actually she said 'and be normal, not a man-hating old hag.' Lillian's bought that hill to the northeast. She says it's for witches' ceremonies, but only for her kind of witches."

"Holy moly. I thought all the witches would stick together." Dane whispered, half hiding behind Chris. "I am so out of here."

"Good idea." Chris retreated, and the girls followed them.

"That nonsense is enough to make me glad I don't have any power genes." Benita grinned up at Chris. "What are you guys going to do, if they won't have anything to do with men?"

"Heave a sigh of relief and date normal girls, like you two."

Dane wrinkled his nose. "We have to marry women with no power genes, to have sons to carry on the magic. Actually they're doing us a favor."

Chris blinked at him. *Because witches can't have boy babies, and if I want a son to teach all these cool things to . . . I have to stop feeling for Iris the way I do.* "Oh, crap. That's right. What a horrible . . . damn those stupid . . . genetic engineers for putting the power genes on the sex chromosomes."

Benita sighed. "Are they prettier than we are?"

"Not on the inside." Chris said. "Nor the outside, now that you mention it. But they sort of glow, magically, and draw us like flies. Lillian really is doing us a favor, showing us the poison in the honey."

The girls nodded, then headed around to the back door. "We've got kitchen duty tonight. We'll probably hear about nothing but the fight all night long."

Chris stayed away for another hour, and returned to find the witches had claimed two separate seating areas, and the two groups were both speaking loudly while pretending to ignore the other group. Chris caught a wave from Lance and tried to stroll nonchalantly to a table in the demilitarized zone. Jamie and Mallory came home from the hospital, and got a recap loud enough to fill everyone in. Or at any rate make their eyes glaze over. Apparently Lillian had the most supporters, barely, among the witches from the bus. The rest of the town's witches out numbered them. The older witches, Phaedra and Muriel, were sitting at Milly and Ariel's table. Lillian had Iris and two other girls from outside the bus gang with her. Roslyn, Katy, Karen and Elinor sat at the next table, more outsider women at another.

"So we're going to have two separate pyramids. Regular and extra-man hating." Milly called over from the far side of the dining room.

"So, where do you stand." Lillian stared at Mallory, glanced at Jamie.

"Ugg. I stand for mental health. You always have had a screw loose, Lillian. Your mother filled you with poison from her three divorces, then sent you here alone while she married yet another man." Mallory turned away, then lifted her chin and walked to Lance and Chris's table, Jamie following. Lance edged out a chair in unspoken invitation.

"Thanks guys. I can't believe we're doing this."

Chris shrugged. "You know, for the level of civilization we've got, we're getting pretty close to the carrying capacity of the local region. Splitting up may be a good idea. Although I don't really think there is any need to be so confrontational about it."

Jamie nodded. "You guys are hunting just about every day, and it goes straight from the butcher to the kitchen."

Lance snickered. "And we don't even want to think about how many septic tanks we've got crowded into this small an area."

"Eww!" Malory wrinkled her nose. "But where would we

go? To start over? Or do we try to kick out the people who came after the walls were up?"

"There's a whole world out there." Chris waved, vaguely. "How about South Africa? Gold and diamonds, and isn't it supposed to have a good climate . . . well, maybe not during an ice age, but there's a whole continent. Or cross the Pacific and settle in California."

Leo Harding looked over, from another table. "No need to go that far, there's most of India, Indonesia, Australia. Or how about the Asian east coast? Catch a warm current up the coast like the Gulf Stream, live in Japan."

"Moving livestock would be easy, just get a god to fix up a bubble for you." Vito joined the general conversation. The witch split was fast moving into second place.

"I wonder how big a town can get, before you start having trouble with sanitation and hunting issues." Chris frowned. "What's the population of Tripoli, now?"

Larita winked at him as she whisked by dropping off plates of what might well be the game they'd killed today. *We need a whole lot more cows. We ought to be having wild cattle roundups once a month. And horses. Breed wild mares to our stallions and turn them loose, get the domestic genes into circulation. How many vets do we have? Maybe we could do artificial insemination of wild cows or something. I wonder if the gods can stun the cows, and from how far away? I wonder if I can do it?*

"Anyway, what we probably need to start thinking about is

having half of us move out to our farms, now that we've got the predators knocked well back. That will spread the strain on water, septic and the wild herds."

He looked over at Lillian's witches and shook his head. *They can do whatever they want to do. I have other things on my mind.* His eyes slid toward Iris, and he jerked them back toward dinner. *Damn Ira Penner and his sexual repressions. Does Iris have any chance of a healthy relationship? Hanging around Lillian isn't going to help.*

Lillian sneered. "I've filed for a hill to the north east. We may just have our ceremonies there, or we may move. But that will be our decision, not *yours*."

Chris nodded. "Yep. Nobody has to move, but anybody can move, to any open area." *Like that nice little bay about twenty miles to the east. A snug little winter harbor and refuge. Careen a boat on the beach and scrape the barnacles and all that.*

Chapter Twenty

December 21, 2118

Tripoli, North Africa, Exile

"I thought being a god was bad when it was sarcasm." Wolf shook his head. "It never occurred to me that being the real thing would be worse." He paced a bit, his attention on the shortwave, and the quiet hiss of dead air. The High Sheriff of Gibraltar was off the air, at the moment, outside with the beacon. It was probably too early for a new gate to have been finished, but running the beacon for a couple of weeks hurt nothing.

"I don't understand why it's just some of us. Is it that we aren't guessing the right God and Goddess? Or are the God of Love and Goddess of Women just not summonable?" Harry sipped his hot tea, and wondered how long Wolf and Romeau's automated kitchens would last. *Good thing we've found tea and coffee trees. And cocoa trees or bushes or whatever it grows on.*

He thought about the kitchen in the bus. Funny, how they hadn't used it in so long. He ought to seal it up and preserve it for emergencies.

Wolf was looking grumpy. "I seem to remember Edmund saying he could be summoned. Why does the collective subconscious think the God of Vice would need to be summonable?"

"So people would get their orgies right?"

They all glared at Romeau. He shrugged. "Maybe you can't summon me because you don't really really need a wedding performed Right Now."

"Point. Maybe the circumstances weren't right. I came when summoned in the middle of a battle, Harry came when that wretched wagon broke down. I was cursing by the 'God of Travelers' and asking for Triple A service. And voila, there he was. Just long enough to make a sarcastic remark."

"Then I popped back home. Just like you return right back where you'd been, after the fights are over. God of War."

"This really stinks. I don't believe in magic, you know? And I don't like the idea of being hauled into every damned battle in the World."

Harry nodded. "At least we showed up with armor. That was interesting. Weird, but interesting."

"But we're not invulnerable." Wolf ran a finger along the scar down his arm. "Bummer, to get killed in someone else's battle."

Harry nodded slowly. "We were summoned, but not controlled. Barry called you, but you helped me. You summoned me, and all I did was twit you about your poorly made wheels. I didn't have to help you. You didn't have to help Barry."

"I suspect we'd better start writing this down, and

analyzing it all. And I think I'd better start giving you some lessons in fighting with that spear, in case you start getting summoned for bandit attacks."

"The spear disappears with the armor."

"I'll make you one to practice with." He cocked an ear toward the shortwave. Still nothing but dead air on the Gibraltar channel.

Phaedra molded an ornate iron spearhead for him, and Harry heated it red hot in charcoal. The "normal" witches tended to gather here, at her cabin for practice, and she had a lot of metal-working tools in the yard, including this little forced air forge.

"I read about how they case hardened chain mail. The carbon combines with the iron to form a hard but rather brittle outer layer, and the interior iron is unchanged. It stays more flexible." Harry fished the glowing spear point out of the fire. "Maybe this will harden it. I really don't know much about making steel."

"I wish I could heat things up with a thought. Not that I need to melt metal much, anymore. All the tools I brought with me, I swear I just tap the metal to focus my thoughts." Phaedra slipped a hand through the crook of his elbow. "What are you thinking about?"

How good you smell.

Her mouth twitched, as if she'd heard that. "When you heat metal."

"Umm, vibration, that's what heat is, after all."

"Hmm. And you men heat huge volumes of air when you make weather, don't you?"

"Umm, yeah." He was having a hard time concentrating on much of anything except her, and he certainly didn't protest when she steered him inside her cabin.

***

Michael only had one dog with him, when he walked into town. The big boxer lay down on the porch of the Fire Mountain Inn, and growled at a cattle dog that trotted by at a horse's heels. Michael grinned at that sign of normality, and sauntered into the Inn.

A couple of kids were stacking chairs sideways, apparently making a fort for some sort of game. Or perhaps the construction was the game.

"Is Harry around?"

The nearest boy shook his head. "He's off canoeing."

"Canoodling," the other boy rolled his eyes. "At least that's what Chris said."

"What's the difference?" The first boy turned his attention back to construction.

Michael managed to keep his face straight, and headed back out. Red was watching some young men, hackles half raised. "Take it easy, Pup, we're trying to make friends here."

The boxer twitched an ear his direction, but kept his eyes

glued on the men.

Michael glanced their way. They didn't seem to be doing anything. *Loitering with intent.* He frowned. Intent to what? Where had that phrase come from? He headed for the winery. So long as he could keep Red outside, and really it wasn't like Wolf deserved any bad karma. His main fault was being too damned good at everything, including being a hero, being nice, being handsome . . .

One of the young men stepped away from the group, walked up and kicked Red.

In one elongated moment Michael saw inside the young man's mind. Jason. A muddle, ill sorted, full of discontent, spitefulness, hunger for trouble, hunger for sex. A flash memory of fights, of sex, of frightened women, of rape. Waiting for a particular woman to leave the Inn. Predatory anticipation.

The dog turned and leaped for the man.

Michael grabbed a hind leg in mid-jump, jerked the dog up sharply. Teeth clicked closed inches from the man's throat.

"No! Down!"

Red crouched, teeth showing in a soundless snarl.

Jason jumped back, face bloodless in shock. "That dog tried to kill me!"

Michael straightened. "Do not tempt me to let him."

He stared down the man's blustery attempts to save face, then turned and walked away. "Heel!"

Red leaped into position, the hair still up on his shoulders and back. Teeth still bared.

Old Wolf was out on the porch, frowning his direction.

"So, are you the local sheriff?"

"Afraid not. Or maybe that's a good thing." He frowned down at the dog. "What's his problem?"

"Like I told Harry, I get flash impressions from people. I just got one from that fellow. Jason. Knife fights and rape."

Wolf looked cynical. "Because the dog doesn't like him? Your dogs don't like anyone but you, and in fact, I think they may be the only creatures on this world that care about you."

Michael bit back an angry retort. *They are, god help them.* "Because I stopped Red, another something will happen to him. Something he deserves. Pity about any women he rapes, between now and then."

Wolf pinched the bridge of his nose. "We're all being . . . controlled, to some degree, by the collective subconscious. You've got the worst of it. Because you get the blame for everything that happens around you. And I really hate the idea of four big dogs attacking everyone who deserves it."

"Shall I move even further from town, live as a hermit?"

"That may be the only way the collective will let go of you." He shifted then, stepped back. "How about some really bad wine and dinner? You can tell me about Jason. Perhaps I will be the thing that happens to him."

"I thought you were the God of War, not Policemen." Michael pulled Red along with him, and shut the door behind him.

"The town has gone and elected an idiot for their sheriff.

He says rape is the fault of the women, wearing short skirts and flirting."

"Oh. What fun. Shall I stroll past his house? I'm not sure just what his Just Deserts might be, so be careful what you wish for."

"I shudder to think of it. Please don't."

He watched the Old Wolf pull the cork on a bottle. "I never figured you for a, oh, farmer of any sort, let alone the upscale snobby sort." He frowned suddenly. "Didn't you run away and join the army, something like that?"

Wolf paused, then poured the wine. "I . . . really don't remember."

"I can't remember doing anything but playing video games and stuff." He glanced at Red. "I don't even remember where I got the dogs."

Wolf frowned, shook his head. "Anyway. You say Jason is our rapist?"

"One of them. That whole group had nasty vibes. Or auras or something. If I'd had all four dogs here, there'd have been a slaughter. I mean it. The dogs will kill, if the person deserves it."

"Dogs? Hell Hounds, more like."

Michael took a sip and grimaced. "Harsh." *He's right about the dogs.* "Needs to age about four more years."

Wolf sipped and sighed. "It seems to be lacking subtle overtones of cherry or vanilla."

"Edmund and Barry have those bubbles, you know? Major

time dilation, and if you think really hard about it, you can change the time ratio. They speed aged some fruity stuff."

Wolf paused again. "Really? How . . . useful. I think."

Michael grinned. "It not traditional, but the results are better than a total lack of aging."

Wolf's autokitchen had a different suite of programming, a welcome change of menu. And it produced wine much more drinkable than the Old Wolf's first attempt, which was about all that could be said for it. And even a faux bone with raw meat attached, for Red.

And not a single glass or plate was broken.

Behind the winery, outside the walls, the Wolf had chairs scattered about a flagstoned patio. And people, friends, came and sat and chatted.

Mostly about the lack of a gate, this solstice. There was an interesting mixture of distress and relief coming from various people.

They all watched the sun set. Michael sat back and listened, wistful. One lady was staying close to Wolf, and had sounded happy at the failure of the beacon to summon contact with Earth. Michael kept a hand on Red's ruff. He felt the dog bristle a couple of times, but apparently no one here was bad enough to compel action.

There was music playing, somewhere back in the village, laughter. Mooing cows.

Red's mouth dropped open and he panted contentedly.

Oh, crap. Someone just got their just deserts.

Abrupt silence. Then voices raised.

Old Wolf and two other men stood and listened. As the volume of distant voices increased, they headed back through the winery.

Michael pried himself out of his chair and walked off into the night. He didn't want to spoil the memory of a nice evening with whatever had just happened. Even though all those nice people had been Wolf's friends, and not his, it had still been pleasant. He needed all the pleasant he could get.

***

Inside, Mallory was singing, with Darren and Neil playing guitars and too many people improvising drums. Some people were even dancing.

Chris was out on the porch, more or less part of the group that included Iris. It was getting pretty argumentative.

". . . don't care what your stick-in-the-mud father says. I'll wear whatever I want. And you'd better believe that when the next election comes around, a good solid definition of rape, and the punishment is going to be on the ballot." Milly crossed her arms and scowled at Iris.

Iris was wearing a skirt that hit her mid-calf, and a blouse that buttoned all the way up her neck. She was still spectacular. Glowing. "Go ahead. I'll bet most of the men vote against it, so they can't be victimized by some slut who changes her mind, after."

That got so many confused and angry replies from enough people that no one was coherent until Ariels' shrill voice rose over the rest. ". . . clout over the head. That's hardly foreplay. Even you can see that violent, forcible rape is rape. She had a concussion."

Snort. No words, just contempt.

Sickened, Chris turned away. So he was the first one to spot the staggering figure. Gasping and crying, her hair yanked out of its usual coif, bloody nose. Lillian.

He jumped down and reached for her. She jerked away in a near panic and threw herself into Milly's arms. "I think I, I think I . . .killed him!"

"I was helping in the public barn. I didn't like the way a couple of the guys kept looking at me, so I hurried out, ahead of them and then there was someone right there. He grabbed me by the hair and pulled me back behind the barn. I tried to bite his hand, he had it over my mouth, and I kicked, and I couldn't, and he was so strong! I tried to fight him, and he . . ." her hand went to her nose. "And he, and he . . . I think he had a heart attack . . . I shoved him off me and ran."

Ira Penner was the worst sheriff ever. He was scowling at her. "So, who was it?"

"I don't know, it was dark . . . maybe, maybe he's not dead?" Her hands clenched. And still trembled.

"Maybe we ought to go take a look?" Chris suggested.

A glare from the sheriff. But the people at the back of the crowd shifted, someone produced a flash light, and suddenly

Penner was elbowing through the crowd and leading the way.

Jason Brachman was quite dead, pants down around his ankles. Chris caught a single glimpse and turned hastily away.

With their limited forensic experience, the doctors could not be sure of what he'd died of.

Ginny Walcomb shrugged. "His blood glucose levels were extremely low, my diagnosis is that he died of hypoglycemia. This is more usual after a diabetic coma of some length, not the few minutes that elapsed in this case. He had not been diagnosed as diabetic, but the symptoms are easy to miss." Penner's threats to arrest Lillian died quickly, as a search of Jason's tiny cabin turned up the missing panties of the other two rape victims. And a lot of other panties as well.

Rumors flew.

Mostly about the possibility that Lillian had killed him with magic.

Tasteless jokes made the rounds, mostly about dying in ecstasy, and black widow spiders. And the God of Bad Karma. Curses and hexes.

"Can a god give someone diabetes?" Chris rolled his eyes. "And I fail to see how Lillian could have, I dunno, turned into a sugar vampire?"

His attempts at humorous reality were ignored.

Michael got dirty looks, and was thoroughly shunned by half the population, on his rare trips to town. All well and good that Brachman had gotten his just deserts, but no one had a completely clear conscience.

Harry shrugged. "It's the collective subconscious. At some deep level, everyone knows it was your proximity that caused Jason to attack a woman who could kill him."

"That's a bit tough on the girl, isn't it?"

"Yeah. You'll never be mistaken for the God of Sweetness and Light. But you'll never get the people as a whole to admit that it's their subconsciouses, working together to cause the effect. You are just the focal point. I don't know why."

Michael sighed. "I probably deserve it. Pity I don't remember why."

After an unusually unpleasant visit to town, four young men rode out to "show the god that he wasn't welcome." Their horses stampeded back into town a few hours later. Ira Penner's posse found no one. The god had departed, taking his mansion with him. Of the young men, there was no sign.

Unfortunately they weren't the only troublemakers.

In a flash of competence, the Sheriff uncovered a fencing operation run by two men who rode between Tunis and Tripoli with "trade goods." They'd kept record of what they'd bought, from whom. But not in enough detail that stolen goods not caught on them could be identified.

One theft suspect was dating Iris. The yelling match with her father had been loud enough to qualify as public.

Two nights later the sheriff's bellowed demand for entry woke half the town. Chris stumbled out, yawning, listening at the back of the crowd. Apparently Iris had failed to be home by her curfew. Ira continued to pound at the door of the young man's tiny cabin.

Chris sighed, and wiggled through the crowd. "Sheriff, calm down. I don't think anyone is there, you're loud enough to raise the dead." He winced. "Some of the youngsters meet at the back of the public barn. Have you looked there?"

The sheriff rounded on him. "Have you ever seen my daughter there?"

"Us bus kids aren't welcomed by that clique. But I didn't see her at the Inn this evening." He looked over the heads of the crowd. Several people were backing away from the scene.

Penner pounced on them, and two girls shrugged. "Iris was there with Basil."

The sheriff loomed. "Doing what?"

"I saw them dancing."

"I think that was after a couple of drinks."

They both shrugged to show their complete indifference to Iris Penner.

An apprehensive crowd followed the sheriff to the back of the barn. This late, just a few men were still there, sitting on crude stools before a makeshift bar.

"Marshal Wallace." Penner growled as he stalked up to the bartender. "You've been warned about serving alcohol to children."

"And your bigoted, restrictive, biblical based, laws were all voted down."

"Where's my daughter?"

"Off somewhere. Try the hay loft."

Chris leaped and grabbed the sheriff's arm. Got cursed for his ". . . interfering ways, probably all your fault from the beginning."

"No, it's yours for being a horse's ass about just about everything." Chris turned him loose and headed for the nearest of several barn doors.

Iris was passed out drunk. Basil was dead.

"I don't understand how having sex with a man can kill him." Gisele stared down at the body on the hospital exam table. "He died due to disbursed small strokes, bleeding points all through his brain, all through his circulatory system. As if he had a massive blood pressure surge."

"Lillian only killed someone when she was raped, and it was her first time." Chris had decided that he'd better get nosy and find out. "She says she's done it since, without a problem."

"Was Iris a virgin?"

"I don't know. But she was also drunk, lacking control. Can magic affect blood pressure?" Chris cast his mind back to a warm Cairo night. *There was magic everywhere, none of us were harmed. But there certainly were a lot of magic surges. But all the guys were magic, too.* "Is it an effect that the magic have on the non-magic? Did Basil have any engineering? Jason Brachman didn't."

Dr. Walcomb stomped in. She must have heard what they were saying. "There's some concern about how consensual it was, whether Iris was deliberately plied with alcohol. She's awake enough to say she was only drinking fruit juice. She remembers dancing, doesn't remember going into the barn with Basil."

The sheriff, stiff as a rod, and with a totally frozen expression, convened a court.

They found insufficient evidence to indict.

"That two young men died in the same circumstances is odd, but in as much as the immediate cause of death was different in both cases, coincidence is as likely as causality. A third young woman with power was also raped, without any negative impact on the rapist that we know of, certainly not instant death." The Jury foreman reddened a bit. "However, as a general precaution, perhaps some of the older women with power genes should council the younger set about controlling their magic during sex, and all authorities should definitely keep records for future analysis and reconsideration."

Iris, and all the girls with power were openly called Witches. They were shunned by the young, powerless men.

"Hey, Chris, C'mere." Lillian was on the balcony, just outside the "wing" of the girls' rooms.

Chris perked up when he spotted Iris with her, and a third girl, Cassie, was it? Not one of the bus kids but he'd seen her at magic practice. He trotted up the stairs, and Dane and Rob trailed uncertainly after him.

Cassie made a face. "Oh, not those babies!"

Lillian waved a hand. "It hardly matters. Chris, we're testing a batch of spells Gisele taught us, and we need a man to test them on. It's nothing permanent, just those spells Harry brought back from Cairo."

Cairo? Oh, not the orgy spells. Surely. "Oh, those healing spells Harry got from the massage therapist?"

"Yeah, and later we'll be trying the rock building spells. But this batch, we're not sure if they'll work the way we want them to." Lillian tossed a glance at the room below and retreated down the hallway. "Come here."

Chris hesitated, but he didn't want to miss an opportunity to talk to Iris. And whatever Lillian was humming drew him, and the other guys like bees to honey, and now all three girls were glowing as they briefly clasped hands. They cast a fast series of spells as a Triad, overwhelmingly powerful . . . Gorgeous. Chris touched Iris's cheek, caressed her lips and then kissed her. *Wait, wait, it's only been a few days since . . .* Lillian was panting, her face flushed, as she pulled at Chris and Iris, tugged them all into her room.

Chris tried to scramble his wits together as Cassie tackled Dean and Iris turned to Rob. "Lillian, that's the orgy spell, did you mean . . . "

"We all want babies, and we can't stand men." She started unbuttoning his shirt. "This sounded like getting a bit of our own back. And by casting on ourselves too, we'll like it as much as you do."

A three witch orgy. Score! Chris started in on her buttons.

Sometime around midnight, the spell wore off. Iris flinched back from him. Cassie looked horrified. Lillian smirked.

Dane looked lost, and a bit hurt as Cassie scooted away from him. Rob, thank god, just smirked back at Lillian.

Not as much fun as with the happy, laughing women in Cairo. Chris cast a quick look at Iris. He'd tried to monopolize her . . . unsuccessfully. Her expression was vindictive, triumphant. And growing a bit fearful. His own sense of victory rolled over and died. He shivered, and picked through the shed clothing for his own. Stopped and thought. "Lillian, you can't do this sort of thing. Oh, those spells are all fun, when everyone agrees. But when you don't ask, ahead of time, it's practically rape. Yeah, yeah, we're guys, we don't think about sex the same as you do. But what are you doing to yourselves? Turning into rapists in turn? Don't do this again. "

"We'll do whatever we want to." Iris tossed her head, anger overriding the nervousness, the fear in her voice.

Dane scowled suddenly. "And will you say it's all right if we just pick on some random girl, toss a spell to make her say yes, rape her for revenge? Don't be stupid, Lillian. Chris, we need to work on some counter spells." The boy scooped up his clothes and walked out, naked.

Rob chortled and followed.

Chris hopped to get his jeans on, and walked out, buttoning his shirt. He was glad there were no witnesses out there, but the other two looked disappointed.

"Damn. Three women in one night. Several times each." Rob was grinning as he dressed in the hallway.

Dane looked a bit embarrassed, but a gleam of triumph was starting to show in his eyes. "Wow."

Chris snorted, then nodded. "But we really do have to stop them. We really don't need a war between the sexes."

And the more he thought about it, the worse it seemed. Sick. *I couldn't even think about Iris the way I had been. With love as well as lust, and sure as hell not sharing her around like this.*

Shaken and a bit sick, he buried himself in finishing the big boat.

And working on a shield that would block sexual effect spells.

They launched the hull as soon as the ice broke.

Lacking a bottle of champagne, they begged a glass of white wine from the Old Wolf's autokitchen.

The eight of them looked at each other.

Chris handed the glass to Lance. "Go ahead."

Lance shook his head and nodded toward Mark, who shook his head in turn.

"No one?" Chris looked around, then took the glass and turned back to the ship. "In that case . . . Gentlemen, I give you The Harpy."

They laughed as he tossed the glass of wine on the bow,

and they removed the logs supporting the earthen wall of their improvised dry dock and knocked holes in the last barrier between the ship and the deep channel of the stream.

Getting the rigging right and learning how to actually sail a boat with this much sail took weeks of practice. But they only ran the keel aground twice, and in mud soft enough to do no damage.

They cautiously applied their weather work to influence the wind, and found it easy, with the Compass. And dangerous, as storms, once summoned, were hard to send away.

They loaded supplies and trade goods and headed west as soon as the ice retreated enough for safe sailing along the southern shore.

Chapter Twenty-one

1 May 2119
Trading on the Lakes

By April they'd ferried goods and people all the way to Gibraltar. In May they turned east and visited both Cairo and Red River.

Thanks to the shortwave, they brought in ingots of refined metal, both iron and copper, with reassurances that they could buy all the grain they could handle. And assurances from Red River that they'd take all the wheat they could carry.

The brotherly gods sauntered down to the dock and observed the young men, and walked off without speaking. Chris blew out a breath of relief and settled down to the business of determining the relative value of iron and wheat.

"Wow, dolls at eleven o'clock high." Lance sounded appreciative. "Despite the encumbrances."

Chris looked further up the bank. The girls from the orgy.

With babies. Big ones. Toddlers.

He swallowed nervously. *Somehow managed to not think about consequences, didn't I?* He glanced at the dock. "I think we'd best be a bit conservative with our first load. I think that's enough wheat."

"We've been talking to Red River, they've got some small

steam engines we'd love to try out for irrigation, running the mill, maybe even a municipal water system, if we can make enough pipes." One of the merchants selling wheat eyed the boat. "Think about making several trips."

"We will, that's an excellent plan." Matt hefted another bag and handed it down to Lance. It all fit, and the boat didn't ride too low.

"It's beautiful. How did you do the woodwork?" One of the young women stooped to run her hands over the bonded planking.

Before he knew it, the boat was over run with women, young men, and there were babies everywhere.

Chris introduced those he knew to his compass, other introductions flew, food appeared on the dock and a party had somehow gotten underway.

"It's the gods," Mica said. "When we're around them, well, anywhere within ten miles of town, partying just comes naturally."

One of the guys glanced over. "You won't hear us complaining, but, well, mainly because we can shield a bit and not get pulled into the scrums they have up on the plaza."

Mica tossed her head. "We just have to not worry too much about who fathered which kid, and get on with life. Which sounds all fine now, but come hard times, the guy's'll probably just walk away. But we don't let the gods influence us any further than that, any more. Which has pissed them off. They threatened to leave, and we all cheered. That . . . got a little nasty for awhile. But it's settled down, now."

"They're plotting something, you can see it in their smirks." Lakisha shrugged. "No doubt we'll find out eventually."

Chris took a quick head count. "Ten guys? Do you know how to work together? You'll need to recruit some more, for complete compasses. And I'd love to learn how to shed a god's influence. I've tried to build a good mental shield, but it barely works."

Sharon held out her hand, palm outward in a "stop!" position. "Picture a mirror, facing out, a bubble. Close your mind, reject outside thoughts and magic, then picture that refusal expanding out to your bubble."

They had impromptu lessons off and on all evening, the party stretched out and a few more people drifted in.

The babies got laid out on blankets, then moved to clear a dance-and-compass floor. Chris picked up a little redhead and felt an odd zing. Almost like a shock of recognition.

Mine.

He blinked at the tiny girl in dismay. Could this baby be his? He sucked in a shaky breath, feeling tingles of magic winding up his arms, and around his heart and soul. He put the sleeping child down and looked around. It was a brilliant night, bright stars and a fat crescent moon. He could see everyone, touch everyone mentally, see their glows, soft, or bright, sparkling or steady. They were all beautiful, and for a long moment he felt like a god, looking down at the brilliant souls below.

He dodged the next dance, and paced around, out in the darkness. *Me? A father? A damned poor one, if I am. But I feel so . . . inflated, powerful. Joyful, like I could laugh and the whole world would smile.* He studied the people around him more carefully. *No. Not the whole world, just this group, both the locals and my Compass, who know me so well.*

He pried himself out of his weird mental state and went back to magic lessons.

He wasn't all that sure how the witches in Tripoli did it, but with a bit of encouragement, the women started experimenting with their last copper bars. "Picture it flowing, like clay. Form shapes with your mind as much as your hands. Think about making pipes, for a water delivery system, all over your city and country-side."

Then he was pulled away to a compass with half locals. They traded around, practiced with all the magicians and they changed around again, finding the best positions for each magician in each Compass, to smooth out the power flow so it could be raised to the highest possible levels. Chris was easily the most powerful, and the best trained of them all. And his compass wasn't far behind him.

Matt eyed him. "You've gotten stronger. Again. Either I'm going to have to start practicing more," his grin flashed, "or get some girl pregnant in a drunken orgy."

Chris snorted, and then waved Matt silent as Red River called them on the shortwave. He took the call, then turned back to the others. "We'll leave tomorrow, come back in a week.

They'll take all the grain you're willing to sell."

Mica laughed. "Excellent. Now stop tending to business and come party. I want to show you how we've refined a few of those tricks we discovered last year. And stop looking so worried. We've got contraceptive spells, now."

On Harry's advice, they didn't volunteer their magical status in Red River.

They made six trips back and forth carrying people, products, and grain.

Then they headed for home, with their profit in the form of two small steam engines.

Not much had changed over the months.

Lillian, Cassie, Iris and a bunch of other girls had been granted title to a square mile in the name of the Sahara Pyramid. It was notable only for the rocky hill in the middle of it.

Muriel Westfarlin pounced on the steam engines, and dived into figuring out how to run her thresher from one, and then started talking about a large mill to take care of everyone's grinding.

In return, the witches filled The Harpy with copper pipes of various sizes, and suggested that more steam engines would be useful.

Chapter Twenty-two

10 June 2119

Cairo, North Africa, Exile

The man in Kuwait sounded desperate.

They'd had very poor rains, and could they bring grain?

A new voice from Red River broke in and said they were still short as well, and as long as they were in Cairo, why not bring all they could handle?

While Kuwait and Red River argued over who ought to get their theoretical cargo, the compass conferred, and decided they'd risk having difficulty getting back up the Red River.

"We might as well find out now if we can make it, you know?" Lance grinned. "We can always yell for Harry to come help us poor stranded travelers."

"How true."

They loaded the hold with sacks of wheat and maize, then piled more on deck for Red River. Then they sailed east.

The Red River was shorter of grain than they'd let on, and while they argued about selling the entire shipment to them and going back for more, the tenor of the Kuwait messages changed. How many passengers could they take? New Bombay had invited them to move there, and it seemed like a good idea.

They sold three quarters of the grain to Red River traders,

and headed down the river.

In the five days it took them to get around the Arabian peninsula, Kuwait's water situation went from bad to dire. By the time they docked, the question of transporting livestock had become moot. The refugees piled in. Frighteningly few of them. Chris was afraid to ask how many had died. *Perhaps there weren't very many people there in the first place. Some of the western villages are smaller than this.*

Even so, there wasn't enough room for everyone. The Harpy was wallowing and ten men stood on the dock, expressionless. All the bags of grain were piled on the dock. There wasn't anything else they could strip out of the boat. A woman sobbed, behind him. *Will they survive long enough for us to make a round trip?*

Chris took a deep breath . . . exhaled. "Matt? See if you can raise Harry on the shortwave. If he can come . . . tell him to grab his mast, hard, and we'll summon him. Can't hurt to try, but we need his boat, not his spear."

Reception was lousy, ". . . can't possibly work, but I've got the mast."

Chris closed his eyes and pictured the old man, standing in the boat. "God of Travelers, help us in our dire need. Come with your boat."

The Harpy rocked a bit, and he opened his eyes. Harry and the Viking bobbed just off their side.

Harry laughed. "I don't think you're supposed to be able to game the system like this!"

They hastily swapped people around, to get families back together, and sailed immediately. The compass formed up and heated air masses to keep the wind in their favor.

**

He was starting to get used to it.

A scary thought all on its own.

But he had no time to think about it, just recognition of what was happening and throwing up a physical shield. For offense, he was, as usual, wagging his damned sword from atop a rearing stallion.

He looked around, sorting combatants into groups. The people on the inside were defending their homes, the people outside were attacking, and doing a damned poor job of it. Jet leaped forward, taking aim at the largest bunch of raiders. They carried torches in the twilight, no, they were throwing torches at the houses. Jet plowed into them as they looked for targets. Torches dropped, a gun appeared. The sword swung and blood gushed. More guns. On the moving horse, he couldn't stabilize the shield by driving it into the ground. The kinetic energy of multiple hits knocked him completely off the horse. He landed in an experienced roll. A flash of memory, a parachute, hitting the ground and rolling back to his feet.

He managed to not cut or stab himself with his own sword and came up swinging. The blade was sharp enough, hard enough, to remove the hand with the gun. He stabbed the next man through the heart. Pulled the sword back and rammed the pommel into the face of the man right behind him. Blood splattered as the nose crushed. He punched out at a man. The sword's cross guard hit the man's throat. Wolf's breath caught as he saw men aiming at Jet. The horse laid ears back and charged. Undeterred by bullets. *Can Jet make magic shields?* And suddenly the bandits were running away instead of toward him. A distant shout of triumph, men running, carrying something between them. A black shadow galloped up, and he reached up to grab the horn of the saddle, and used the horse's speed to aid his leap to the animal's back.

They crashed down in his wine tasting room, heavy hooves booming on the wooden flooring.

The big video screen was still playing the movie he'd started.

"Well, horse, I wonder where we were that time?"

The horse snorted, and he dismounted stiffly and led him out. They both needed a bath, or perhaps a midnight swim in the stream to get all the blood off.

On his return, he clicked on the shortwave. Everyone was talking about the raid on Gibraltar.

About the beacon.

Stolen by two men, large, running to fat, one with red hair, the other a blonde.

***

The wallowing, overloaded boats sailed into the harbor at New Bombay at noon.

Chris felt like kissing the marble quay.

He suspected some of his thin, seasick passengers did kiss it. Might have just been stumbles after a week on a boat. They'd balanced speed against their over loaded condition and magicked up enough wind to cause choppy seas, but not large waves.

"Pitiful, just pitiful."

Chris looked up from handing his last passenger ashore to see an exquisite woman looking them over. The yellow silk robe she wore glowed in the sun, and her deep honey tan glowed with it. Lustrous black hair rippled down her back. She looked to be perhaps, sixteen. Her large dark eyes met his gaze and left him gasping for breath.

She walked past him to where the Viking was just now tying up. "Oh Harry, you risked your life for these pitiful creatures? They'll take some feeding up before they'll even be decent factory workers. The women? Well, I suppose we need some servants."

Harry bristled. "I didn't rescue them so you could make slaves of them. They are our fellow Americans, with all the rights and privileges of all people."

A masculine laugh from the other side. "You are so soft, Harry."

Chris gawped again. The boy, young man, was golden. Hair, skin and eyes. He wore an open vest and loose pants, brilliant red silk embroidered with golden thread. Chris closed his eyes, and the pair glowed to his inner senses as well. He held up his hand, blocked, pushed the block out into a bubble all around. The searing light of the pair dimmed.

Even frowning down at him they were still spectacularly beautiful.

"Better soft than arrogant, Mercy." Harry helped his last passenger off the Viking. "Use a bit of common sense and build up supporters, not frightened and angry subjects. Barry and Edmund are about to face a rebellion, you could be next." He stepped back into the boat and faded.

Water slurped hastily into the hole left by the boat, and slopped back to rock the Harpy.

The woman snorted. "I didn't realize he knew how to teleport. He could have saved himself a bit of distance." She sighed dramatically. "Well, all of you get up here. We'll sort you into some work groups and assign you a place to live." Mercy frowned as the former mayor of Kuwait helped his wife toward the steps.

Chris winced guiltily. She'd been a bit dehydrated and suffering from heat exhaustion when they'd picked them up. The week at sea hadn't been what she'd needed to recover, even though she had at least gotten all the water she needed.

"We'll split you men and women up, can't have the dregs reproducing."

Even sick, that caught everyone's attention.

Chris stepped ashore, and felt his compass coming with

him.

They scooped up the children, and helped the others. It was a dozen steps up to the street that ran along the shore. Chris swept a look over the bright white city. *As beautiful and cold as its mistress.*

"Practical, young man. There's no mercy in the helpless bringing children into the world, so they can suffer and die."

Chris shivered and stiffened his shield. *Harry said Mercy was merciful by her own standards.* Three other men were walking down from the city to join them. No, two men and a woman.

The new woman eyed them dispassionately. "I think for now they had best be domiciled in the hospital. It is nearly empty, in any case, and the doctors can handle any illnesses.".

The older of the two new men shrugged indifferently.

The younger of the two men looked even younger than the golden boy. He eyed the refugees and wrinkled his nose. "There aren't enough of them to worry about, just feed 'em up a bit and let them find a place to do whatever they're good at."

The former mayor nodded. "We lost all our livestock. But we can hunt and fish. Just . . . the last of the water went so fast, those last two days . . . but we'll be back on our feet and working in no time."

Pax laughed. "And you'll owe us some work, for the care we've given you."

Chris shook his head. "Mayor, do you want us to sail you another day or two down the coast? These people don't seem very welcoming."

"You dare to criticize me?" Mercy's glow started showing the gleam of collected power.

The other woman snorted. "A rather obvious observation. Slavery is abhorrent to the civilized, stop trying to edge it into your society."

"You. . . !" Mercy cast a look at the golden boy. "Pax, why don't you deal with the refugees, while I explain a few things to Little Miss Logic, here." She turned a baleful glare back on the woman. "Abrams, you are so open minded, one is tempted to wonder if your brains have fallen out."

Chris dropped them from his consideration, watching the three men as they strolled a bit closer.

"We're gods, little boy. Get back in your boat and go away." Pax's head turned suddenly, as something else snagged his attention.

As one they turned, looking around.

Two figures stumbled out of thin air, one with his arms wrapped around a four foot cylinder.

Large men. One blonde, one redhead. Barry and Edmund.

The brothers were grinning through grubby smears and smelled of smoke.

"Hey! Look what we got!" Barry grunted, and his muscles all stood out as he lifted the cylinder. It had a base to hold it upright, and solar panels like the petals of a flower at the top.

A second chunk of realization dropped into place. *The beacon.* Chris stepped closer.

"How did you get here? How did you jump to somewhere you've never been!" Mercy snapped. Then the cylinder Barry was holding registered. "*Is that the beacon?*"

Edmund swaggered forward. "The one and only. I figure, one of those unnoticeable spells, and I can walk out of here, through the gate, and do anything I damn well please, back home. On Earth." He leered. "Want to know how much I'll charge you to join me?"

Mercy raised her eyebrows. "Why would I want to go back? I'm a Goddess here. Speaking of which, if you'll excuse me for a moment, I was right in the middle of putting down a minor rebellion."

"Ooo! Can we watch?" Barry smirked and set the beacon down, keeping a possessive grip on it.

Mercy laughed. "Of course, unless you'd like to join the fun." She turned to look at Logic. "Well, you're all alone, now you cold-blooded fool. Do you really think you can beat me? Me?"

Peace turned away from the women, and started raising power as he walked down to the miserable huddle of refugees. "I think you lot need to learn your place here, then we'll all get along perfectly well."

Chris stiffened. And stepped between the god and the refugees, starting to gather power.

Pax eyed him contemptuously, Marty and Richie looked amused. Their smiles widened as the other mages stepped up to join Chris.

Marty sauntered down toward them. "Do you really think you can stand up to a God?"

Lance stepped to Chris's right. "We have to. Otherwise the half of you that are so full of yourselves will turn the rest of us into slaves. And that just isn't going to happen." He turned and stretched his hands out to the other mages.

Pax gestured to his fellow gods. Richie shifted uncertainly, then shook his head and walked away.

Barry and Edmund laughed. "Run away, Baby!"

Richie shook his head. "Perverts and slavers. Go play with each other. No one else wants the pair of you."

Chris turned his attention back to the Compass.

Lance was pouring on the power in the East position. Matt was South, strong and solid. Vince was West, excited, but in control. With Tyrone sandwiched between Lance and Matt, he couldn't get into much trouble. Hugh was the weakest magically, but he was safe beside Chris. Dane and Javier were young, but strong. They worked so well together you'd never guess their inexperience.

Power flowed around the compass, strengthened, flowed faster. Lance held a physical shield over the compass as a whole, Matt took over the mental shield.

Chris held the beautiful spinning loop of pure power and turned his head to gaze at the two gods striding down the street towards them.

No.

Problem.

He could see clearly, as Pax flicked out power in the form of a fireball, and batted it away. He braced and absorbed the quick shock of a stun spell. He reached out with a delicate slice and the red vest dropped away from one shoulder. Pax jumped in shock, flicked a glance at his shoulder, then turned and threw a wave of kinetic energy at them.

Lance shifted the base of the shield out, sank it into the marble, and the blast of energy screamed up the slanted shield and passed over them.

Dane created heat, up high, and the air rose. Clouds formed with uncanny speed.

Chris sent another precise slice, the vest dropped. Another, and Pax yelled in pain, scrambling backwards, clutching his pants, blood on his side and his hands.

"Oh, damn, sorry! Very clumsy of me," Chris called. Thunder grumbled like deep, distant laughter. The day darkened.

"Damn it Marty, do something," the golden boy snarled.

Chris looked over at the other fellow.

"Engage in a dock-side brawl? Oh, I don't think so." He turned away, and Pax lunged, grabbed him.

"You're going to let them get away with that?"

"They seem to be getting away with it."

Pax's grip tightened as he swung the man around, between him and the Compass. What he threw had aspects of mental magic in it; the part of the Compass that was Matt threw everything he had into that shield. Black and poisonous, the magic seeped around, under, through . . .

The Dane part released the lightning. It struck the apex of the nearest building, danced down to the fence. Too fast to see the strokes and return strokes, it bounced down and left scorch marks as it was forced toward the gods. Pax and his shield scrambled backwards, and abruptly disappeared. Dane let the lightning go. He and Matt leaned on each other, barely keeping the circle intact.

The poisonous spell seeped away.

Chris eyed the remaining gods, and goddesses.

Edmund was laughing. "Oh, good show, but now we could blow you over with a huff and a puff."

Logic pressed her lips together, then raised her voice. "God of War, I summon you!"

Chris barked out a brief laugh . . . Barry and Edmund were both grabbing for the beacon. Chris threw a push, staggered them. Pushed again. Threw a flash of light.

Light gleamed off sword and armor, the rearing horse touched down.

Chris yelled and pointed. "The beacon!"

The black horse leaped for it, the warrior leaned to grab. Barry and Edmund tackled the beacon. And they were all gone.

Chris cursed under his breath and looked around.

Mercy turning back to face Logic, Richie watching from up the hill.

Logic's mouth quirked up in a grim and confident smile.

Mercy stepped back and disappeared.

Chris straightened in alarm, as he felt a wave of powerful magic.

"Not to worry, that was just Mercy taking her whole house with her. I do hope she doesn't come back." Two more waves of power swept over them. The goddess nodded in satisfaction. "Just as well. Those five are not suited to be leaders." Logic dusted her hands. "I must say you young men were impressive. Why don't you stay for a while? You can get your refugees settled, and train some of the people here." She cast a judicious gaze toward the embarrassed Richie. "Set a good example for someone who needs one. And I will show you how teleportation works."

Chapter Twenty-three

19 June 2119

New Bombay, India, Exile

Teleportation, the conscious control of it, involved holding precise patterns in one's head. The recognition of where you were, the recognition of where you wanted to go, and a bridge of spells that swapped mass, momentum and orientation.

Chris learned first how to jump around New Bombay. Then he brought up his memory of the Inn. The front porch. *Home.* He stepped there.

Jamie yipped in surprise then grabbed him and kissed him. "How did you do that! Good grief. Everyone isn't going to start popping in and out of places are they?"

"I hope not." He swayed and grabbed for a chair. "It . . . takes a bit of energy."

She stuck her head in the door, Long enough to yell something, to someone. "I see that. And how far away were you?"

Chris grinned. "Very. Look, did the Old Wolf get back? Did he get the beacon away from Barry and Edmund?"

She shook her head. "He came back empty handed. Everyone's in an uproar about it, and over-reacting to everything else. Ira Penner tried to—oh, grumpy old Vito caught your mares in a cattle drive and they have the cutest little black foals—and Penner tried to have them put in the auction, and Vito, can you believe it? Stood up and said, no, they were your mares, branded with your registered brand, and they and their foals were yours. They nearly came to blows over it. And Lillian is pregnant. Cassie and Iris too, which isn't helping the situation with Penner."

Milly hustled out then, and handed him a glass of what proved to be apple juice. With the first swallow Chris could very nearly feel the energy flowing back into his body.

"Dinner for you in five more minutes. Honestly, Chris! We might have known you'd learn how to teleport."

Sky and Sea blasted out the doors and climbed all over him.

"You came back!"

"What did you bring us?"

A snort from the street was Vito.

"Hey." Chris struggled to sit up straight under the lapful of kids. "Vito. Thank you, I understand you caught those wretched mares."

The man gave him a surly shrug.

"Tell you what. Why don't we breed them both to another stallion, your choice, and you take your pick of which foal you want, next summer."

The grumpy man blinked. Opened and closed his mouth a couple of times. Finally found something negative enough to get his voice back. "Most likely some wild stud bred them already."

Chris grinned. "There's always the year after. And, you know, you really ought to come along to the winery, learn how to use that power you've got."

"Me? Do your weird shit? No way."

A laugh behind him. Harry and Wolf.

"Vito you might be surprised."

"Huh!" Vito faded away as more people started their direction.

Phaedra and Miriam were apparently deep into an argument.

"It hardly matters."

Harry looked over at them.

Miriam scowled back. "Tomorrow is the solstice, a bit over two years since we were marooned here. But we don't have the beacon. So it doesn't really matter, does it?"

Wolf nodded. "But having a choice really does matter, doesn't it?" He pulled absolutely nothing off his arm, reached in and hauled the beacon out.

People started crowding around as he unfolded the solar cells.

"You can juice it up a bit, plug it into a generator right there."

Chris pried himself out of the chair and wiggled through the crowd. "But what are you gods going to do?"

"Go away. When I get back, you can tell me all about it." The Old Wolf glanced at Harry, then over the crowds' heads to where Romeau and Gisele were walking down, attracted by the hubbub. "Us."

"But, but. . . " Miriam looked worried. "What should we tell them?"

"I'd recommend the truth, it's easier to keep track of. But it is entirely up to you. You are free to do or say whatever you wish. That is the one principle we must always cling to." He shifted his gaze, and met Muriel's.

She glanced from him to her children, back to him. She looked panicked, and pale, tears shining in her eyes as she shook her head.

Chris winced in sympathetic pain. *Not even for him will she abandon her house, uproot her children, again.*

Wolf turned and walked away. Harry followed. They joined Romeau and Gisele, and spoke briefly. Then Wolf went to the winery, and Romeau and Gisele to the Temple. Both buildings vanished. Harry walked out the north gate, toward the wharf.

"Humph. Ought to have arrested them!" Ira Penner glanced north, shrugged and stomped away.

Chris looked around for the bus kids.

He jerked his head to the west. "C'mon. We got a couple of holes in the wall to fill up. Mark, Derry? Can you guys go cut trees? Erik, you lay out the lines and I'll start the ditches . . . "

He could hear snatches of conversations as he walked away.

"We should revise that list of things we need . . ."

"Now we can finally have the store . . . "

"... will they come back?"

George Wilson was volunteering his generator if anyone had fuel.

Milly hustled over, looking worried. "But where did they go?"

Erik shrugged. "Stop worrying about those . . . gods. They can take care of themselves."

"But, but . . ."

"And if we have an emergency, I suspect we could call them, and they'd come."

Vito was talking about not telling any police or military that the gods had ever lived here. "Just play dumb."

"I'd tell them where to look, if I had a clue." Ben's voice over rode the background chaos. "I'll bet they can find Mr. Bad Karma. And I'm sure going to tell them to shoot those hell hounds on sight!"

Chris grabbed Darren's sleeve as he turned toward Ben. "Everyone is free, including the gods. Including the assholes. Free to act, move and speak. And that must never change, no matter what else happens."

"And what if nothing happens?"

Chris grinned. "Then we keep on the way we have been. Building a very strange new world."

All the Little Gods
118 years post exile
Pam Uphoff

Chapter One

2235 Winter Solstice

New Miami, Southern tip of the Indian subcontinent

Two magic globes glowed on either side of the door, too dim to light the courtyard. No sign of dawn lightened the horizon. The night sky was a dark dove gray, eerie and unnatural.

"I hate Comet Winters." River tried to make out the constellations, but the pervasive faint glow of the comets' tails erased too many of the middling bright stars.

The beautiful woman beside her shrugged. "It's just a few weeks, every three or four years. I admit I haven't seen it this bad for decades. The astronomers are saying that there's been a few collisions and further breakup of a few of the larger bodies. So fresh ice is now exposed to the Sun." Her warm voice drew one in. The Goddess of Mercy, glowing with power, connected at some deep subconscious level with every person on the

World. "The astronomers think there's a small trailing cluster that could be a problem next year as well. I'll have to store more food, if these lazy supercilious merchants won't listen to me."

A bright streak flashed across the sky, then two more.

"The astronomers say those are just dust, burning because of their high speed." River watched as the next streak expanded into a bright fireball and crossed the sky with deceptive slowness. "And a few pebbles. It's probably a hundred miles high."

"All in all, just a pretty show. Now, about the Witches of New Tokyo?" Mercy turned in the darkness and faced her.

"We had a telepathic conference early in the night. They will support you, as always, this time by backing up the God of Art. They will gather power for him, and thus strengthen him. That should nearly double the number of trained magicians who are aligned with your side."

"Excellent. Come back inside, now, this sky is unnatural." The Goddess turned; her figure brightened suddenly.

River spun and winced back from the brilliant line of light in the north. A last bright flash from below the horizon. "Did that one hit? I've seen some of the old craters . . ."

The ground shuddered beneath their feet.

The Goddess stepped out beside her. "Yes, that one hit. Pity it wasn't further west. A meteor hitting New Bombay would have solved half our problems so fittingly." She cocked her head thoughtfully. Shook it. "The meteors are out too far and come too fast. I doubt I could touch one."

River shivered. "But, you wouldn't kill a whole city. And the Goddess of Logic is there." *And I thought the problem was the "King" of the Mages, in between here and New Bombay?*

"Indeed. Killing her with so much power would bring all these stupid mortals to heel quickly, with, in the end, less bloodshed." The Goddess looked at the witch, and the last glimmer of light from the north showed the hint of contempt in her smile. "Mercy is not something you would truly understand. Its scope is larger than you can see. Come inside and pack. I'll just add some last thoughts to a letter for you to deliver to Art. It is time you were on your way home."

River stopped to watch a sputtering trio of meteors, but they all died out quickly. *I hate Comet Winters.* She packed quickly, shedding her sari and donning the sort of pants suit that business women wore as a declaration of their professionalism. A tossup whether she'd get more unwanted advances in this or the other, but negotiating ship's ladders would be easier in pants.

She carried her two cases, one large, one small with multiple locks, both ordinary and magical, on it, out to the vestibule. She opened all the locks on the small case and added the two letters Mercy handed her.

The building shuddered. For a moment, River thought another meteor had hit, then she heard the moan of the wind and swallowed to equalize the pressure in her ears.

Mercy sniffed. "Air blast. It travels more slowly that the ground shock. I'll walk part way with you. I need to keep up with the mood in the street. We gods are too influenced by the people as a whole to ever ignore them. Unfortunately." Mercy walked off as she spoke, leaving River to negotiate the door with her cases. None of the goddess's cowed servants rushed to hold the door.

Good thing I have long legs and a thick skin.

The streets were strewn with wind blown debris, but there didn't seem to be any serious damage. The few street people about looked a bit nervy, and most of them shifted away from the goddess. Only one approached.

"Support the new hospital, Mistresses?" The beggar was female, young, with big dewy eyes. An hour yet till dawn. What was the girl doing out on the street already? The girl's eyes lit suddenly with recognition, and she went to one knee.

River lowered her shields enough to see the flaring, untrained glow of the girl's magic. One of the Little Gods, caught up in an archetype straight from the collective subconscious.

The Goddess waved an arm, and despite the intervening three feet of empty air, the beggar was tossed out of their way. The girl rolled over and scuttled away, uninjured physically, but probably shocked by the actions of her goddess.

"Mercy is swift, and stops suffering, it doesn't prolong it. I'm getting tired of all these miserable little whiners calling themselves Angels of Mercy. I thought they'd be a good buffer, but they've turned into more of an annoyance."

River nodded obediently. "They don't follow your

guidelines. Fortunately the Witches have outlawed those spells to allow them to have male children, and they're talking about forbidding congress with both mages and wizards, so there shouldn't be any more of these overly magical children, these little gods." She marched along after the Goddess, suitcase getting heavier with every step. The smaller case with letters and packages was too light to counterbalance the heavier case. She switched sides.

Mercy sniffed. "I'm sure it sounded like a good idea at the time. Foolish witches dreaming of having male babies with god-like powers. And a few of them are nearly that strong. But most are like these soft-hearted idiots! No real training or goals, they just absorb what the collective subconscious sends their way. I make mine drill, so they have some competency. We'll need them in this war." The Goddess of Mercy curled a lip at the three men in the next intersection, each claiming to be the God of Travelers and capable of blessing their journey. "They couldn't bless a horse as far as the City Limits. But, like Harry himself, they are loyal to their homes. Loyal to us. When we call, they will form the magical branch of our army."

A very poorly trained branch of the army. River smirked. "What about all the Army mascots? Every company has their own God of . . .War." Her voice stumbled to a halt. *Big mistake, girl!*

"Do not mention that man to me." The Goddess's brown eyes burned as hot as the dawning sun for a moment.

"I mean, all these little gods take a tiny bit of, well, the focus of godhood or something, away from the real god, don't they? So the more mascots, the weaker he will be. I'm sorry, Mercy, I thought you'd find it amusing." *The God certainly does.*

"I do, but there's going to be a war, and it won't be amusing if the Real God shows up. The little ones don't take nearly as much ability from us as people think. The people don't realize quite what we are. How dangerous we are. Especially War. He has trained for mindless violence all his life. And he will support New Bombay, he's always had a soft spot for Logic."

"I can't see why. She's cold and well, practically asexual." River bit her lip. "Anyway, you won't let it come to an actual war, will you? I mean, where's the mercy in war?"

"War is not about mercy, girl. It's about power. Those idiots, letting the people who ought to be their subjects govern themselves! The ideas are spreading as fast as their new cities, and this plague of little gods isn't helping at all. They undermine our authority, people have started treating us as if we were no more than those street corner beggars. Something amusing. Well, we'll use them up at need. Little gods and people alike. They'll all find out what a god truly is."

Trained and deadly, honed by over a century of experience. Unlike these sad beggars, flailing around with a bit of instinctive magic. "I don't understand why they're all out now, so early."

Mercy waved dismissively. "Comet winter. None of us

sleep well. We have premonitions, clairvoyant dreams. Sometime far in the future there will be a horrible disaster, but I can feel that it's hundreds of years from now. Now, go back to your witches coven, or pyramid or whatever you're calling it these days, and convince the witches to continue to support us. Me. Certainly they won't want to be on the side that is controlled by *males*."

"Oh no. We don't let men have any say in our affairs." *Nor gods nor goddesses, unlike the sniveling witches you have under your control, here in Miami. Art may get a bit of a surprise, if it comes to open warfare.*

"Good. Then they should be easily persuaded to continue their support."

River ducked her head respectfully, and turned off toward the docks. She should have no trouble finding a trader heading north. No matter what rumors of war were spreading, trade would carry on until the shooting started, and probably past. In New Tokyo she would deliver her report on the Goddess of Mercy to the various people she owed allegiance to. It would be a relief to be done with this trip, however much she generally liked travelling.

"Try your luck with the dice or cards, Miss?"

River looked up and shook her head. The little gods, as people jokingly called them, weren't physically little. They were just ordinary people endowed with a lot more of the magical genes than the rest of the population. The magic put them more in touch with the collective subconscious. They could influence the psyche of the whole of mankind—or could have if they'd all pulled in one direction. Instead they were controlled by it.

Like the original gods, the Old Gods, they were divided in their desires and goals. Pulled by the influence of the collective subconscious, they were rarely able to resist the strong impulses from outside that tried to shape them into the form of one or another of the Archetypes.

Only the Archetypes, the things nearly everyone believed in, survived coherently to emerge from the collective subconscious and shape the most powerful magic users.

This pretty girl was Lady Luck; something in her personality had biased her magical talents, and now she worked in a casino. River had met the God of Chance, and "Lucky" wasn't one of the words she'd have applied. "Random." "Unpredictable." "Unreliable," more like. River fished out a coin and tossed it to her. "For luck on a trip."

The girl laughed. "You should give to the Traveler for that!"

She even looks like Chance, I wonder if she's a descendant?

Some of the Old Gods had children, others didn't. Mercy had a daughter, tucked away somewhere, rarely mentioned, rarely seen. The Gods of Virtue, Vice, and Chance had bastards spread over the world. The God of Eternal Youth was said to occasionally give children as well as renewed youth to the women who slept with him. The Traveler had a few. The God of War had a habit of marrying widows with children, she hadn't heard of him having any of his own, but that might just be a desire for privacy. The love between the Goddess of Health and Fertility, and the God of Love had never been blessed with a child. The God of Peace claimed to be above common physical desires. *They are such contradictions! Who would think that a War God would strive for peace, and the God of Peace rant about uniting all people, forcibly?*

In the harbor she scanned the notices pinned to the board outside the Harbor Master's office. There were two ships that would be heading north on the tide. Both claimed to have cabins for passengers. She noted their moorings and walked to look them over, and bargain for her passage. The first was small, but bore the blue pennant of the Traveler on the foremast. The second was an ornate fat tub. She sighed wistfully and advanced on the boarding plank. She'd much rather have travelled under the protection of Harry Traveler, but she'd be much less conspicuous, and checked less carefully in New Tokyo if she arrived on the larger ship.

The Kittyhawk's purser was delighted to take her money and fill the last bunk in a cabin already occupied by three women.

River stowed her case under the last cot. "I'm Sally Reardon. Visiting family in New Tokyo." She swallowed carefully. *Seasick before we leave the dock. Not a good sign.*

"Oh?" The older woman looked her over, her gaze lingering on River's perfectly flat abdomen.

Wondering if I'm pregnant and being sent away to hide

the disgrace? Or wondering what business I'm in, wearing trousers. River knew she looked younger than her twenty-five years, but apparently she passed inspection.

"I'm Mrs. Jasmine Gardener. We escorted my son to the University here and saw him settled in. Now we're returning home."

"It's an excellent University. Competition with New Bombay keeps everyone keen." River looked over at the two younger women, neither looked above twenty.

"My daughter Heidi. I brought Heidi along to keep her out of trouble. And the maid. Mary."

Her daughter looked embarrassed, their maid, tired.

"I think I'll step out and watch the sunrise. Did you see the meteor earlier?" River stepped the very short distance to the door.

"I suspect it was just some silly magician trying to impress someone with illusions." Mrs. Gardener didn't glance at her daughter, but the girl flinched.

"I don't think so, but . . . " River shrugged and let the door close behind her. She stood still a moment, telling her stomach—and her head—that the power of Earth was still there. Just a few feet away beneath the water. No one was convinced. Witches were notoriously bad travelers on the ocean, and River was no exception.

On deck, a few last boxes were being toted toward the hold. The Captain had his watch in hand, the crew was standing by the lines.

River leaned on the wall of the forecastle, as much out of the way as possible, as the hatch was barred and the Captain closed his watch with a snap and nodded to the officer beside him. The crew leapt into action. "Cast off!" was the first and last command she completely understood. The ship drifted away from the dock with no tendency to get washed back against it, as she'd expected. Sails rose, snapping in the breeze and filled. Hundreds of ropes were loosened, tightened, or moved. The ship picked up forward speed, and took aim for the opening in the breakwater and the open sea beyond.

She controlled her stomach with stubborn willpower.

To her surprise, they turned north and sailed up the bight for the better part of the day. An ominous cloud covered the sky to the north, and the scent of burning reached her as they tacked wide of the shore, then cut in closer.

The mate answered her query. "That meteor, the captain wants a closer look. It'll settle the crew down as well. Nothing like the unknown to scare a grown man."

In the later afternoon a fine ash began floating down on them.

"There don't appear to be any settlements up this way." A passenger at the rail nodded politely to her, and turned back to his friend. "And the winds don't indicate a firestorm, so it must have been a small one."

His friend nodded. "This time."

River frowned. "I've always heard that while there was a chance of meteors reaching the ground, it was very rare. Am I overestimating 'rare?' Is this likely to happen again?"

"Well, the risk is higher when the comets are closer, lots of debris in their vicinity." The first man shrugged. "We can only track the ones that are large enough to see through this damned tail gas. Or, of course, the very large ones that we can see with telescopes from a very great distance."

She nodded. "I took in a lecture of Dr. Havier's. He said they were following a hundred and twelve solid bodies, hopefully all the large ones, and that none would actually strike the world, although every time they come close to Earth, they're diverted again and they have to recalculate their orbits. According to him the largest comets will eventually spread out so far that nearly every winter we will be at risk of a dangerous meteor strike."

"Yes. I'm surprised they didn't see this one coming, it must have broken off recently from Comet Cow." He jerked his head skyward, where a paler patch of the creamy sky marked the position of the last big comet. "I'm Dr. Simon Golan, this is Dr. Neil Frasier. We're actually from Cairo, although we rather downplayed that while in New Miami. We're both picking up and disseminating up-to-date knowledge." He cleared his throat. "Selling our textbooks." Golan was probably in his mid forties. Thin and fit, brown hair and eyes.

Dr. Frasier was older and larger. Plump and pale. "I'm a geologist, Simon's a physicist. Good thing the Captain's the curious sort, otherwise I'd be frustrated to have been so close, and not investigated this phenomenon."

"Yes. I have that itch of curiosity, myself. And who knows? It may be good for another textbook." River's eyes drifted toward the rising smoke column. What had the Goddess said? *"The meteors are out too far and come too fast. I can't touch them."* River shivered and hoped that did not indicate a desire to try. *But I will mention that to the Boss, when I report.* She shook herself, and introduced herself to the two scholars, and when her cabin mates joined them, added them to the round. More passengers were coming out to watch the smoke and speculate. The only other women traveling were with their husbands, the majority of the men were traveling on business and not much pleased by the detour.

The sun was still above the horizon when they came opposite the impact site, but the light was dimmed by the pall of smoke.

The Captain lowered two boats over the side, manned by rather frightened looking men. *Is this actually going to reassure them?* Several passengers joined them, and seeing an open spot in the bench beside Dr. Golan, River pounced on the chance to set foot on dry land. She eyed the boxes on his lap.

"It's called a camera. It focuses light on a sensitive film deposited on a pane of glass, and creates a permanent image."

"I've heard of such thing, from the Exile. I didn't know any still worked."

"They don't. I made this one. Some chemists at. . .various universities have come up with the sensitive films."

The boats grounded on a beach of white sand, with

blowing drifts of darker ashes leaving lines on the sand where the sea water had dampened them and stopped their progress. Beyond the beach, what had been thick subtropical forest and brush was now a charred wasteland.

Dr. Fraiser surveyed it triumphantly. "See the tree trunks, all snapped and knocked flat the same direction? The meteor's kinetic energy transformed into a hot blast wave, not unlike one of your experiments with black powder, Golan."

"It certainly seems so." Golan climbed onto the trunk of a palm tree and walked down it, crossed to another . . .

Their progress wasn't fast but the crater was less than a mile inland. And more than a mile across, as she paced it out. No sign of the meteor. Dr. Golan set up his camera, hustling about doing things under a heavy black cover.

Frazier was climbing about, exploring the crater. Golan climbed out from under his shroud and wiped sweat from his face.

"Did the meteor bury itself?" She frowned at the empty crater.

"No, I expect it shattered, or the part that wasn't molten did." Golan shot her a look. "Think of it as the reverse of a seasick witch. Instead of a body without power, what did this damage was very close to a huge amount of energy, without a body."

She raised an eyebrow, and didn't respond to his implicit assumption of her magical status. He didn't have much glow about him, but he didn't feel like a magician with closed mental shields. *Powerless or* extremely *well trained and controlled?*

She got her feet down onto the scorched ground and meditated, looking for density concentrations. She managed to track down half a dozen small blobs of still hot metal and rock, much to Dr. Frasier's delight. He was talking about chemical analyses and how to determine which were meteor and which were local material, melted and thrown out of the crater. How much they might have mixed . . . Dr. Golan didn't quite have to manhandle him back to the ship.

"I should be spending days here, not a few hours!" The older man looked wistfully back at the devastation.

The sailors seemed impressed by the crater, but less afraid. *The Captain knows his men.* Still, it was a thoughtful group that returned to the ship. They raised sails and anchor, and headed southeast with a good following wind. River picked at her dinner, and spent two hours on deck afterwards. Just in case willpower failed. Sleeping in the enclosed room made it worse, and she rose early and returned to the deck. When the sun rose she felt a bit more energetic, if just as queasy.

With the wind behind them now, they made good time down and around the broad peninsula of Indonesia, and standing well out from the coast they found favorable winds and currents to carry them up the coast to New Tokyo.

Chapter Two

February, 2236

New Tokyo, Pacific coast of Asia

All told, the voyage consisted of three weeks of borderline queasiness and eating more dried toast and biscuits than anything else.

She staggered ashore in New Tokyo and simply stood on the bricks of the sidewalk, enjoying the sensation of being whole and able again.

People converged on her. She recognized the sleek black carriage and stooped to her luggage. Dug out the package and letter and handed them to the God of Art as his driver stopped beside her. He tossed her a little bag and the driver cracked his whip and took his master off.

Simon—Dr. Golan—had stopped dead to watch the interchange. Now he approached more cautiously. "Perhaps I should have been calling you Lady Sally all these weeks?"

River laughed. "Heavens, no! He'd have offered Lady Sally a ride home, instead of tossing her a tip. I'm just a lowly messenger, and glad to be done with it." She nodded toward the two advancing witches. "But you can amuse the other parts of my Triad by calling me that, instead of River."

"Ha! I knew it. No one gets seasick quite like a witch."

"Oh, I thought I had quite a minimal case of it. I never lost my lunch overboard."

"That's because you never ate much of it." Simon turned his eyes back to the pair of witches.

"Simon, may I present Amused and Flattered? Guys, this is Dr. Simon Golan. He's a physics professor."

"Oh my." Amused was a well named young woman. "We have been talking about advancing, haven't we?"

Simon turned beet red.

River felt her own cheeks warm and Flattered laughed.

"A pleasure to meet you, but I'm afraid we have to grab River and run off. Our Senior Sister wants the news from the south."

Simon bowed to them, as Amused and Flattered grabbed her and hauled her away. *Drat, I didn't even get an address where he's staying.*

"Did you guys see the meteor, three weeks ago? It hit about two hundred miles north of New Miami."

"That close? Wow." Flattered released her arm, apparently realizing she wasn't trying to escape and chase down the handsome man. "We saw the fireball, and felt the earthquake. There've been rumors about impending disasters circulating."

"And the mayor called for the Old Gods to intervene." Amused smirked.

"That must've hurt." River grinned at the thought. Mayor Brigham had often claimed that with so many gods about there was no longer anything special about the old ones. He and Art disagreed about nearly everything. It livened up local politics to no end.

"Anyway, what are the odds that it will happen again?" Amused shrugged the subject away.

"Go north, away from the city, go north." It was the familiar voice of an old woman, Lady Gisele, everyone called her.

"Go north, away from the city, go north." The warm bass rumble of the War God.

"Go north, away from the city, go north." Another man, worried.

"Go north, away from the city, go north." A woman, detached emotionless advice.

"Go north, away from the city, go north." "Go north, away from the city, go north." "Go north, away from the city, go north." The voices tangled, male and female, recognizable and strange.

"River? River! Are you all right?"

River blinked and looked around. New Tokyo. Just after noon. "Umm. I guess the seasickness took more out of me than I'd realized." *Please tell me I'm getting sick. I don't like the idea of pre-cognition. That couldn't possibly be what that was.*

They pulled her along to the next street and then aboard the cable car, to be hauled up the hill. Steam engines, underground, kept the cable moving, and the cars hooked on or released at need. It was all very handy, and less messy than the horse drawn trams.

The Top of the Hill District was very well to do. An empty corner, fenced, with landscaping surrounding a bare rock hole showed where Mercy moved her home for a part of every summer. Art stayed here most winters but occasionally summered in Scandia; his private museum was an unlikely upside down step pyramid. Edmund Vice had a spot here, rarely used, she was pleased to say. The God of Just Deserts came and went irregularly, unwanted and unloved, his home well down the hill to the south.

She'd never heard of the other Old Gods moving their homes about with them. Even Pax, who ran with this crowd, remained in New Miami most of the time, occasionally visiting Mercy when she was here.

Over the hill and down the west side, a large private park, landscaped and trimmed at the edges, a near wilderness in the middle, with little private cabins tucked in here and there. The home of the New Tokyo Pyramid.

Most witches stayed with their birth pyramids, but a few wandered, visiting other places, and working with other pyramids. River's mother had been a wanderer, but passed on the enjoyment of travel to only one of her own daughters, before returning to her home here. River's sisters had stayed in New Bombay, Red River, and Scandia. River had been born in Sahara, and grown up there. Apart from shorter visits here and there. And eventually she'd escorted her mother home. Then traveled down to New Miami, to New Bombay. More than one person had looked her over and muttered about her being too pale to be a daughter of the Traveler. She sighed faintly. *Wrong Old God.* Her mother had sought a return to youthfulness, taking the usual path of seducing the God of Eternal Youth. River spotted the vigorous white-haired woman striding up the path toward her. *And she does look closer to forty than seventy.*

"Mother!" River trotted down to meet her, hug her. "You look terrific."

The tall woman looked smug.

"Oh, you didn't!"

"Well, your father was in town to talk to Art, so I whipped up a good illusion, not to mention an aphrodisiac that has to be experienced to be believed, and gave him a private welcome to New Tokyo." She frowned down at her daughter. "I'll give you the rest of it, you really do need to advance."

"I don't want to be held down with a baby, right now, Mother! I'm doing a lot of traveling for the Pyramid. Even you had to stay in one place when we were small."

"Bah. I stayed because there was something to learn there. I was usually back on the road within a year or two." She sniffed dismissively. "Generally leaving the baby with someone. You were a good traveler, so I kept you with me for a few trips. But Sandy was raised by the Red River Pyramid while I came and went five times, trying to track down the records of the Twin Gods. And Fantasia and Raw were nearly as bad."

"And I've barely met them." She shrugged. "Do the Elder Sisters want me to report to them?"

"Of course. And then we need to talk."

She eyed her mother with trepidation, but held her peace.

The warm offshore current kept New Tokyo warmer in winter than an inland city at the same latitude. The Eldest Sister was enjoying the late afternoon sun in her garden, the other Senior sisters with her.

River delivered Mercy's letter to the Eldest, and stepped back to be unobtrusive, and hopefully not dismissed, while it was handed around the oldest triad, and then her mother read it and passed it on to the two other witches of her triad.

Her mother spoke first. "As we expected. This so-called King Kelso has declared his city to be independent of New Miami. New Bombay is supporting him."

"So, it's Mercy against Logic." Sister Elm was a tiny wrinkled woman, over a hundred years old. Born just five years after the Exile. "Pity those people won't either get along or ignore each other. Thought we'd gotten them separated enough to stop any fights. Well. Can't have kings, now, can we? We're going to need to support Mercy, which means helping Art and Peace." Her old eyes swung over to River. "We may need to be sending you about. You need to be stronger. You must learn how to channel power. It's time for you to advance." She looked over at River's mother. "Firefly, instruct her, and her triad. They should all advance together."

Chapter Three

March, 2236

New Tokyo, Asia

"Mrs. Gardener, Heidi. What a pleasure to see you again." River's brain caught up with her tongue. Mrs. Gardener didn't look pleased at all, but her scowl was aimed at her daughter.

"Miss Reardon." She nodded stiffly. "We were strolling and admiring the flowers."

Heidi was pale, apart from the red spots on her cheeks. She looked furious. "I like to crowd watch. I've met the most fascinating people along the river walk."

Now her mother colored up. "Most of them just fascinated by the balance in your Trust."

River stepped back from what looked to be heading for a nasty family fight. "Enjoy your walk." She turned and walked away.

A man was watching them from the far side of a fruit vendor's stand. He turned on his heel and matched her steps as she passed. "Excuse me, you're a friend of the Gardeners?"

She looked him over. Younger than she was. Dark skinned, bright intelligent gaze. Not actually ragged, but his clothes were built for work and had plenty of mileage on them. A solid glow. "I met them aboard ship, and don't even know where they live. Traveler."

"I'm not . . . that influenced. I'm an independent Mage. I write books." He scowled. "About far away places."

She shook her head. "I really cannot help you, even if I were inclined to get a young girl in trouble."

His jaw muscles clenched. "I am not trouble. Besides my writing, I've got a job as a drover, a share of the business. I can support a family."

"Heidi is nineteen. And her mother is not about to let go of her. If you don't want her crying kidnap, you'll have to wait until she's twenty-one."

"That's barely over a year and a half from now." His aura rippled and darkened.

"Haven't you had any magical training at all? You've no shield what-so-ever."

His eyes narrowed. "You're a witch!"

"Yes."

"You don't know anything about Mages."

She sighed and steered him down an empty alley. "Picture a piece of glass. Now picture it with a faint rime of frost on it. You can still see through it, but your undirected thoughts are trapped back behind it."

The scowl deepened, but she could see the drop in brightness even as he dismissed her visualization.

"Now think of it as a mirror. Keeping other people's thoughts out."

He opened his mouth to say something and she flicked a

tiny needle of pain at him. He flinched back.

"Mirror. Reflect it."

He ducked. Scowled and crossed his arms. Winced at another hit. Bounced the next needle.

"Nice. Study those two, and you'll be a lot less vulnerable to anyone with a desire to use you, or attack you." She sighed. "Of course, as you gain power you'll be pulled more strongly into the Archetype. You'll be a little god, not a Mage."

"I am not a god. Nothing controls me, I go where and when I wish."

"Control you, no. You'll just have a hunger to go places and see new things. You already feel it, don't you? It will get stronger."

"Nothing controls me." But his eyes shifted, and his rudimentary shields stiffened a bit.

"Then practice those basics hard."

She left him standing absolutely still, attention inward, and his glow dropping steadily. Independent mage indeed. Abandoned, more like, to have had what looked like no training whatsoever. He'd picked up visualization quickly enough. What he needed was a list of the basic charms to memorize, then training in how to apply power to them, how to combine them, then how to gather more power . . . *Mother would kill me if she caught me training a male in magic usage.* She smiled wryly. *Add it to the list of things for which I'll some day find myself expelled from the pyramid.*

Chapter Four

April, 2236

New Tokyo, Asia

River finished the report, and charmed it with the God's name. Folded it carefully, then dug down to the bottom of her wardrobe, where the carelessly discarded pouch lay among her shoes. She slid the report into the pouch and sealed it. Some sort of dimensional shortcut, the god had said, the day he gave it to her. The twin of the pouch was in his office, along with several dozen others, one each for his far flung web of spies. No doubt all the gods had them—spies and pouches.

And what am I going to do about that one? Simon. Who is he spying for? River blew out a long breath and glanced out the window. *Almost time for lessons. Do I really want to advance? What man do I use to bump my skills up a level? Or two levels, if I get pregnant, as well as lose my virginity.* She blushed a bit, remembering a good looking professor of physics. *From Cairo, he said. I wonder how long he'll be in town.*

She kicked out of her shoes and stripped down to bare nothing. "Bloody theatre, no reason we have to wear these damned robes, and nothing under them other than to make us feel naughty or something."

"I heard that!" Amused's voice filtered through the door.

Flattered's giggle followed. "I thought it was so we'd feel insecure and unready, so we don't jump the gun and grab the nearest man without worrying about his well being afterwards?"

River opened the door as she finished tying the belt. "I think someone was trying to set up a mystique about witches and gave up when the sexy robes turned out to look like ordinary bathrobes."

"You can't make up rituals and the proper trappings, River. And don't go quoting something about the Exile, either!"

"It's only been a hundred and eighteen years since the Exile. So there aren't any rituals older than that." River scowled at the mirror. Her hair was an unremarkable lightish brown, shoulder length, her eyes blue. "They might at least let us put our hair up. It keeps getting in my mouth."

"That's because you cut it, what, two years ago? Honestly River, what were you thinking?"

"That if I expected to get out of Athens alive, I was going to have to look like a boy. I thought I was quite dashing with the mustache." She led the way outside, turning for the amphitheater of the Crescent Moon.

Flattered snorted. "I can't imagine why you went there in the first place."

"Because Edmund Vice had a reputation for throwing magic all over the place. I figured I could pick up some readings and analyze them. I didn't realize how often the God of Vice indulged his baser desires."

Amused widened her eyes, trying to look innocent. "But River, think about how you could have advanced, two years early, and with a God!"

"Not with him!" River hunted around for a way to distract them. "Now if Pax had been interested . . ."

Two matching sighs.

"Oh, those golden eyes!"

"His voice! It's just mesmerizing."

"Well, I see two of you are ready to advance." Firefly eyed River and shook her head in resignation. "Come in girls, you need to understand the dangers, and practice as much as is possible beforehand."

The so-called amphitheater was actually an open patch in a grove of trees. Stones had been set in the ground in a hit-or-miss pattern that kept it drained and usable most of the year.

"Amused, tell me about the tiers of knowledge."

"The tier of the New Moon is for the daughters of witches. They learn the usual academics and receive additional instruction and training to prepare them for the advent of their power. Most girls are New Moons until their fifteenth or sixteenth year. The Crescent Moons are girls who have evinced their power. They are trained and drilled until they are deemed ready to advance, generally between the ages of twenty-five and thirty. The witches of the Bright Quarter Moon tier have lost their virginity and can channel the power. After advancing they learn skills that require channeling. Full Moon witches have given birth, so they can learn to heal. Most witches stay on this tier until they are forty-five. As witches approach the Change, they become capable of stronger magic and move to the tier of the Dark Quarter until they are around sixty. The Dark Moon tier is where witches learn the most powerful spells, including things once thought only the province of the Gods."

"Right out of the text book. Very good. I will just add that the ages are approximate, and depend on many factors, such as an early loss of virginity, infertility, and early menopause. What else, River?"

"Basic strength, and the mix of magic genes each individual possesses. And the mix of normal genes, that influence the way the magic genes work."

"Explain about basic strength, Flattered."

"There is a gene that enables the collection of power. It is an artificially engineered version of a naturally occurring gene that energizes a person in a crowd or through music. Depending on which of numerous alleles of the natural gene a witch has can change the amount of power than she can collect, and the velocity with which it can be collected and used. The artificial gene was added to the X chromosome, so a witch can have one or two copies of it. But because it is strongly dominant, having two is only a slight boost to power collecting abilities."

"Good, River, the mix of genes?"

"There are one hundred and five artificial genes besides the Power collection gene. We can have one or two copies of them, on the paired chromosomes. So a maximum of two hundred and ten special genes. Some of the genes are dominant, some are recessive, some share dominance or influence other genes. And for about half of them there are multiple alleles. So while the power gene influences the strength of spells, these other genes determine what sorts of spells any given witch can actually do, and which of those they can do best."

"Close enough. Amused, tell me about the other power collection genes."

"Our power collection gene is located on the X chromosome, and is usually called the witch gene. It catches a bit of the power of gravity. The wizard gene is an engineered gene, much like the witch gene, but unable to collect as much power. It operates on light, over part of the electromagnetic spectrum. The Mage gene is again similar, but it is located on the Y chromosome. It is very powerful, collecting from the lower electromagnetic spectrum though heat and vibration and kinetic energy."

"Yes, although we've had information about what is being called a Golian wizard, apparently fairly strong. River, the gender differences?"

"The witch gene is linked to an artificial gene that primes the immune system to attack Y bearing sperm. That is why witches mostly have female children. Like anything, it can be got around. The mage gene, being on the Y chromosome is inherited father to son. The only instances of it occurring in female children involve irregularities, XXY babies with hormonal changes so the baby is physically female. The

Goddesses are like that. The wizard gene is weak in males, but when doubly inherited by a female the resulting magic can be strong." River hesitated. "This isn't according to the text, but I've heard . . ."

"Please restrain yourself from unproven gossip, River."

River opened her mouth, then shut it.

Her mother sighed. "Oh, go ahead. You'll tell the girls outside of class anyway. I might as well hear it."

"I understand that girls with one witch and one wizard gene are strongly magical, and often wind up as these little gods."

Her mother grimaced. "That's actually probably true, and why we have amended our rules, so we don't produce any more of them. Pay attention. Witches should not cross with wizards. Nor do we use any of the various methods of circumventing the female selection gene, *especially* if we mate with mages.

"You've all seen the pathetic results of these crosses. There really is such a thing as too much magic. While mages and wizards have psychic glow, and are very attractive, I recommend against intercourse with them during your fertile periods."

Amused squirmed. "Is it true that witches have more trouble getting pregnant than ordinary women? Is that why some people call us mules?"

Firefly sighed. "There are numerous incompatibilities between some of our artificial genes, and normal chromosomes. And among the different artificial genes for that matter. But we are not sterile hybrids. But yes, we do have a lower fertility rate than normals. But frankly, we're busy enough that we wouldn't want endless strings of children interrupting our studies. So it hardly matters."

Flattered was sitting up straight and bright-eyed. "What about seducing gods?"

"The Old Gods and the little gods have both a witch gene and a mage gene. So long as you do not use a spell for a male child there is no problem. Of course, you'd best be careful they don't use one on you. Not all of them are considerate of *your* desires." Firefly nodded. "Good. You have the basics. Now, River tell me what danger you face."

"When a witch loses her virginity, there's a leap of psychic energy which can cause her partner's blood pressure to spike. Then as she begins channeling, if she doesn't control the energy flow quickly enough, she can drain the man, and then herself, of personal energy, umm, glycogen, causing anything from a slight weakness to severe debilitation or death."

"Amused, how will you avoid this problem?"

"I will pick someone with moderate glow, because their nervous system can handle the zap with less effect on their blood pressure. Then I will choke down the energy flow and shut it off before either of us is drained."

"Exactly. Now we will start with meditation, and then we will practice shunting power. This is not too different from channeling. By learning to control the rate and amount of shunting, you will come as close to practicing control of channeling as we are capable of. Any questions?"

River nodded. "I can already do some healing."

Firefly snorted. "You can suppress pain for a short while, and press wounds together, sometimes long enough for the cause to resolve itself. After you give birth you will be able to detect the cause of the pain and cure it, and micro manipulate wounds, rebuilding the injured tissues. The difference is quite striking. As you shall see, hopefully within a year."

They were already sitting cross legged, and dropped into a light mediation state easily. Or should have been able to. Amused and Flattered were both uneven and spiking with excitement.

Firefly sighed. "You will not advance for at least a month, so settle down."

River settled in, easily enough, but now she had things to meditate about. Simon.

I'd hate to hurt him. Quite apart from the criminal penalties, I rather like the man. Pity, he's good looking and obviously intelligent. Not the worst fellow to pick as a father for my witch daughter. But that little bit of glow he has might mean he's a wizard. Hands off.

But if I did it off-cycle, so I didn't get pregnant . . .

Chapter Five

May, 2236

New Tokyo, Asia

"In theory, every winter we should be sweeping up the small debris, and altering the orbits of the larger chunks. Eventually we'll have cleared the orbit of all the comets." Simon had a glass of wine in one hand, a tiny plate with two hors d'oeuvres in the other, leaving him with the usual party dilemma of how to eat the goodies.

The God of Art sniffed dismissively. "And we should waste our time helping the astronomers, why? We couldn't do anything about it if our own doom was bearing down on us."

The other god raised his eyebrows. Art was a good looking man. Peace was drawing the eyes of every woman in the room, irrespective of age or marital status.

"We could raise shields, for a brief period. Or perhaps those dimensional bubbles would be useful. But all things considered, that's not the route to peace I'd like to see."

Simon raised an eyebrow. "Peaceful coexistence of city-states seems to be working for the most part. Although I really wish Kroll or whatever his name is, would have moved further away from everyone else."

Art snickered. "Kelso. Only a university professor would

say something so foolish to the God of Peace. What do you say we turn him into a toad for the evening, Pax?"

Simon stiffened, but Pax gave him a look of utter disinterest. "Why bother?" He turned away, nodding to a tall boy. "Richie, I didn't know you were in town."

Richie? The God of Eternal Youth?

"Just got here a couple of days ago." He looked around the room. "Edmund's here, but not Barry? Do you suppose he finally killed his brother?" His eyes tracked toward a slinky platinum blonde and he left without so much as a wave.

"Never did have any manners." Art curled a lip and turned to bow to an exquisite little woman. Colorful silks shown against her deep tan complexion. "Mercy, so good to have you back for the summer."

Simon stayed where he was, trying to be unobtrusive and overlooked. *Five gods here tonight. At least.* This was the first time he'd seen any of this batch up close, and an opportunity to listen in as they spoke . . . Richie was getting excessively friendly with his pale blonde, but she seemed to be encouraging it. Simon choked faintly. The three young women watching the scene were Sally, or rather River, and her two fellow witches, Flattered and Amused. And River looked a whole lot like Richie. He hauled his attention back to the nearer group with an effort.

"The main problem with Zapolo, is that he thinks he'll be in control. His plan to put everyone, worldwide, under one government is excellent. We should support him, and once he's got everything together, take over." One corner Peace's mouth turned up. "Oh, I know you don't like the idea, Art, but think long term. You're much too limited."

Simon boggled a bit. Quietly. Zapolo was a nut case in Scandia, trying to organize a world government while campaigning to be elected President of the World, himself. Kelso paled in comparison. He had simply founded a town and crowned himself king of it.

"Don't like it! That's understating the case by several orders of magnitude." Art scowled. First at Peace, then across the room.

Mayor Brigham was the center of a swirl of people. He looked belligerent, and not at all in a party mood.

"I'd like to hear from him about it, though. Man's got a nasty tendency to call the city his. Bet he'd like the idea of a President of the World."

Simon's attention drifted again. A big red haired man with two young men, obviously his sons, in tow, had approached Richie.

The three redheads were notable for their leering attention to the young witches. Richie stiffened. One arm around the platinum blonde, he turned her away from the group.

The older redhead stepped up close to River, and she retreated. His laugh boomed out. The younger men and the other two witches seemed to be finding each other interesting.

River kept retreating, and the older man stalked after her.

The tiny Mercy looked over her shoulder. "About time you

showed up, Edmund. We need an update on your side of the world." She walked over to him, the other gods trailing along. Simon found himself standing alone, with no reason to follow.

River retreated right through the group of gods and kept going. She did a double take when she spotted him, and veered his direction.

He looked at her, his heart sinking. "That was a fast retreat. Know him, do you?"

"The God of Vice? I regret to say I know him well enough to run at first sight. And keep going. Excuse me." She turned and he caught her elbow.

"And the other one, that was Richie, the God of Eternal Youth, eh? Perhaps I should ask you how old you are."

"Eww. No. I am not on those sorts of terms with him."

"That blonde is."

"That's not blonde, it's gray. White. *That* is my mother." She pulled her elbow from his grasp and slid off behind a crowd of people.

Her mother. And no doubt Richie is her father.

He felt a faint pang as he realized the young witch was solidly in the enemy camp. *Girl's lucky she hasn't been pushed into being a little god, she must have double witch power genes and at least one complete set of the rest of the magic genes. No wonder she's so damned attractive. And I need to leave her completely alone.*

He closed his eyes in pain. *Or use her. She might be a valuable information source.*

It was one thing to realize that you'd be using people in the course of your espionage career, and quite another to use a woman you were pulled to. Simon braced his shoulders and looked around for more interesting people. *I'd better get to work, I've got another unpleasant duty later tonight.*

***

Amused and Flattered seemed quite taken by the brothers. Her mother's admonitions swirled around her head. Witches could mate with mages. Which is what these two would be. Probably nothing on their X chromosomes, since they hadn't been pulled into little god roles. But they'd have at least one complete set of magic genes from their father. So long as they didn't slip her triad some sex selection potions, they were a pretty good choice.

She shrugged and slipped down the stairs to check the second floor. And here was the supposedly virtuous brother, holding court with some other gentlemen. River stayed on the far side of the room, edging toward the stairs that continued down on the far side of the room. A trio of men mounted those stairs with haste and hustled across the room. The man who strolled up after them had hair so pale it was nearly white, and eyes so blue they looked artificial. She didn't look around at the tinkle of broken glass. That was pretty much inevitable around the God of Just Deserts. *Mr. Instant Karma, himself.* He nodded politely in the general direction of Virtue and sauntered across to the next stairs. At least he'd left his dogs at home. Probably. River eyed the stairs down. A trip to the buffet was in order. She loaded a plate with meatballs, dribbled on a bit of sauce in case she wound up eating them herself, and descended the stairs.

Art's museum home was an upside down step pyramid. This level was the smallest of the three layers. But not small. A group of four bronze horses galloping, tails high, necks arched in high spirits. A bull, menacing and huge, horns lowered. Two young women, heads together, arms around each other's waists, giggling. All bronze, no marble. River turned to the double glass doors and pushed through to the warm twilight spring air.

Movement from the side. Large low shapes, about the size of ponies . . .

"Ah, he brought all four of you? Would you *nice* doggies like some meat balls?"

They would. She shared them out, got sniffed a bit more thoroughly than she would have liked, then they drifted off into the deepening shadows. She hunted around the garden, veering at the sight of a couple of very realistic statues, and found a bench to sit on. Mother, Amused and Flattered would be along eventually. But they weren't who she was waiting for. What was Simon doing, in the gods' inner circle?

As if she didn't know. The question was, which one was he working for.

A gust of magical potential swirled.

Edmund Vice again? Perhaps she ought not have isolated

herself. She looked for a line of retreat as a tall form materialized out of thin air.

"What are the odds that the World will be hit by a large meteor next year?"

River looked at the man cautiously. Not Vice. Chance. This was the real god, the inspiration of all the lucky ladies in the casinos. "Low, I hope. But I don't know. What are the odds?"

"We don't know either, but we're collecting data. We're getting so many premonitions, we're worried."

She straightened. "How large? How much damage? Next year!" Her voice sharpened as his meaning sank in.

"Half a mile, in my dreams. It will kill everything in a ten mile circle, at least. There will be serious damage, deaths, out a hundred miles, further. Once the observatory has cataloged the asteroids, the dark pieces, Logic and I will refine our numbers as it closes in. That's all I can do, but the others say we should do something, not leave it to chance." His smile went crooked, and he walked away.

She heard giggles and male laughter, going the other direction. It seemed the rest of her triad had found what they wanted. *Mother will be furious, to have attracted the attention of the God of Vice. Or maybe not, she ought not have brought them along if she didn't want them to meet gods and their children.*

River sat, disinclined to move for long enough to recognize the unnaturalness of her state, and hunt down the tiny delicate spell Chance had used to avoid her following him, questioning him further. She memorized it first, then snapped it.

She looked around. The garden was empty, a few of Art's guests walking away down the driveway. And there was Simon, now. Bowing his head politely to Art as he stepped out the doors. He walked briskly, some destination in mind.

River slipped quietly after him. Her pale dress blended into the local stonework; she hardly needed the unnoticeable spell.

Simon was easy to follow, never looking back. She wondered about his tense shoulders and tendency to stomp. He passed through a middle class neighborhood into one with the slightly larger houses of the educated professionals. He stopped dead in the middle of a block, shoulders hunched and hands jammed in his pockets. She studied the houses beyond him. Prosperous, large, well landscaped yards. One stood out as larger than the rest, but not to the point of being odd. That was the one Simon finally approached.

River backtracked, found an alley and walked down it. From the back there was clearly a connection between four of the homes. There were no dividing fences. She caught glimpses between the tall fence slats, of a lawn that ran the length of the four houses without restraint. There were children running around, playing tag in the dark. *Up at midnight? Not much parental supervision around here.* The large house was the northern-most of the four. A cross fence divided it from the next, a quiet place with a neglected looking garden, and a few fallen fence boards. She slipped through a hole and staying close to the fence, crossed to the narrow side yard between it and the large gray stone house. She eyed it wistfully. Dare she trespass further?

"I wouldn't recommend it."

She spun around. The voice had been quiet, with a bit of a shake to it. The stooped gray haired form was barely visible through the netted window, a tiny shape in a big chair.

"Er, sorry. I was, well . . ."

"Wondering what really goes on with those people? I'll bet you're one of those new professional women reporters, aren't you?" The old lady leaned forward. "Well, let me tell you, those wizards are sick. Child abusers, in my opinion. They want the boys to get the girls pregnant when they're young—when the boys are young, they don't really care about the girls. Then on the boys' sixteen birthday—they cut 'em!" The grey head bobbed. "Eunuchs, every one of them. That's what gives them their power. The old ones marry the pregnant women, and raise the children as their own, but most likely they're grandchildren, through the boy or girl, or both. They don't really seem to care." She pounded her fist on the arm of her chair. "It's evil, I tell you, evil, what they do." She leaned forward and glared. "Now you get! I don't want those evil people to notice me. Get!"

River retreated. Wizards. Simon Golan, Golian Wizards. Why hadn't she made the connection? She slipped through the hole in the fence and walked away.

So. There it was. A connection between The God of Art

and the wizards. Which got her nowhere. What could the wizards do that Art and his Little Gods couldn't? Of course Art was also collecting the witches' support. *So he's lining up* all *the magic users.*

Perhaps she should do a bit of research. If that little old lady was right about the castration enabling the wizards' power . . . what a hideous choice. In the unlikely event the boys were given a choice. But would it explain why the Golians were as powerful as most witches? A fourth organized group of magicians. Gods, witches, mages and now wizards. With the little gods scattered about, and about to find themselves used by their older but less numerous Archetypes.

Simon. Well, if he was a wizard, and not an ordinary go-between, she could just stop thinking about him, couldn't she? Damn. He hadn't acted like a eunuch.

***

Simon had to consciously relax his jaw before speaking. "When I got your message, I hoped for some show of friendship, family. I should have known better. No. I will not perpetuate the family. I will not give you children to mutilate. If you would at least let them decide for themselves . . ."

"They'd all say no. At that age, I would have. But now, oh, now, the power I have, the things I can do . . ."

"I don't care." Simon huffed out a tight breath. "I'm glad to see that you are doing well, *Father*. But I won't be back."

"Take this. My man said you were drooling over a witch. It's an aphrodisiac, a fertility aid, and forces a witch to have a boy."

"Force. Always force."

"You don't want to pass your X to a daughter, do you? And it is also a truth drug. The little bitch will tell you just what she really thinks of you, and how she's just using you to advance her own powers."

Truth drug. *Oh Hell. It could be useful. And I will not take advantage of her, even if she is a follower of Mercy.* He hesitated, then picked up the vial. It tingled in his hands. One of the few magics he was capable of was the detection of magic.

And this magic was strong. All he had to do was figure out how to get a witch to drink it without noticing.

Chapter Six

June 2236

New Tokyo, Asia

It was a frustrating three weeks since the party. She'd located Simon's home, a small apartment just outside the university, and followed him. He was frequent visitor at Art's museum, and even ventured into Just Desert's territory. He'd been limping once, but hadn't seemed to have drawn the God's dogs into a personalized delivery of karmic justice.

Amused and Flattered had been disappointed that their swains had disappeared the day after the party. The witches who had trained in health matters shook their heads. Neither of them were pregnant. Keep trying.

And they all looked pointedly at River.

"I'm a messenger. How am I going to do that, waddling around pregnant, needing to stay near a midwife and then with a baby?"

"Really, River." Her mother shook her head reprovingly. "The Senior Sister wants you to advance in power. I think you should try for an immediate pregnancy, you'll be back in shape by next year, the baby can stay here." Her mother's nose wrinkled. "Amused and Flattered are just advancing to keep the triad together. They weren't supposed to get ahead of you. But they'll be handy to keep your baby while you're away. But! If you don't want a baby, fine. But you must learn how to channel." Her mother rattled around in her cupboard and pulled out a small vial. "Here, take this. It's an aphrodisiac, not a fertility aid, since you don't want children yet. A couple of drops in your wine, a couple in his and you'll see that it's all good fun."

River closed her eyes. *Damn it all! I don't want to use Simon. I want . . . I want to take my time and find out how much I like him. Except. Who is he working for? University of Cairo my ass. No longer than it took to form a legitimate sounding background, I'll bet. Where would he have been before that? Athens? Maybe. Maybe New Miami. Next time I get down there, I'll have to ask around about this "professor."*

She smiled wryly and took the vial. *After all, I don't have to worry about* hurting *him, he's the enemy. Maybe he'll babble in bed.*

So. How do I get him to drink some wine?

At this time of day, the Sea View Restaurant was quiet, even though far from empty. Perched on a headland with two hundred and eighty degrees of floor to ceiling windows, it lived up to its name.

Simon looked over the wine list. "Daring. I wouldn't have thought Art would want Wolf's Head sold in his premises."

River chuckled. "Art says keeping the Old Wolf busy with his wine is for the good of humanity." *And the Wolf laughs and agrees.*

That got a snort from Simon. He ordered a white wine, and opened his menu. The waiters whisked around with silent efficiency, pouring a smooth fruity Pinot Blanc.

Go north, away from the city. River blinked to clear her head.

"I heard that Art owns thirty percent of the restaurant, the windows being his entire investment." Simon's gaze crossed from the busy harbor on one side, lingered on the offshore islands, and moved on to the rough, rocky coast stretching to the south. He settled back in his chair and eyed her.

River suppressed a grin; he hadn't seen her pour the vial into their glasses. "I've heard he charmed the refrigerated boxes as well. But all this glass is impressive."

His eyes crinkled. "So long as it doesn't make you seasick."

"Not as long as I have my feet firmly on the ground. I thought you were a physicist, not a magologist." All it had taken was a chance meeting in the street to turn into an invitation to dinner. A bit to her relief, not in a venue where she could easily seduce him. She was undecided about whether it had been wise to use her mother's potion. *No matter how strong, it can't make me leap on him and ravish him in public.* She slipped the vial into a pocket by feel, while she admired the view.

Embarrassed, he fussed with the silver ware and then shifted the wine glasses back out of elbow-knocking range. "I'm incurably curious. Take your witch name, for instance. River, where the two women you introduced me to are Amused and

Flattered. River doesn't fit the theme; am I correct in assuming that means you aren't a native?

"So to speak. My Mother, Firefly, is from here, but she traveled a lot when she was younger. My oldest sister was born in Red River, the next in Scandia and the next in New Bombay. Then all the way back to Sahara, where I was born. I think I'd traveled the world before I was ten. At any rate, I gained my witch name from the Sahara Pyramid at birth, and kept it, even though I've been in five pyramids since gaining power." *Ha! My mother's amblings are well enough known to be checkable, so he can research and realize I told the strict truth.*

"Huh. And still traveling. Despite the sea sickness."

"I like going places." She took a sip of wine. The spells just about knocked her out of her chair. She hastily spun out a mental dampening, even a wizard might pick up on something like this. "Well, not the seasick part."

"Does it get better or worse as you get older? I've heard about all the witches steps to power." He reddened a bit and reached for his own wine glass.

She tried, and most likely failed, to suppress a smirk. "Get the twinkle out of your eye, I'm not going to discuss advancement through major life experience stepping stones. I expect I'll get more seasick with advancing power. Pity overland travel is so slow." She took another sip of wine. *Mother should have warned me!* River turned her attention to the menu.

Simon glanced at his, and settled back, still with the expression of a researcher on the hunt.

River jumped in first. "It's very odd, the three new sorts of people we have around, the last two generations."

The waiter reappeared to take their orders. Simon included an appetizer, and a Wolf's Head shiraz to have with dinner.

"Three? Gods, Goddesses and what?" His fingertips traced a line down her arm, pulled back.

"No, those are the standard. Now, just in two generations, we have Little Gods, Golian Wizards and the Sea Kings. Not that they're really kings, in the old literary sense." She turned, and her knee rubbed his.

"They're certainly lords of all they survey. Did you notice anything odd about our voyage north?" He retreated a bit. Damn, hadn't she got enough into his glass?

"The way we never sloshed back against the dock, nor had a seriously unfavorable wind? The crew seemed ordinary, the captain very sure of himself."

"And barnacles won't grow on his hull and his ship will never sink, nor can he be drowned. If you believe everything you hear." He smiled at her, then nervously shifted his gaze out the window as she reached for her glass.

She swapped it for his nearly empty glass, then touched it to her lips. "Well, people who aren't witches tend to disbelieve what we can do as well, so I shouldn't be too skeptical." She paused while the waiter delivered a platter of little tidbits. "And I wasn't even as sick as I usually am. So, maybe there are mages with an affinity for the sea."

"Ah. Magic users, sticking together. Do you believe in mermaids?"

"Umm, I've seen some very impressive transformation experiments, but witches that can change into dolphins? Who have lived in the sea for generations? Umm . . . I'm a bit skeptical."

"And the Little Gods?" He poured more wine for her, and sampled his own. He didn't seem to notice anything so the damping of perception spell must be working.

If I were already a Bright Quarter Moon, I'd have power enough to be sure. But then, I wouldn't be here trying to seduce this man . . . Right? "Poor things. They're really being dumped on by the collective subconscious. But I know a bunch of them who have resisted and have reasonably normal lives. Someone being pressured into the mold of the God of War can be a soldier or a guard. No need to make a spectacle out of oneself. One of the 'Gods of Chance' is a stockbroker, another a speculator." River shrugged. "And the Travelers, well, some hang around cities, but most find jobs that involve traveling. 'Travelers' is nearly a synonym for freight haulers, these days."

Salads arrived and they crunched vegetables for a moment.

"As I understand it, when there were only the thirteen old gods, you could pray to one of them, and he'd appear. Or at least the God of War and the God of the Roads worked like that. But now the prayer gets absorbed by the little gods, and the old, original god stays home, fat and happy." It was definitely his knee drifting over to bump hers, not the other way around.

River raised her eyebrows. "Huh. I didn't realize the little gods interfered with prayer reception. So actually there would be a practical reason to have a little war god as a troop mascot—he'd keep the real thing from being used against you." River leaned forward a bit. Extra cleavage couldn't possibly hurt.

Simon removed his gaze from her. "I hadn't thought of it that way, but it makes sense. The other old gods I've seen always have a 'God of War' in their private guards. I thought they were amusing themselves."

"Instead, it was practical. Huh. I don't know why so many magicians with two power collection genes are . . . eccentric. I don't know why the collective subconscious isn't satisfied with the Old Gods. Or why they don't invent something new." *He's fighting the potion, drat.* River sat back and shifted her knee away.

"That would be more interesting." Simon flashed a quick grin. "Why not a God of Music? A Goddess of Beauty?"

The white wine was gone, and Simon shook his head at the offer of another bottle.

"God of Thieves; goodness, look at all the Robin Hood and Black Bart tropes around." She ran her hand up his arm. Strong wiry muscles. "The God of Spies."

"Yes, think of the stories about the Super Spy. He out fights, out talks, out magics everyone. He's got the fastest horse, working equipment from the Exile. Always gets the girl, but never finds true love."

River met his warm gaze for a long moment. "Unless she gets killed, so the Super Spy goes off to get revenge. That's not fair!" She leaned back and got a grip on herself, and her hands off Simon, as the waiter took the salad plates away and delivered her steak.

"God of Assassins, God of Scumbags."

"Not all the Archetypes are gods. Think about women. The Girl Next Door. The Perfect Wife."

"Dumb blonde. Trouble Maker. The Other Woman. Ice Queen. The Black Widow."

River snickered. "You seem well up on the negative stereotypes."

The waiter brought the shiraz and poured.

And her knee was back where it belonged, but she'd dropped a shoe and was running her foot up and down his boot. She made herself stop. Concentrated on the steak and searched for a change of subject.

"I haven't heard of any updates from the astronomers, about the comet swarm. Do they still think we'll have more next year? I thought they were in a four year orbit."

"Yeah, well any given comet comes back roughly every four years. But the comets aren't evenly disbursed along the orbit, they clump up, all in roughly one quarter of the orbit. There's debris all along the whole of the orbit, from some original collision in the asteroid belt, but definitely a concentration. All the comets and asteroids are in approximately the same orbit, their perihelion—closest approach to the Sun—is close to the Earth's position every Winter Solstice. Any individual comet comes around every four years and fourteen days, so it falls gradually behind us. But the comets being spread out, means that one comet or another is close just about every fourth winter for about twenty-four or twenty-eight years. Then we get a break of seventy-four to seventy-seven years with just a few and generally small asteroids whizzing by at the Winter Solstice. Then we're back to the start of the thick, heavy stuff."

"Asteroids and comets—it's just a matter of whether they have exposed surface ice, right?"

"Yes. They're mostly conglomerates, rocks, sand, dust and ice, loosely bound together. Some larger, solid rocks or metals in there, too. If they've got ice, they show up like a beacon. We have trouble seeing the ones without ice, because of the glare of the sun off the sublimating ice of the others."

"So there are surprises lurking amongst the comets?"

"Yes. Nasty ones. We're almost done with this century's major encounters. Unfortunately, the astronomers spotted a wild card, a comet that came so close four years ago it affected its orbit drastically. I think we had a near disaster, and it'll be swinging past right when we're in the area, next winter. It just broke up. There must have been a bit of heat expansion splitting or something, because three small comets lit up unexpectedly."

"Oh. I see. So we don't have much information on these three? Other than they've got ice on the surface?"

"Exactly, and it's badly placed for observation. We'll get a better grasp of it now that we're past the summer solstice, we should be able to see it in the early morning hours, any day now."

"Humph, just when we thought we'd ditched these bad winters for a while. Two late spring plantings in a row could bring our grain reserves to a dangerous low." Damn, her knee was back where it didn't belong again. Or was it his that was encroaching on her territory?

He leaned her way. "Maybe we need a God of Comets?"

"But is that good or bad? Think about Just Deserts."

"Ooo. A God of Celestial Disasters instead of individual ones? How big would his dogs have to be?"

"Dragons. I think they'd have to be dragons, to fly up and drag rocks and fly ice cubes around. You know?"

He blinked. "I know I should have stuck with one bottle of wine."

"Probably sensible." River blinked at her empty plate. She sort of remembered the steak being outstanding. "But too late."

The waiter brought the dessert tray around.

"Death by chocolate." She managed to not imagine rubbing it on him and licking it off. Almost.

"Yes, that's how I'm going to feel tomorrow. Bring two."

They ate, eyeing each other warily as the dinner came to a conclusion. Knees touching. Simon paid the bill and they walked out. He'd picked her up in an open carriage. The bay mares yawned as he boosted her into the seat.

I can't take him home to the pyramid . . . will he invite me home?

They stared at each other uncertainly.

"Maybe, maybe we ought to go look at the stars, or comets or whatever from Fuji Point. Sober up a bit, so we don't do anything either of us might regret, in the morning." Simon looked like he was regretting those words even as he spoke them.

"Hmm, I, yes. Sober up. Good idea, God of Gentlemen."

"Ouch! Are you a Good Little Girl?" Simon hoisted himself into the seat beside her.

"Let's define 'Good' as a starting point." She scooted a bit closer.

"Ooo. Goddess of Double-entendres." He leaned to pick up the reins, and settled back, closer. Touching.

By the time they'd reached the point, she was the "Good" in quotes Goddess and he had decided to be the God of Perverts.

Being far away from anything resembling a bed proved to be no barrier.

The pre-dawn hangover was brutal, the pain spell effective, the embarrassment extreme.

But the goodbye kiss lingered.

Chapter Seven

August 2236

New Tokyo, Asia

Four weeks later, Simon was sipping water at an afternoon reception at the Mayor's House. And wished he wasn't reduced to reading lips from across the room, and the body language of the gods and goddesses with their backs to him was even more opaque.

Nods. Shrugs. "We need to keep on top of this."

"...my personal representative..."

"You should go, yourself."

A disagreeing lift of one shoulder and Mercy was turning to summon River with a preemptive gesture. The girl, woman, responded instantly, nodded twice, and departed.

Simon thought about following her, and felt himself blush. And in any case, she was moving with decisive speed. He'd draw too much attention if he tried to catch up with her. *Should have brought the carriage, could have offered her a ride.* He kicked himself mentally. Last thing he needed was for everyone to know he had a fast team at hand. *I am a destitute but brilliant professor. The gods keep inviting me to parties because I agree with their vision of what the universities should be indoctrinating their students with. I cannot step out of that role.*

But River would know what the gods were all so excited about.

He eased out of the group he'd been pretending to be listening to while reading lips across the room. Thinking invisible thoughts, he ditched his glass and wandered out.

He emptied his mind and let his feet take him wherever his erratic and weak talents desired. Wizardry was very different than the other magics. It consisted of noticing things, of coincidences and luck. Being in the right place, meeting the right people, saying the right thing. All apparently by accident. But at a nearly subconscious level, and erratic at best.

But today it was working, because there was River up ahead of him, talking to two other women . . . passengers from the ship, that girl and her maid, and a stranger. The man glowed a bit, and was smiling at River. Simon dodged behind a fruit stand, and walked behind a fabric booth with hanging swatches of cloth.

"How can you talk about going off with her?" Wailing, hurt, feminine, tones.

River sounded exasperated. "I'm offering him a job, not eloping with him. I need to get a bunch of very fancy camping gear up Mount Tambour to the observatory. It should be a three week trip, each direction."

"Oh, yeah, two months alone together with this silk tent and fancy rugs and cushions and . . ."

"Old Gods! I'm not even going to set it up until we get

there. I'll be bringing a little camping tent for my use, and I assume Mike has something of the sort for himself?"

"Of course. Heidi, it'll be fine. I need the money, *we* need the money, for next year."

Simon took a peek. The man was good looking, tall and muscular, standing nearer Heidi than her mother would have approved of. Black hair, dark skin . . . Traveler's Child, which, as a category included not just children, but grand and great grandchildren, plus the little gods that had picked up the archetypical characteristics of the God of the Roads, whether or not they were related to *The* God. This fellow looked like one of Harry's children. The maid was standing back, arms crossed, frowning. Heidi was pouting, and oozed closer to the man.

So. River was taking a silk tent and various fripperies to the observatory. And not for her own use. Heh. Typical of everything he'd read about Mercy. Make the girl do all the work, then the Goddess would teleport up there and harangue the astronomers for whatever information the gods were looking for.

They want to be certain that there will, or will not, be a second comet winter in a row. They can play the market on food stuffs, buy up a lot of the late harvest. They don't have any worries about storage. They'll be even richer, or more in control—or both—by next spring.

He eased back and followed River at a distance. Mike departed, Heidi at his side and the maid following. They returned with an open wagon pulled by a pair of horses. Simon eyed the beasts with a horseman's eye. Not youngsters, but good strong animals. If they kept the load light, they'd have no problem getting up the mountain. River started loading the wagon immediately. Large rolls of fabric, rugs, oil cloths. A small tin charcoal grill, and charcoal. Lots of canned foods. Some dried. *Heaven forbid Mercy should eat beans!* They left the market and headed for the Pyramid's little self contained community.

Simon gritted his teeth. *I can deduce what they're going to ask the astronomers, so I don't actually have to go there myself.* He turned and stomped off.

And failed to see her the next day at a garden party given by the God of Vice. Amused and Flattered were there, climbing all over the redheaded brothers, and pulling them away into the extensive maze the god had brought here, along with a three story stone mansion.

Vice himself was looking over the other women, and with a nasty smile turned his attention to the Mayor's wife. She sidled away nervously, trying to keep her husband between herself and the god. Pax and Mercy were together again, verbally dissecting politicians. Art circulated, talking about inconsequentialities. A wave of unease rippled across the garden as the God of Just Deserts showed up. One of his dogs pissed on the mayor's leg before the mayor noticed and moved away. With his teeth gritting, but too much control to kick one of *those* dogs. The huge boxer grinned and trotted away. The other dogs wandered off, one stopping to poop in the middle of the sidewalk, before trotting off into the maze. People started moving toward the central plaza, not wanting to risk a solo canine encounter.

Simon circulated, briefly touching base with a number of influential people.

Shrieks and screams from the maze focused everyone's attention that direction. No one seemed inclined to see who needed to be rescued. Simon looked the other direction and saw the Mayor's wife walking off on Vice's arm.

This party could take a nasty turn. Or is that, nastier?

The shrieks turned to cursing, died down. Everyone turned away, tried to resume a normal party air.

Amused and Flattered stumbled out of the maze, supporting each other. Dresses torn and showing a few streaks of mud, but reasonably dry. Hair dripping pond water.

Amused looked furious and stalked up to Michael Omega. Stuck a finger in his face. "Those damned dogs! The next time I see one, I'm going to kill him!" She staggered a bit as she tried to stalk off. Flattered was crying, but also looking mad. She glared and followed the other witch.

Simon looked over at Frasier. "Do you suppose we ought to go look for their young men?"

"I'm not setting foot in there."

Other people around them nodded.

Simon bit his lip.

"Your curiosity is going to get you into trouble one of these days." Frasier sighed. "All right. I'll admit I want to know just how bad those dogs are too. They can't possibly live up to their reputations."

Simon led the way. A small crowd followed. *Sick thrill seekers, every one of us.*

A few wrong turns, then they followed the sounds of masculine curses to a central pond. Two naked and wet redheads were chasing four dogs with clothing in their jaws. The two women in the crowd almost managed to turn their laughter into exclamations of horror as their husbands hastily guided them away. The dogs dropped the clothes and ran off, fortunately in the other direction.

Simon assisted in the hunting down and delivery of torn garments. "What on earth did you do to deserve that?"

The slightly taller one, Dangelo if he remembered correctly, snorted. "The girls couldn't keep us straight, so we swapped."

Ristophe grinned. "And then swapped back. I'm not sure what *they* did to deserve the dogs humping them and chasing them into the pond. I'll bet it was almost as amusing as watching them get humped was."

"That is disgusting, young man." Professor Frasier dropped a ripped pair of pants on the ground and marched off.

The rest of the observers started moving off. ". . . he didn't mean those dogs actually . . ."

Simon shook his head. "Would you like me to inform your father?"

"Gawd no! We'll get ourselves inside, thanks awfully. A

touch of illusion and we're out of here. I suppose the girls are gone?"

"And out of the mood, anyway." Dangelo shrugged and concentrated. A fog concentrated itself around him and firmed up into an illusion of intact clothing. His brother did the same and they headed off through one of the other paths.

Simon shook his head, looking around the muddy, stirred up pond, the wet grass with shreds of clothing still laying about. "Personally I prefer horses." He walked off, keeping his eyes open for large dogs, although what he could do if they decided he deserved a dose of karma . . . All right, he knew it was really the collective subconscious, sans any civilized restraint of the conscious mind, that moved the god and his hell hounds, but man and dogs got the blame, and were shunned by most sensible folk. Back at the central plaza the mayor was frowning at his wife. She looked half asleep with a sweet smile on her face.

Well, Edmund is the God of Vice. Attend his party at your own risk, because most judges are too damned scared to take action against any of them.

***

River tried to avoid thinking about how much trouble she might be sideswiped by when they returned. Heidi was cuddled up beside Mike on the driver's bench. Mary was splitting her time glaring, looking reproachful and hauling Heidi aside to lecture her on the lack of wisdom she was displaying. Mike had pushed the pace the first three days, no doubt hoping to outdistance anyone Mrs. Gardener might send after them. The big harness horses could walk along for hours at four miles an hour. Add trotting on the few down hill portions of the road, and occasionally on the flats and they made sixty miles a day, easily. But the ground was rising steadily and the climbs were only going to get steeper as they headed into the mountains proper. Their daily mileage started dropping fast. Mount Tambour was the eastern most peak of the Himalayas. River had seen maps of the other Earth, the one the Gods and her own ancestors had been exiled from. Here, the Himalayas were taller and extended further east. The Indo peninsula was much larger, with all the islands and part of a continent called Australia shoved up against it. The area called India was smaller. Shoved further under and up on Asia, hence the larger mountains.

Tambour was a modest peak in comparison to her sisters to the west, but still a substantial climb.

Just sitting in the wagon, River felt exhausted. It was very unlike her, and she wondered a bit uneasily if she could be pregnant. *It's only been five weeks, I shouldn't be tired already, should I? And the timing was wrong to catch, but my monthly . . . hasn't. But it's only barely overdue. Just a few days, really. Damn, damn, damn! And a wizard for a father, poor girl!*

And she hadn't even spoken to Simon since that parting kiss. She'd cured their hangovers magically . . . well, doused the pain temporarily. Nothing could douse the embarrassment. She sighed. Rolling around in the grass all night long. Pity she hadn't thought of a reason for Simon to haul her up the observatory. A couple of weeks of rolling around in the grass . . . She pulled out a book on astronomy and forced herself to start reading.

***

Three weeks. River should be nearly to the observatory by now. Simon sighed. *With her damned handsome son of the Traveler. I don't know why she wanted me, with little gods all over the damned place.* He winced suddenly. *Apart from that potion I dumped in her wine. Oh damn it, what did Father say? Aphrodisiac, fertility aid, guarantee a boy child, truth potion . . . What was I thinking? Oh yeah, that I'd behave. Just take advantage of the truth spell. And then I drank too much, forgot I was being responsible, and didn't even ask her any leading questions. We just played silly gods and made love all night long.*

Why didn't I go talk to her, the next day? Or the next? I wasted weeks, and now it's been almost a month, and what if she is pregnant? Old Gods! Well, wasn't that what witches were supposed to want? But when she has a son, she'll know I dosed her. I'll be lucky if she only ignores me. I have to go talk to her.

He eyed himself in the mirror. Nice suit, but obviously not

very expensive. Very nice silk tie, that he'd worn to dozens of parties so far, as if it were his only really good tie. *Playing my part.* He stalked out into the twilight and walked down to the corner to catch the horse tram. The party was at Mercy's tonight. And no doubt with the same batch of people. He switched to the cable car and dropped off at the top of the hill. Mercy's home, transplanted from Miami.

What did my ancestors do to deserve to be exiled along with these thirteen beings? Even the ones I like and serve can be so strange and inhuman sometimes.

He bowed to the Goddess. She smiled charmingly and he melted under the regard of those brilliant brown eyes, so deep a man could drown in them. She turned away from him and he staggered back a step. He shook his head and walked carefully away. He took a drink and hid in a corner to observe and regain his senses.

"She likes doing that to men." The high pitched voice came from down around his belt buckle.

A girl, eight, maybe nine?

"A hundred and seventeen. Mother keeps storing me away and forgetting about me."

Simon winced. The girl had plain brown hair and eyes, sallow skin with none of her mother's dark honey glow.

"Every time I wake up, everybody I knew has died. Or grown up. It's a good thing she doesn't let me have any friends." The girl's voice was aching with loneliness and there were tears in her eyes as she looked away.

"What about the other gods? Is one of them your father?"

She shrugged. "Mother says she teleported sperm to get me, that she's still a virgin. And the only one that even cares is Harry, and I don't look at all like him. If I ever grow up, maybe I'll marry him."

Simon shivered. *Four generations since the Exile. And she's been allowed out only enough to grow to eight or nine years of age.*

He heard a giggle over the background noise, and tracked its source. Amused, with her constant companion Flattered. They were in a group of youngsters, no red heads in sight. A few of the older generation were looking askance at them. No one quite knew how to deal with a pair of witches who hadn't sense enough to be both traumatized and ashamed of, well, whatever had really happened.

To his left Art strolled in. The young woman on his arm looked very much like him. Mercy smiled deeply into his eyes and he smiled back. *Is that how she stays so powerful, despite all the vicious petty incidences? And the not so petty, but every bit as vicious, major actions she sometimes takes?*

Edmund and Barry walked in together, one brother golden blonde, the other a flaming redhead. Otherwise identical. According to rumor, Barry attempted to restrain his appetites, but they were the same appetites his brother reveled in. They both had children en-train so to speak. The redheaded brothers were eyeing matched triplet girls. Sixteen or seventeen, breathtakingly beautiful, as blonde as Barry.

"They're witches. Mother says I'm a Goddess, not a witch. I wish I was a witch."

"Are all the gods bringing their children tonight?"

"Some of them. They're trying to show off, prove they're better than Pax. But Mother likes Pax best. I'm glad I don't look like him."

Simon looked down at her. "You don't look like any of them. You look like yourself. Which is the best thing, anyway." He squashed his thoughts and kept observing. Richie came in, alone this time. Then another man who teased at Simon's memory.

"That's Chance."

"Ah. I'm Simon Golan, by the way."

"Pleased to meet you, Dr. Golan. I'm Grace." Her forehead crinkled. "I don't know if I have a last name."

"Well, if you were a witch, it would be Mercydaut. Otherwise I expect it would depend on who your father is."

"Ick. I don't like any of those. I'll be Mrs. Grace Traveler."

"Hmm, Well, until you marry, perhaps you should be Miss Grace Determined."

She laughed out loud, and clapped a hand over her mouth, with a guilty look toward her mother. Mercy was too busy, in a circle of male gods, to be paying her daughter any attention.

The halo of youngsters around them was clumping to one side now, and Simon spotted Amused and Flattered closing in on them.

"Oh, this is going to be interesting." Simon edged a little

nearer.

Amused had a tight smile on her face. "Oh, do introduce us to your *cousins*."

Grace snickered. Then sobered as Mercy looked around with a frown. "Got to go. I'm sorry you won't be alive next time. You're nice." Then she wove through the thin crowd and walked up to her mother. Ugly duckling, beautiful inside. The opposite of her mother. And far enough away that the girl couldn't pick his brain, Simon noted the resemblance of her features to the God of Peace's. She may not have gotten either parent's spectacular coloring, but her face spoke volumes.

"I don't see why we have to go now, Chance! In the middle of a party?" Mercy sounded seriously put out.

Chance just spread his arms. The redheads grabbed Amused and Flattered. They all disappeared. Air whooshed in with a sharp snap, to fill the space where sixteen people had stood.

Simon hissed in annoyance. "Did anyone hear where they were going to go?"

One man turned and stared at him. "They were talking about the observatory, but that's nearly five hundred miles away."

A woman leaned into the open space. "Should we leave this space open, for when they come back?"

Everyone drew back a bit.

"Good idea." Someone in the crowd said.

"Better idea. Where'd the wine go?"

"Damn, damn, damn." Simon bit his lip. Stay or go? Would they be right back? If he left now, it would be weeks before he got there, and well over a month before he returned. Was he about to destroy his ordinary appearance, the only thing that kept him safe in this nest of vipers?

He turned and strode out. Dr. Frasier turned up on his heels. "What are you going to do?"

Frasier was exactly what he looked, but he knew Simon wasn't.

"Get to the observatory as quickly as I can." Simon hopped the tram for the trip down the hill, and jogged for his apartment. By the time he'd gotten the much folded bit of metal out and grabbed his always-ready-to-run smaller case and returned to the street, Frasier had caught up to him.

"What's that? Oh . . ."

Simon unfolded, and unfolded and unfolded the metal, leaned the resulting big square frame up against the wall and led the mares out. They were harnessed, and pulling the light carriage.

"I've always wanted to see one of those trans-dimensional bubbles." Frasier sounded wistful.

"I'll let you play with it when I get back. For now, tell people I'm ill. Or had some crazy idea and ran off to check on it, who knows where." Simon folded the metal frame that sealed the bubble and stuck it in his coat. Tossed the bag into the carriage and climbed in himself.

Frasier was gawping at the horses. "They're pretty. Are

they fast?"

"They are crosses of some of the fastest thoroughbreds and arabians, crossed back twice with the War God's stallion. I've never found their limits, but I'm going to try now. Later, Frasier." He picked up the reins and the mares moved out quickly, picking up his nerves. "God of Travelers, be with me tonight, I need to get someplace fast, with no holdups.

Chapter Eight
September 2236
On the Tokyo-Miami Road

For better or worse, the only excitement on the trip was when Mary caught Heidi and Mike naked in the bushes.

"I can't believe you're so stupid. You aren't even married. You aren't even eloping."

"Yes we are. We just haven't had an opportunity to get married yet."

"And you trust that, that *mage* to marry you?" The maid scowled over at River. "He spends too much time listening to her nonsensical magic lessons. Good grief, all the silly kids' songs and rhymes? There's got to be more to magic than *that*!"

On the twenty-third day they made it up the last climb to the long level ridge that was the top of the mountain. By the time they'd crossed the last two miles to the white dome of the observatory, they had been spotted.

"You're not our supply wagon." The man looked baffled to have visitors.

River gave him a compassionate smile. "I regret to inform you that you're going to have even more visitors. The Goddess of Mercy, I'm sure of. How many other gods? Who knows. This new cluster of comets has everyone worried and wanting more information."

"Huh. Well, for starters, this clump has mostly de-gassed. It's mostly asteroids, we've found eighteen of significant size. So far. The last bright comet just quit, so we can finally over-expose plates and see all the dark ones. We took a bunch of plates over the last few days. We've been measuring them, comparing them to the plates we took last month and calculating the exact orbits of the biggest ones. Should be done in another week or two. No good bothering us until then."

"I'll set up camp, umm, just over the rim, so as to not block anything."

"No campfires. Can't have any light at night. At least camp to the south. The comets are rising slightly to the north." He shook his head. "Good grief. Go camp or something. Let the rest of the crew sleep. We work all night, you know. What am I supposed to do with you?"

"Umm. Right. Sorry, but the gods just don't consider anyone else's convenience."

He rolled his eyes. "Chance comes by, now and then. I know what you mean."

She shivered, remembering the God of Chance's colloquy about his premonitions. Half a mile wide. Time to find out the reality of the situation.

Mike turned the horses south, and they started looking for a good spot to camp.

River picked two spots, well separated. "Trust me, you do not want to be camping right next to the gods. I'll need to be within hailing range, but you want to be over there. Honest."

The little swale was a brief steep climb down from the crest, and would easily hold three tents the size of the one she had for Mercy. She moved stones to smooth the ground, and mentally sliced off big protrusions and softened and molded the rest of the stone. River smiled as she felt how easily the earth power flowed, now. *Wonderful. Bright Quarters are so much more powerful than mere Crescent Moon witches.* Then the oil cloths, then set up the tent, again molding the rock to place the tent pegs. Unroll the padding, the rugs, pile the pillows, shake out the down comforters. She pulled back the front drapes and unrolled a last rug in front of the tent. Unfolded the folding chairs and table, and Mercy had her colorful, civilized backdrop.

River set up her own tent—large enough for one person to crawl into to sleep—the grill, the food, the plates and everything else around to the side, mostly out of sight, handy when summoned, easily able to hear everything through the silk walls.

Mary stomped over and glared at her. "Now what do we do?"

"Wait for the goddess to show up, wait on her hand and foot, and when she leaves, pack up and go home."

"I'm going to be fired—with no references, you know."

"That's not my fault. Heidi ran away from home, and that is her decision. You decided to come and try to talk sense into her, all the way here." River shrugged. "You could have stayed

Pam Uphoff

in New Tokyo. Been shocked when you found Heidi gone, supported Mrs. Gardener as she tried to get her back. You are here by your own decision, own up to it."

"But they keep running off and, and . . ."

"Tell you what. The Goddess of Mercy could probably use a maid."

Mary's eyes widened.

"Beware, she is not a nice lady."

The astronomers started wandering out from the low buildings as the sun set. They gawped a bit at the colorful silk tent, then took themselves off to the observatory. River followed them, and sat quietly as they opened the slit in the roof and aimed the long main scope at something in the east.

A chubby young man looked at her uncertainly. "The Comets won't rise for an hour. We have other observations to make, until then."

She nodded. "Go ahead. Just ignore me until I get in the way, then tell me to move."

He laughed a little uncertainly, but skittered off to crouch over a table, taking careful measurements on something there. The others moved around efficiently, the telescope moved several times.

The sudden clatter from outside was startling. Loud voices, feet tromping on the stone. The door crashed opened and Chance led the way in. Mercy was right behind him, demanding to know why the telescope was inside.

The head astronomer came at a trot. Half the new people

318

took a look around then stepped back outside, leaving the astronomers at the mercy of seven of the old gods.

Mercy snapped her head around and speared the old astronomer with a piercing stare. "Well? Why isn't it outside?"

"To protect it from weather. It get very windy up here, and a big lightweight tube like this would be twisting and turning. We couldn't get anything done." He waved at the open slit. "This is just perfect."

"Humph. Makes sense. Now, we're all having premonitions, but they aren't exact enough. Where is the meteor going to hit? Which city?"

"City!" There was a general recoil from the scientists drifting their way.

Art stepped up beside Mercy. "All our dreams are about it hitting a city, killing thousands of people. But we have conflicting recognition points. There's no consensus as to which city it will actually hit. We need to know, so we can evacuate in time."

"Old Gods! Well, we don't have the instruments from the Exile. Or those calculating machines. I remember one still working when I was a trainee." He sighed. "But we got some good plates last night. We'll start our measurements and calculations, and get, hopefully, their movements exact enough to satisfy your needs." He raised his hands, but hesitated to shoo them out.

River eeled between Pax and Barry and stepped up behind Mercy. "I have your tent set up, if you'd like to take refreshments while these gentlemen work."

Mercy scowled at her, and then over at Chance. "I have a better idea. I'll be back after my party is over." She disappeared with a faint pop. Chance laughed and raised his arms. River leapt away from the group and they all disappeared.

"Thank Gods." The old astronomer glanced at River. "Begging your pardon."

"No need. I'll leave you as well." She stepped through the door, and found the gods' children milling about. And Amused and Flattered.

"Didn't dodge fast enough, eh?"

Shoulder to shoulder, the two of them were glaring at the usual redheads.

"Dodge, nothing, they grabbed us and hauled us along." Flattered's attention was distracted by a giggle.

Three blonde witches, just youngsters barely settled into their power. Two others were beyond them, a grown woman and a girl, probably under ten.

"Ooo! Eight women, and only two men." Dangelo swaggered past the trio of blondes and homed in on the dark haired woman. "I don't believe we've met."

"Unfortunately your reputation precedes you." She was tall and good at looking down her nose. She gave him the full treatment, then turned to the rest of them. "Regina Art."

One of the blondes nodded. "I'm Rose, this is Chrysanthemum, and Peony." The three of them eyed the older triad.

"I'm River, this is Amused and Flattered. We're Bright Quarter Moon witches of the New Tokyo Pyramid. Where are you training?"

"Father is training us. In Rome."

River eyed Art's daughter, and then the little girl. "Are you two witches as well?"

"Mother says I'm a goddess. I'm Miss Grace Determined." The little girl advanced fearlessly. "Can goddesses train like witches?"

"They ought to, they have the Witch gene on their X chromosome. I wonder what's on your other. Do you know?"

"No. Mother doesn't talk about me very often."

Now the other red head spoke up. "I'm Ristofe Vice and this is my brother Dangelo. We're mages. Y-chromosome from Dad, right?"

"I see." River bit her lip. "Do any of you know how long we're going to be up here? I brought stuff for Mercy for a week. Food, you know?"

"Wine, I hope." Dangelo looked her up and down. "You're that witch Dad is after. What does he see in you?"

"Richie's daughter. Does tupping a rival's daughter give a god points in some fantasy game of theirs?"

"Fantasy game? Darling they play the real thing. The fantasy is that ordinary people have any rights."

"Well, did you realists bring any food along?"

The blondes had a whole room in a bubble. With pantry.

The men had a bubble each, loaded with plenty of

drinkable supplies. They popped corks, River produced glasses, and a small but rowdy party was underway.

"Mother doesn't let me drink wine." Grace took a sip and choked.

River tasted it, removed a pack of spells, leaned and removed them from the kid's drink as well.

"What was that you just did? I could almost see it."

"Watch." River circulated, removing spells. The blondes thought it was funny and she had to demonstrate taking them off while the brothers put them on. Then she left them to their own peril and shifted the little girl a bit further away.

"Have you had the basic training?" Nope. River showed her the starting meditations and the basic charms.

When she checked the party, Mike, Heidi and Mary had joined in. Mary was standing by Regina, both of them looking appalled. The blonde triad was judging a three way kissing contest. Heidi and Mike were doing a good job, but Amazing and Flattered had gone beyond kissing to foreplay.

"Yuck." Grace turned away and Mary and Regina joined her.

River grabbed a bottle of wine and took them down to the tents, and they sat at the folding chairs and played cards with a tiny bit of light. "So we don't mess up the astronomy." The ridge kept most of the noise from the other party away. She heated water and brewed tea. Raided the supplies she'd bought for Mercy, for cookies.

After a while Mike and Heidi wandered by, arms around

each other, and waved as they passed.

Mary scowled. Regina'd had enough wine to look a little wistful. River sighed and wished Simon was here. *Even though I ought not have anything to do with a wizard.*

It was well past midnight when Mercy stormed into the campsite. She stopped dead at the mundane sight of the four of them playing cards. River swallowed, glad she'd brought out the tea set and tossed the wine bottle.

The Goddess visibly relaxed, and smiled. "River, I might have known you'd be more sensible than that triad of yours. Not to mention Barry's and Edmund's children."

River shook her head. "It's unfortunate, how witches advance, but that doesn't excuse . . . well. When we get back to town I'll speak to the Eldest about those two silly girls." She quickly changed the subject. "Have the astronomers finished their calculations?"

"I dare say we'll find out later today when they are sober and back working."

"Oh. Dear. I suppose Barry's triad felt they needed a few more men around."

"They appear to have gotten seven. At least they didn't kill any of them." Mercy eyed the quiet girl. "Well, Grace, it's definitely past your bedtime. And mine, for that matter. Good night, Ladies." She ushered Grace into the tent and released the curtains.

River picked up the tea service. "Do you have anyplace to stay, Regina?"

"If my father is here, I'd best check with him . . . Oh." She looked up the hill a bit.

Art looked around, nodded his approval to his daughter, and pulled an amazingly ornate little house out of nowhere and set it beside Mercy's tent.

"Thank you for the tea, and the card game, River, Mary." She raised her voice a bit. "Goodnight Grace, your ladyship."

Mary trotted off, but returned with her own bedding before River'd cleaned up.

"Tomorrow I am going to be the world's best damned maid." She kept her voice very low, and laid out her blankets beyond River's tiny encampment.

She was the World's best damned maid for two weeks, while the astronomers recovered from their introduction to witches and Chance helped calculate the positions of the asteroids.

The wilder set dropped down to a lower altitude, and returned with wild goats for the slowly expanding field kitchen.

Just as well. When the four huge dogs showed up, River had a pile of offal and bones and apparently gained good karma from the God of Just Deserts, who mostly stayed away from the dome and harassed the other Gods and their children until they presented a united front and sent him away.

River found herself teaching Regina and the blondes as well as Grace. Grace had grasped power very young, and Regina hadn't been trained in anything specific to witches. Amused and Flattered were thrilled to be the most advanced witches and readily took the others under their wings. Ristofe and Dangelo just laughed and grabbed Mike for some mage practice, frequently roping in one of the gods so they could form a lesser compass.

River poked her nose into the dome, when she found the time. The problem there was not so much the calculations as making sure which asteroid was which between any two photographic plates. Plates taken twice a night settled that, and the calculations contained the bad news. One definite impact. Probably off the tip of Indonesia.

"In the ocean. That's good, we can warn ships away . . ." the astronomer broke off. All the gods were shaking their heads.

"Tsunami. Isn't that the right term?" Edmund scowled up at the telescope as if it were its fault.

Art nodded. "I remember. A wave of water, usually from an underwater earthquake, but this . . ."

Chance looked down at his figures. "It'll be slow, as meteors go. But if it's as big as we think it is, the energy . . ."

The old astronomer nodded. "New Miami will be the closest. If it hits a bit to the Pacific side of the peninsula, New Tokyo could see the wave. Probably won't wrap the tip of India. New Bombay should be safe. Let me calculate. You know, sometimes we've had dangerous waves, that's why the building codes keep residences back from the shoreline. I wonder how many of those are caused by meteors hitting the ocean." He was still mumbling as he sat down and picked up a pencil.

River shifted uneasily, she could feel an undercurrent but

couldn't tap in. Time to stir the pot. "Could we move it a little? Get it to hit on land? No one lives on the peninsula."

The gods exchanged looks, the astronomers perked up. "It looks like just a hundred miles north and the problems would be so much less."

Mercy frowned and looked at the map. "That puts it a bit closer to New Miami."

"Go north, away from the city, go north." "Go north, away from the city, go north." The voices tangled, male and female, recognizable and strange. River blinked; the voices went away. No one else appeared to have heard them. She looked at the map, the circles were labeled with percent certainties that the meteor would hit inside it. New Miami was just outside the northwest edge of the ninety percent circle. The ninety-five percent and ninety-eight percent circles made it look unlikely New Miami would be hit . .
.

"Still far enough away for safety, and the air blast will be much safer than the water wave." Barry ran his fingers over the map. "I remember things like this, now that my memory's been bumped. How about if we could move it even further north, get it north of you, and further away that way."

"And New Bombay's far enough west we don't have a worry there." Pax put in. His eyes were narrowed in thought and he and Mercy exchanged silent glances.

River shivered. *They can do it, they're gods. But New Bombay's much further west, they couldn't move it that far.*

Wouldn't. Surely. A hundred miles, two hundred. Sure. But a thousand or more? She rubbed her arms, feeling the goose bumps that had nothing to do with the cool temperature.

Pax stepped in and rolled up the map. "This is what we need, what we came for." He disappeared, and the rest of the gods popped out as well.

The old astronomer grumbled something under his breath, then spoke up. "Don't just stand there, get another map. They left all the calculations here."

The staff startled back into movement. River slipped out and looked around. No one around. She walked down and found the silk tent standing alone, Art's little house gone, and Regina with it.

Amused and Flattered were standing with Grace, looking around. They spotted her and walked over. "Virtue and Vice came and got their children, Regina grabbed Mary, saying she needed a sensible maid and ran off too."

"How about Heidi and Mike? I guess it's time for us to all pack up and head home." River frowned at the silk tent. "And now I have to pack all of that. Oh well. If Mrs. Gardener won't accept that those two are married, I'll give them the tent. They'll need it."

Grace sighed. "That's so romantic. But, the best thing of all is that my mother forgot me. *I* can have an adventure."

"Well, I hate to poke holes in your expectations, but I hope we don't have an adventure. Bandits and storms and such . . . Oh, don't look so hopeful!"

The girl grinned. "Bandits! Maybe they'll kidnap me. But instead of being ransomed, I'll join the band and be the most vicious bandit ever!" She danced around, almost helping with the packing. The witches returned with a scowling Mike and Heidi.

"We don't want to go back to New Tokyo."

River blinked at them. "I see. Well, there's no other roads until we're down off this mountain. Then the road to New Miami splits off to the south, so why don't you plan on taking us at least that far. Then we can see if the rest of us can hire a ride with a merchant caravan or some such."

Grace started bouncing. "Caravan! A caravan!"

By the time they got everything packed, it was noon. And when they climbed out of the little vale, they spotted another vehicle. River narrowed her eyes. Those bay horses looked awfully familiar, and the light carriage very out of place.

Chapter Nine

October 2236

Mount Tambour

A week to the top of Mt. Tambour was unheard of. Simon figured his prayers to the God of the Roads had something to do with it. Even the mares were tired.

And the place was deserted. He slumped in disappointment. The mares kept going, and stopped by the dome.

Midday, most likely the staff is asleep.

He climbed down and walked stiffly over to the door. The dome was closed, the huge circular room hushed and quiet in the daylight from the open door. A table bore a map, several maps. Piles of papers full of calculations, some spilled off onto the floor. Simon studied the map. Concentric circles with percentage marks were centered off the tip of Indonesia. A line was drawn up the broad peninsula, marked off every hundred miles.

"What the hell?"

"An asteroid."

He spun around. He recognized the voice. "River! I thought everyone was gone." Silhouetted in the open door, she was a bit . . . less slender?

"You should have seen the mess. Seven of them, eight for a bit, but they ran Just Deserts off. I guess the other gods are immune to him. They all popped back home just before dawn. I've just finished packing everything up." She'd walked down to the table as she spoke. She looked down at the map.

Simon pulled his eyes away from an examination of her figure and looked at the map. "An asteroid?"

She touched the center circle. "They think it will hit here. Apparently water collisions are bad, start huge waves. So they, the gods, are going to try to push it north. A hundred miles, and it'll be on land. Three hundred and it'll be safely far from New Miami." She drew her hand westward toward New Bombay, and shook her head. "So, what are you doing here?"

"I . . . I wanted to talk to you. I should have, immediately. I . . . We. . ."

"Simon . . . I'm a witch. There isn't a 'we.' There never can be."

"But. I mean, I know that, but, I hadn't intended . . . sorry, I rushed here, but it still took long enough that you'd think I'd have had time to figure out what to say."

"That we had a lovely night together. That any time you're in New Tokyo you should drop me a note."

"I didn't mean to. Well. Umm."

"If you extend regrets I *will* hit you."

He started laughing. "I'm sorry. I'm an idiot. It was a lovely night and I want more of them. I guess I'll just have to find lots of reasons to find myself in New Tokyo." *Dear gods, am I going to keep using you? Maybe I'm cold blooded enough to be a proper spy after all.* He didn't feel very cold-blooded, though, as he leaned and kissed her.

"Eww, gross!" A familiar little girl voice.

"Oooweee! Go River! Your cute professor came to save you from the dissolute gods."

River pulled away from him and glared at her fellow witch. "Simon, we're about to head back to New Tokyo, except for those who will be splitting off and heading south. How about you?"

"I, umm, think I've concluded my business here. May I offer you a ride?"

"Absolutely."

And while they went off to finished their packing, he unharnessed the mares and gave them a good feed while he hastily pulled supplies from his bubble and stuffed the leather boot with horse and people food and an oil cloth and blankets.

When the others drove the wagon up to the road, he added Grace to his passenger list and let the mares dawdle behind the bigger wagon as they started down the steepest part of the road. And that was because he liked the little girl, not so River would have to sit closer to him, as claimed by the other two witches.

They stopped early, the worst slope safely negotiated. A north facing scarp protected a snow bank from the sun and even now it was barely melting, a trickle of water filling and spilling from stone hollows with a natural beauty that would be the envy of rock gardeners everywhere, had they ever ventured this high.

A delighted Grace helped brush Artemis and Diana. "Mother thinks horses are smelly and dangerous. She won't even let me have a pony."

They raided Mercy's supplies to house Amused, Flattered and Grace . . . and somehow River's bedroll ended up right beside his.

"Is that nice? With all these people around?" He suspected he wasn't keeping all the whine out of his voice.

River grinned. "Two weeks until we're back in civilization sufficient for inns and privacy. Big tough guy like you can handle it."

"I'm not a big tough guy. I'm a university professor."

She snickered and headed back to the wagon. "I hope you like tough, stringy mountain goat. It's what we've got the most of, and needs to get eaten before we're out of the chillier altitudes."

"Yummy. For me. I have a suspicion you lot may be sick and tired of it." He blinked at the lump of meat River unrolled from a paper wrapper. It was coated with spices and smelled vaguely of wine and something citrus. "I'll get a fire going." He swallowed saliva. *All this and a good cook besides. Maybe I can lure her over to the good side. Despite her mother, father, triad, pyramid . . .* He sighed and fetched the charcoal and grill from the wagon.

The temperatures warmed as they dropped down to the North Road that stretched from New Miami to New Tokyo.

332

Four hundred miles to New Tokyo one way, and twelve hundred to Miami the other.

The Old Wolf had explained to him, years ago, that the names of the cities were taken from Earth cities, some because they were in approximately the same place on this "Earth" and some from nostalgia. The god had said that the original Tokyo was located on an island a thousand miles further northeast, and Miami on another continent altogether.

At the crossroad, they put their heads together and split up their supplies, River fussing over Heidi and Mike like a mother hen.

"We'll be able to buy stuff in another four or five days. You guy's will have to get most of the way to Miami before there's any place . . . oh, stop laughing. I know you can hunt. All right. And no, Grace, you cannot go with them. I have no wish to be incinerated by your mother. And this way you'll get at least another week of magic practice."

Simon winked at the girl. "And the bandits are thicker on the ground to the north."

Her eyes brightened at that.

Two days later, Grace got her wish.

The twenty riders must have felt invincible. A light carriage with one man, three young women and a child? Four of them rode out to block the road in front of them. Simon glanced back and spotted more riders blocking the rear, as an even dozen horsemen galloped down from the trees to the left. They didn't rush, and Simon could see their grins.

"I've got a shield up, in case they decide to toss some arrows around." River didn't sound too worried. "Go forward another twenty feet, that'll spread them out the most."

Simon eased the reins for a few more strides, then pulled the horses up, hoping that the young witches weren't over confident. "Didn't realize there were large companies working the roads." *Wish I was riding.*

He reached under the seat and pulled out a crossbow, a case of bolts and his sword.

Grace's eyes widened, and the looks she was darting toward the approaching men was apprehensive.

Reality crushes dreams, again.

River jumped down from the carriage, and Simon blinked a bit at the sight of her bare feet. *Does their contact with Earth need to be that immediate?* He tied off the reins and stood to cock the bow. Little flicks of movement; he turned his head in time to recognize darts bouncing off of absolutely nothing. "Can I fire out?"

"Umm, I can't make it one way. But once we start attacking, it'll be down." River reached out to the other two witches. Simon blinked at the sudden burst of glowing power around the three of them. River dropped the other witches' hands, turned and thrust her left hand, palm out. A horse in the lead crashed suddenly to the ground, flinging his rider under the hooves of the other horses, tripping the horse behind; two others veered and bumped.

Simon's mares stomped and tossed their heads. "Whoa!"

Poor girls, trained to fight and all harnessed up and hitched to the carriage.

Simon aimed, hit the rider furthest to the right, cocked, slid the bolt into place, turned and got the one trying flank the witches to the left, cock, slide, lift, another to the left. Cock, drop bow and draw sword as a bandit reined his horse around the mares and came at Simon from the other side. Simon deflected his sword, lunged, but the bandit was already out of reach, reining around to come back.

The bandit's head jerked and he slid limply off the horse, as the horse stumbled and fell.

Quick survey, only four bandits still mounted in that first group; the ones on the ground didn't look very belligerent. But both the front and rear blockers were charging in to join the fray. Simon set the sword down on the seat, picked up the bow, slid the dart and took out the leader of the front group. Cock, slide, lift and aim.

A feminine cry twitched his attention, the bolt flew wide. Cock, slide, lift, aim.

"Grace, will you hop down here and help us." River sounded like she was serving tea.

Cock, slide, lift, aim. Simon couldn't see much, the next man was crouched, trying to hide behind his horse's neck. Simon dropped his aim, and the horse threw up its head with a shriek, then collapsed. Cock, slide, lift, aim . . . at a rider reining hastily around and spurring for safety. Simon turned.

The rear guard was close and at a dead run. River stepped

forward and slashed her hand horizontally. Blood exploded from four horses, the bodies tumbled, the witches dodged. One rider rolled to his feet. Jerked as Simon's bolt hit, and fell.

One of the fallen horses was screaming. River stepped into the horrible mess, drawing her knife.

Silence fell.

Muffled hoofbeats as the loose horses galloped away. A few of the bandits were moving, only two on their feet, and they were running. The others were hitching painfully away. A horse staggered to its feet and hobbled off.

River turned and grabbed Grace in a hug.

"I'm sorry, sweetie, there were too many of them to do anything else. I wish you hadn't had to see that, though."

Grace's voice caught in a sob. "I don't want to be a bandit any more. I could hear what they were thinking. They were *ugly* inside."

Simon jumped down to where Flattered was hovering over Amused. A long slash down her arm bled freely. She was pale with shock, crying.

Simon grabbed his first aid kit. A bottle of iodine. He poured it on, ignoring her indrawn scream. A roll of bandage, a long strip of gauze. He started at the top. River reached in, pressed the wound closed and covered it with gauze, while he wrapped. The roll was soaked through as fast as he worked, but it wasn't dripping when he was done. He pulled out a second bottle. "One swallow."

Flattered steadied Amused's hand and she took a swallow.

And relaxed, her eyes widening. "Oh, wow, who made that? It's marvelous." She leaned her head back against Flattered and her eyes closed.

"Is she dead?" Grace whimpered.

A loud snore from Amused, and the girl burst into tears.

Simon brought out a jug of water and they washed hastily. He circled the battle field, freed two lamed horses of their tack. Cut the throat of one with a broken leg. One horse and two bandits appeared to have been magically stunned. He stripped the tack from the horse. If it recovered first, the bandits wouldn't have him to ride. He found and pulled four of the eight bolt's he'd fired. Although he certainly hoped this was the only bandit gang working the road, and he wouldn't need them again.

"Ordinarily I'd bury bandits, spare the next travelers a really nasty stinking mess, but there's more than a dozen of them and six dead horses. They're just going to have to stink." Simon picked Amused up and settled her on the carriage seat. River waved Flattered up with her, and lifted Grace to sit on the boot before climbing up beside her.

Several miles down the road, Flattered turned her head and eyed River's back. "What on Earth was that last spell? It was horrible!"

"Slash. It's like the hardest shield possible, super thin, thinner than a razor, thinner than an oil sheen on water, and you . . . slash it across. But you've got to be so close you can almost touch what you're slashing. I didn't have anything else left. Tomorrow I ought to be able to do . . . something. Maybe."

Simon put another five miles behind them, then stopped where the road forded a small river, reduced to a trickle in the summer heat. "Let's get some food into you witches. Can't have the lot of you fainting on me. Two's my limit for dealing with fainting beauties."

Grace smiled a little bit at that.

Two days later they passed the first farm villages, all with defensive walls. And found the first inn.

"Hot baths!" Flattered sounded starved.

Amused looked a bit apprehensive, and the other witches led her away to soak the bandage off. An hour later they joined him at the table. A bit wide-eyed.

Amused flexed her arm. "What was that potion?"

"I picked it up ages ago when I passed through Sahara. The Goddess of Healing is credited with it."

Grace was wide-eyed. "Are you from Sahara?"

Simon shook his head. "I was born in New Tokyo, ran away from home when I was fifteen."

Grace looked up at that.

"Only if you're truly desperate, Miss Grace Determined. Which you may well be, someday. But remember the bandits. It's got to be bad enough to face that."

She nodded. "Yeah. I'll need to be older." She heaved a deep sigh and looked wretched and glum for the rest of the trip.

But she didn't argue when Simon stopped outside her mother's mansion.

River walked in with her. The doorman blinked at the girl. "Lady Grace! I hadn't realized you were out."

Grace just shrugged. "Is mother here?"

"No, Mi'lady, she's attending an afternoon soiree at the Mayor's House."

"Good, tell cook I'll take an early dinner in an hour." Grace looked up at River. "I hope I see you again."

River was quiet the rest of the way home.

The goodbye gaze lingered, then she turned and walked into the parkland.

Chapter Ten
November 2236

New Tokyo, Asia

"The Mage Kings. Not content with their new city, they are organizing rebellion in New Miami!" Mercy paced, a furious glowing figure. "They want to drive us out, take our places. Well, I won't have it! Even Pax concedes that perhaps they'll need to be put in their place sooner rather than later. Zapolo and Kelso. Two trouble makers, trying to make themselves kings.

"I say, we should do it now, before their poisonous ideas spread any further." She finally stopped, turned and glowered at her audience.

Edmund and Barry exchanged glances.

Barry shrugged. "It was a lost cause within a few years of the Exile, Mercy. We simply aren't enough stronger than they are to control them when they band together. There are too many of them. If you'd just live in luxury and let them go their own way, you wouldn't have these problems."

"Your stupid demands cause too many problems." Edmund grinned. "You need to just give opinions. And the people who try to rule otherwise need to have unfortunate accidents. You'll find very few people will bother you, after a few years."

"Generations of children brought up as independent thinkers isn't a good thing. It will lead to strife and even more wars." The golden boy shot a glance toward Simon. "We need to get control of education."

Simon nodded obediently, and wished he were across the room, where River and her pals were sitting quietly behind the senior witches, here for this meeting.

There was snort from the head witch. "This is a matter that touches on all magic users. It's not just you gods who are receiving less respect and a smaller place in the power structure. The Mayor actually had the audacity to criticize our family structure. Some of the possible voting restrictions the city council has considered will impact us especially harshly. The rule has always been one vote per person. Not per family-as-they-define-it. Not limited to individual property owners, which would exclude ordinary wives, not just group ownership situations, like the Pyramid. And this inheritance only to the children of legal marriages? Obviously aimed directly at witches. *And we will not stand for it.*" The old woman's voice was strong, and had dropped to a threatening growl by the end of her speech.

The Archmage curled a sarcastic lip, but remained quiet. There were a dozen full Compasses in the city, and their reputation for orgies and revolving marriages was based on fact, not rumor. They'd been thoroughly criticized as well.

Art stood and stepped out to stand with Mercy. "This city

used to realize that we were above them. They respected us. But all the news, and worse, rumors, coming from all the new little towns, all the constitutions and civil rights . . . and now this 'King Kelso' moving beyond New Bombay and building a town, a large town, less than three hundred miles from New Miami? We're being treated like pariahs. We need to remove that town, and make it clear that they cannot encroach on our area of influence."

Peace shook his head. "Yet we don't want to foment war. We are not violent, antisocial men. We should return to New Miami, and talk to these people again. Perhaps a show of force. There must be a way to remove that town without resorting to violence." His eyes slid to meet Mercy's and they exchanged knowing smiles.

Mercy stepped forward. "The second thing we need to talk about can be made to be of use in this matter. As you all know, there's an inbound asteroid. We're going to shift its impact point from the current ocean impact, which could raise damaging waves, to an impact on uninhabited land. Perhaps our selfless use of power will shame them into obedience once more. And so I think we all ought to practice making magic together. " She dismissed the issue with a wave of her hand. "But enough of that. Please join me in taking refreshment, and we'll exchange ideas, plan on magical practices and so forth."

Mercy swooped down on Pax and took his arm to lead the way into a parlor with doors open to a broad, stone paved patio.

Simon nibbled while watching the gods interacting with the other powerful magic makers. *I'm probably the weakest person here.* His eyes drifted to the small knot of "Golian Wizards." His father and three other men, their body language a combination of wariness and aggression. They glowed as strongly, no, more strongly than the top witches and mages. For just a moment envy twisted at his emotions. His eyes tracked to the young witch triad. River. *For her, I gave up power.* Then reality reasserted itself. *I ran like hell to keep from being castrated. River's just the most marvelous reason yet that I'm glad I did.*

He glanced back at the wizards. *Is that Dennis? That mean-faced old grouch? Has my older brother had a moment of joy since that horrible day when he regained consciousness and realized what they'd done to him? He's only three years older than me. He looks like a poisonous toad.*

A stir of magic pulled his eyes back to River. Her triad glowed in the center of the patio. He'd seen them in practice and then in battle. This was practice, and now he knew it wasn't a third of what they were capable of, at need. Was it his imagination that River was dampening her glow much more than the other girls, to stay down at their level?

The gods, the male gods, Pax, Art, Vice and Virtue, strolled out and surrounded them. Edmund leered at River's definitely expanding belly and was ignored. He scowled as he stepped back and the flow of a Compass oozed into existence and swooped around the four of them. As it sped up and grew higher, the triad's glow deepened, reached upward, higher, touched the clouds and grew further. Golden light spread through the cloud. Brightened. And disappeared with a audible snap.

Seven people staggered away from the center, variously clutching their heads or cursing. Or both.

The three witches moved as far as the stone wall around the patio, then slid down to the ground. Simon ducked inside to load plates and took them out to the trio.

River blinked at the plate he held under her nose. "Chocolate? Now I know I'm in love."

Amused managed a snicker before she bit into the fudge. Flattered followed suit.

Simon, greatly daring, sat down beside River. Just because it got him nearly out of the sight of everyone else. Not because he liked the way she was leaning on him.

It was, however, a very superior way to watch the older witches try to coordinate with the mage compass. The wizards coordinated not at all, even with each other.

"So, Professor Physics, how high are those clouds?" River stretched, then wiggled around to get her head back on his shoulder. Somehow his arm had gotten around her shoulders.

"Ten thousand feet, give or take. I couldn't tell how far further up you were reaching, but, well, even being generous, four or five miles won't be high enough to shift a meteor."

"We have to reach out at least a hundred, just to get out of the atmosphere. Ouch."

"The closer the asteroid is when you try to move it, the harder you'll have to shove it. It'll be a balancing act between reach and the power you can apply to redirect it." Simon stared at the cloud and wondered if it was even possible.

"And we've all trained in close work, because that's where we can apply the most power." She narrowed her eyes. "At a hundred miles up, to divert it a hundred miles north, we'd have to change the angle of descent forty-five degrees to the north. A chunk of rock a half mile in diameter? We couldn't possibly do it."

Simon shivered. "Half a mile?"

"That's what Chance said he'd been seeing in his dreams. If we could reach out two hundred . . . four hundred miles or more. Old Gods! We need to be practicing extending our reach. Hugely."

"Yeah." He sat back and watched the mage compass and the oldest witches push a giant blossom of power upward, punching a hole in the clouds and seeming to reach for the stars. *But actually, still not out of the atmosphere.* "They're wasting too much energy low down. They don't need a pillar, they need a needle."

"Oh?" A chilly female voice. Mercy loomed over him. "And do you think you know more about it than we do? Our weak little Professor?"

"I'm used to analyzing things involving physical energy. We may not be able to measure magic, but we can measure the effects, and many of the same laws of physics apply."

River stood up, abruptly. "Let's test it. As if it were volume of effect verses the amount of energy we put into it. A subjective measurement, to be sure. But an interesting idea." She looked around, then led the way to one side of the patio. "Right. A scale, or something."

Simon stooped and picked up a flowerpot. "Just for a first order test. I'll stand a quarter of the way across the patio. Envision a square cross section of push, two inches by two inches. Push the pot. Then we'll do it again with a one square inch push. Then we'll repeat when I'm halfway across, three quarters and all the way."

It was subjective as all hell, and even with his quick reactions, tough on the flower pots. But the power required increased with distance, and with the *square* of the cross section. More mages came and watched, then tried reaching upward with smaller columns.

Simon made himself useful, and found himself included in the working group.

He tried to avoid compromising River's reputation with the Goddess or the pyramid. While spending as much time around her as possible.

River found it amusing, exasperating, and finally sad. "Witches don't have husbands, witch babies don't have fathers. Simon, I'm sorry. I understand that this is going to be painful for you."

He just hid the hurt and sniffed dismissively. "I may be a professor of physics, but I assure you that I took enough biology to be quite certain . . . "

She snickered. The eavesdropping Amused and Flattered laughed so hard they had to prop each other up.

But later, alone, it hurt.

I ought to kidnap her, haul her away . . . Except she'd kill me. And . . . her position of trust is so valuable . . . Simon thumped his head on the wall of his apartment. And sent a report to his boss.

They moved out of town and started knocking down nearly invisible targets on distant mountains.

No one explained why their encampment—two mansions and a hundred tents—was called Los Alamos by the gods. But one morning late in November, Simon woke, and found most of it gone. A few servants were packing. River had gone with all the other magicians and gods. He drove quickly to New Tokyo. No mansions. He sent a quick message to his boss, and headed for the water front. There must be a ship heading south. Must.

Chapter Eleven

December 2236

New Miami, India

The New Miami Pyramid had a triad of Full Moons. With the Blondes in one corner, and River, Amused and Flattered in the other they formed a widespread base for the pyramid's power gather. Technically not yet trained to Full Moon status, but able to channel and all six of them pregnant, the Bright Quarter Moons were close to the Full Moons in power. In the last weeks of practice they'd worked out the best combinations for raising and projecting power. And this was it.

The courtyard was dim in the setting sun, then painfully bright as the magic gathered.

Two triads of the Dark Quarter, and one of the Dark Crescent stood just inside them.

The eight men, gods and mages, formed a Compass inside that. In the center, Mercy and the two Eldest sisters formed another Dark Crescent Triad.

The power they held was *enormous*. Spinning, glowing, painfully bright. As one they reached out into space with a tiny needle. As the Earth swung, for a brief moment they were directly beneath that asteroid. They touched it. Pushed it to slow it. Began to shift it north.

And under the gestalt of the whole, River saw both the intent and the results.

A slower approach would move the strike zone west.

"No! Pull it faster, away from the City. You're making it hit the City!" Her voice wrenched her loose. Power sparked, flashed from the walls around the open courtyard, crackled like lightning. A blast knocked her off her feet, reverberated off the walls.

River scrambled back to her feet as Mercy descended on her, fury and death in her eyes and in her upraised hand.

River backed away. "You've changed it's course. It's going to hit the City."

"That was the plan, you traitorous bitch. Who do you work for? Wolf? Yes!" The death spell leapt from her hand. River shielded. The spell crashed through, physically throwing her back, into the stone wall. The residual power in the wall flashed. As everything went dark, she heard Barry's voice. "Perhaps we should check with the astronomers. We may have managed enough change already."

"Go north, away from Miami, go north." "Go north, away from Miami, go north." The voices tangled, male and female. Always the same voices. The War God. Logic. Fertility and Healing. The God of Love. The God of the Roads. Who were the others? Her own father, perhaps? Chance, Just Deserts?

God of Chance, I'm sorry! I think I just made your premonition come true. They wanted to destroy New Bombay,

350

but now they've targeted New Miami.

"Lock her up. Put a guard on her who can't be over-powered magically. We'll deal with her later. Pax? Have we moved it enough?"

"Yes. There will be no war. I can feel it."

Art's voice cut in. "The astronomers said that the earlier we moved it the less change we needed to make. We touched it immediately."

"We should check." Barry again.

"There's no time." That sounded like Edmund. "The Army marched three days ago. We need to hurry if we are to be outside Kingston when New Bombay is hit."

Pax's irritating drawl answered. "I sent a marker. We'll be able to teleport directly to them. Let's eat, then we can leave at dawn. We have most of a day before impact."

Hands grabbed her, tried to make her stand. Ristofe and Dangelo. Her legs didn't seem to be there. They gave up and dragged her. Once outside the courtyard, they called in the guards and made them do the carrying. Sent someone for the Commander. In fact, most of her body was gone. And there went her brain spiraling down into the dark, after it.

The pain woke her. The cramping agony she identified immediately. *Miscarriage. Mercy didn't kill me, but she's killed my baby.* She curled up into a knot as another wave of pain swept through her. *And I came close to dying with you, my unknown, unnamed, child. I'm so sorry. I could not protect you.* River managed to focus mentally for a moment, to send something, some wave of love, of comfort, but there was nothing to receive it. All that was left was for her body to expel the fetus, the already dead child.

She could see the results of Mercy's attack on her own body, patches of dead tissue, mostly small. Too much for the baby to survive, too little to kill River. Very odd, this perception, as if her body was translucent. *I'm going to be very sick, as those dead patches . . . do whatever they're going to do. My heart is fine, lungs good. That one on the liver is not good . . .* She paced. She cramped, and bled. She cried. In the end she held a tiny bald thing in one hand. And cramped, and bled while the placenta passed. And then cramped and bled more.

She'd had some vague impression of guards looking in on her occasionally. She'd tried to be laying down and still every time she heard them coming. She had no idea if she'd managed it. The tiny high slit of a window brightened, the night had passed before she was done.

She ripped up her bedding, for pads, for a tiny shroud. For washing and for a towel. She heard footsteps coming closer, again. She staggered over to the corner where she'd left most of her clothes and dressed hastily.

I have to get away. I have to warn people. I have to escape.

The window slit opened. She moved into the center of the cell, and looked back. Recognition bloomed. Mercy's commander, her pet War God. A tall muscular woman, eagle eyed, proud.

"God of War. Do you hear me?"

The commander's lips peeled away from her teeth as she laughed.

"God of War! Anyone has always been able to summon you. But you were always the one who decided which side you were on. Remember? Have you heard the voices?"

"Go north, away from Miami, go north." "Go north, away from Miami, go north." The voices tangled, combined. Male and female, recognizable and strange.

The memory of the voices echoed in between them.

"An asteroid is going to hit New Miami. At nightfall. Everyone needs to leave, now. To get as far away as they can. God of War. Let me out!" River put all the power she had into that command, a curiously intricate and complex spell. *I never saw the complexity before, never twisted the little bits to fit into the lock of another person's mind. However disastrous the results, I have given birth, and I am a Full Moon witch.*

"God of War! Unlock the door."

For a second the shadow of the real god was there, looking out of the commander's eyes. The lock clicked open, the bars slid.

She walked out. Up a flight of stairs that had her legs quivering. Across a stone paved patio, around the corner of the building and across the front garden of the mansion. At the gate she turned. The commander had followed her.

"Do you understand? The city will be destroyed. Get all

your people out of here. Send all the citizens out there away. Tell them to leave the city and keep going." River turned and walked out the gate. Down the street, around two corners. The plaza was bounded on one side by the Mayor's Residence, on another by the Assembly house. The north side was the start of the market. West were the better homes of the rich.

River walked out to the center sculpture. A simple slice across the ankles and the marble effigy of Mercy toppled. She stepped up to take its place.

People were turning to look at her. Some ran off to the mayor's. To the assembly. More just came close enough to see her, hear her.

"A meteor is going to hit the city. Get your family and get out of town."

"Go north, away from Miami, go north." "Go north, away from Miami, go north." The voices tangled, male and female, recognizable and strange.

"Go north, away from Miami, go north." The God of War's deep voice echoed across the plaza.

"Go north, away from Miami, go north." Goddess of Health and Fertility, Gisele's voice was commanding, for all it was also sweet and beautiful.

"Go north, away from Miami, go north." God of Travelers, God of the Roads.

"Go north, away from Miami, go north." A warm baritone that had men and women alike leaning toward it. God of Love.

"Hurry." A command, devoid of emotion. The Goddess of Logic, of course.

River climbed down and started walking. Everyone scurried away. *Everyone. Everyone heard the gods, that time.*

Behind her, staff and solon alike were fleeing the government buildings. The merchants were folding their canopies, harnessing the donkeys and old nags that had pulled their wares to the market. By the time she was three blocks away, light carriages, suitable for the city, were passing her, piled with a few possessions snatched, families and servants. The roads were filling fast. *How far away do we have to be? A ten mile wide area of total destruction, a hundred mile wide zone of diminishing danger? We'll be lucky if most of the people make it twenty miles.* She felt the quiver in her legs and knew twenty miles was beyond her ability.

***

Simon stepped off the ship in the early morning. It had been a fast trip. Now all he had to do was prove his insanity by once again showing up to woo an agent of Mercy's. He picked up his case and headed up the hill toward the City Plaza, and the site of Mercy's mansion (in the winter.) He angled through smaller streets, circled Mercy's abode at a block's distance, then retreated to eat lunch at a small neighborhood diner. *Am I insane? What am I doing here?*

"Go north, away from Miami, go north."

"Go north, away from Miami, go north."

The voices, male and female, were recognized deep in the psyche of *everyone.*

"Hurry!" The Goddess of Logic snapped the trance.

And everyone started moving.

Simon hauled out the folded metal frame and opened the dimensional bubble. Led the mares out, right there on the street, in full sight of everyone. Closed the frame, folded it and leaped in. The mares took off at a trot, and he let them go, dodging the early traffic. Opportunities for speed were going to be few today. People were boiling out of their houses, small sacks of possessions in their arms, distressed children clinging. Simon could have stopped, given a ride to one family, perhaps two. But he was driven to hurry. To go *that* way. Down that street.

And there she was. Walking. Plodding. Wavering a bit. *What happened? Why isn't she with Mercy?* The mares couldn't make progress in the crowd of people, but River was slow. Slowing. Leaning against a street sign. Looking up as the bay horses halted beside her.

She met his eyes, reached, took his hand and let him pull her into the carriage. She leaned wearily against his shoulder. "I tried to stop them. But it took so little to move the asteroid. When I broke the pyramid, it made the premonitions come true. It's going to hit here." She slid down, head in his lap. Her eyes blinked uncertainly, her skin was cold, pale and clammy.

"I'm all right. Miscarried. I just have to sleep, rest." She closed her eyes.

He checked that she was breathing, then let the mares move out again. A woman trying to herd three children caught his eye. He gestured for her to put the children up on the boot. A street waif, thin and frightened, fit in once he scooted closer to River. A man with one leg stood on the step for a few miles, then gave up his place to a young woman with a baby.

The crowd squeezed through the city gates. There were no guards, they'd fled with their own families hours ago. They picked up speed on the open road. One of the roads the God of Vice had built between every major city. *Just goes to show that the worst of all the gods is in some ways the most useful.* River stirred, sat up. She looked around, squinted at the setting sun. "How far have we come? The asteroid will hit near midnight."

"Fifteen miles, maybe. It's hard to judge, when people move so slowly, sometimes. What happened to you?"

"They were trying to shift the asteroid so it would hit New Bombay. When I realized they weren't trying to make it less dangerous, I broke the pyramid. Mercy hit me with a death spell. I barely . . . I didn't block it enough. You risk your life helping me. You don't really love me, I put an aphrodisiac in your wine, at dinner."

He blinked down at her in a chaotic churn of emotions. "Umm. I put one in yours. Because it was also a truth serum. I needed to ask you a bunch of questions."

She snorted, winced and wrapped arms around herself.

"Ouch. I thought that stuff was awfully strong, and you rather immune, until I swapped my half full glass for your empty one."

"Oh. No wonder I lost control of the circumstances." Simon looked behind. The mother of the three children was looking desperately tired, a death grip on the leather of the boot, keeping her walking with the carriage. Simon stopped the horses, and hauled the oldest child up to the front, reached back to pull the woman up beside the other two. "Hold on. The road is clearing a bit, I'm going to speed up a while." The waif slipped silently down and ceded her tiny sliver of the seat to the girl who had clung to her baby and balanced on the footstep all this time. The fat moon was giving enough light to offset the dimming twilight from the east.

"Is this the northwest road, or the north road?"

"Northwest. It was the fastest way out of town. Does it matter?"

She shook her head. "The army is ahead of us, but I doubt we can get far enough to need to worry about them."

The mares were only a little tired, five hours of walking . . . "God of Roads, everyone on the road tonight needs desperately to get away, give us strength and speed, for these few last hours."

River squeezed up beside him and pulled the boy onto her lap. "Don't let Art know you prayed to Harry. He'll probably do a less emotional, more thorough job of killing you than Mercy managed with me."

"I don't work for Art."

"Umm. Pax?"

"War."

"Don't be silly. *I* work for War, and I've never seen you."

"Of course not, I had a cover to protect . . . wait. *You* work for War? But, you're a witch. You're a part of the New Tokyo pyramid. How could you fool them?"

"By never thinking about it."

Simon shook his head, then steered the mares around a last group of families and let them trot. For five minutes, until they caught up with the next group of people. Then it was back to walking. The pedestrians stumbled slowly out of their way, so at least the mares could walk out at their normal pace. A bit of clear road, another brief trot. At times it seemed like the countryside was blurring a bit, moving past too fast. Simon sent heartfelt thanks to the God of Travelers, old or little, any and all that could help put distance between New Miami and the fleeing residents of the city and the homes they were about to lose forever.

They stopped at a bridge over a stream, and Simon climbed down to dip buckets and hand them up, for both people and horses. Other people on the road stopped, some coming partway down the rocky hill to help lift buckets. Shod hooves rung on pavement up there.

"You!"

Simon's head snapped around; that voice had come from up there, and it had sounded like the Goddess of Mercy. He dropped the bucket and scrambled up the hill.

There were screams and yells, the crowd that had stopped for water scattered. A whip cracked and he caught sight of a closed coach disappearing into the night beyond the bridge.

River was gone.

Chapter Twelve
December 2236
New Miami, India

"You've got a good shield, girl, to survive that spell. Well, it won't happen again."

River was almost thankful for the paralysis spell that held her up. The army of new Miami had been just an hour ahead of them, marching doggedly toward Kingston. They had stopped now for a breather. Water and rations were being passed out.

"Are you going to walk your army all the way to Kingston? They'll desert when the asteroid hits." Her mouth felt stiff and clumsy, but was mostly free of the spell.

"Nonsense. Why should they, it's the sign of our power."

"Haven't you slept? Dreamed? Don't you know what we did?"

"We've moved the asteroid. It is going to hit New Bombay."

"Mercy . . . no. All the dreams, they've come down to New Miami now."

The Goddess scoffed. "As if I'd believe you."

"Mercy, I've tried to evacuate New Miami, to get your people out of there."

"Bah." The Goddess raised her hand.

Is there anything this woman cares about at all? Think, witch, or you're going to die here. "Mercy . . . Where is Grace?"

The exquisite little woman froze. For one second something real, some human terror showed through. She disappeared.

River felt her muscles unlocking, and held very still.

"Should I kill her, sir?" The man looked like Edmund Vice, but moved and held his sword like the God of War. Pax's commander, another little god.

Pax looked around in irritation. "No. She'll want to do it herself. We don't have time for this sloppy sentimentalism. Pick the witch up and throw her in one of the wagons. Get us moving again."

River locked all her muscles, fought to stay stiff, awkwardly posed, as two soldiers slung her on top of the nearest wagon. The wide eyed drover opened his mouth to say something, perhaps to protest, then closed it and faced forward. The little god ignored him, walking off to chivvy his troops into order and get them moving again. River watched Pax pace by; the wagon lurched into motion. She turned her head slowly. Guards there and there, a file of troops three wagons back.

The wagon rolled under a tree. Deep moon shadows. She rolled off the wagon and staggered as quietly as possible around the tree. Spotted a thinnish spot in the brush and kept going.

***

The refugees from New Miami quit when they reached the cross road. Simon blinked in disbelief. This road cut across the lowland, linking the North road to the Northwest Road. They were nearly two hundred miles from New Miami.

Simon turned the mares up the cross road and stopped when he'd put a low hill between them and New Miami. "Stay here," he told his passengers. "You're safe for now. I've got to try and find River."

Where would Mercy be? Would she have passed the army, gone ahead, or was she staying back from the hostilities? Up ahead there the lead elements must be setting up their siege on Kingston. "I need to hurry." He rubbed the two mares' foreheads. "I'm sorry to do this to you." In the dark, no one noticed him pull the saddles out of an empty metal frame. He rubbed the mares down, watered them, fed them. Saddled them and headed back for the northwest road. Tired people were everywhere, spreading out, collapsing. Whatever god had given them energy, had kept them going, was gone. *And we're at least four times further along than any of us walked or rode. Thank you, Harry.* He mounted Artemis and led Diana up the suddenly empty road. He hesitated, uncertain who to pray to for a lost witch. "God of War, I suppose. Or Health, she looked so weak. Oh damn Mercy!"

In the dark, Simon heard the arguments before he could see the guard post. He reined Artemis to a stop and listened.

"But we have to keep moving. We have to go north, the gods said so."

A male voice, exasperated. "All that's north of here is going to be a battlefield. You don't want to take your family there. Back off a couple hundred feet, I think there was a stream, camp there. After our gods have put this upstart Mage King back in his place, you can move on."

Simon looked around. The local semi-tropical forest was fairly open here, and his night adjusted eyes showed a faint track off to his left. He turned Artemis and actually had to give her a nudge with a heel to get her to move out again. "Sorry, lady, I know you're tired." The clink of the horses' shoes was loud in the night, then muffled as they left the hard road. He let the mare pick her way along the track, and extended his mental senses forward. The little glows of animal life were overshadowed by the brighter glows of humans. The human glows varied enormously, from those with no special genes to some who were, no doubt, Little Gods. *I wonder what it was like, before the Exile? When people with no magic whatsoever were the vast majority. Surely the genetically engineered must have stood out, obviously better than the ordinary human.*

Simon pulled his wandering thoughts back to the present. The mares weren't the only tired ones around.

A brilliant glow at the very edge of his perception. He recognized Mercy, and put up a cautious shield to keep his thoughts inside, but allowing him to see the army, and keep track of Mercy. She was further to the left . . . would that be where she had River imprisoned?

Simon pulled his sight back into the real world and looked

for deer tracks turning right. Deer being small creatures, he soon dismounted, and finally gave up and dropped the mares' reins. "Remember that you are trained to ground tie. I'd prefer to not have to chase you all over the country in order to make a quick get-away."

They pointed their ears at him, then dropped their heads to scavenge for bits of not-too-winter-dried grass.

Simon checked for glows; three gods now. Mercy, Pax and Art, he'd bet.

The forest ended in a fringe of brush. He eased through, staying low.

The meadow ahead was swarming with the bright dots of campfires, the dull glows of lanterns inside canvas tents . . . and centered on the west side, two large buildings. Mercy's and Edmund's movable mansions.

Right, no Art, this isn't pretty enough for him.

He blanched at the thought of River in Edmund's hands, and slid back into the forest. He ought to be able to get around behind those two buildings . . .

There were two sentries pacing behind the buildings, and another glow just inside the line of trees. Very dull, almost animal-like. Simon caught a brief silhouette and couldn't stop a snort of amusement. *Or a powerful witch shielding hard.*

She'd heard him, and turned, hand raised to throw what was probably a really nasty spell.

"You just don't know when to quit, do you?" He got ready to dodge, if she threw a spell.

Her glow wavered, dimmed again. "Simon. How did you find me?"

He slid up next to her. "I was planning on burgling Mercy's home, to rescue you. What are *you* doing?"

She nodded toward the building. "Amused and Flattered are in there. They feel frightened."

Right, her Triad. Mercy can't hide them from that bond. Or perhaps she doesn't want to. "Even odds it's a trap."

River shook her head. "Mercy's too busy to really worry about me right now. I need to help them *now*, later will be too late."

He looked at her, nearly invisible in the dark. "You sound like you're about to keel over in a faint." He sighed. "So let me get rid of the sentries and scout ahead. Please?"

"Certainly. Couldn't deny you the chance to show that you're the God of Heroes, now can I?"

"Just so you don't do the archetypical fainting maiden routine. I don't know the layout of Mercy's mansion."

"The dungeons are in the basement, of course. Unfortunately, the stairs down are outside and near the front left corner. We're going to have to get rather uncomfortably close to the gods, to get down there. I was waiting for the big distraction." She leaned her head briefly on his shoulder. "And trying not to faint."

Simon dropped a kiss on the top of her head. "I think we'd best do the burgling now, and escape when the big distraction hits." He moved up to crouch and watched the movements of the sentries. Careless, their attention inward, toward the camp. As they reached opposite ends of the two mansions, Simon eased out of the brush and crossed to the house . . . paused to wait for River as she staggered after him. "This is not smart!"

"I know the house. If they aren't in the dungeons, I can find them faster than you could." She reached out and propped herself against the wall of the house, then staggered around the corner.

A low wall bordered the stairs down. Open to the front. No sign of a guard. Simon slipped forward and took a good look around. And froze, his attention riveted to the north.

He hadn't noticed the wall of tree trunks, the hasty forward fortifications of a town about to be attacked. At the top of the wall, on some sort of platform, three people. The God of War and the Goddess of Logic flanked a man who glowed nearly as brightly as they. This King Kelso, perhaps? Another figure joined them, glowing, handsome . . . the God of Love.

Below, far enough away from the barrier that they didn't have to crane their necks, five bright figures. Even at a distance Simon recognized the tiny figure of the Goddess of Mercy, the bulks of the Virtue and Vice twins, the taller, slimmer figures of the God of Peace and the God of Art. Other glowing figures were moving, forming up in an arc behind them. All the little gods. Scores of them. Perhaps a hundred, and more were scattered among the troops.

"You're outnumbered, whether you count Gods, Magicians or soldiers." Pax's clear voice carried unnaturally. "Why don't

367

you three just go home and let us take care of these upstarts?"

"They aren't upstarts. They are people, and they have the right to build on any open, unclaimed land they want." Logic's voice was magically amplified as well. "Try to remember your roots, the precepts of the society that raised us."

Mercy laughed. "Oh, you mean their empty prattling about civil rights and freedom, while they called us sub-human and enslaved us?"

War's deep rumble rolled over the meadow. "They fell short of their ideals, but you? You have only your pride and desire for power."

Peace laughed. "Indeed, and you let your power spread and dilute. A few of us had more sense than that."

"Probably wise, although for all the wrong reasons. I thought I was spreading strength and courage, but it was only madness." The God of War took a step forward. "And so it ends."

The god glowed, blindingly bright as he lowered his shields. Simon could feel Mercy gathering power for a strike, but her gaze met Logic's cold watchfulness, and she shrank back a bit. And behind them, screams of pain and loss. Simon's eyes jerked to one nearby. A little god, looking like Barry, but his stance and gear that of a War God. Some extra shine faded as Simon watched. The man fell to his knees, panting, now. Struggling back up to his feet. Now he looked almost awkward in his armor. His hands were clumsy as they patted his sword hilt, his face.

Simon wheezed as he realized what had happened. Whatever divine spark the little god had held was gone. *And they never had any training in arms. They simply* knew *how to fight.*

"And now they don't." River finished his thought for him.

They looked to the platform, where the God of War glowed so brightly he was painful to look upon. And dimmed as he raised his mental barriers again.

Mercy looked fearfully at the Old Wolf and suddenly clutched for all the power she could pull from all the Little Mercies around her. Women staggered, looking around suddenly baffled by their participation in this insanity. No lingering ties to the goddess; she'd never cultivated a following.

And that quickly, over half of Mercy's Little Gods were destroyed. As such. The remnants, the people without the overlay of power, backed away, through the puzzled, or perhaps horrified, ranks of Travelers, Lady Lucks and Gambling Men.

The witches and mages were pulling back too, away from the group of gods. Could Mercy drain them as well? Surely not. Whatever effect the collective subconscious had on them, there wasn't much Mercy in any of them. Simon heard sharp commands in a high voice, and the retreating witches wavered, stopped. Did he recognize Firefly's voice? Someone was rallying the witches, getting them back in line with Mercy.

"C'mon." River eyed the confusion out on the field, and scattered thinly through the army. She turned her back on it, and tottered down the steps. A quick look showed all the cells empty. The door at the far end yielded to a tiny spell. A thankfully normal basement lay on the far side. Shelves loaded with gleaming jars. Large crocks probably full of grain. Wooden barrels. Floor to ceiling wine racks, mostly full. And stairs leading up to a kitchen.

River paused and glanced down a hallway. Shook her head. "Staff. Hiding under their beds, like sensible people." She kept going, pausing to scan an ornate dining room, and then a huge reception hall before she turned and tackled a double height graceful curve of stairs.

Simon wrapped an arm around her and half carried her up. "I hope you have an escape route planned out. I really don't want to go traveling with Mercy, when she flees the battlefield."

"No kidding." River turned and headed down a back hallway. "The 'unimportant guest' rooms are back here. Hideous woman always put me up like a poor relative." She staggered, and Simon guided her to a bench.

"Sit a moment."

She slumped, and nodded at the cross hallway. "To the right. They're close."

Simon took a look. A row of closed doors. Magical locks. He closed his eyes and studied the twisting . . . he triggered it. Simple, for someone with the right training. Carefully eased the door open. And blinked at the tearful Heidi.

Heidi leaped up, "Let me go, please! Just don't hurt Mike, he didn't know they were Mercy's enemies."

"I'm trying to rescue Amused and Flattered." Simon

interrupted. "Are they here?"

"Oh! Simon! It's you!" She gulped and nodded. "Mercy's out to hurt everyone River knows."

Simon tried the next door—same lock. He hustled down the corridor, uncharming every lock. By the time he'd run out of locks, he had Mike and five witches pestering him with questions. Amused and Flattered abandoned him abruptly to smother River with hugs and tears. The three blondes hovered. Did Barry know Mercy was holding his daughters? Would he really care?

"We need to get out of here." River struggled to her feet and headed for the front of the mansion.

Simon led the way, backtracking through cellar and dungeon. He edged up the stairs from the dungeon carefully. No guards in sight. He stepped out and spotted the parley still underway, across the camp.

Sudden movement, closer. A woman wearing the livery of Mercy's troops. The tall woman's eyes gleamed oddly, her mouth moved, but made no sounds until she swallowed. Hoarse and rasping. "I didn't believe in HIM. I believed in the Goddess, not some damned MALE! How can he have done this to me? I never worshipped, I was none of his. You called him to me, and that let him in, you bitch." The sword in her hand was still sharp, her grip strong, and she looked as if she had drilled for years.

"Mercy's Captain." River's voice was low, then she spoke more loudly. "Did Mercy get your family out of Miami? Is everyone safe?"

Simon could see that the words had no impact. The Captain was past all hope of being talked down.

He saw the madness in her eyes with sudden clarity, in the bright light that blossomed around the corner of the mansion.

Pain stabbed through his head, and he shielded as hard as he could. It wouldn't be enough, even shorn of her touch of the God, the captain was still a much more powerful magician than Simon.

Except that she was clutching her head, too.

He realized what had just happened, and stepped out and looked. A brilliant streak of light still lingered in the sky. A glowing line of yellow, orange, red; cooling. A hellish red dawn rose to the south east.

"No. No!" The big woman staggered out to stare, shaking her head in denial. "What have the Gods done?" Her head whipped back to River. "You! Who are you? *What* are you, who has done this?"

Then a roar, a rumbling. The ground heaved, threw Simon into the air and dumped him onto shivering pavement.

Red lit clouds like hell's own thunderstorm rose to the south, a column of superheated air and vaporized stone.

And buildings and people who didn't heed the gods' warning.

Simon crawled hastily around the corner of the mansion. "Get down, get against the wall."

River melted down beside him and he rolled her up

against the foundation, covered her body with his . . . Furnace hot air blew debris over the house, swirled around the corner and dropped leaves, twigs, sand . . . in the unprotected open area of the army camp, larger branches and stones hit unprotected targets, overturned wagons. Panicked horses thrashed and broke their picket lines, terrified soldiers covered their heads as they were flattened and rolled . . .

Behind the blast front the air was hot and dry, burned. The air had cooled too much to start fires, but the fires in the Army camp had been scattered, and hot coals were kindling flames in a hundred spots.

And in the dying light, Simon saw an army that believed their families dead, turn on their masters.

"Run!" River gasped, hauling herself to her feet. The others took heed and they ran for the back of the mansion, across the field without a thought of concealment. River started collapsing halfway. Simon grabbed her and hauled her across his shoulder and staggered on.

Through the brush, and into the forest. A waft of air. He glanced back. Mercy's mansion was gone, and as he watched, Edmund's disappeared as well.

No chance of those Gods standing up and taking what they've earned.

Simon sank down and eased River from his shoulder.

Out in the meadow, the soldiers milled about. Ugly in their grief. Starting to look at the barricade, and the only gods left to vent their rage upon. Starting to look at the Little Gods, even those drained and abandoned. The witches and mages bunched up and started moving west. The army was all clumped directly in front of the barricade, the magic users ought to be able to escape.

Amused and Flattered hovered. River reached for their hands. "There's one more thing I need to do." She closed her eyes.

Simon could feel her dragging weariness, and with no shields, hear her call across the chaos of the army camp.

:: Wolf! Can you hear me?::

:: River. Where are you? ::

:: West of the Army Camp. Can you tell them that most of Miami evacuated? North and Northwest roads. They should go find their families. ::

There was no answer, mentally.

But the god's voice rolled over the soldiers. "Miami was evacuated. You will find your families on the North Road and the Northwest Road. *Go.*"

The army swayed, buzzed. Turned south and started moving. Some immediately. A few voices rose in commands, and the tattered tents started coming down, loose horses collected.

Supplies for the refugees. Yes. Dear gods, what are all those people going to eat, until they clear new fields, plant, and harvest?

"Each other, most likely."

374

Simon jerked around. The God of Peace rolled a crackling ball of power in between the fingers of his left hand. Simon eased away from River and stepped toward the god. *Keep his attention on me.* "You don't think the other cities will send food?"

A sarcastic snort. "You lot make me sick. Always thinking that scattered and chaotic individuals will spontaneously act for the greater good." His eyes focused past Simon. "Go away, little wizard. I have a bone to pick with this witch."

River wavered to her feet, clutching a sapling for support. "Messed up your attempt to kill a hundred thousand of the enemy? Turned it into flattening your own city? Old Gods, I can only hope I was successful beyond belief in evacuating Miami, because it *is* my fault."

"You won't feel guilty for long." The god raised his hand.

Simon swallowed. Raised his voice, as if volume mattered. "God of War! I summon you!"

Pax spun and drew back his arm to throw.

Small cross-section.

Black on black, a huge rearing horse, a golden gleam of distant disaster on polished chain and plate mail. Uplifted sword.

Peace threw his fireball.

Simon's left hand extended, pointing. A needle of power zipped across the night. The fireball jumped, exploded.

A squeal of equine pain and a thud as a heavy weight hit the ground. Cursing, thank the Old Gods.

Simon blinked flash blinded eyes. Staggered, knees weak. The second squeal was angry; a gasp of fear, vegetation crunching under heavy hooves. The glow of Pax's magic disappeared.

Thank the Old Gods! I can't do that again.

Simon bent to help the God of War off the ground.

"Damn. I haven't been summoned like that for a couple of decades. Gotta remember to have the shields all up when it happens."

"Are you all right?" River's grasp on the sapling looked pretty tenuous.

Simon's head whipped from rising god to collapsing witch.

"A bit scorched around the edges. I think I'd best . . . " the half-seen form staggered over to River, and disappeared.

"Where'd River go?" Amused sidled up behind him.

"Wherever the god took her."

Flattered's voice spoke from the dark. "I know the god is supposed to come and fight, then return to wherever he was. But I didn't know he could take people with him."

"And I think he's left his horse behind." Amused sat down abruptly. "I'm not going anywhere until I can see what I'm stepping on."

That was the most sensible thing Simon had heard in a good while. He collapsed against a tree and closed his eyes.

A horse snorted in his face. He started awake, and blinked at Diana. "You don't look very ground tied." But rubbing his eyes, he could see that she'd managed to not break her reins, although her saddle was listing a bit. He pried himself off the ground and looked around. They were just a few trees inside the forest, the sun was just clearing the horizon. A couple dozen horses, Artemis included, were milling about. He pulled Diana's saddle off, and tied her up, walked around a big work horse, wasn't that one of Mike's mares? He grabbed Artemis's bridle. "At least you acted like a real horse and stepped on your reins." He led her over to Diana and unsaddled her, dug a halter out of her saddle bag. All nice and ordinary every day activities. He passed a rope to Mike, to catch his horses . . . "Why are there so many horses here?"

One of the Blondes, Rose, he thought, snickered and pointed. "I think your mares came to you. He made all the rest follow them."

Oh. Of course. How had he missed the black creature towering over the rest? *The* War Horse. Collecting mares like any other escaped stallion. Of course, it was mid winter, unlikely any of them were in season . . . Pity. The god didn't bring the stallion out very often, even Simon's mares, for all his bragging about them being double crosses, the nearest cross was three generations back.

Where had he put that fertility potion of his father's? Surely there were a few drops left . . .

He dug out his innocuous looking bit of metal from Artemis's saddle bag and opened it up. Food for people, grain for horses, and the little vial of potion. He added water and drizzled it over the mares' feed. What the heck, Mike and Heidi were going to need a classy team in the future . . .

It was midday before the last of the army pulled up stakes and headed south. Then Simon led his group across the meadow to the log barrier. He lost Mike and Heidi halfway, when they spotted their wagon, abandoned with a number of others, for lack of horses to pull them. The five witches exchanged uneasy looks and followed. *Even Logic and War are going to be shunned after this.*

The War Horse snorted in disgust, then turned his loose mares to follow Mike's pair. Diana and Artemis cast wistful looks back, but didn't protest too much.

A score of people huddled around a tiny fire. Big men, pretty women . . . shorn of the touch of godhood, they looked ordinary and frightened. One woman stood up, and took a few steps toward Simon.

"Please . . . if you know them, it wasn't our fault, we didn't want a war . . . We don't have anywhere to go, no families, and no home and . . . everyone blames *us*."

Simon nodded. "The gods won't blame you. They will understand."

One of the men rubbed shaking hands over his face. "I can't even remember how to hold a sword."

"So? You'll learn again. If that's what you want. If you'd rather learn farming, or weather making or anything that ever took your fancy, you can do that now. You are free of compulsions, now."

None of them looked over forty, a couple were teenagers.

"You'll be all right, now. I'll talk to War and Logic."

The Old Wolf met him at the gate. The god was looking his age, hair and beard white, skin a bit scorched.

"Don't look so appalled. I heal." The god looked amused, and waved in a man to take the mares.

The god glanced out toward the little encampment of former gods. "Kelso isn't keen on them staying here. I'll take them with me, when I return to Sahara. They are all powerful magic users. And untrained at it, which can be dangerous." His eyes crinkled. "I know just who to put in charge of training them."

Simon snorted and followed the Old Wolf to what was evidently a field hospital. Several wounded were on cots.

From here, he could see that the wall ran in an arc, both ends in the water of a fast flowing river, protecting a ford.

"There were a few early skirmishes with scouts." The god sighed. "We tried to keep an open path of retreat to the north, with messengers ready to ride out and warn the town to evacuate. It's not in a defensible situation. They had enough people to overrun us, if they were too impatient to try a siege. And Mercy was too bloodthirsty to take the time for that. Bloody arrogant woman."

Gisele, Goddess of Healing was bending over one man.

Simon suddenly recognized the Eldest of the Saharan Pyramid, sitting beside another patient. Kendra Star, the Old Wolf's, well, sort-of-wife.

She looked up and smiled. "Simon! Look at you! It's been, what, fifteen years?"

He stiffened as he recognized the form she was kneeling by. "River?"

Eyelids twitched, nearly opened.

"Oh, you know our little girl?"

"Your . . ."

She waved a hand dismissively. "Her mother practically abandoned her, so we raised her. I suppose she was nine or ten when you left, much too young for you to notice. Then when she was sixteen, her mother showed back up to claim her."

The Old Wolf chuckled. "River leaped at the chance. 'I can be a spy!' she said."

Kendra snorted. "So we had to let her go. Now, of course, *Dear,* since she's known to be yours, *my* pyramid will claim her and *you* can go train a new spy." She glanced at Simon. "Or two. I dare say the University could use a well traveled professor."

"Looks like you two have my career path all sorted out. Thank you."

They both grinned.

"We know you'll do whatever you want, Simon." Kendra frowned at the God. "Including pretending to be a nice little brown-noser. But I think all the wrong gods will recognize you, now."

River's eyes fluttered open. Checked the people around her. When her eyes found Simon, she smiled.

Good enough. I'll worry about the details later.

Chapter Thirteen

New Years Day 2237

River Wall, West Coast India

River stayed back, observing. Barely within hearing range.

Logic and War were looking down at the draggled remains of the army encampment. There were remarkably few bodies. The soldiers had, mostly, abandoned their attacks on the little gods when they abandoned the camp.

"Makes me glad I don't have any actual children."

The goddess nodded. "We subtly encouraged the magically talented to marry talent. And of course they worked out how to have sons. But the strongest of this last generation of children . . . We tried to shed the attention of the collective onto them."

The Wolf's quick grin flashed. "And *some* of us succeeded."

Logic glowered at him. "We must not do that again. The little gods who survived should marry the most common people they can find. And your attempts to dilute the attention of the collective must not happen again."

"I'll talk to Harry and Chance. With Mercy, we four were the worst offenders. And perhaps the Goddess of Fertility can whip up a spell that makes the talented be faintly repulsed by the talented."

A man stepped out of nowhere. River started, but the Wolf just nodded politely. Chance, the God of Luck, or Chaos or Statistics.

"Leave it to chance, now. You know we always, eventually, regret it when we load the dice."

"Spoken by the expert. Yes, perhaps so." Logic turned her back on the desolate battleground and walked away.

Chance sighed. "We really are stuck with this god thing, aren't we?" A rhetorical question, apparently. He looked down at the little gods scampering around, helping wherever they were pointed. He glowed brightly, briefly. Two young women staggered, hand going to their heads, looking around as something intangible, but always with them . . . disappeared. The God of Chance disappeared as well.

The Old Wolf, the true God of War, looked over at River. "Would you like to get home quickly?"

"Thank you, but no." River looked back at the battleground. "There were people I should try to find . . ." She caught a distant curse, and squinted. "Ah. They appear to be arguing with Jet over the possession of several mares."

Her foster father, the man who'd raised her, laughed. "I'd better go tell the old horse the bad news. I'll send your friends up here."

"Thank you. If the God of Love is still here, tell him there's a marriage to perform."

The god paused.

"No. Don't be silly, *my friends* need to get married. Witches don't do things like that."

"Don't worry, sir. I'll work on her." Simon spoke from behind her.

"I was raised by Kendra Star. Who is a very traditional witch." She pressed her lips together, trying to suppress a smile before she turned.

"Who lives in a winery with a god. I only have to persuade you to live with a penniless physics professor. Can't possibly be too difficult."

River cocked her head and thought back. "I hope you don't live in a tiny apartment just off campus, because not only do you have two expectant mares, I seem to recall Professor Frasier saying something about experiments with explosives."

"Well . . . Actually, not having been back to Sahara for nearly fifteen years, I don't have a home at all. So the possibilities are wide open. Perhaps you could help me choose the sort of place that a rather independent witch would find attractive . . . "

Thieves and Horses
333 years post exile
Pam Uphoff

Chapter One

June 4th, 2449

Scandia

Mikey Flicker had done several jobs for the Golden Boy and been paid promptly and in a business-like fashion.

So he wasn't the least bit concerned until he learned what the God of Peace wanted him to steal this time.

"A statue of a horse from the private museum of the God of Art?" He boggled a bit.

"Oh come now, you know we aren't really gods. We're just very powerful magic users. Artie was unconscionably rude, and I'm going to take his favorite horse statue. He's got three—one of a horse standing alone, a pair of foals playing, and a group of four running. I want the single horse." He pulled out two metallic buttons. "This one will keep you unnoticed by people, this one will unlock the door and turn off all offensive and defensive spells. You'll need some way to lift and move the statue, which weighs roughly a thousand pounds. In three days, Artie will be attending the opening of 'Romeau and Gisetta' and should be absent from six in the evening until midnight."

It actually sounded easy. The God had never steered him wrong before.

"Right. Friday night, then. And where do you want the statue delivered?"

He pointed out the window. "To my garden."

Mikey nodded. "Right. Will you be here?"

"No. I'll be attending the wretched play. Just leave it." Pax, God of Peace, the Golden Boy, call him whatever you wish. He was three hundred and fifty years old, more or less, and could easily be taken for less than twenty. And like all the thirteen Gods, he was "just" a powerful magician.

"Yes, sir." Sounded easy. Really it did. Now, moving a thousand pounds . . . Igor and a pallet on wheels? Umm. Half a ton. A very, very heavy cart. An engine hoist. That would do it. A box truck with a long ramp. Ramps in case of internal stairs. "We'll try to have it in your garden by the time you get home."

The butler showed him out silently.

He started up his little runabout, and whizzed away. Electric cars were so economical when one had the power to charge them oneself. Mikey knew he'd never qualify as a powerful magician, but he could pull power from movement and thermal differences and convert it to electricity. He could detect spells and charms and wards and traps. Disarm them if the magic user hadn't put too much power into them. But apart from being able to charge his car batteries by sitting half in the sun and half in the shade for three bloody damn whole hours, there just wasn't any *use* for magic any more. Hell, they didn't even test the kids these days.

If it got much worse, he might have to work for a living.

He drove past the target on the way home. A showy building with three cantilevered floors, each larger than the one under it. The god, if he recalled his society scream sheets correctly, was one of those who moved their entire homes with the seasons. Bombay for the winter, New Tokyo for spring, Scandia for the summer and Sahara for the fall. Not only was the building an upside down pyramid, it was up on a bit of a mound, with steps and formal landscaping.

But if he backed the truck up to the steps, he might be able to avoid pushing a thousand pounds up a ramp. Or at least as far up. The signal changed and he drove off, making plans.

Igor Benny was lifting weights when he stopped by. His best buddy from school, they were both brown haired and twenty-two. All resemblance ended there. Mikey had always been average in height and appearance; his father had been known to comment that he hardly needed an unnoticeable spell. Igor bulged with muscles and was nearly two meters tall. And agreeably ugly. Well, ugly.

"So, want to lift a thousand pound statue?"

Igor grunted, and racked the five hundred pounds he was bench-pressing.

"Only half of it." The big man scratched his flaky scalp.

"Does it come apart?"

"I figured we'd get an engine hoist to help."

Igor's eyes lit up and he nodded. "Dan has one."

"So we wouldn't even leave a rental record. Excellent. Let's go talk to him."

Igor's older brother was a practical mechanic, unable to hold a job for long, as the alcohol always sucked him back under. He mostly fixed the cars of friends and acquaintances, and fixed up junkers to sell. At that he was doing better than Igor, who simply didn't seem to be able to manage anything but manual labor, under supervision. At least Dan had a wife and kid. Or somebody's kid, Mikey seemed to recall Vera'd already been expecting when she took up with Dan. Or maybe she had been expecting by the time Mikey noticed she'd become a part of his circle of friends and useful people. Who cared? The Kipper was a cute little thing, eight years old now.

Dan was quite happy to loan out the hoist for a few bucks. Vera took half for food, the little girl jumping up and down at the prospect of a shopping trip.

Mikey got another friend to rent a truck for them, and by Friday they were ready to go.

At seven in the evening he backed the truck up the driveway and hopped out, clipboard in hand with a delivery slip to another address as he knocked and waited for an answer. He pounded, to be sure. Nothing. Excellent.

He walked back to the truck while sizing up the steps and rolled up the back door of the truck. "We'll need just three of the step ramps, once we back the truck around. I'll get them, you bring the hoist."

Mikey climbed into the front of the truck and got the two buttons, activated both and dropped them in his pocket.

Ramps in place, he touched the door pad, and they swung open for him. Slick, having a God to do the tricky bits.

There were pictures and statues all over the place.

The single horse was, unfortunately, up on a pedestal. Mikey cursed and went back to the truck for another ramp.

Igor was petting the statue of the two foals, one rearing and one kicking. "Aren't they purty?"

"Yeah. I gotta say this guy has good tastes in art. Look at that bull!"

Igor sniffed at the angry bull and patted the foal good bye. He pushed the engine hoist up the ramp and looped the chain around the horse. Mikey worked the lever, and the hydraulics did their thing. The horse came off the pedestal, and they very carefully rolled it down the ramp, Igor straining, and Mikey standing by with a wedge in case the hoist started rolling too fast. Igor started rolling the horse across the floor, and Mikey grabbed the ramp and hauled it back to the truck. He hustled back to help maneuver the horse through the doors, then Igor stopped while he backed the truck around and up to the steps. The ramp was more of a bridge, not too much of an uphill fight. As soon as Mikey had it secure, Igor walked across it, grunting with the weight of a foal statue.

"Igor. Bad idea. We can't sell something like that, we'll get caught and end up in jail."

"It's for Kipper."

The little girl. His niece, or whatever. Good Grief.

"Oh, what the hell . . . " Mikey got back to the horse and started pushing it along the sidewalk. Igor walked past him, and he looked back in disgust as the big man went back inside. "Igor . . ."

As he'd feared, the big man came back with the other foal. As he strained and walked, Mikey went back and shut the doors, hitting the lock pad. He pushed the horse halfway to the truck before Igor got back and helped him push it the rest of the way, up the slight incline of the ramp and into the truck. Mikey wedged the wheels of the hoist, stowed the ramp and rolled the doors closed. He climbed up to the cab and drove away. The first car to almost hit him reminded him, and he turned the buttons off. Sometimes being unnoticeable was dangerous. But when he turned into the God of Peace's street, he turned it back on. No need to attract the attention of the neighbors . . .

The Golden Boy's damn rock paths were a real pain to roll the hoist over. But Igor grabbed the horse and pulled it upright as Mikey released the hydraulics, and there it was. All done.

They wheeled the hoist out and drove off. They dropped the engine hoist and the foal statues off at Igor and Dan's place, and Mikey took the truck to his friend, who would return it in the morning.

He walked home, feeling a pleasant sense of accomplishment. The two foal statues in Igor's back yard were a bit worrisome, but it wasn't like he was going to try to sell them or anything.

In the morning, a messenger came by with a package for him. Mikey tipped him and sat back in satisfaction to count his money. It was even more than he'd expected, and he split it up and hid it in various places, and took a wad to the friend to reimburse him for the truck rental, with a nice bonus so he'd jump at the chance to do Mikey another favor sometime.

Then he drove to Igor's, and joined the family in admiring the foals.

Their house had been their parents'. Igor lived mostly in the big master bedroom, and Dan used the three smaller bedrooms and the garage. Back and front yards were for spare parts and projects being worked on. But the corner that had been cleared out to be Kipper's play area sported the two foals, and the little girl was delighted. She climbed up and rode on the rearing foal, then climbed across to the kicking one, giggling maniacally.

Vera was shaking her head. "They must be worth some money . . . "

Mikey shook his head. "Nah, perk of the job, but I'd get into trouble if they showed up for sale. Some people you just don't want to look unappreciative around, you know?"

Vera nodded. Like all petty crooks, they lived in the cracks between the law of the land and the law of organized crime. And sometimes the law of gangs and gods, too. You had to get along with all of them, else you got crushed between them.

Scandia was no worse, and from all he'd heard, a bit better than any of the other large cities.

With his new found prosperity, Mikey figured he was set for the rest of the year. No taking chances, he'd scope out some possible high return targets, do a really thorough job and . . .

"Hey! Mikey! Man wants to see you."

Oh hell, one of Doscompos's men. Just what he needed.

Not that he was stupid enough to ignore the summons.

"A little birdie whispered in my ear." The big man leaned forward in his chair and put his elbows down on the desk. "An' you know what he said? He said you'd made a big score, and hadn't even remembered your old friends, who keep you and your good friends and their families safe in their beds."

"Ummm . . . "

"Why don't you go think about it? Think about the local widows and orphans, and donate generously to them."

"Uhh . . . " Mikey could see his money swirling down the drain. "I, uh, got some real nice stuff that needs a buyer, but you know, maybe being the smart man you are, you'd appreciate the art, know where it could be sold for more money. For the widows and orphans, you know?"

"Really." Doscompos looked unconvinced.

"I'll, uh, bring it by tomorrow, you can decide for yourself. I mean, what do I know about art?"

Snort. "Now that's the truth. Show me what you've got."

Oh. Bloody. Hell.

As he walked out, Mikey started turning explanations over

in his head. Actually, it was easy. Wait until school was in, and offer Vera money. All he'd have to do then was get one of those damn heavy foals into a vehicle of some sort.

He caught a horse drawn tram for a few blocks to save his strength, and cut over a street to his apartment . . .

The big steamer limo was waiting for him. The door opened as he walked by. "Get in." The chauffeur drove off with a hissing from the steam cylinders.

"Sir?" Mikey looked at the Golden Boy uncertainly.

"It's not often that I admit to a mistake, but some news I've received makes it necessary for Artie to rejoin my circle of friends. I need to completely divert his suspicions of me. Do you have any ideas about how to manage that?"

"Hmm, gotta pin it on someone else. There's a fellow, mex syndicate, big cat . . . he'd be easy to blame it on; he collects art. Maybe if you just mentioned his name, as someone you'd heard was in the black market? Even though he didn't recover his statue, he'd think this fellow was responsible . . . I still have that button that opened the doors, I could drop it off there, to make it more obvious . . . I don't see why my name should come into it, but I could take a vacation, maybe a cruise or something . . . "

"What an excellent idea. What's his name?"

"Estaven Doscompos. He has a warehouse, Ed's Storage on East Halleluiah Street. I'll, umm, have everything there by noon tomorrow."

"Excellent. Perhaps I can manage lunch with the man." The Golden Boy simply handed over a box and tapped on the chauffeur's window. The man pulled over and Mikey stepped out, and walked away without looking back.

"I am in so much trouble." He reluctantly turned up the street to Igor and Dan's house.

"I don't like the kicking horse." Kipper met him halfway down the block. "He's no fun to ride."

"Hmm, maybe I should take him away and bring back one that would be fun?"

"I want a pinto pony. A real live one. But Mommy says no, and Daddy's in trouble again."

Once he made it inside the house, it was clear that Vera was upset.

"Dan won't ever be able to hold a job. He's never going to overcome *this*. We can't pay the taxes, we just *can't* and we're three years behind and owe more than the house could possibly be worth and I don't care how big the houses are that they are building three blocks away. It not fair!"

Vera usually saw the sunny side of everything, so Mikey started worrying seriously. "What is it this time?"

"He got a bit of work at Milt's garage, because they had two mechanics out sick. He was test driving a car after fixing the brakes and crashed it. It wasn't his fault, but they said he'd been drinking."

And Dan always does drink. Mikey bit his lip. Could he use this?

His eye caught something in the paper scattered around the living room.

He picked it up and tapped it. "How about emigrating? This George Scooner Company has a pretty good reputation, and you know there won't be many organized shops out there."

"The Western Hemisphere?" Vera bit her lip, and Kipper started looking big eyed and scared.

"Heck, I'll bet you could get a real pony, if you moved there." Mikey told her.

"I doesn't matter." Vera said. "We don't have the money." She pulled the advert away from him and smoothed it on the table. "See? Eight fifty a piece, four for kids. Nearly three thousand dollars, for all of us."

"Thirty eight hundred, if I went too." Mikey plopped the box down on the table, and started counting. "I've gotten myself into a bit of a fix and was going to leave town, but you guys are all the family I've got. Igor an' me, we've been buddies since, since, well, I dunno. Babyhood or somethin'."

It was true, too. Without Igor he'd be lost. Who else could he depend on?

There was five thousand in the box. Vera bit her lip. "I'll go talk to Dan, see if there's a fine, or if it's the stocks again."

"Take five hundred, in case it's a fine, and I'll get Igor to help me with something . . . then we can pack and go." He tapped the paper. "Last call. They're leaving in five days."

And they'd better have room, 'cause I seem to be burning bridges and I'd hate to be left standing on them.

He walked home to fetch his car and drove it back to Igor's.

"Kipper doesn't like the kicking foal. I know a guy that will just love it, and then when we get to the New World, we'll buy her a real pony." He didn't give the big man any time to try and think about it, just had him carry the statue to the car, and cram half of it into the boot, and wrapped and tied a tarp around it.

It was a slow, harrowing trip to Doscompos's place, and he backed up to the office door.

The goons in charge strolled down. "In a hurry, eh?"

"Yeah, why don't you two show the boss how strong you are by carrying this in there."

"We gotta see it first." the blond one said. "It might be dangerous."

Mikey blinked, and removed the tarp.

They pulled the statue out and tipped it up on its nose.

"Huh, well it's got, uh, detail."

Mikey sniffed, and walked over to open the door. "It's a work of art."

The goons hefted it and staggered inside. Doscompos walked out of the inner sanctum and circled the foal.

"Well! Mikey, you surprise me. This is excellent, a bit realistic, but there are subtle expressions of human feeling in there. I *like* it." He clapped Mikey familiarly on the shoulder and started chatting about where he should put it.

Mikey fingered the button in his pocket. The key to Art's museum. He dropped it into Doscompos's pocket and whined a bit how he couldn't sell it very easily, so he hadn't gotten any money, and surely Doscompos would like to *buy* . . .

Mikey got himself thrown out and drove away.

"I am in so much trouble. I am going to be squished like a bug." He thought about buying dinner, but his stomach knotted and he decided to pass on it.

Vera had brought a banged up Dan home, and she was on the phone chatting to someone about emigrating when Mikey walked in.

Dan looked up, hungover. "I'm going to have to pack up all my tools. Crate everything. *Everything*."

"Don't worry. I'll help." Mikey assured him.

They wandered out to the garage to look over the situation. The hoist was the largest thing. "I know where to get some crates." Mikey said, and left again. It was so late it was early when he got to the wharfs. The boxes and crates were piled even higher than he remembered, and with the touch of the unnoticeable button, no one paid any attention to him taking all the empty crates he could get inside the big one for the hoist. He hesitated, then got another one that he thought could fit the rearing foal. Igor and Dan could try and argue her out of it. He had enough to do already. He tied the unwieldy load on top of his car and drove carefully.

His shopping spree started with tools. *Can't tackle the untamed wilderness without an axe. Or a saw, a shovel . . . oh hell. I'm going to need a tractor, aren't I?*

He sold his *car*. His little beauty.

The tractor was neat though. Also electric, and he got a plow, disks, rake and baler. Then he started talking to the salesman, and wound up buying a seeder *and* seed. Perennial wheat in bulk. Then a whole load of other seeds in small amounts to experiment with, find out what would grow.

And books. He doubled his book collection.

And Vera said they were all paid up and could start delivering goods to the dock warehouse immediately.

He had Malcom's Hardware deliver *everything* to the warehouse. Packing his apartment was a bit random. He still had some of his dad's stuff . . . He took his bookcases and books, of course. Clothes. Another shopping spree. All his cooking stuff. He hired a truck and delivered it all, checked that the hardware delivery was all there and properly labeled as his. Dan and Igor's stuff was there.

"You lot sure do have heavy goods." The longshoreman complained. "Not that I'm complaining, mind you. Beats the hell out of trying to load horses and cattle, and their feed takes up an incredible amount of room."

Mikey slipped him a big bill to ensure no unfortunate accidents happened to those heavy crates.

The fourth day, Derrick Hasten tried to kill him. Man never could shoot worth beans.

"Why?" He loosened his grip on the goon's neck enough for the man to take a breath.

"Doscompos put out a contract. Two thousand dollars for your head. You shouldn't have done that, man. He's pissed."

"Done what?" *Oh shit.*

"Started a war with a God, man. Doscompos don't back

down to no God and he's fingered you."

I knew that was a bad idea. I knew it. He squeezed until Derrick passed out, then tied him up and left him. He took the tram and taxi to Igor's and helped them finish packing. Slept on the couch, armed. Hustled them in the morning and got them aboard the ship early.

"Mikey," Vera sounded exasperated. "We're going to be onboard for fourteen days. The ship sails on the tide, in eight hours."

"I know, I just got anxious and kept dreaming all night long about missing the boat." He scanned the dock anxiously. Surely anyone looking for Mikey would look for Igor first thing, and the neighbors probably all knew about the boat . . .

He kept the little Kipper amused watching them load horses for hours, and cattle too. And the tide turned and they were off.

It was a miserable sixteen days. The storm delayed them, and the Kipper cried every time a dead horse got thrown overboard.

"Sea voyages are tough on them honey." Dan tried to explain. "Horses have delicate tummies."

They all had delicate tummies, in the big rolling waves. But they did finally pull into the big bay where George Scooner had his land grant.

The Colony was leasing the Government built dock, built by one of the Gods working with other magic users, when they started the transcontinental road. That massive boondoggle and waste of taxpayer's money was now complete, and another road across the southern part of the continent was under construction. The Scooner Company had built warehouses at the dock and a road to the main town site, and the accountants were all prepared to deal with the new colonists while all the goods were unloaded.

The land was broken up into pie wedges centered on the town site, and then split into blocks. Everyone got a single block of land as part of their membership fee. The sizes varied according to whether they were in town or out, and the farms according to the soil quality.

They all liked the sound of 'High Top', and they wanted to be far enough out to have that pony for the Kipper. And Mikey had all the farm gear . . . they inspected the land and then took a strip of four lots—one for each adult—that reached from the south side of the hill that gave the section the name, east toward town. That put them out on the outskirts, with no one beyond them.

Mikey took the furthest west lot.

"It's big because the soil is a bit thin and rocky," the woman registering parcels mentioned.

"No problem." Mikey smiled, thinking of the fun he'd have with his new tractor.

Then back to the dock to start the move.

They uncrated the tractor first, and Mikey sat and charged the batteries as Igor and Dan collected the rest of their goods. It was an impressive—and heavy—pile.

Various of his implements had wheels, and being careful to not overload them, Mikey and Igor made several trips to their land and back. They finally managed to borrow a trailer for the last load, and then take the trailer owner's last load to *his* place. Some time around midnight they were done, and collapsed while Vera poked through crates and finally found her cooking gear and the rather small amount of food they'd brought along.

Mikey worried a bit about that. It was late summer . . . He got out his farming books, and found the crop tables. It appeared to be time to plant hard winter squash, and too late for pretty much anything else. Maybe he could do a bit of green housie stuff . . . all he lacked was the greenhouse . . . Was anyone going to be making glass?

Maybe he should just grow his squash. Get his fields planted and have a hands on learning experience, as his father used to say. He sighed. His father had been a mage, a powerful one, and Mikey had learned all the endless, useless . . .

Hmm, or not useless? A lot of it had involved weather. Maybe, finally, out here in the wilderness all the crap his father had filled his brain with would be worth something.

They were all stiff and sore the next day, but they warmed up exploring their new empire.

Dan and Vera chose a slight hill to be the site of their future home, and Igor moved one hill over. Mikey started shifting his stuff three miles further down the road and fell in love with High Top hill.

His parcel was two square miles on the south east slope, climbing up from the road to a spot just below the apex.

It was rocky, as the lady had said, but he stopped at a flat spot three quarters of the way up the hill and just sat there admiring the view, and knowing he was grinning like a fool.

Then he unloaded the first crates and left the plow there.

He had to stop and charge batteries before he could make the second trip, and Vera had breakfast ready.

"We're going to have to hunt, aren't we?" Dan was looking a little worried.

Mikey nodded. "I've got more money, but I'll bet food is going to really get expensive."

Hunting. Hunting magic. Hmm, he'd have to remember stuff about that.

The Bennys were unpacking, and taking apart the big crates carefully. The hoist crate had already turned into a shelter for the Kipper, and the rearing foal crate was going to provide the sides of another room.

Thinking about magic, and the gods, and how the hell he'd suddenly gone mad and wound up out here, he poked the pretty statue. "It's kinda big, isn't it? I mean, bigger than a real foal?"

Dan wandered over and shrugged. "I dunno, I never had anything to do with horses."

Kipper hopped over and petted her statue. "It's got a funny rough spot right here under his head."

"Well, all those jaw bones and . . . " There was something *very* odd about the rough spot, and Mikey scratched at it, peeled it off like it was glued there . . . and something popped like a soap bubble and the foal touched down and threw his head up, startled.

Not half as startled as the people. Mikey backed away carefully, and swallowed nervously. What had just happened? The Kipper held her hands out and cooed to the oversized dull gray and black creature. It snorted and sniffed her, then trotted off a bit and looked around.

Vera wrung her hands. "I do hope he's old enough to eat grass, because we don't have a milk cow."

Keeping half an eye on the colt, Mikey went back to work, loading up everything that would fit onto his reaper. The colt followed him to the hill, and grazed while he was unloading, then followed him back to the Bennys' place. Kipper ran around with him, and they explored the back of the property where there was a creek.

By the time Mikey got back from the third trip, girl and horse were both wet and muddy and getting scolded.

Mikey's tractor crate was dismantled, but the rest he took himself, and lined out in rocks where he'd build his house.

Thinking about it, he moved the crates to the side where his equipment storage was going to be. That way his first house wouldn't be in the way of his second.

He slept there, alone and free, and hungry. Thinking about magic and hunting. In the morning he surveyed the lands to the south, and spotted some herds of large animals. Domestic cows? Or something wild? He set out to discover which, reviewing his selection of spells.

Unnoticeable. Definitely. Slice or fireball? Hard to say, neither was useful beyond about four meters. That was pretty close to get to a wild animal.

The animals were wild cattle, not the plump short horned variety he was used to. These were big, lean and possessed large horns.

He eyed them from a safe distance. "Lots of steaks and hamburger, right there," he muttered. The nearest cow flung up her head and looked his way suspiciously. *Good hearing.*

On the far side of the herd he could see some movemen— men on horseback, with rifles. They were holding them up as if already primed and ready . . . aiming them and then a volley of shots rang out.

Four cows fell, and the other fifty turned and ran straight at Mikey. He leaped up onto the tractor and banished his unnoticeable spell. They were still coming! He sliced out at the first big cow, then threw a fire ball at a huge bull. Then he put up a shield, and was knocked completely off the tractor as another cow ran straight into the shield. Then they were gone, except the first cow and the bull, and a staggering calf that must have hit the shield and practically knocked itself out. He jumped up and grabbed the calf and found himself fighting with a critter that weighed more than he did and had hard things on the ten or twenty appendages that seemed to be striking him.

Then it was suddenly jerked away.

"Sorry about that."

Mikey staggered back to his feet and blinked up at the man on the horse.

"We didn't realize there was anyone over here to get trampled."

Mikey looked at the carcasses, and grinned. "Hey, it wasn't how I was planning on hunting, but whatever works."

The man had the wild calf roped and tied off to his horse, and now he dismounted and grabbed the creature. "Heifer, excellent. I expect you'll want her?"

Mikey nodded. *What am I going to do with a cow?*

The man threw the critter down and had her legs all tied up in nothing flat. "Can you hold her and drive?" He seemed to assume an affirmative, and transferring his attention back to the carcasses, he simply roped their horns to the tractor. "There you go. Really sorry about the stampede."

"No problem, " Mikey repeated weakly. Fortunately it was mostly a straight shot, all the way back to the Bennys'. If he'd had to do much steering, he'd have given up on the struggling calf.

Vera had met the neighbors across the way, and they all came and exclaimed over the carcasses and the calf. The two families with side by side plots were farmers, or at any rate planning on being farmers, and they knew just what to do.

Wild Thing was quickly put into a pen with their own cattle, and the carcasses attacked with knives and reduced to hide (a bit the worse for wear after being dragged five miles) and chunks of meat. Fire pits for roasts, smokers for jerky, using leaky tents made of the hides over poles, and of course, a steak dinner whipped up on the spot.

The men chatted about hunting, and the women about cooking and preserving food, and the kids—the other two families had six between them—played with the big colt and named him Foggy.

The farmers considered the Bennys to be woefully lacking in needed skills, but Dan's ability to improvise when spare parts weren't available was approved.

Mikey's ability to hunt, as proved by the lean, mean steaks they were chewing, was considered proven. As a single man, that was fine. But Dan, and by association, Igor, had family responsibilities.

Next thing you knew, they were chopping down trees for a house.

Mikey hated his new axe within four strokes and stepped back to *slice* the tree. Worked like a charm, and he noticed that it fell in the direction of the partial cut he'd made.

Branches, dead easy. He was panting and drained by sundown. But happy. Magic. He'd found a use for magic.

That first log cabin was crude, and the fence for the Wild Thing and the dun colt too low. The colt jumped out, and Hastings gelded him. "Before he gets you into serious trouble."

The electric tractor was put to good use. The Hastings and Turners had larger and more powerful machines, but were already starting to have trouble getting fuel.

They did the first ground breaking for the Bennys' fall

garden, and left the rest of it to Mikey and his machine.

Squash, tomatoes, beans, peppers, lettuce, chard . . .

Once planted, they turned back to building, and got up some good barns for the Hastings and Turners, a good equipment shed for Mikey, and a shed for the dun and the wild heifer.

Then the farmers introduced the poor city folk to the concept of "haying".

Mikey spent every morning charging batteries so he could mow, rake or bale in the afternoon.

The Turners and Hastings were proud of their protégées, and a larger barn was built.

Then there was firewood.

Collecting acorns, as a flour extender. "Just this year, we'll have plenty of wheat next year."

Berry picking and canning jelly happened. Mikey avoided the process as much as possible, and started building his house. He started small, with what he decided would eventually be his library. A roaring fireplace, absolutely necessary. Four walls, with the windows mostly high up for good reading light, but leaving plenty of room for book shelves. One larger window to take in his favorite view.

On inquiry, he found glass almost impossible to find, and searched through his father's books for information. The purest quartz sand possible and heat it till it melted. There were various additives to help clarify less than completely pure silica, none of which he had, or had any idea how to get. Spells for the heat and the levitation so it would cool smooth and not stick to anything. He practiced on pure sand, shattering a lot of glass until he built a rocky beehive shaped oven he could heat, and stack with glass so it could cool down slowly.

The first glass he produced was awful, but he made thick blocks he could fill his high windows with, and with three times the trouble, a bunch of small panes for his big window. The distortion was bad, but the window was weather tight. He finally unpacked all of his books and turned the old crate wood into rough shelving so all his books were out and he could find them.

This winter he would be studying magic.

And improving his glass.

Chapter Two

15 October 2450

Scoone, East Coast of North America

They called it High Top Road, and 'his' family, the Turners and the Hastings were the only families living there as the winter slowly set in. It was not very cold, and the dun and the wild heifer kept grazing, as they enlarged the pastures and the gardens produced an abundance of squash and tomatoes.

Hunting had gotten a lot more difficult, as the local cattle migrated south and the deer learned about the new predator. The mounted hunters he had encountered on his first hunt lived down the Scarlet River, a mesh of siblings and cousins and in-laws that were all horse mad and had brought lots of brood stock, both bovine and equine.

By heading due west, or even north-west, he could avoid the ranchers and stalk the slowly migrating cattle under his unnoticeable spell. He practiced stun and sleep, but didn't want to feed more cattle through the winter. He'd just see about catching some yearling heifers next spring. In the mean time, they had plenty of meat, and had preserved a whole lot of it. In late December he managed to get some wild birds, for the holidays, and they got together with the Turners and Hastings around a bonfire and sang the old carols.

None of them ventured as far as town. The big church that had gone up was, according to who you believed, a revival of the True Religion or the New Religion.

None of them felt good about the fiery denouements of the Old Gods, in favor of some disembodied Creator that the Preacher was fond of. What was there to denounce? Nobody actually worshiped the old gods, did they? Mikey was even less comfortable when the human users of magic were added to the denunciations. So they celebrated at home and settled down to a nice quiet winter, with a little snow, frequent rains, and an early spring.

The electric tractor got a workout then, as Mikey plowed his flattest stretch and planted his perennial wheat amongst the rocks. They all helped each other, and at some point Mikey was astonished to realize that not only was he working hard and completely honestly, he was enjoying it.

Well, not the rock picking, perhaps. He gradually assembled long, contour following heaps of rock, and with some more digging and piling, the start of something that might eventually be some hybrid of terracing and stone walls.

Vera produced a little brother for the Kipper and Mikey and Igor tried to pick up the slack in the garden for a bit, but were chased out of her kitchen when they tried to relieve her of that burden.

The wild cattle migrated back northward as the grass sprouted, and he stunned and then charmed two heifers. They never calmed down like Wild Thing had, and he regretfully ate them both. He'd have to start with fairly young calves, and handle them regularly or it just wasn't going to work.

Kipper was riding, a little, the dun yearling, just bareback with a loop of rope from one side of his halter to the other for reins. Dan rigged up a pair of leather hoppers to lay across his back, and the pair of them were given the chore of hauling ripe veggies from their extensive gardens to her mother's kitchen.

Wolves raided a few outlying farms, and Mikey joined the hunt for them. Fifty miles to the west he found a boy living with wolves, and suggested that if the boy didn't want his four legged family killed they should move further and never raid farms again.

The boy scowled. "You shouldn't have been able to see me."

"I'm a Mage. You glow like one, too. If you send the wolves away, you could come and live in the town."

The boy growled. "My father would find me, come and claim me. Never. Never again."

"What's your name?"

But the boy slipped into the brush and disappeared.

The wolves weren't seen again.

The hunting party had to be satisfied with driving the wolves off.

"Teach them to fear man," a sheep rancher growled.

Mikey made lots of glass jars and glass stoppers that minimized the amount of bees wax needed for canning. He was quite proud of them, and sold as many as he had time to make.

In the late spring the second shipload of colonists arrived. And the accumulated news from the Old World.

The political maneuvering sounded pointless and unimportant.

The crime reports barely touched the apparent feud between organized crime and an old god.

The burnings of magic users alarmed only a few.

The high society news was meaningless.

The rumors of looming war with any of four other polities seemed empty.

The colony turned back to important things, like the three widows and their six daughters who had bought nine shares, every single one on or just north of High Top. The rumors whispered that they were witches. The matchmakers, delighted at such a balancing of the majority male colony statistics, got right to work.

Mikey rather hoped they weren't going to build their house on the very top. He didn't like the idea of anyone looking down on him, like they were sneaking around behind him.

But he really didn't have time to worry. He was too busy looking through his father's books for something to deal with the bugs that were all over the garden, and eating his wheat sprouts.

He and Igor did go around the hill and introduce themselves, neighborly-like, but got a bit of a cold shoulder.

"If they are witches that means they won't ever marry.

Anyway, we're introduced and all. I hope they're friendly. We lucked out with the Turners and Hastings, I hope our back neighbors are half the friends the front ones are." Mikey shrugged.

They rode the tractor back to the Bennys' houses and reported in.

"Lady Best and her daughters, Muddy and Salty. Lady Driven and her daughters, Last, Puddle, and Rippled. Lady Motivated and her daughter, Vapor."

Vera giggled. "I'll bet those aren't the names on their birth certificates. They're just playing old fashioned witches with their silly names."

"How old are they?" Kipper asked, looking a bit hopeful. The Turners' and Hastings' kids were a bit heavy on males in her age range.

"Umm, Last looked about sixteen, and Vapor was maybe two. The other four are in between. Maybe you and your mother should go over, you can borrow the tractor if you want."

"I should take over some fresh vegetables." Vera handed the baby to Dan and started assembling lunch. "You two men might have looked a bit scary." She smiled up at her brother-in-law and shook her head. "I remember thinking I was in trouble the first time I saw you, poor Igor. And Mikey, all you need is a knife clenched between your teeth to look like a vicious pirate."

"Me?" Mikey tried to look hurt instead of complimented. *Pirate? Me?*

Kipper liked the idea too and called him Captain Black,

despite his brown hair.

His regular hunting trips continued, and he started bringing home calves as they started looking old enough to wean. He bought milk from the Hastings regularly for them, but there simply wasn't enough grain to supplement the grazing. Petting and taming the calves was added to Kipper's chores, and by mid-summer she had six of them following her around like puppies.

The day before the Summer Solstice, a rather stiff Lady Best walked around the hill to inform him that the Pyramid of High Top would be holding a meeting on the crest that night, and that they would appreciate not being disturbed.

He nodded. "I'll bunk with Igor for the night. No problem."

She blinked a bit in surprise. "Because we . . . umm, sorry. I had my arguments all lined up."

Mikey grinned, hesitated. "Well, I mean, I understand the importance of a Solstice to you, and tonight the mountain belongs to you."

She opened her mouth and hesitated. "Umm. Thank you. Both for your honesty and your understanding. For your respect."

Mikey shrugged. "Hey, it costs nothing, is very valuable, and tends to get returned. Happy Solstice, Sister Best."

Of course he and Igor wound up at Dan and Vera's for dinner, and after planning the enlargement of their house and admiring Kipper's training Foggy to pull things—the yearling was clearly a draft horse—they slept in the barn and started the foundations the next morning.

Lady Motivated came by in the afternoon. "I wanted to thank you for not, well, either laughing at us or being deliberately disruptive. We moved here because we couldn't seem to ever be left alone for a single night. We were tired of hiding."

Mikey nodded, and walked back down the road a bit with her. "Look I know the various magic users haven't always gotten along. I don't see any point to it. I'm a mage."

Motivated looked startled. "Oh. Goodness, I hadn't even realized. I'm afraid I don't know much about mages."

"I'm not a very strong one. My father, err, well, there were problems and I never had a Compass. About all I do is glass, and a bit of hunting magic. And charge batteries."

She giggled at that. "Oh dear, and we spent so much time wondering how you kept it charged with no windmill in sight. Did you leave the Old World because of persecution?"

"No. I wasn't really afraid of exposure, I don't have any rites, no Compass, no Orgies. So no job either, mind you. Moving here has been wonderful, I can use magic and just not mention that that was how I did something, and everything is fine. Mind you, I could do without that Church of the Creator. I refuse to believe the Creator of all this beauty is so vindictive and cruel."

And it was beautiful. The lush green grasslands were dotted with groves of trees, and wildflowers were blooming. To the west it seemed like he could see forever. The slim brunette walking with him helped improve the view as well.

They chatted about various of their different magical traditions, finding a large amount of overlap, and it just seemed natural to invite her up to see his library, and somehow they wound up in bed instead of reading.

"I like this. Sleeping surrounded by books." She nestled up against him, content.

He nestled right back, grinning like a loon, most likely. He hoped he hadn't been too obviously amateurish.

She finally got up, and books were read, and the construction of the house admired. He volunteered himself and Igor to help with their own house raising in a few weeks; they were apparently still living in tents.

In fact, all the neighbors came, and three houses and a barn were built around the meeting corners of four of their parcels. Other neighbors from further north drifted in and were recruited, and food appeared and was consumed during a break, and polished off after the roofs went on.

As the youngest of the 'widows', Motivated garnered a lot of masculine attention. Last and Muddy, the oldest girls, both claiming to be seventeen, scooped up a lot of the remaining ogles. Heck, Lady Best and Lady Driven were fine looking women too.

Igor was getting a fair number of return ogles, Mikey hauled him aside and informed him of the known dangers of deflowering a virgin witch. Igor laughed, and nearly flattened him with a friendly swat on the shoulder.

It seemed like every family that had emigrated had brought at least one unmarried brother along, and there were plenty of single men who had emigrated alone as well. A group of them were sizing up the witches.

Mikey caught Motivated's eye and grinned. "Don't hurt them *too* badly."

She snickered, but glanced toward Last and Muddy. "I hope they don't try anything with those two, they know they aren't trained yet."

Mikey nodded, contemplating another piece of chicken. However good, he simply didn't have the room for it.

"I didn't believe any number of people could build three houses, even small ones, in a day." Lady Driven walked over and sat on a log.

"Well, you ladies had the foundations ready, and the logs cut." Gerald Gibson, a married man from a knot of farms a few kilometers north, eyed the three cabins. "I guess with those straight cuts, I'll have to take your being witches seriously."

Mikey started to open his mouth and take credit, but Motivated elbowed him.

"Oh yes, and after we magically felled them, we went around magically putting saw marks on half of them." Lady Driven chuckled. "It's taken us four months of off and on work to get to the point of being ready to raise the walls."

"They did go up nice and fast." Igor said. "We've got lots of practice now."

Mikey nodded. "How are the rest of you doing?"

They all had houses up already, and there was some chatter about needing barns, expanding plowed fields and pastures. They were all interested in Mikey's wild cattle.

"The oldest is just a yearling. I figure to breed her this fall to Harvy's beef bull and see what the result is. I suspect that they'll just be a stop gap, until the domesticated herds are big enough that we don't need the wild ones."

That got a fair amount of nods.

"I suppose I could catch more calves, if anyone's interested?"

They all were, and Mikey was kept busy, between harvesting, haying and cutting firewood, and putting in the fall crops again.

With more children around, they petitioned for and got a small parcel to build a school on. Several other schools were built as well, but the witch children came across the hill and attended theirs. Sally Turner taught the littler children, and Lady Best the older, and except for the most stormy days, the school was open for nearly all winter, and the kids were expected to read a little bit every week the rest of the year.

Chapter Three

10 May 2451

Scoone, North America

The town proper was growing. The city hall, a polished granite edifice imported in pieces, was finished. It faced the Church of the Creator across a pretty green square, and shops filled the other two sides.

The wear and tear of a year and a half's use was catching up to much of the first colonists' machinery, and Dan was kept busy. And spent too much time too close to sources of liquor. Mikey was appalled the first time he had to hunt the man down and drag him home. This whole new life, all this wonder and beauty, and Dan was still crawling into a bottle.

His own life was wonderful, apart from Motivated living two miles away. She was expecting a baby, and despite her firm warnings that baby witches didn't have fathers, he was determined to be at least a frequent visitor. Heck Vapor was a cute kid, and liked him. Motivated laughed at him when he tried to dodge Last and Muddy's attempts to corner him for kissing practice.

"They have to learn to flirt, and sorry, my pirate, you are a safe person to kiss. Most of the other men here are either married to women who wouldn't understand, or who would want to do a lot more than the girls are ready for."

So he got lots of kisses, and then Motivated hauled him off to harvest his sexual arousal.

"Umm, but you're always so . . . energetic." she laughed at him. "I think the three of us are almost giving my mage the orgies he desires."

Indeed. And in fact he was finding that he could do a lot more, magically, then he'd ever expected. Charging the tractor batteries went much faster, and after a long day on the crest of the mountain the large storm off the coast turned away and went out to sea.

But perhaps it would have, anyway.

His daughter was beautiful, and in the witches' way, named Whirlpool.

The third colony ship brought a whole lot of rich people.

The news was all about the unrest in the southern colonies, the Forre's colonies clashing with the Al Guerros's Colonies.

Rumors about the stratified Al Guerros society having trouble digesting the New Lords from the colonies, and the Forre Colonies had outlawed magic and accused the Al Guerros of supporting it.

The new rich people were acting like they were Lords in fact rather than in title, come to that. When they started using the titles as verbal weapons, rather than the courtesy that, for instance the witches were afforded, Mikey really got pissed.

"Are you sure you don't want to plow on the contour,

Franklin?" Turner had his biggest tractor out and would break ground, with Mikey coming after to further condition the soil.

"That's Lord Franklin to you." The man stared down at Turner like he was an insect in need of swatting.

Mikey snorted. "Well, I'm the Duke of High Top, and I don't need to put other people down, Frankie. Now do you want this field plowed straight or on contour?"

Not at all apparently.

Mikey apologized to his neighbor for losing the job, but Turner laughed and the story about just how far Lord Franklin's eye had bugged out when a mere peasant called him Frankie was all over the colony the next week, and the Duke of High Top was greeted by title all the time. Rather a lot of titles popped up over the summer, and the new people gritted their teeth and their attempts to regulate titles was voted down, firmly. So firmly that one rather suspected their own hired laborers must have voted against it.

In the rare slack time, Mikey and Igor worked on building a wagon. It was a bit trial and error, but in the end they produced a nice working rig that the huge Foggy could pull. It helped immensely with the grain harvest. His perennial wheat's second year harvest was impressive, and he built a small silo.

It was the scent that caught his attention.

West northwest of the town proper the flats got a bit too flat for good drainage, and people had skipped the muddy areas and settled a bit further on. But one little hut was there, absolutely surrounded by lush herbs. He let the tractor coast to a stop and just sat and inhaled all the wonderful smells for several long moments. Then shaking himself, he reached for the switch when he noticed the little old lady in the garden, watching him.

"Good morning. Your garden smells wonderful."

She stumped over, smiling to show worn but good teeth. "Why thank you young man. The local climate seems to agree with them. I sell spices, and also medicines. I'm willing to trade, and I can always use some extra hands to pull weeds."

"Do you need bottles and such?" Mikey asked. "I make them, whenever I have the time, which isn't very often these days."

"Oh yes, bottles of all kinds. Does your wife need spices?"

Mikey grinned. "I see I'll need to find time for glass making again. What size bottles do you like?"

Then he was off to bale Leander's timothy.

There was half a riot in town as he passed back through. He cut through alleys and got around it, but parked and walked back to find out the cause.

A group of men had a rope over a large oak limb, and were apparently prepared to hang a young man lying in a bloody heap at their feet. Their putative mayor, George Scooner himself was arguing with them.

"This is a law abiding town. We have courts of law, and as Judge Wittaker told you, what this young man did isn't a crime. Your daughter is sixteen and if she wants to screw the stable boy, she can. You have committed assault and battery of the most appalling sort, and now you think you can commit murder without anyone lifting a finger?"

"Anyone who lifts a finger, is going to lose it." Growled the so-called Count Valasi. He was immaculate. No doubt he'd had flunkies beat the young man . . . a brief parting of the crowd made it unfortunately clear that 'man' was perhaps no longer the correct term.

Mikey cringed. The kid looked maybe eighteen. He looked over the crowd at the rope and made some tiny slices in it, not quite enough to break it . . . hopefully enough that it couldn't hold any weight to speak of.

He sent a flick of fear into the horse a flunky was holding. It reared and lunged away, breaking the tension between the Mayor and the Count as everyone shifted away from the unruly animal, including the Count.

His teeth barred, he sneered. "You want him? He's all yours."

"You'll receive your summons to court, Valasi."

The Count glared, but spun away and stalked to his horse, which was still unsettled, and made mounting a bit of a trial.

The crowd disbursed, leaving just a few people standing around the stripped and castrated boy on the ground. The boy at least didn't appear to have been dragged here.

The others edged away, making spectators-only of themselves. The Mayor eyed Mikey. "Well, Duke?"

Mikey shrugged. "Yeah, I'll take him. Can you walk, kid?"

The kid didn't want to get up, didn't want to show his

mutilation. Mikey looked over at the spectators. "Fenny? Go get a pair of pants from Madam Handal. Medium size, soft fabric. And a shirt." He pulled out his wallet and sorted through the paper money the colony used for local business, and handed over more than he should need.

"What's your name, kid?"

"Jeremy Fentris. He had no right, he, how could he . . . why blame me? Why didn't she . . . "

Mikey sighed. "She dumped the blame on you, and he is an arrogant ass that thinks the law doesn't apply to him. And you're the idiot that got caught in between and you're the only one that'll pay for it."

The Mayor cleared his throat. "Actually this all fired up because the girl's pregnant."

"Ah, yes." Mikey sighed. "So bloody stupid, all around."

Fenny returned with the clothing and Mikey helped the boy put it on with minimal titillation for the audience. The boy stood shakily and hunched over, and Mikey walked him off to the tractor.

Sitting in the seat was less uncomfortable than any other possible method of transporting the boy, so Mikey showed him how to drive and directed him from the rear perch.

At home he got more practical, with some ointment he used on the heifers, and some padding, and some of Mikey's older, softer clothes while the new pants had the blood stains washed out.

He put Jeremy to work, small things at first that wouldn't

physically tax him, but would keep him busy. But in a few days he started the kid on moving rocks and dirt to build up a new foundation and floor. It was time to expand his house.

He'd seen plenty of examples now, of fireplaces and ovens and kitchens, and knew just what he wanted. The front was open and grand with a big room, and the back was designed with feeding a family in mind. A big spacious kitchen, with lots of pantry space, because here on the rocks of High Top there was no chance of a basement.

The dining room, and a loft over it and the kitchen for a boy he seemed to have acquired. The furniture that had been crammed into the library spread out over the empty space and he even moved his two best book cases to the front room. All farming and fiction, where anyone might see them.

"All right. You need a bed, and I finally have room for a big dining room table. Let's go shopping."

Jeremy paled. "I'd rather not."

The house raising had been a bit harrowing for the boy. He'd attracted a lot of pitying looks. Last thing he needed. Mikey shrugged. "All right, but don't complain about the colors."

Jeremy smiled at the thin joke. The local plants hadn't turned out many dyes, so the color choices were pretty limited.

For this Mikey walked down to the Bennys' and borrowed Foggy and the wagon. There were three carpenter's shops in town, and Mikey put in his order for the dining table and chairs, and bought a simple bed frame, and from the shop across the street, a wool stuffed mattress, linen sheets and blankets. He chatted with friends, shrugged away the lascivious concerns expressed about 'that boy'.

"There's plenty of us single men that won't ever get married. It isn't the end of the world, no matter how much it gives us the cold grues to even think about."

"Valasi says he won't show for court."

"Valasi ought to go back home, where he'll have to obey the law."

"I heard he was going to send his daughter home, but there wasn't a ship he could trust."

"You mean there weren't any people he trusted to travel with her. He doesn't want to do without his wife for a year, after all." Mikey corrected.

Jeremy was fretting and uncertain as he helped unload. "It's Sicily." He finally said. "I shouldn't care."

"But you do. I haven't heard a thing. Just gossip about how he hadn't been able to send her back." Mikey nodded. "I'll try and pry some information out of someone."

***

A ship full of colonists docked in the late summer.

"Moving way west, across the Blue Mountains." Mark Hastings reported. "I dunno why they want to go so far inland."

"The surveys show good soil." Mikey had ignored the transcontinental road up to now.

But he inspected it after the colonists had passed through. It rather put his glass making into perspective, as he listened to the mayor talking about how the god had formed and melted it as he walked along.

"The surveyors just staked out the route, and he walked along . . . never seen anything like it. There was a whole bunch of people along, but they were just there to keep him happy." The mayor's lips thinned. "There was no call for him to . . . he had his wife and kid along. He just took Miss Faloni because he could, and he *enjoyed* hurting her."

Mikey sighed. "Gods are just powerful men, George. No different than Lord Valasi. How's his daughter doing?"

"No one's seen her, everyone says she's pregnant, but maybe he thinks if no one actually *sees* her, it didn't happen?" He snorted. "Nobles."

But Jeremy continued to worry.

Chapter Four

28 January 2452

Scoone, North America

And so in the middle of winter Mikey was borrowing Foggy and riding carefully around Scooner to the far side of Scooner Bay and wondering how to approach someone on Count Valasi's staff for information.

The air was crisp and cold, and just above freezing. He tied the placid young horse in some trees and wrapped an unnoticeable spell around himself and walked over to see if he could find anything out. One wing of the Count's house was well lit, and Mikey discovered that his timing was impeccable. Lady Sicily was in labor. He was puzzled by the absence of staff in the kitchen, and walked around to the front of the house. He caught the sound of voices from a ground level basement window.

" . . . why the Countess is so sure the baby will be stillborn, the girl's full term."

"Oh, I'm sure the Countess has ways of knowing." The other woman's voice was dry.

Mikey shuddered and walked on. Yes, one could be quite certain of a stillborn child, if one was prepared to ensure it never breathed.

The Count's house was easily the largest in Scoone, and

had plenty of ways for an enterprising former thief to get in and out. He took his time and explored a bit, finally picking up some clothing that probably belonged to the Countess and bundling it up into something roughly the shape of a baby . . . not heavy enough . . . a couple of jars of some beauty product took care of that. Then the spell . . . he stood at a window and felt the breeze, harvested its energy and built up Power. An illusion. A baby, still and unbreathing. Dead. Wrapped like they expected, but unimportant, they didn't need to look. Embarrassing, deal with it quickly. But hard and secure, the idea that this was a baby. He looked down at the bundled jars and hoped it worked. He never could see his own illusions.

He moved to the room all the noise was issuing from.

"Now bear down, dear, we need to remove this poor dead baby, and then everything can get back to normal."

"Stop lying . . . At least have the guts . . . to admit that you . . . are going to murder . . . your own grandchild. Aergh!"

Mikey wrapped unnoticeable around himself as hard as he could and stepped in. He stood quietly in the corner through another half hour of the girl resisting labor, the Count stomping in to order them to finish up this disgraceful episode quickly. And inevitably, the birth. The Countess sighed and curled up on the floor, sound asleep, and Mikey stepped forward to support the baby's head, as the rest of her was born.

"What, what . . . ?" the girl squinted trying to see him.

"Your baby will be fine." He tried to whisper in a high tone. "Hold her, just this once, and know that she will be loved."

The girl held the baby, tears running down her face, while Mikey unraveled some thread and tied and cut the cord.

"We were going to marry, we had plans. We were going to be so happy." Babe and mother stared at each other in wonder, and she nursed the baby one time then handed her to the blurry thing she couldn't see.

"What I leave is not a real baby, but everyone will think it is."

He wrapped the dummy in the small blanket that was all the preparation for the baby that he could see, and placed it in her arms. She gulped. And he shed his jacket, wrapped the sleeping baby in it, and left. Behind him, the Countess stirred and rose.

"You were right, Mother. She's dead."

He hugged the small bundle to him and walked out the front door.

Jeremy touched the baby as if he was afraid she'd break. "What are we going to do? How can I feed her?"

"Ever hear of these things called cows? And sheep, goats and horses, for that matter. I'll take the horse home and bring back some milk." As he turned, he very nearly ran into Motivated.

"Or you could ask a passing witch for help." She said. "I wondered what you were up to, I could see you being unnoticeable so strongly even I couldn't see all the way through it."

Little Whirlpool was a healthy big six month old, and sound asleep in a pack on her mother's back.

"Do you want to raise her yourself, Jeremy?"

The boy nodded. "This is the only child I'll ever have . . . isn't she beautiful?"

"She is. Mikey, you'll be bringing back cow's milk? You'll need to get a milk goat, soon, it's better for babies, and I'll come and nurse her now and again. She'll do well, being truly loved. Now, go get the milk, I'll help with a few practical matters here."

By the time he returned, Imp had not only gained a name, she had a bed and a diaper on, with a stack of clean ones waiting and a pail for the dirty ones.

Motivated was sewing something out of thin leather. "Boil it after every use, and you'll probably want to make a lot of them and toss the old nasty ones away frequently." She stayed long enough to demonstrate bottle feeding a baby, then hugged them both and left.

Mikey bought an expectant nanny goat the next day, and between Motivated's frequent visits, and Vera's additives for the cow's milk, Imp thrived.

The goat surprised him with triplets, but still had plenty of milk for a little girl.

Wild Thing calved and after a week of revision to wild, remembered the dispensation of grain and returned to the barn. She wasn't much in favor of being milked, but then Mikey didn't really want much, and wasn't about to wean her little heifer, or butcher it for meat and the cheese making enzymes in her stomach, like the Hastings did to one calf every year.

They all got through the winter, and with the spring the work built up and they were so busy Mikey nearly missed Whirlpool's first birthday.

He didn't miss Last's increasingly frequent presence in Igor's vicinity, nor her swelling belly as the year progressed.

"Muddy should advance too," Motivated fussed. "The winter after this will be the Winter of the Comets and I'd like them to have advanced enough to be able to feel them."

"They'll be back four years later." Mikey told her, setting down a basket of pea pods. "So, what's the difference?"

"Barbarian mage! Pirate!" Motivated kissed the top of his head as she passed. "Some years they are closer than others. Next year they will be at their closest for four hundred years." She put Whirlpool down beside Imp and picked up a basket.

"Oh, great, so we can look forward to the Great Fireball that destroyed New Miami?"

"Bah! That's a myth and you know it. You nasty Mages were fighting with the Gods for supremacy and killed thousands of people."

"Bah! That's a myth." Mikey echoed. "There are a few records of local mage authorities giving the bums rush to some people who set themselves up as gods, complete with shrines and contributions, please. But they didn't make fireballs that burned entire cities."

Jeremy snorted as he carted another full basket of pea

pods to the porch, and grabbed an empty one. "You two are hideously funny to listen to. You don't carry on where normal people can hear, do you?"

"Certainly not, having no desire to be burned at the stake." Mikey stood up and joined him in the garden. One thing or another was going to be ripe from now till fall, most likely. The witches had planted fruit trees and they'd be swapping fresh and canned this-or-thats all year.

"Oh, Mikey, we need more jars, and Lady Gisele says she needs more bottles."

"Lady Gisele?"

"She said she knows you. Little old lady, herb garden?"

"Oh, her. Yes, sorry, I guess I never actually got her name, and Vera took the bottles I made around to her."

"I want to watch, this time." Jeremy said. "It sounds like real, actual magic, not this 'make the bugs go away' stuff you claim to be doing all the time."

"Claim! Oh I'm wounded. Old gods! Why did I plant so many peas? And look at the beans. They're nearly ready too."

Jeremy looked cautiously at him. "Do you believe in the old gods?"

"Well, yes and no. They're handy to swear by, and certainly no one I'd want to cross. Again. Very powerful magic users, and if you think Count Valasi is arrogant, well, let me tell you, the reason I'm here is because I got caught between the God of Peace and the God of Art, and running away very, very fast was the only thing that looked remotely survivable."

Motivated looked at him thoughtfully. "Do you mean that seriously?"

"Oh yes." Mikey nodded. "I could see which way it was tipping and just bolted."

Jeremy nodded. "Wish I'd been as smart. We marched right up to the Count and informed him that we were going to marry."

Mikey raised his head and stared. "You didn't!"

"I have been accused of naivety before. I figured a horsewhipping would be the worst possible outcome." He huffed out a breath and waded back through the lush garden.

Mikey made a pass through the picked over tomatoes and found more, and some early squash. "I swear, next year, I'm planting half as many veggies."

Motivated giggled. "Your wheat looks quite good."

"Yes, two more weeks, maximum. At least that's tractor work."

"And the silo's full of oats. We need to build a new one."

Mikey moaned. "All this honest work is ruining me. I want to go back to a life of crime."

"Did you enjoy it?"

"Hell no, I was miserable, but my father had taught me all about magery, and diddly about how to make a living. Don't mind my griping, I love it out here. But sometimes I think I need to specialize a bit."

"If you can get bags, we could bag the wheat, makes it easy to sell."

"Umm, yeah. Sacks for grain. What an excellent idea. I can escape for the rest of the day. And really Mo, if you guys want more vegetables, come pick all you need. The Bennys have planted easily three times what I have, so if for some reason I run out and actually want some more, I can get some." Mikey looked at Jeremy with raised eyebrows.

The boy shook his head. "I'll stay with Imp, and maybe think about where to put another silo."

Chatting with people around town, Mikey found a fellow up the northwest road who had put in a water wheel, and a mill. He'd be delighted to mill the wheat and then bag it, and hunting around a bit Mikey found buyers for about half his calculated crop if it was milled and bagged first. He also found Dan in a tavern and hauled him home.

After some discussion, he went to work on the glass, digging out the white sand along the sides of the stream, and heating it and forming bottles and wide mouthed jars and plugs for both. And then very large glass jars. Enough to hold a whole lot of wheat.

"How do you learn to do magic?" Jeremy looked wistful.

"Well, it's an inborn talent, and most people can't do anything but the simplest sorts of things. Back before the steam engine and electric motors, magic users used to be, well, useful. They'd test kids to see if they had any potential." Mikey grinned at his hopeful expression. "Here, hold out your hands, like this. Feel the breeze, the moving air? Picture capturing the motion, but not the air, just strip the movement right out and hold it in your hands."

Jeremy snickered. "And that really could work?"

"That's where I get the power to do things like melt glass." He shrugged. "I think we can skip the witch tests. Hold your hands out in the bright sunshine, like you're holding a cylinder of sunshine, and then squeeze it down, like strangling, only what you are doing . . . old gods! You're doing it!"

Jeremy yelped and tried to get the sunshine off his hands, and Mikey laughed helplessly, and finally grabbed him and pulled a bit of power out of the heat of his body. The lights on the boy's hands flickered out and died.

"Mikey?"

"Looks like you've got some wizard talent, there. Now, everyone can do a bit of magic, but wizards are about ten times more powerful than someone with no power source abilities. Mages are, oh, three to five times that strong. And witches are probably double what most mages can do. Mind you, there's a range, between weak and strong for each group. And the old gods can outdo us all. Keeps us humble if nothing else."

"So I won't ever be as powerful as you?"

"Well, probably not, but I'm not really strong." Mikey frowned. "I'm stronger than I used to be. Constant use, maybe." They'd taken Foggy and the wagon, so Dan could use the tractor today, and the big horse pulled up to their house without directions. "Smart damn horse."

They unloaded most of the glass and took the rest to the Bennys', and sat out in the hay field beside the dead tractor, and chatted with Igor and Dan while Mikey charged the battery. The Kipper rode the big horse over, Dan junior in front of her.

"Mom says thanks for the jars, and she'll send some of them back with vegetables in them."

Mikey shuddered and got laughed at, and baled hay until the batteries died again at midnight.

He charged the batteries from the early morning breeze the next day, then with a list of desired herbs, took bottles and jars down to Lady Gisele.

The summer smells were a bit different, but still nearly magical in their ability to pull him in. She was talking to a young woman, but broke off when Mikey stopped outside her gate.

"Ah, just what I need." The women helped him unload and filled the work shelves with the new bottles.

He stared around his armful of glassware at the shelves of colored . . . stuff. Long shelves. Longer than the hut.

Mikey stared at her carefully.

The old crone cackled. "Aren't I exactly what you'd expect the Goddess of Health and Fertility to look like?"

"Health and Fertility?" He gulped. "Pretty much, I suppose . . . "

The girl nodded and looked hopefully at the old woman. She had classically beautiful features, but looked pale and unhappy. Mikey blinked as he realized who she was. Lady Sicily.

"Umm, my, well, I suppose he's not really my fiancé now,

not after what father did to him. But you, can *You* help him?"

The goddess didn't seem to have any trouble understanding what the girl wasn't actually saying. "Oh, yes, stable boy verses noble, the usual result. Well, not the castration, although this is hardly a first. Umm, a regeneration spell for the gonads. Have to go all the way back and start with the embryonic development stage for that, I suspect. I'll have to think on it. That one will be a bit of a challenge. Good for me."

"Thank you, thank you." Tears, a hug, and the girl fled.

Mikey felt breathless, and took Vera's herbs home, along with a bit of quiet hope.

Last gave birth to a tiny girl they named Xanadu.

Mark Hastings tromped over to say that he'd seen wolves, but his brother Derrick argued that they must have been dogs, because there was a boy, a teenager maybe, with them.

Mikey slipped out that evening and sat out in the open, clearly alone, until the wild boy appeared at his side. "Something bad is happening. So we came closer. The pack won't raid."

"If they get too hungry, come to me. I have meat, dried and salted."

The boy looked suspicious and faded away. Mikey told Jeremy and Motivated, but no one else.

Chapter Five

The little old lady looked littler than before. Mostly because of the contrast. A man built on Igor's muscular model, but even taller, loomed over her. "This is that young mage I told you about." She took his list.

The man shifted and Mikey froze in shock. He recognized the general class partly from the height, but mainly a deep primal recognition. One of the old gods.

"Yes. War."

And with the same tendency to treat surface thoughts as if they'd been spoken out loud.

"How good are you at levitation?"

"I can almost float glass well enough that it can almost be used for windows."

"Hmm. Probably can't help us then."

Fortunately.

The god lifted his eyebrows, then smiled a bit. "Sorry, I forget that everyone doesn't know about the comet."

Mikey hesitated, a horrible thought returning. As he'd teased Motivated, the fireball that had destroyed New Miami.

"Yes, only we think this one is larger. Very dangerous, so

we're trying to organize a good hard push and get it to miss."

Mikey nodded uncertainly. "Good idea, but I don't think I can do anything . . . do you know where it will hit?"

"The range of error is still larger than the World, so it may miss all on its own. When it gets closer, we may have enough time to figure out more precisely and at least move it enough to minimize deaths."

Mikey shivered. He had so much to lose, now . . .

The god nodded at him. "We all do. We must try our best to prevent this." He looked around into the hut. "I'll let you know, Gisele." He disappeared.

Gisele hustled back out, little paper packs in her hands. "I'll have something for that boy of yours, in another few months. I'm testing it on animals, right now."

He dropped spices at the Bennys' and drove on up the hill. He parked the tractor in its usual spot and sat there staring into space for a long moment.

"What's wrong?" Jeremy's voice was sharp with concern. "You look awful. What happened."

Mikey took a shaky breath. "Good news, bad news, and too much time to think about the bad news.

"The bad news is that there really is a chance that a comet will hit the World and kill everyone that can't get out of the way. Year after next. At the solstice, just a few months, really. Fourteen months. The gods are getting together to try and steer it away."

Mikey put his head down and pondered a World that

depended on the likes of the Golden Boy and Barry Virtue to save it.

"All right. What's the good news?"

"Lady Gisele is the Goddess of Healing and Fertility. Lady Sicily asked her if there was anything she could do to help you, by way of regeneration. She said today that she's testing something on animals."

"Sicily . . . The Goddess of . . . "

"So look forward to that." Mikey straightened. "After all, what are the odds the comet will hit Scooner, eh? And if we know ahead of time, we'll just haul ass down that pretty road."

"Yes. Exactly." Jeremy raised a smile. "Hopefully carousing all the way."

"Right. Nothing to be so damned concerned about." Mikey tried to smile. "So, let me show you some shielding spells."

"Just in case we need them? Good idea."

"The problem with shields is that the more things you shield from, the thinner the shield. So you can't shield for everything, because then anything can get through if it's even middling strong. So you generally pick the most likely threats and shield specifically for the top three—if you're strong enough. And you are. I don't know why everyone says wizards are weak."

"Wishful thinking? Or maybe the wizards hide how strong they are to avoid the sort of nonsense some mages and witches get up to."

"Never did figure out why mages and witches don't get

along. It's like a tradition, but they forgot the reason." Mikey pondered. "I suppose this impact . . . Are comets hot? Let's see, to shield against heat . . . "

They stored food as if expecting a decade long famine, and practiced shields all winter. And talked to the witches and practiced shielding with them, trying to see how large an area they could cover, and for how long.

Lady Gisele approved, and they worked on a three point shield. The Goddess could shield the whole settlement, briefly. The Goddess could hold one point herself, the Pyramid another and Mikey and Jeremy working together could hold the third point for almost two hours.

"We need two more magically inclined men. A minor Compass." Mikey gritted his teeth and tried harder. Longer.

Then they started trying to hold two shields at once: kinetic and heat.

"I don't think we'll need to hold the kinetic shield for very long. But there may be a wave of fire, and then forest fires."

"What about the air? Will we be able to breathe if the fires are worldwide?"

Gisele rubbed her wrinkled forehead. "A shield that could use the heat to convert carbon dioxide to oxygen . . . "

"I can use heat, and Jeremy can use fire. But how do you convert . . . You'd have to pull the carbon atom out of the molecule . . . " They talked over ways and means, and Mikey started teaching Jeremy the theories behind the fun spells, the methods for analyzing problems and testing possible spells.

It was a long spring, and the nervy wild boy moved closer. And admitted to a name.

Dace was a mage, and even had some training. Jeremy could hold up his point, when they tried to work together. Mikey cursed his father and his own lack of group practice, but it worked. Limpingly. They could hold a single shield for eight hours.

"We need one more mage. Just one more, so we'd have a minor Compass."

They stored so much food they were very nearly short. They killed wild cattle, salted and canned the meat, caught wild birds and rabbits, hoping they could release them in the spring.

And Lady Gisele handed over a small bottle that looked familiar. "Drink this on an empty stomach, and come and see me in two weeks."

Jeremy looked at it, then reluctantly shook his head. "What if it means my magic gets weaker? We can't afford that now. I'll try it when we're safe." He glanced skyward. "It's only another month, after all."

They almost became accustomed to Gods popping out of nowhere.

Mikey fled when he spotted the God of Art's upside down museum blocking the road outside of Lady Gisele's garden. He kept a wary eye out, but didn't see Peace.

The God of Just Deserts was the worst. Or the best, depending on one's point of view. His four dogs were infamous for doling out the instant karma.

They attacked Lord Valasi in public, stripped and humped him in the town square. Lady Valasi's nasty little dogs got eaten. Fights broke out all over. Several rapes, two murders. Dan got beaned by a whisky bottle and only Lady Gisele's immediate intervention prevented him from becoming the third murder victim. The God of War popped out of nowhere and told the God of Just Deserts to get out of town, and not come near any of their collections of power while they were trying to divert the comet.

"Did you see that?" Mikey hunched his shoulders and glared across the square.

"And enjoyed every second of it." Jeremy sounded more angry than amused, though.

"No, not the dogs, what Lord Valasi was trying to do to get away from them. He's a mage."

Jeremy frowned down at him—when had he grown so tall? "Valasi? Mikey, we can't . . . " He turned and walked off a short distance.

Mikey just waited.

Jeremy stalked back. "Well, I said I'd do anything necessary to hold the shield. And I meant it. So let's go talk to him."

Valasi snarled at them, swore when Mikey persisted. Finally said his father had been a mage, but that he, himself had never practiced.

"Pity. Gods aren't actually that much more powerful than a really strong Mage, and even a small Compass can beat one." Mikey smiled faintly. "Come to where the south road crests Butler Ridge at daybreak. We've got two days to practice coordinating and shielding so we can save the town if the gods can't save the world. I'll teach you how to fight a god, if you still feel inclined to do so, after the comet." He turned and walked away. *Give the man time to think it over.*

Valasi was waiting, pacing, at dawn. He recoiled from the wild boy's unwashed scent, but seemed even more leery of Jeremy. But with four men the Compass soared.

Mikey felt drunk with power, when they finally stopped.

He perched on the back of the tractor and let Jeremy drive them home. Imp wasn't with the group of kids at Vera's, so they drove on up the hill. No Imp.

Mikey yawned and headed over the hill, too tired to try to reach Motivated mentally. Besides, he could use a hug. The next two days were going to be scary.

He looked up at a rattle of stones.

Motivated waved. "Mikey! I was coming around to collect Whirlpool."

"She's . . . I was going to come get Imp. I didn't see either of them at Dan's."

"But . . . "

They searched all night. No one had seen either of the girls since lunch.

Chapter Six

31 December 2455

Scoone, North America

"We can't close the town off yet." Mikey stared at the old woman. "If they're out there, they'll die."

Her eyes were damp. "Possibly, if the gods can't divert the comet. But so will millions of other people." Her eyes swung between the two men. "Think about Scandia, Mikey. All those people. Everyone you know, except the few who came here with you. Every single one of them is going to die. We must be ready to save the few who are here."

Jeremy nodded jerkily. "I know they're all going to die. But Imp! Why now, where could she be? I searched Valasi's place. I looked everywhere."

"I searched the houses he and his people have moved into. The girls aren't anywhere. We had lunch with them, dammit. I thought they went with Dan, he's sure they stayed home." Mikey wanted to barf, cry. Break something. He looked up into the sky. The pearly fog bank covered most of the sky. The comet was coming from sunward, the solar wind blowing the tail of the comet over the world. It was nearly midnight. Noon in New Tokyo, where one group of Gods and Mages was already trying to push the comet core. Dawn in Sahara, where the other groups would be starting. Did they need line of sight? At that distance did it matter? And if they failed, the people in Sahara had best be prepared to move their homes and people. Fast.

"I saw Dan, but no children. It was dark already, and I was arguing with Marty. Again." The old woman shook her head. "I'll go home and pray that they can shift the comet. But if they can't, if you four aren't out on the south road and ready to hold your corner, then everyone will die here. Everyone. You have an hour. At the most."

Mikey wiped his face. Everything he'd left behind. *The gods will protect it, they were talking about all sorts of things to try. Everyone won't die. Not everyone. The gods will save people, when, if, they cannot divert the comet. Lots of people.* He drew a breath like a sob. Old pals, old girlfriends, old clients and old enemies.

Mikey swallowed. "Let's check at Valasi's again, then we'll pull back up the south road. We'll be in position in an hour."

Jeremy's fists closed. "They'll divert the comets. Wherever the girls are, they'll be fine."

Streaks of light shot by overhead, ominous heralds of the main body.

Valasi's place was empty. House, barns, sheds. Empty.

Dace and Valasi waited on the South Road. Valasi pacing, Dace jittering.

Mikey took the North Position, Dace South, as if he couldn't bear to have anyone between him and the wilderness. Valasi East, Jeremy West. Valasi glared across at Jeremy.

Jeremy looked beyond him gazing up and searching the morning sky for something more than the dim sun. Rays of bright light flashed across the pearl gray light. Then a long slow-seeming fireball.

"We won't see the main body. If they can't divert the comet, well, it'll be hitting right about now." Mikey cut his left wrist, passed the knife to Valasi. "The ground shock, in probably fifteen minutes. The blast wave in four something hours. We should hear about it . . . " He clutched his head at the searing mental scream.

"Mikey, Mikey! What is it?" Jeremy was holding his shoulders.

What was he doing on the ground? The pain was gone.

"You know. It's a good thing you three are all defensive sorts, with natural mental blocks. That wasn't very pleasant. The comet hit. It's time to get our shield up around the village." He climbed to his feet, and held his hands out to the other men. *My little Whirlpool, Imp* . . . He crushed the emotions, opened his mind again and pulled power from the wind rustling past them. He felt Gisele, crying, but determined. The witches, their pyramid strong and beautiful.

They raised the kinetic field. Mikey pulled power from the wind striking it, felt Jeremy up above it pulling fire from a small pebble just before it hit. Absorbed the kinetic energy from the strike. And two more. Tiny, insignificant, pieces shed by the comet. And suddenly a shower, a torrent of molten pieces. Jeremy tried to take the fire and divert the power into the shield. *Easy, you don't have to do it all. This must be . . . splash. Rocks that blasted back into space, and were pulled back to earth.*

An incoherent mosaic of thoughts joined with his. The sudden pain of realizing the deaths of friends, relatives that he'd never had. Running with wild animals. A memory of holding a baby in his arms, and the pain of loss. Anger, pride, insecurity, temper . . . shame.

Concentrate. Hold. Relax and lean into the shield, hold it on the ground. Just concentrate on the shield.

The ground started quivering, tried to throw them into the air, break their grips. He was never sure how long they held the shield. Long enough for two deadly waves of super heated air to pass. Long enough for a dark pall to fade into true night. Long enough for Valasi to collapse, for Dace to panic and run away with his wolves.

And Mikey and Jeremy leaned on each other and held the shield, and cried for those lost, now and forever.

About the Author

I was born and raised in California, and have lived more than half my life, now, in Texas.

Wonderful place. I caught almost the first bachelor I met here, and we're coming up on our thirty-third anniversary.

My degree's in Geology. After working for an oil company for almost ten years as a geophysicist, I "retired" to raise children. As they grew, I added oil painting, sculpting and throwing clay, breeding horses, volunteering in libraries and for the Boy Scouts, and treasurer for a friend's political campaign. Sometime in those busy years, I turned a love of science fiction into a part time job reading slush, unsolicited manuscripts, for Baen Books (Mom? Someone is *paying* you to read??!!)

I've always written, published a few short stories. But now that the kids have flown the nest, I'm calling writing a full time job.

Excerpt from The Black Goats

Book Three of the Wine of the Gods series

By Pam Uphoff

Chapter One
Late Winter 1352
Village of Ash

Picking rocks was only fun for the first half hour. Pity it was such a good way to practice magic.

Never walked barefoot through the mud, feet chilly in the early spring. Her blonde hair was braided back out of the way and her skirt was her shortest and scruffiest. She stopped and centered again, and reached for the Earth power. It flowed up sluggishly from the wet soil, and showed her the bright spots of more rocks. The annual freezes and thaws in the valley caused the slow and inexorable displacement of rocks in the fields, and removing them was a necessity before the fields could be plowed. The witches had the advantage of seeing the rocks that were near the surface, and so prevented a good deal of damage to the plow, not to mention saving the farmers a bit of time. Never could see the bright sparks of rocks in her immediate area, and one by one drew them up to the surface, and flung them down to the road.

She was careful to miss the people on the road. Her grandmother Answer was showing the teenagers how to break the rocks up into gravel. None of the three younger girls had grasped her abilities yet, but they would soon.

"Never! Mostly! I've got a big one!"

Never chucked her last stone down the hill and joined Likely around the boulder that was just peeking out of the dirt.

The Triad of the Crescent Moon joined hands briefly, then stepped back and lifted the boulder free. It rolled and bounced down the hill, and as it approached the road, Never reached out with a spider web of heat and the joined power of the triad. The boulder landed, and the impact and unequal thermal expansion combined to shatter it.

More or less where it ought to be.

Mostly giggled. "Show off." She elbowed Never, and headed back for her own transit.

Likely wrinkled her nose. "I don't know how you manage to control things that far away. You haven't even lost your virginity yet."

"More practice, less time in front of the mirror." Never dodged the return mud ball and got back to her own transit. It was spring; if they were going to have any people passing through, it would be in the next month or so. The problem was, there really wasn't much of anyplace to go to, north of Ash. To advance to the next level of magical ability she needed to lose her virginity and have a baby. The other members of her triad were a year older than she was, and had ventured down to the town of Wallenton to find suitable men. Most likely she would have to as well.

The sheep and cows were out nibbling at the new sprouts of grass that were quickly covering the slopes that rolled up to the forest. The sheep were kept in loose order by the nasty goats the Sheep Man kept. Solid black, with an even more evil mien than ordinary goats possessed, and big. They ranged from one that could have passed for a pony to the nearest one that probably only weighed two hundred pounds. She shied a dirt clod its way, just on general principles. The cows were mostly the local milk supply, although two of the mage-farmers had small beef herds. They kept three teams of horses. Those horses and the elderly dun gelding that pulled the muck cart at the tavern were grazing in a clump across the road.

The valley was very close to self-sufficient.

Its inhabitants were certainly independent.

To the best of their knowledge, they were the last surviving magic users on this world.